Choose your Lane to love!

Fish Out of Water

"…I will promise you this, you WILL be left with one hell of a book hangover."
—Rainbow Gold Reviews

Red Fish, Dead Fish

"Packed full of action, suspense, and of course steamy goodness, *Red Fish, Dead Fish* is the sequel we have all been anxiously waiting for."
—Love Bytes

A Few Good Fish

"*A Few Good Fish* is a riveting page-turner with high-stakes action scenes, an intriguing plot and two compelling, incredibly likeable central characters."
—All About Romance

Hiding the Moon

"This whole series is amazing, and this book is the cherry on top!"
—The Novel Approach

By Amy Lane

Published by DREAMSPINNER PRESS
www.dreamspinnerpress.com

By Amy Lane

Published by DREAMSPINNER PRESS
www.dreamspinnerpress.com

FISH
ON A
BICYCLE

Amy Lane

Published by

DREAMSPINNER PRESS

5032 Capital Circle SW, Suite 2, PMB# 279, Tallahassee, FL 32305-7886 USA
www.dreamspinnerpress.com

Fish on a Bicycle
© 2019 Amy Lane

Cover Art
© 2019 Reese Dante
http://www.reesedante.com
Cover content is for illustrative purposes only and any person depicted on the cover is a model.

Trade Paperback ISBN: 978-1-64405-677-6
Digital ISBN: 978-1-64405-676-9
Library of Congress Control Number: 2019942796
Trade Paperback published October 2019
v. 1.0

Printed in the United States of America

This paper meets the requirements of
ANSI/NISO Z39.48-1992 (Permanence of Paper).

Mary—okay, you have so many more awesome things to do than to give a wackadoo weirdo advice on her books. But you make me feel like I'm doing you a favor. I love you to pieces. Thank you.

Mate—always.

Chicken—plotting with you is the happiest part of my week.

Karen—you are a goddess and you inspire.

Acknowledgments

So Karen Rose and Geoff Symon answer my random questions all the time. They are also both spectacularly inspirational when it comes to murdering people in print. Thanks, guys!

Author's Note

YOU MAY recognize Henry Worrall—but if you don't, and you like his brother, David, and David's husband, Carlos, you may want to check out the Johnnies series, starting with *Chase in Shadow*. Also, for everyone asking for Henry's story—you're welcome.

Prologue
Donuts in the Morning

THE ALARM went off and Jackson Rivers groaned. "Really? You made the appointment for eight in the morning? Really?"

Ellery Cramer grunted. "Yes, really," he said. "I'll shower first if you want, but we're going."

"Augh!" Jackson pulled himself out of bed, and Ellery watched as he fumbled for the phone. "I'll shower first, Counselor. This is my damned doctor's appointment. There's no reason for you to have to get up too."

Of course there was, Ellery thought grumpily. Because if Ellery, personally, didn't ride Jackson's case about this doctor's appointment, Jackson quite simply wouldn't go.

They'd just gotten back two days ago from a case that had almost cost them their lives and had resulted in a lengthy hospital stay down in Southern California. Ellery's body felt battered and bruised, just from the drive back to Sacramento, but he and Jackson had wanted to be home in Ellery's gracious American River Drive ranch style so badly, they'd left as soon as possible, even though they'd had to split the trip into two four-hour stretches.

It was just so good to be home.

Ellery stood up and stripped out of his pajamas, wondering how cold it was outside. It had been mid-January when he and Jackson had gone south to investigate a rogue military megalomaniac who had been training assassins and turning them into serial killers. Karl Lacey had left one too many bodies in his wake. And after cleaning up a mess so gruesome that even one of his pets couldn't stomach it, Jackson and Ellery had felt honor bound to stop him.

But the physical toll—on both of them now, but mostly on Jackson—had been brutal and long-lasting.

As Ellery made his way to the bathroom, he tried to count how many weeks Jackson had spent in the hospital. He didn't bother to count the year Jackson had spent nearly a decade ago when a sniper had tried to take him out for wearing a wire to catch a dirty cop—that was old news.

No, Ellery counted the times Jackson had been under care since they'd first gotten together in August.

Well, it had been three weeks from the drive-by on that case, the one that had rendered his shoulder mostly useless for the better part of a year.

Then there had been ten days from a raging infection in November, when they'd taken down the Dirty/Pretty killer and had been alerted to Karl Lacey's presence in the first place. The infection had been bad—but the worst part was that Jackson had fallen into a swimming pool with a raging fever and his heart had seized. He'd been told he'd have a heart murmur for probably the rest of his life after that, and that eventually he'd need surgery to clean out the scar tissue left from the attack.

Jackson was still a thin, pale version of himself. Between the heart attack and the infection and seeing his mother dead in the morgue—God rot her junkie's soul—he'd been left with a violent phobia of hospitals that, as far as Ellery was concerned, had occurred a day late and a dollar short.

And even that phobia hadn't kept him out of trouble. Before they'd left for So-Cal, he'd had a planter fall on his head and, hey, hello, a concussion.

And then there was So-Cal.

Ellery paused at the bathroom door, leaning his head against the frame. His fault. This last one had been his fault. They'd been chasing down Karl Lacey and his partner in crime—some asshole named Hamblin—and in the chaos of a battlefield, and Jackson had given him a gun.

God, Ellery had been so proud. He'd only just learned to use one, and he'd listened to Lacey taunting the two of them, talking about "breakage" and "collateral damage" to dismiss the swath of carnage his serial killers had been leaving in their wake. And Ellery—Ellery Cramer, the defense attorney with the nice house in the spendy suburb and the educated liberal parents, who was known for being smart and sharp and never losing his cool—had fired on the guy blindly, through a tin wall.

And Lacey had fired back and almost taken him out.

Jackson had been wounded in the hospital when one more goddamned assassin had tried to finish the job.

Adjoining beds. They'd shared adjoining beds for two weeks.

Ellery sighed and stripped, then threw his stuff in the hamper before getting creakily into the shower with Jackson.

"This is nice," Jackson murmured, wrapping his arms around Ellery's shoulders. They were both thinner than they had been—but

Jackson's heart needed more weight at this point. That had been one of his promises upon leaving the hospital. The hospital itself left him too freaked-out to eat, to heal. He'd promised to eat regularly, to keep himself healthy, if they'd let him go. And they had.

"I felt like you needed me," Ellery said weakly. He was tired. He really just wanted to sleep today. But God, even though Jackson liked Dr. Keller, the cardiologist he'd been seeing since November, Ellery just didn't trust him to go to the appointment. Not right now. Not when even saying the words *outpatient clinic* made Jackson's hands tremble.

"I do," Jackson soothed, rocking them both back and forth. "I do need you."

"You think maybe we can go out to lunch after this?" Ellery asked. "Maybe call up your sister? See if her boyfriend's working?"

"Mike's coming by *with* lunch," Jackson laughed. "Probably about an hour after we get back." Jade wasn't, strictly speaking, Jackson's sister. They had, in fact, dated during much of their early twenties. Or as Jackson put it, "booty called." But Jade and her twin, Kaden, had been Jackson's only family after Jackson's mother pretty much bailed on the job in grade school, and the three of them were tighter than most blood siblings Ellery had known. Jade's boyfriend, a redneck with the habit of saying the wrong thing politically while he was doing the right thing as a human being, was as devoted to Jackson as Jade was.

If Jackson didn't need so many people looking after him, Ellery might be jealous.

As it was, he was just grateful for the help.

"Whatever we got them for Christmas, it's not enough," Ellery murmured. Jackson was soaping his scarred body, and Ellery fought the temptation to hide. Jackson's scars were legion and horrific—and there were a shit-ton more now than there had been when they'd met.

"I'll make a note of that," Jackson said, nuzzling his ear. "We need to add Ace and Sonny and Burton and Ernie to the Christmas list."

Ellery groaned. "Seriously?"

"We'll just send them something," he said. "Or, you know, send Ace and Sonny something and have them give Burton and Ernie's thing to them. Way way way in the future."

Ace and Sonny owned a gas station in the middle of the desert, slightly south of hell. But they'd been there to help Jackson and Ellery take down Karl Lacey and his band of mercenaries, so Ellery could definitely agree to that. Ellery had seen much less contact with Burton and Ernie—and he wasn't sure he wanted more.

Burton was a government assassin. No, he didn't have business cards that stated that overtly, but after Jackson had recounted the parts of their adventure that Ellery had been unconscious for, Ellery would take it on faith. Burton had saved their bacon, and he'd saved Jackson's family, and Jackson had apparently sworn fealty to him while Ellery had been in surgery.

Fantastic.

Ernie—Burton's boyfriend—was a flakey psychic with no record of existence. And Ellery thought Ernie liked it that way. Once upon a time, Ellery got up, put on a suit, did paperwork, and only assassinated people verbally, but now, after knowing Jackson Rivers slightly less than a year, this was his life. Putting together a gift list for hit men and their psychic boyfriends.

Color him surprised.

But like Jackson said, Christmas was a whole ten months away.

"But first we recover," Ellery said.

"Yessir." Jackson squirted some soap in Ellery's hair, and Ellery welcomed the warmth, the contact, the cosseting. Jackson was good at it, which wasn't a surprise. The scars on his body were only the tip of the iceberg. His psychological damage was way, way worse. Jackson Rivers had been having nightmares for close to ten years now, and before Ellery, he'd kept them at bay with an endless parade of faceless people. At least, with anyone else, they'd be faceless. But with Jackson, the people he slept with were friends—just friends who didn't get too close, who didn't know what the nightmares were about, whom Jackson would never feel indebted to.

Ellery was, on all counts, the exception.

Jackson was, as a result, a stunningly good lover—good enough to use sex as a distraction, to try to pull the focus away from himself, often, but very, very good.

Ellery wanted some of that right now. Not the sex, but the good-lover thing. They both needed it. It had been a rough patch of road since August. It was time to recover.

"So," he mumbled, holding his head back while Jackson used the showerhead to rinse his hair, "we go to this appointment, we come back for lunch, and then what?"

Jackson chuckled weakly. "Then we sleep."

"What about tomorrow?"

"We stay awake a little longer."

"And after that?"

"I know where this is going, Counselor." Jackson gave his head one more pass and nuzzled his ear before putting the showerhead back. "You said it yourself. We're finding a venue and starting up your practice. I'm sure there's more to it than that, but I figure it'll take four months or so before we get up to speed."

Ellery smiled. "We're going to spend a lot of that time naked. You know that, right?"

Jackson chuckled and turned off the water. "Looking forward to it."

"Good," he said, and they proceeded to dry off and dress casually. Jackson's wardrobe hadn't changed much in the last ten years, but Ellery had bought him a fleece jacket for the winters because he was tired of seeing Jackson wearing holey sweatshirts that should have been torn to shreds and used to wipe down cars.

They eschewed the "urban assault vehicle" that Ace and Sonny had gifted them with after their adventure down south and took Ellery's Lexus instead. It wasn't until they were pulling away from the house that Jackson saw the pink box on the doorstep.

"Hold on," he said, waiting until the car stopped before going up to get the thing from the porch. He came back with the oddest look on his face.

"What?" Ellery asked.

"Breakfast?" Jackson said blankly.

"What?"

"I swear to God, Ellery, there's fresh donuts inside. Sprinkles and old-fashioned's and the regular glazed—"

"My favorite," Ellery said, perking up. "Was there a note?"

Jackson shook his head. "Well, there's a message."

"What's it say?"

Jackson looked at the words block printed on the pink bakery box. "It says, *He told me to tell you, every day is recovery*."

Ellery grunted. "Who's he?"

"Ernie."

"No, seriously—"

Jackson sighed. "No, trust me. It's Ernie. He brought us pastries when we were in the hospital, remember? And Burton has the means to get them here."

"But isn't Burton...." He looked at Jackson unhappily.

"Still tracking the serial killers Lacey trained? Yeah. There's plenty of bad guys for Burton to kill." Jackson still had Burton's number memorized, of that, Ellery was sure. Burton's entire unit had changed focus to chasing down Karl Lacey's monsters—and Jackson and Ellery seemed to be trouble magnets.

"Then why do we rate donuts?"

Jackson shrugged. "I don't know, but I'm not looking a gift donut in the mouth. Ernie's a baking genius, remember?"

Ellery had to laugh. "Fine. But no coffee until after your appointment."

"What do you suppose it means? Recovery is every day?"

Ellery sighed. "I'm not sure. I just know we have to get through *this* day before we can get any further."

"Then let's hurry," Jackson told him. "The quicker we get this over with, the quicker we can get on with our lives."

Fish on a Bicycle
Go Fish, Go.

ELLERY KEPT a very neat garage—Jackson would give him that. Three shelves, which kept things like basic tools, duct tape, and a few storage boxes for off-season clothes, all of it perfectly aligned. Jackson looked under the one on the far left and... woot!

There it was.

He picked up the skateboard that had sustained him on short-term trips around his neighborhood while he'd been young, and then through the academy when he'd been broke, and then after his time in the hospital, recovering from the shooting that had ended his career in the force, when he'd been pissed off.

Yeah, this skateboard had been his one faithful mode of transportation, if you didn't include the car Jackson had gotten right out of high school that had been shot to pieces during a case the year before.

He gave that car the moment of silence it deserved and then moved on to the triumph of finding the board. He spun the wheels a couple of times, grinning, and turned to Ellery, showing it off.

"See?"

"What am I seeing?" Ellery crossed his arms over his chest and eyed the thing like it was a jumbo-sized dead rat. "I can't believe Jade and Mike saved that when they brought your stuff over in November." Jackson had been in the hospital at the time when his sister-of-the-heart and her boyfriend had cleared out the garage of the duplex Jackson used to live in.

"Well, of course they did!" Jackson grinned at him. "Me and this board go way back. It's perfect. I brought my backpack—I can go get stuff from the store, takeout, whatever, and then board back to the office without taking the car!"

Ellery stroked the hood of his beloved Lexus—five years old now and purring like a kitten—as though soothing it from the insult. "Why would you even need to do that?"

"Because finding parking is a big furry bitch. I'm not sure if you've noticed, but our office is not exactly centrally located."

Ellery grimaced and Jackson tried to keep his face neutral. That end of F Street boasted a lot of converted Victorian houses, most of them hosting businesses. The effect was lovely—and the office Ellery had chosen was classy, if small, and very much suggested they were successful, even though they hadn't opened yet.

But it was four blocks from so much as a 7-Eleven, and Jackson was tired of driving to go get paint or food or office supplies or even toilet paper, for sweet fuck's sake, and having to park farther away than the store he was heading for on the way back.

He didn't want to blame Ellery for not getting something newer and less classy and more centrally located to anything but converted Victorian law offices, but he had told Ellery this was a problem when they were looking and… well.

It was Ellery's fault.

Ellery didn't make many missteps—Jackson had, in fact, been trusting him to know what the hell he was doing since they'd gotten together the year before—but this had been one.

"So you're going to take a skateboard?" Ellery practically whined. "Isn't that… I don't know. Dangerous? Juvenile? Embarrassing?"

"Convenient?" Jackson rolled his eyes. "Now pop the trunk and let me put it in there. It's getting hotter by the nanosecond outside, and I'd like to get some painting done before we have to close the windows and turn on the air-conditioning."

Jackson wouldn't have minded just keeping the windows open and painting all the way through the day, but Ellery had already brought in his computer equipment, and he had a couple of towers. Without the AC, the towers could overheat, so AC it was.

Ellery popped the trunk, grumbling, and Jackson sighed. This was just one more way he and Ellery didn't seem to fit together. The skateboard had seemed like a good idea—yeah, sure, there were laws against it, but Jackson was more of a guideline-not-a-rule kind of guy.

He put the skateboard in the trunk and slid into the car before Ellery backed it out of the garage and into the blistering morning sun.

"C'mon, Ellery, nobody needs to know I know you. I promise I won't even give away any of our business cards!"

Ellery paused as the garage door closed and then continued to wind his way through the posh houses of American River Drive.

"You had nightmares," he said shortly.

"Sorry," Jackson muttered. He'd been working on it—he had. Had been talking to a rabbi, of all people, in an attempt to not let his emotional baggage strangle the best and longest relationship he'd ever had.

"They were getting better." There was no recrimination in Ellery's voice—just acknowledgment that once again, Jackson was broken.

Jackson growled and threw his head back against the seat. "I don't want to talk about it."

Because last night's nightmare had been more of a memory. Considering all the times Jackson had gotten shot or stabbed or beat up, you'd think that was what was haunting him. But no. What was tormenting him now was the memory of Ellery, his body blown back by the force of the bullet that penetrated it, because he'd stepped in front of an aluminum wall recently ventilated by a bastard with a gun.

And then, oddly enough, there had been the face of the guy who'd shot him, after Jackson had emptied a clip into his chest. A waste of good skin, really—a megalomaniac who thought turning soldiers into serial killers made them better at their job.

The guy had shot Ellery and Jackson had taken him down, end of story. Jackson didn't regret it, really—but of all the things he'd done, all the ways he'd failed as a human being, it had been the first time he'd taken a human life like that. But that wasn't the worst death.

The worst one had been when he'd finished off the guy who'd tried to take Ellery out in the hospital. Jackson had killed him, up close and personal, a scalpel in the heart, before almost bleeding out himself from the kidneys.

In his dreams, as he pushed the scalpel in, the man's face—a blank, automaton expression, a man wrecked so horribly, his humanity didn't even return in the moment of death—morphed into Jackson's mother's face, as she'd lain on the slab.

And in the dream, he was just so damned grateful they both were dead.

Then he'd kept waiting for the announcement from God that he'd had his human-being card revoked. He'd let Ellery get shot and he'd killed somebody in retaliation—two somebodies—and he wasn't sorry. Even when his mother had been murdered last November, all he'd felt was relief.

"No, you just want to go skateboarding down a busy road in the middle of the day."

Jackson wrinkled his nose. "It's not really that busy. I mean, I know it's downtown, but everybody parks at the levee and then walks. Seriously. Not nearly as much traffic as you'd thi—"

"Why won't you talk to me?"

Jackson grunted and closed his eyes. "You know why you don't get bad dreams?"

"I do sometimes."

It was true—sometimes Ellery did. Now and then, he woke up with a start and told Jackson he didn't want to go back to the hospital, and Jackson would hold him until he was asleep again. It happened maybe once a month.

"Why you don't get them all the time?" he asked.

"No, why?"

Jackson looked at Ellery—his hair slicked back, khaki's pressed, polo shirt crisp and bright. They were going in to paint the new office. The license to operate would be coming through in a week, the space was leased, and Ellery's old desk from Pfeist, Langdon, Harrelson, and Cooper had been installed two days ago. They had a conference room, an office for Ellery with a smaller desk for Jackson, two vacant offices waiting for partners, and an office manager who was dying to come in and schedule them both to their last minute in the bathroom, if Jackson knew his sister-of-the-heart at all.

Ellery had made that all happen. Jackson had helped, but it had been Ellery's vision of owning his own law practice, of being his own boss, that had driven them both.

Jackson was tired of working for bosses who cared more about the bottom line than the truth. Ellery was tired of limits, as he should be, because Ellery was a first-rate defense attorney, and if they could clone him, they could probably get all of the innocent people off death row. From what Jackson understood, there was an appalling number of them.

It might not be the best way to make money, but the two of them wanted to make a difference.

Before he'd met Ellery, Jackson hadn't been sure that much idealism existed in the world.

"Because you shouldn't," Jackson said weakly, not enough words to explain the fullness of his heart when he took in Ellery Cramer—a shark-in-a-suit lawyer who slicked back his hair on his day off and had never worn cargo shorts that Jackson had seen, not even in August, a man who had skeptical eyebrows and a beak of a nose and a pair of sharp, shrewd brown eyes that could assess a case without blinking.

And the most steadfast heart Jackson had ever known.

"I shouldn't?" Ellery stopped at the intersection, taking the left from Fair Oaks to J Street. Some people took the freeway, but Sacramento freeways were like clogged arteries, and the surface streets were the shunts that kept them from being permanently blocked. He used the pause to risk a look at Jackson, who looked away quickly. "What does that mean?"

Jackson stared out into the overbright sunshine before pulling his sunglasses from the vee of his T-shirt and sliding them on. "It means you don't have anything to be ashamed of," he said softly. "And it means you have faith in the universe, and that's okay."

Ellery shouldn't be afraid, because if someone was going to come after him again, they'd have to go through Jackson first.

Jackson wasn't good for much, not really, but he'd already proven himself as an excellent piece of cannon fodder.

"You haven't done anything wrong." Ellery frowned. "I mean, you cleaned the cat box, right?"

Jackson chuckled a little. "Yes, Ellery, Billy Bob's box is pristine." Jackson had even given old Billy Bob a bath—and contrary to what most people might think, the battered, snaggletoothed, three-legged tomcat actually loved the water, when it was warm and soapy and somebody was petting him. Ellery had finished up the bath with a long brushing using his silicone brushing mittens, and when they'd left that morning, Billy Bob was on top of Ellery's bed, practically comatose with too much attention.

"Then what?" Ellery negotiated the morning traffic with the aplomb of an elderly spinster. If Jackson's car hadn't been a tank that guzzled gas like a sprinter downed Gatorade, Jackson would have insisted on driving, but it just felt wasteful to take that thing anywhere but on a mission across an apocalyptic wasteland to bring water to the thirsty masses.

"Nothing," Jackson sighed. He didn't want to get into it. He hadn't brought up the new dreams to Rabbi Watson because… gah! He was tired. He was tired of opening up his insides, letting the rabbi see all his damage and then waiting for the man to tell him how to fix it. He was just so tired of being damaged.

Ellery grunted—a habit he'd picked up from Jackson—and then swerved into a Starbucks line that didn't appear to be moving at all.

"Here?" Jackson eyed the joint. "But it's going to add twenty minutes to—"

Ellery threw the car into Park and undid his seat belt. "We're the bosses. We can be late."

"What are you—"

Ellery—in his khakis and his polo shirt—was practically climbing on top of Jackson, and as Jackson stared, at a loss for words, Ellery lowered his mouth and kissed him.

Brutally, without reservation, and without pity.

For a moment, Jackson's defensiveness, his pissiness, his irritation, all of it disappeared. Ellery—prissy, irritating Ellery, who was afraid of what people would think of Jackson skateboarding to the store—was kissing him for no rhyme or reason. And his kisses did what they always did, pumped endorphins through Jackson's battered body and fed him the nectar of life.

The car behind them honked, and Ellery slid off Jackson's lap, moved into his seat, and put his seat belt on, while Jackson tried to catch his breath, adjust his shorts, and fix his brain, all at the same time.

"What the actual fuck?"

"How you doing?" Ellery asked, taking the car out of Park and edging forward.

"I'm very confused."

"You've been pissy for two weeks, all defensive and 'Nothing,' and 'I'm fine, I can deal.' I mean, I thought we were over this bullshit, but I guess we're not, and that's fine. I just thought you should know."

Jackson blinked hard, and Ellery sidled up to the drive-through speaker and ordered a giant Frappuccino with whipped cream for Jackson and a small cup of iced coffee, one sugar, one cream, for himself. He topped it off with hard-boiled eggs for himself and a couple of chocolate croissants for Jackson, and then rolled the window up again to capture the cold air until they made it through the absurdly slow-moving line.

"Know what?" Jackson could barely talk.

"I love you, even though you're being a complete and total pain in the ass."

Jackson growled. "I'm trying not to fucking whine here. Do you have a problem with that?"

"I do if it's going to make you a flaming asshole. Just tell me what's wrong and get it over with!"

I killed two people, and I'm not even fucking sorry!

"Not before we go into work," he muttered. "Because then you and I will be hashing it out all day, and Jade and AJ are coming over to help, and… just fucking Jesus. It's private."

Ellery turned that perceptive brown-eyed gaze on him. "Understood. Is that why you haven't told the rabbi yet?"

"I haven't told the rabbi yet because he's a really sweet guy and I don't want this to ride him. He can deal with the hospital phobia and the dead mom who was a junkie hooker bullshit. I'll save the rest of it for myself."

Ellery let out a little laugh. "I'm not sure that's how it works, Jackson, but okay. Are you really going to ride the skateboard to go get drinks and takeout?"

Jackson shrugged. "Where it's legal."

"You don't even have a helmet!"

"Oh, dammit, *Ellery*—"

"No. I can't let you go talk to a witness with a concussion. Can we make that a rule? No boarding without a helmet and pads?"

"No, Dad. We cannot."

"Well, good luck getting me to give you the keys to get it out of the trunk."

Jackson was still sputtering as Ellery pulled up and paid for their order. Jackson nursed his pleasing sweet freezy in sullen silence and tried to plot how to get around Ellery's damned super-controlling tendencies. He still hadn't figured it out when they pulled up to the pretty converted Victorian house that was their office now.

The houses down this block tended toward colorful, if tasteful, paint schemes. Dark gray and white, pale yellow and navy, forest green and eggshell—each building was an individual confection of turrets and crenellations and pretty-colored siding, but taken as a whole, the block was almost a fairy tale of enchanted houses. Ellery's chosen office was painted dark gold with forest-green trim, and Jackson thought that alone was why he'd picked it.

It was pretty on the outside. Of course, Jackson knew the place had a lot of good features—decent plumbing, internet, adjoining offices in case Ellery ever took in partners, an elevator from the ground floor to the second floor to make it accessible—all of it made for the perfect location for a starter business. But when they'd driven under the giant shade trees and Ellery saw the address, his first words were "Oh, how pretty."

They'd looked at three other properties, even one with a Starbucks on the corner, but Ellery always found a reason to love this one most.

It was one of the many very dear things about Jackson's shark-in-a-suit that made Jackson not want to bother him with the blood on his hands.

But Ellery had stopped in traffic to kiss Jackson stupid, which meant Jackson was getting on his last nerve. Jackson had sort of promised himself he'd stop doing that. He really didn't want to push his luck and have Ellery decide he wasn't worth all the trouble.

Ellery pulled up into the last available parking space in the covered carport, and Jackson gestured violently. "See?"

"I said no, Jackson!"

"But a skateboard—"

"Will get you killed!"

"We didn't get to the store last night," Jackson justified, "and we have no water, no snacks, and—"

"Lunch delivery. You could always call Jade and have her bring beverages. We're getting the refrigerator today."

"Maybe I just want a little freedom. Has that ever occurred to you?"

This office—for the law practice of Ellery Cramer, Esquire—was Ellery's baby. He and Jackson had worked a case in late January that had cost Ellery his job, and Jackson and Jade had quit too. Jade was a paralegal—she was very necessary to Ellery's little operation—but Jackson was a PI, one at odds with most of the cops in the city. What good was he going to be to Ellery as he tried to fix the world?

About all he could do was keep the walls painted and be the muscle of the operation. Unfortunately the last year had been hard enough physically that he wasn't even as good at that as he used to be.

Ellery cast him a skeptical look. "Not really," he said, arching an eyebrow. "And I'm starting to doubt the strategy of letting you talk about this when we get home. Come on, Jackson. I'll take us right back home if you don't spill one thing, one honest thing that's on your chest."

Jackson grunted. Ellery would do it too. "I'm not a lot of help," he said apologetically.

Ellery's turn to grunt. "Of course you are."

"Any idiot can paint!" Or lay carpet or rewire the small kitchen area or install Ellery's computer tower.

Ellery cocked his head. "You need a case, don't you?" he asked, as though he'd just discovered that sunrises were pretty.

Jackson almost cried. "*Yes!*" Oh dear God, was that the problem? "Yes! Oh my God, aren't you losing your shit? How can you not be losing your shit without a case?"

Ellery flashed him an entirely unfettered grin. "*I* like decorating," he said primly. "But don't worry. I have the feeling as soon as our business license comes through, we'll have all the cases you can handle."

Jackson's job was to check out alibis, run down histories, generally look up information on the people Ellery was trying to defend and the misdeed they were alleged to have done. But Jackson—and Ellery—had a long history of going above and beyond to get to the truth.

Jackson shook his head. "No, I don't want to be full up." He gave a faint smile, knowing Ellery deserved to know this much at least, after his emotional unavailability of the last couple of weeks. "I mean, I know we're on medical leave for a couple more weeks, but seriously, being on vacation with you hasn't been bad, Counselor."

And Ellery's grin turned wicked. "I've never had this much sex in my life," he said smugly. Jackson leaned over in the seat, and Ellery met him halfway. A kiss—short, sweet, personal—and Jackson's pissiness faded.

Yes, parts of him were still broken, but the part of him that worked best was about to kick it into gear.

A FEW hours later, Jackson dabbed at the navy-blue trim he was painting and moved his lips to the new Outbreak Monkey song coming from the Bluetooth speaker on Ellery's new desk. The band had been one of his favorites ten years ago when they'd played dives in Sacramento, and they weren't getting any worse.

"Jackson!" Ellery stomped into the room. "Jackson! Jackson!" He hit the volume on the speaker. "Jesus, what is that noise? There are people standing right behind you, and you couldn't put on your shirt?"

Jackson almost dropped his brush, instead fumbling it so an arc of paint spatters covered his chest—and hit Ellery across the ironed polo shirt that he considered casual wear at an office that wasn't quite open yet.

"Who in the fuck is here?" He looked over his shoulder and blinked. One of the guys had casually mussed curly brown hair and a neatly trimmed goatee, as well as a linen suit that screamed "shark" just like Ellery's blue pinstripes did. The other was stocky but trim, with wide shoulders, a military haircut, and was… oddly familiar? He had blond hair, blue eyes, a square jaw, and a flat grim mouth—it seemed like his lips should be fuller, plumper, and the eyes should maybe be not as hostile. The blond one was younger by a few years and dressed in cargo shorts and a close-fitting T-shirt, and even if he'd had hair down to his shoulders, his bearing screamed sir-yes-sir.

The shark stepped forward, extending his hand. "Allow me to introduce myself. I'm Galen Henderson—esquire." He paused for a moment, which was all Jackson needed to stick his foot in it.

"You're a lawyer looking for a lawyer?" He scowled. "I mean, I thought most of you were pretty shady to begin with, but that's amazing."

Galen Henderson turned his attention to Ellery as though he was the only person in the room. "I recently took the bar exam in California for corporate law," he continued smoothly. "The results have not yet been reported, but I spent nearly a decade practicing law in Florida. I'm here on a criminal matter, though, and you come highly recommended."

Jackson and Ellery exchanged looks. "By, uhm, whom?" Jackson asked. "We haven't even moved shit in."

"By your old firm, of course," Mr. Henderson said, deigning to notice him. "Mr. Langdon, in particular."

Jackson sighed. He'd liked working for Lyle Langdon, and no matter how badly things had ended, he hadn't been as bad as Sac PD, where Jackson had worked as a beat cop before literally getting blown out of the water. "Well, fine. He's not a complete douchebag. Let me put on a shirt and we can talk to you in the foyer. The windows are open and the paint smell won't kill us." But not for long. The rooms were getting hot and close, the breeze through the windows notwithstanding.

He went to the counter behind the reception stand and grabbed a towel, grimacing when he saw the paint. "See?" he said to Ellery. "This is why I wasn't wearing a shirt."

"Yes, Jackson, because that thing you're hauling over your head is made so much worse for the paint."

It had holes in it. So sue him. They weren't supposed to be meeting clients. They were supposed to be painting.

"At least he's got good taste in music," the kid in the cargo shorts said, as though unused to making peace between complete strangers.

"I'd be more impressed if he was listening to Seth Arnold," Henderson shot back dryly.

"He's next on the rotation." Jackson raised his eyebrows, feeling the surprise roll off him. "He and his husband are friends of ours." He and Ellery had gotten invites to the very private, very informal wedding that winter, but they'd been recovering then and had needed to decline.

Henderson took a deep breath and tried not to look impressed. "Friends?"

Jackson shrugged. "Old case. Here, I know there's only camp chairs, but you caught us early."

"I'll get my briefcase," Ellery said. He kept it in his office, but while the desk was there, the office chairs had belonged to the old firm. New ones were supposed to be delivered today.

"This will be quite a nice little place," Henderson said, looking around. "I see you've got some room back there for two more lawyers."

Ellery nodded. "The idea was to pick up a couple of partners, yes. But first, I need to get the business license to clear."

"You can practice law, though, right?" Henderson asked anxiously.

"Yes. Full standing with the bar."

"Then why'd you leave your old place?" The kid in the cargo shorts wasn't really a people person. He had laugh lines in the corners of his eyes like he might have been once, but everything out of his mouth now was hostile and irritating.

"We pissed off the wrong people," Jackson said mildly, meeting Ellery's eyes. Ellery shrugged. That story was going to have to be refined—secret military branches and trained assassins sounded a little too extraordinary to the denizens of Sacramento. "Ellery was invited to practice law elsewhere."

Blond-cargo-shorts kid grunted skeptically, but Henderson nodded in appreciation.

"You sound like exactly the people we need," he said, stroking his goatee thoughtfully. Ellery made his exit to his office, and Jackson gestured to the camp chairs set up around a table made of milk cartons.

To his surprise, Galen Henderson sank down gratefully. He looked up at the young man in cargo shorts and said, "I'm going to need help out of this," as though asking for help with what appeared to be an old injury was not a problem at all.

The kid nodded. "Copy that."

Jackson's eyebrows went up as the kid confirmed what he'd already suspected. "Military?" God, they made 'em young—or maybe the kid just looked young.

"Infantry. Just got out," the kid said. Which could make him anywhere from twenty to twenty-eight. His familiarity was starting to bother Jackson on a molecular level.

Jackson nodded. He didn't thank the kid for his service—although that had always been his go-to. He'd met servicemen who were not particularly excited to be thanked, and this guy seemed like he'd rather have his teeth pulled than talk.

Jackson could identify.

"So," Ellery said, entering with his laptop and the inevitable yellow legal pad. "What brings you here?"

Jackson's phone buzzed, and he checked it as Henderson opened his mouth to answer. "Also, we can offer you beverage service in about five minutes, in case you thought we were rude," Jackson added.

The kid's eyebrow twitched, and finally Henderson acknowledged his presence. "Water would be appreciated when it arrives," he said, and Jackson detected a hint of Southern gentleman in his voice.

His bonkers meter was working overtime, because these two men did not appear to like each other much, one of them needed a lawyer and the other one *was* a lawyer, and this situation was bonkers.

Ellery gave Jackson the sort of look that said he'd been raised by wolves and continued on. "So if you called my old firm, you know I'm a criminal attorney. What can we help you with?"

Henderson gave a sigh. "So, my boyfriend runs a company—"

Blond Cargo Shorts gave a disdainful snort.

"Henry Worrall, I do not give a good goddamn what you think of me, but you will be quiet and respectful until I am done speaking, do you hear me?"

Henry grimaced and tried not to roll his eyes. He failed. "Copy that," he managed, and Henderson continued.

"So, my boyfriend runs a company, which you may or may not approve of. Regardless of your approval, it's honest, the books are in order, and he employs upwards of two-hundred-and-fifty people, with health and dental—and options for upward mobility."

Henry's eyes grew huge. "For *what*?"

"You heard me," Henderson told him, ignoring Jackson and Ellery in his irritation with the younger man. "For a chance to move from phase one of the company to something partially skilled that offers the same health and benefits. John's a good man. He does what he can to make sure his people are well taken care of." That said, Henderson made eye contact with Ellery. "This does not mean that unsavory elements don't seep in. One such element—a Mr. Martin Sampson—actively sold drugs and terrorized two of the other employees."

"And your boyfriend let this happen?" Ellery asked, eyebrows drawn.

"My boyfriend is a recovering addict, and he was Mr. Sampson's number one client," Galen said, and Ellery's eyebrows popped right back up again.

"Oh."

"Bummer," Jackson said softly. "That's a shitty position to be in."

Henderson's eyes—fine, brown, steady—landed on Jackson's face as though seeing him for the first time. "Indeed. John regrets so much about that time, you have no idea. But since then, Sampson has worked hard to make life… difficult for John's employees, Sampson's ex-boyfriend in particular."

Ellery had his head tilted as though trying to remember something. He shook himself and said, "I'm sorry, this is a criminal attorney's office. You know that, right? We can help you file a restraining order or fight a blackmail attempt, but you still need to file an actual police report."

It was Galen Henderson's turn to snort. "As though the police would help *us*," he said, a fine layer of disdain falling over the office like construction dust. "No. That is not why we're seeking your help."

"What do you need?" Jackson asked. "And what's the cops' problem with your boyfriend? I mean, I get that they don't always help, but usually a local business owner—"

"It's porn," Henry said bluntly. "This 'legit business' he's talking about is a porn shop."

"Oh!" Jackson said, relief cascading over him like cool water. "*That's* why you look familiar! You look just like Dex from Johnnies!" It was his favorite porn site—pretty boys, lots of laughter. It looked like the guys were having fun and not just fucking for money.

Henry's grim disgust turned nuclear. "That's so gross that you would even know that!"

Jackson shrugged. "He's cute. I'm bi. Every boy has a spank bank. You're not him—what's it to you?"

"He's my brother," Henry growled.

"Well, he's retired," Jackson said mildly, and was on the receiving end of a ball-boiling glare from Ellery. "He's *been* retired for over a year and a half," he said, batting his eyelashes. "So, you know, back when I was single and would be watching porn, I would have known who he was."

Ellery's glare turned bored, but Jackson caught the little smirk that said he was mildly charmed. Well, he tried very hard not to be jealous of Jackson's promiscuous past—and Jackson worked really hard not to give him anything to be jealous about in the present.

Then everything Galen had been saying hit him. "Wait, if Dex is retired, does that mean he's one of those people who have moved on?"

Galen nodded. "Yes. He and his husband, in fact. Dex got his business degree and has been running the shop with John. He's a full partner, actually." A grimace. "John was afraid of relapsing. He wanted somebody who would make sure the boys would be taken care of, just in case. Anyway, Kane, Dex's husband, has been doing odd jobs around the shop—holding lights, moving furniture, that sort of thing—as well as going to school."

Henry snorted before Jackson could get all swoony about his two favorite porn models being married, and Henderson's temper snapped. "You will show respect to that kid. He's going to school, and he works his ass off. Just because it's been easy for someone like you, that doesn't mean it's easy for everybody. They're good men and good parents, and they put a roof over your sorry ass when you turned up on their doorstep. And I know you think you're a military badass, but Kane could pretty much put you in the ground with a backhand. The only reason he doesn't is because he loves your brother. So if you could please try not to piss me off here while I work to save your ass at their request, I would really fucking appreciate it!"

Henry glared sullenly out the window, and Jackson tried really hard not to look at Ellery.

"Parents?" he said delicately.

Henderson nodded. "They are raising Kane's niece. There is, in fact, a little collective of babies—something in the water, I guess, because suddenly an ex-girlfriend and the receptionist, Dex and Kane, everybody's got a kid to raise. It's this really weird *Romper Room* thing going, where all these ex–porn stars with muscles that bulge out of their cars are raising teeny tiny children." Henderson shuddered. "I am just as happy with a cat, thank you."

Jackson smirked, and Henderson shot him a grateful look. "My cat would have to vet any child personally," Jackson said, thinking about Billy Bob's possessive streak where he was concerned.

"Well, it is their job to rule their domain," Henderson said, dry wit at the ready. Jackson thought he could really like Galen Henderson, but he'd like to kick the shit out of Henry.

"So this sounds… unusual," Ellery inserted. "Why come to us? What has Martin Sampson done lately to your little collective?"

"Well, other than trying to blackmail them over the drugs *he sold them*," Galen spat, "not much. That was over a year and a half ago, and he went dark. I'm not sure if he was in rehab, jail, on the streets, had moved to another state, or what. But about two weeks after Henry hit town, freeloading on his brother's good graces—"

"I was looking for a job," Henry muttered.

"Fast food is hiring," Galen retorted. "Anyway, Dex put Henry up in what we call the flophouse. It's not really associated with Johnnies, but it's sort of an apartment where guys pay into the kitty and sleep wherever they can. Or I should say, it *wasn't* associated with Johnnies, because Dex apparently gave his brother a job keeping the place up and babysitting the guys—a thing that hasn't really been necessary until right now, if you know what I mean."

Jackson made sure Henry was looking at him. "So nepotism is fun as long as you keep it in the family?"

"Fuck you," Henry muttered.

"Not if you paid me," Jackson snapped back, "because nobody should have to work that hard."

Ellery and Galen made the same sound at the same time, but Jackson ignored them. He still wasn't sure what the problem was, but he knew that Henry—whatever his term in the service—had a chip on his shoulder that needed to be knocked off.

"Look, Henry?"

Henry glared.

"I don't know why you're being an asshole. And if you tell me it's because your brother's a porn star, I'll call bullshit. A living is a living."

"What about working for a drug addict." Henry glared at Galen spitefully. "Two of them!"

Galen didn't even raise an eyebrow. "I never denied my recovery," he said. "We are broken people, Henry. That doesn't mean we're not people at all."

And finally, the kid had the grace to look ashamed.

"Look, can we get this over with?" Henry snarled.

"So back to Martin Sampson," Ellery steered, and Jackson had to laugh. Ellery tried hard, but he really wasn't happy when conversations got away from him.

"He showed up again," Henderson continued, "this time hanging around the kids in the flophouse. The kids are clean—John does HIV and drug testing, especially after he almost lost the shop to Sampson—and he made sure there was a super-spiffy rehab special in the health insurance he bought. Anyway, the kids reported Sampson to Henry, and Henry had an altercation with him."

Henry snorted. "Poser. Scrawny addict poser. I kicked his ass in three hits."

"You must be so proud." Jackson would have taken longer and enjoyed it.

"His brother drove the guy off by flinging CDs at his head." Galen's snark was at the forefront. "Sampson was Dex's ex-boyfriend. Apparently, he could be a real hero if he thought he had an advantage. He took out all the windows in his ex-girlfriend's apartment too." Henderson shook his head in disgust, and Jackson picked up on the time stamp.

"Thought?" he clarified.

Henderson nodded grimly. "And *that* is why we're here. Henry's altercation with Sampson was a week and a half ago—no police notified, none needed. This morning, Henry was taking the trash out of the apartment when he made a rather grim discovery."

Henry grimaced. "That is an understatement."

"Don't tell me…." But Jackson knew. Ellery was a criminal defense attorney with a reputation for defending people who looked guilty.

"Freaky little asshole was in the same dumpster I kicked his ass behind," Henry confirmed. "But this time, his head was cracked open and he was dead."

"Ah." Jackson heard Ellery's exhale too.

"Have you been charged yet, Henry?"

Henry shook his head. "But they asked me and the boys lots of questions. I mean, seven guys show up on the stairs without shirts, looking fucking ripped, and I think they looked suspicious."

"You think, huh?" Jackson asked, feeling like this needed to be pounded home. "As though, maybe, people would be distracted by what they looked like or what they did for a living and wouldn't focus on who really killed the guy in the dumpster?"

Henry grunted, obviously not ready to concede the point.

"Was it one of those guys?" Ellery asked, missing the nuance completely because the only person Ellery really got was Jackson.

"No!" Henry denied fiercely. "Look, yes, they're porn stars, and I think most of them could do better—"

"Like you?" Galen asked, and Henry shot him a killing look.

"Anyway, they are generally sweet guys. They're gym trainers and yoga teachers, and one of them helps adult special education students go on outings, but that's only three days a week. And med students. There's one med student. They're not... not killers. And they're not drug addicts. It wasn't them, it wasn't me, but once the police make the connection between the guy who found him and me, the guy who kicked his ass.... Not to mention what everybody does for a living—"

"How would they?" Ellery asked quickly. "I mean, I appreciate coming forearmed, but how would the police know to even ask about a connection?"

Galen let out a slow breath. "Because Mr. Sampson used to work for Johnnies under the name of Scott before he did too much blow and too much blackmail and he got fired."

"Scott?" Jackson said, feeling oddly vindicated. "He's our dead scumbag?"

"You watched his porn too?" Ellery asked, slightly horrified.

"No. Seriously, he may have had a nine-inch dick, but he fucked like he was drilling holes through the bed. I mean, no. Just, you know. No."

"Well, that's reassuring," Ellery muttered.

"Technique counts," Jackson said with dignity. "If the guy doesn't act like the other person in bed is a real human and everything, it shatters the illusion."

"See?" Henderson said in complete seriousness. "That's what we think too. Anyway, Scott was sort of everybody's asshole for a while. He knocked up the receptionist, did some mild stalking, some blackmail, and then, like I said, he disappeared."

"Wait." Jackson held up a hand. "Who did he stalk?"

"The receptionist. Apparently he got some jail time for vandalizing her house and terrorizing her when she was inside, and that's on the record. What's not on the record is that he stalked Henry's brother for a short time too. Hence the CDs being thrown at his head."

Jackson's eyebrows went up. Galen had said two employees, but this was a surprise. "Why didn't it go on record?"

"Dex's husband scared the boy off," Galen supplied, a grim smile on his mouth.

Well, if Jackson remembered correctly, Kane had shoulders like a moving van—he would have scared Jackson off too.

"So that's another connection," Ellery said, frowning. "Does Dex have an alibi?"

"He was home with Kane," Henry said, sounding irritated for reasons known only to him. "Kane's niece had school the next day. They've become fucking model citizens now."

Jackson made eye contact with Galen. "Do we have any clue why this pisses him off so much?"

Galen gave an evil smile. "Guilty conscience and unrequited love."

"Fuck you!" Henry yelled. "Fuck you and fuck off and fuck this fucking bull—"

Jackson got behind him and grabbed his ear. It was a gamble—the guy was decked and he was military, and he could have gone ballistic on Jackson's ass and taken out the entire brand-new office, Galen and Ellery included. But Jackson had the feeling there was something of a mama's boy in this guy. And getting grabbed by the ear was a mama's boy's secret weakness.

Sure enough, Henry flailed, his arms windmilling, but he never once sucked it up, stood still, and tried any of the thirty things he could have done to debilitate Jackson.

"Let me go, motherfucker!" Henry snarled, still flailing.

"No!" Jackson kicked him in the back of the thigh and sent him down to his knees. "Now shut up and let the grown-ups talk, Junior. This nice man is trying to keep you out of jail, and you're being a complete twat. Do I care why? Well, only if I've got popcorn and a soda and a big screen—and it has *something to do with the case.* In the meantime, check your chip in at the door and let's hear what Mr. Henderson has to say."

"I'm twenty-seven years old," Henry muttered.

"Shut up. If I roll my eyes back in my head any further, they'll pop out." Jackson let go of Henry's ear, and Galen Henderson beamed up at Jackson with a beatific smile.

"Mr. Cramer, do you and Mr. Rivers come as a package deal?"

"We do," Ellery said, lifting an eyebrow. "I do the lawyering. He does the investigating."

"Excellent. Are you interested in taking the case?"

"We are," Ellery said, after eyeball-checking with Jackson first. "But I'm not sure if you'll need us. So far the police haven't made contact with anybody but Henry here, have they?"

Galen shrugged. "Between Henry and Dex, somebody is going to become a person of interest, I have no doubt."

Jackson didn't either, and by the look on his face, neither did Ellery. "Jackson?"

"I'll do the legwork. You look up the victim's record?" Jackson suggested, and Ellery grunted.

"Are you sure—"

At that moment, the door burst open and a force of nature blew in. "Gentlemen, I have drinks, and there's a nice man with a refrigerator to store them in on the way in fifteen, but we need help here!"

"Excuse me," Jackson said courteously. Realizing Galen and Ellery needed to speak lawyer-to-lawyer for a moment, he added, "Henry, would you like to remember your manners and help us out here?"

Henry stood up reluctantly and glowered. "Sure."

Jackson turned to his sister. "Jade, my darlin', we have here our first client. This is Henry Worrall, and the guy talking to Ellery is Galen Henderson. If you can pull out some paperwork and shit, Henry and I will start hauling supplies."

Jade—curvy, strong, and vibrantly beautiful from the crown of her straightened magenta hair to the tip of her scarlet-painted toes—had lovely dark brown skin with hints of bronze, round cheeks, and a solid bullshit line between her elegant eyebrows that had been put there by assholes just like Henry.

"There are drinks in my car, which is parked on the street, and boxes of paperwork in the trunk." She tossed Jackson the keys to the little Toyota she was driving these days, and Jackson caught them midair.

"Did Mike not lend you the SUV?" he asked, and she snorted, tossing her ponytail over her shoulder.

"Do you know that thing has no air-conditioning? He can drive that piece of shit to his own damned job. He says the heat is meaningless without humidity. I swear, that man makes Virginia sound like fucking Mordor, the way he talks about summer in the South."

"He is not wrong," Galen said, struggling to his feet. Ellery hopped up and gave him a hand, and Galen shot him a grateful look—and then rolled his eyes at Henry. "Ma'am, pardon me for not rising sooner."

Jade's bullshit line eased as she recognized an attempt at graciousness in a room in which camp chairs were the prevalent furnishings. "Hello there, I'm Jade Cameron, receptionist and paralegal here at…." She paused in the act of shaking Galen's hand and scowled at Ellery. "What in the hell are we calling this place?"

"Ellery Cramer, Attorney at Law?" Ellery shrugged. "I mean, that's what my business cards say."

Jade harrumphed. "Those are the interim cards. We need something with a logo—something flashy. But we'll work on it."

"I'm sure you will," Galen said, dimpling at her. When he smiled deeply, Jackson could see that he had some scarring on his face, partially hidden by longish dark hair and the scruffy beard. "In the meantime, I'm Mr. Galen Henderson, also an attorney but in corporate defense, and my client here is Henry Worrall. And he *will* help you with your burdens."

"Why thank you," she said, and Jackson loved how she could be all that was gracious in the middle of the chaos in the room. "Jackson's mostly housebroken—I'm sure they can make themselves useful."

Mostly. Mostly he loved how she could be gracious. When she was *being* gracious, and not being the sister who would throw him under the bus at a moment's notice.

"C'mon, Henry," Jackson muttered. "We've got shit to do."

Henry gave him a fulminating look, but he followed Jackson out the door, where Jackson skipped the elevator, which was slow as turtle shit, and took the stairs down to the curbside to get to the car.

"I don't know why we're here," Henry said, as Jackson opened up the car and started shoving cases of water into his arms. "I haven't even been charged."

"Oh, it's coming," Jackson said with confidence. He shut the door of Jade's white Toyota and moved around to the trunk to look for the boxes of paperwork. "Oh, Jade, you lovely woman, you bought soda." He put the case of soda and one of vitamin water on top of a couple of file boxes, lifted everything out of the back, and managed to shut the trunk with his elbow. "Don't worry about the cops—they'll find out just enough about you and your brother to draw the wrong conclusions. Give them two days before they come knocking on your door again. One if Sampson's got any connections."

"His parents are rich," Henry said, and Jackson nodded.

"So, tomorrow, then. You may want to warn the guys in the flophouse. If they've got any other place to flop, they should go there."

Henry let out a breath. "They're not going to come after my brother, are they? I mean… there's a little girl there. I… I guess she's living there because her father was abusive and her mother sort of picked him. Anyway, she's a cute kid. I don't want her upset."

"But your brother and his husband can go to hell."

Henry grunted. "You know, in the house I grew up in, if we talked about a guy having a husband, it was an insult to both of them."

"The world's moving past that bullshit," Jackson said soberly, leading the way back up the stairs. "You should too. Being gay's not a bad thing, you know?"

Henry let out a bark of bitter laughter. "You should try telling that to my father. He hasn't said Davy's name in our house in two years."

"Davy?"

"Dex. It's weird, Dex was his porn name, I guess, and everybody knows him as Dex here. The only ones who call him Davy are me and his...." Henry let out a breath as they cleared the landing on top of the stairs. "His husband," he said in mild defeat.

"Is Kane *his* real name too?"

"No. It's Carlos. It's...."

Jackson paused with his hand on the doorknob, his load of boxes balanced against his shoulder, while Henry said something human.

"What?"

"It's like they call each other their real names as an endearment. Like they're the only two people who know who they are. And a part of me wants to think it's sweet, but a part of me feels...."

The doorknob turned under Jackson's hand, and he almost fell through and lost the load of crap in his arms. He gained his balance and made it inside, and by the time he'd set the boxes on the counter and the cases of beverage on the floor, Henry was back to scowling again and looking irritated he was even there. Not even a vitamin water could cheer him up, but Jackson downed his thankfully. The pavement was steaming outside and it wasn't even noon yet.

And in the back of Jackson's head, he kept hearing that final word from Henry, as if he'd said it under his breath just when chaos had erupted.

Jackson couldn't be sure, but he thought the word was *guilty*.

Esquire

A YEAR ago, before he'd worked closely with Jackson and seen his compassion for everybody—recovering addicts, prostitutes, spacey psychics, damaged warriors, everyone—Ellery would have regarded Galen Henderson with a great deal of suspicion. And that would have been a shame.

Galen was as Southern gentleman as Ellery was Massachusetts liberal—both of them bred from the cradle to do something serviceable and honorable with their lives and their profession as they grew. Whatever Galen's story was, and of course Ellery was curious, that didn't stop Ellery from admiring his sharp presentation of the facts and the extent of his organization as he listed home and business contacts for the people Ellery or Jackson would need to interview on top of giving Ellery some gentle pointers about running his own law firm.

"So, you have the paperwork for us to fill out ready?" he asked, as though this was a test Ellery needed to pass.

"I have your forms right here, Mr. Henderson," Jade gushed, pulling a clipboard out of the box Jackson had carted up. It had the forms Ellery and Jade had hammered out the month before, the clearances, the permissions, the form promising to pay Ellery's retainer and the fee sheet for Ellery's time as a lawyer, as well as Jackson's time spent on the case. Jackson's name wasn't going on the door, but Ellery knew from the last year that he didn't want to do his job without Jackson's help doing what he did best.

Galen scanned each form before he signed it and then twinkled up at Jade. "Your organization is perfection, my dear. I worked in Miami Beach at Spencer, Cohen, and Harris, and I have to tell you that this is some of the cleanest paperwork I've seen."

Jade beamed at Ellery. "I like him," she said, nodding vehemently, and Ellery held back a flash of resentment. It had taken her *months* to warm up to Ellery, and he was pretty sure that if Jackson hadn't followed him when he'd been let go from Pfeist, Langdon, Harrelson, and Cooper, Jade would have been still working there—maybe a little sad, but not devastated.

"Of course you do," he said mildly. "Jackson, did you get everything from the car?"

"One more load," Jackson said. "Henry."

Ellery watched as Henry followed Jackson outside again, his permascowl not even lightened fractionally by the shared task.

"Well, isn't he special," Ellery muttered under his breath.

"You have no idea," Galen responded, because his mild limp didn't seem to impede his hearing in the least.

Ellery glanced at him sharply. "Do tell?" He tried to keep his shark sense from tingling, but Galen's droll look told him he'd failed miserably.

"My boy, do you have no idea how gossip works at all? You are supposed to wait until the second time I come to visit your office—wherein I shall comment on the lovely décor that will undoubtedly be here in place of this rather temporary setup that is not your fault because we surprised you, of that I am aware. Then, while you are occupied with your next client, or with the delightful Mr. Rivers, who does cut a fine figure without his shirt, I would casually engage your lovely receptionist in conversation, dish everything to her, and she would relay the information to you."

Ellery choked on a sip of warm water at the mention of Jackson and continued to cough as Henderson finished. "I'm sorry?"

"What? About you and Mr. Rivers? Did you want that to be a secret? You failed."

Ellery took another sip of water so he could stop choking on the last one. "You caught us unaware, like you said." Oh, how embarrassing. He and Jackson had been sleeping together for months while working at Pfeist, Langdon, Harrelson, and Cooper, and Langdon had only begun to suspect toward the end because Jackson had dropped off the grid and Ellery was losing his mind. "We are usually very professional."

Galen's snort was far more elegant than Ellery's choke. "*You* may be," he said. "But your Mr. Rivers is exactly who he is, and that's a good thing. Trust me. I have one of those. Don't trade him for gold."

"I won't, or for information. So when would I ask you about Henry?"

"You," Henderson said distinctly, "have no finesse."

Ellery just looked at him. "I win cases. What's his damage?"

Galen's eyes flickered up to the closed door, and Ellery looked over his shoulder, where he could see out the window, down to where Jackson and Henry were still unloading the car.

"You've got two minutes," he said lowly. "We need to know."

Galen's grimace was not reassuring. "I know you do. And I know it's going to come up. It's just that it's personal. Dex only knows because he got a phone call from someone in the family. If the boy finds out Dex told me, it could make everything… worse."

Ellery opened his mouth to press, and the door opened, revealing AJ, struggling under a mountain of packages and grocery bags. Ellery popped to his feet, going in for the assist.

"Sorry, Mr. Cramer," AJ murmured, spilling bags into Ellery's arms. "It's just Jade said I needed to hurry because we had clients, and I know the fridge and furniture people are coming and—"

"No worries," Ellery told him, working hard to project gentleness. Usually he failed miserably at it, but with AJ—maybe because he'd seen AJ at the lowest moment of his life and the young man had worked so hard to climb out of that hellhole—he managed not to scare the kid shitless 90 percent of the time. "Here. Let's get this behind the desk where the fridge is going to go. AJ, this is Galen Henderson, a fellow lawyer and friend to our first client. Galen, this is AJ, our gopher and go-to guy, who is pretty much helping us out for free until we can afford to pay him."

AJ was slightly built, with mixed genetics—skin of pale ochre, dark freckles, and tightly curled hair the color of a faded sunset. He gave Galen a shy smile and ducked his head.

"Nice to meet you. It's more fun to work here," AJ said, turning that smile to Ellery, and Ellery tried for a wink. He didn't fail too badly, because the kid didn't jerk back in disgust.

"Jackson will be up in a minute," Ellery told him. "He was painting the reception area, but I think he's going to have to go make some calls after he and Henry come back up."

AJ nodded. "I'll finish up the kitchen so it's ready for the fridge."

With that he turned abruptly, probably anxious to get away from the stranger who was regarding him as mildly and unoffensively as possible.

Ellery turned back toward Galen, hoping to get Henry's backstory before Henry got back upstairs, only to find Galen regarding him thoughtfully.

"So about Henry—what?"

"I'm just… pleased," Galen said cryptically. "I contemplated not returning to law, you know. I was out of the game for a few years after a motorcycle accident." Which explained his careful walk and the scars on his face. "But I took the bar when I came out here to join John, just in case he needed help."

"Why'd you leave?" Ellery couldn't imagine doing anything else.

"I usually don't like lawyers."

Ellery's mouth dropped open, and at that moment, the guys came back in with one more load of file boxes and cleaning supplies, arguing hotly.

"I don't see why!" Henry snarled as Jackson opened the door. "Why do you gotta go poke your nose into everybody's business? I'd just as soon none of them even know I'm fuckin' here!"

"Well, I'm sure your brother would just as soon you not be, you shitkicking little punk. But if we want to keep you out of jail, we need to have an idea, at least, of who else might have killed your drug-dealing scumbag and what the people around you were doing when he died. So yes, I'm going to go talk to your brother and his boss and your roommates at gay-fucking-topia, because that's my job. And if I'm not mis-fucking-taken, your lawyer just talked to my lawyer, engaging our services for me to do that exact goddamned thing. Suck it up, buttercup, because whatever nasty crawly secrets you've got, I'm about to kick over the rock they're hiding under."

Henry barged in, past Jackson, and dropped his boxes in the middle of the room without ceremony.

"Galen, I'm fucking out of here!" he bellowed.

Galen cocked his head, raised his eyebrow, and looked actively bored. "I have the car keys, Henry. Enjoy the walk."

Henry pulled up short, his chest pumping, sweat running down his back from his short time outside, because the day was that ugly. "Fuck."

"Mr. Rivers?" Galen smiled charmingly at Jackson. "If you would like, I can give you a ride to the offices. I do believe John is there, so you may speak to him. But you will have to catch Dex and Kane at home later this evening. They're currently at a volunteer event for Kane's niece."

Jackson frowned in thought and looked at Ellery. "I'll text you when I'm done," he said. "Somebody can come pick me up."

"I can bring you back to the damned office," Henry growled.

"Or you could choose life, because after two hours in your company, the trip back might be the final trigger," Jackson snapped. "Now if you could do me a favor and let me and Ellery plan a minute, I'd be forever fucking grateful."

"I'll be outside." Henry slammed the door on his way out, leaving Jade and AJ in the office, giving him the side-eye of death.

"Wow." Jade gave Jackson a sympathetic glance. "I know I give you an awful lot of grief about being barely housetrained, but that guy is going to need a rolled-up newspaper and a spray bottle before we let him through that door again."

"He's a big boy," Jackson said, winking. "With that one, I could use a baseball bat."

AJ snickered, and Jackson turned to Galen.

"Mr. Henderson, if you don't mind, I'm going to talk to my boss for a moment, and then I'm going to abandon him to the refrigerator guy and the furniture people, who will probably take all his time."

"You bastard," Ellery said, with no irony whatsoever.

"Jade can defend you from the big assholes with muscles," Jackson said with a smirk. "Don't worry. You'll be safe."

AJ snickered again, and Jackson turned and led the way to Ellery's office. While Jackson had been painting, Ellery had been setting up his computer and stocking his desk with supplies, as well as arranging his law books up on the shelves that had arrived the week before.

"What?" Ellery asked as soon as the door closed behind him.

Jackson shrugged. "The kid's hiding something. I don't think it's the murder, but he's got something he doesn't want to talk about."

"Yeah, I know. I was trying to pump Galen for information, but…." He shrugged.

"People," Jackson said succinctly. "I don't think it's something related to the case, but damn if we don't need to figure it out, all the same."

"Agreed." They both knew that suspects and persons of interest often hid things that they didn't see as relevant but that would prejudice a jury—or the police—against them. In order to keep a client out of jail, it was Ellery and Jackson's *job* to know the things their clients least liked about themselves. Sometimes it made the job interesting, and sometimes it made the job dangerous, and sometimes it made the job heartbreaking.

But it was always the fucking job.

"I'll look up Martin Eugene Sampson," Ellery told him.

"Aka Scott."

Ellery made a grimace of distaste, and Jackson called him to task.

"Don't make that face. You need to look up the porn," Jackson said. He grabbed a pen and a Post-it note from Ellery's big solid oak desk and jotted something down. "It's under my home email, and this is the password—"

"BillyBobs2Balls," Ellery read in stunned disbelief.

Jackson grinned. "Feeling guilty?"

The year before, Ellery had made the call to get Billy Bob neutered while he was under general anesthesia for the wound that took his leg. Jackson had been shot in the same incident, and Ellery refused to feel guilty for an operation that had probably saved the cat's life twice—once to stop the bleeding of the crushed leg, and once to keep the animal from wandering away from home and into traffic.

"Not even a little," he said, scowling. "What about you? You said you stopped watching a year ago!"

Jackson chuckled. "But I didn't let my subscription lapse for reasons!" He sobered. "Look, they run a clean site—don't laugh, we're not twelve. There's porn that's exploitive and porn that's functional and porn that shows happy consenting adults having sex so you can get off and pretend you're one of them. Galen's boyfriend runs option C. But we need to check out our vic, see some recent photos. Henry called the guy scrawny, which means he's not living the same life he was a year and a half ago when he stopped showing up on the site. We need to fill in the blanks."

Ellery nodded. "Copy that," he said, his lips twisting with recognition of Henry's military speech. Jackson turned to leave, and Ellery stopped him with a hand on his wrist.

"What? What'd we forget?"

Ellery pulled him closer. "Really? You're going to ask me that on your first run in five months?"

Jackson's eyes widened, and he swallowed hard. Five months ago, Jackson had gone out to investigate a client's story and had ended up in the hospital because a planter had fallen on his head. And that wasn't even the worst thing to happen to him and Ellery that week!

Jackson threw his body fearlessly into whatever task he had at hand, and Ellery loved him for it and would probably love him for it until the day he died. But he would also be afraid—terrified—because Jackson didn't seem to have the Stop button in his head that told him to save at least a part of himself to come back to Ellery.

"I'll be careful," he said, smiling a little. "I promise not to let the big scary porn stars jump me."

Ellery rolled his eyes. "You're hilarious. We should sell tick—mmmf...."

Jackson pulled him forward abruptly, showing as much roughness as he'd shown before the climax of their last case, when Ellery had been shot and Jackson had been stabbed and they'd both had to move very, very gently indeed.

But for the first time since then, Jackson's mouth on his was hard, voracious, like Ellery was now strong enough to take what had gone on between them almost since their first case together, the August before. Ellery groaned softly, returning the kiss with interest. Like this morning at the Starbucks, a part of him needed so badly to know that Jackson's passion hadn't died just because they'd both been injured and had only now come back.

Jackson thrust his tongue inside Ellery's mouth, plundering, taking, and Ellery melted against his chest, trusting Jackson to bear Ellery's full weight for the first time in months. He opened his mouth and let Jackson in, then met him stroke for stroke until they were both panting, grinding against each other, groins swollen, sweat dripping down their backs.

Jackson pulled away, and Ellery actually whimpered with the loss.

"That what you wanted, Counselor?" Jackson asked gruffly.

"Oh my God, yes." Ellery rested his forehead against Jackson's shoulder, and Jackson brushed his ear with soft lips.

"I love you, Ellery. I'll be careful for you. Can't promise it'll all go according to plan, but I'll treat your property right."

Ellery nodded and gave him a brief, hard last kiss to seal the deal. "It's all I can ask," he said. "If you really don't want the ride from Henry, text me when you're done."

"Deal."

Then Jackson let himself out and strode down the hall, yelling, "Jade darlin', give me your phone charger if you have it. For fuck's sake, I'm gonna want to send that fucking text!"

Jackson paused to help Galen out of his chair and kept his arm out to escort the man down the stairs. Galen took the help without comment, but Ellery did spot a rather barbed glance in Henry's direction, and Henry had the good grace to look ashamed.

Oh yeah. Ellery needed to do his own research, quickly, because if Galen Henderson hadn't come in to vouch for that boy, Ellery might have had him arrested on attitude alone.

The door closed behind them, leaving Jade and AJ looking at Ellery expectantly.

"I need to get my computer set up," he admitted. "We need the vic's financials, his address, and we need the subpoena ready for the police report in case they pull Henry in for questioning." He paused to gather his thoughts, but Jade interrupted with some thoughts of her own.

"I can finish putting the office together and dealing with delivery men," she offered. "AJ, you up to help?"

AJ nodded enthusiastically. "I only work at the firm three days a week now," he confessed. "They cut my hours because they hired Harrelson's useless nephew to do my job."

Ellery grimaced. "Well, as soon as we get a few more cases, we can pay you," he said, feeling wrong and exploitive, but AJ shrugged.

"Crystal's paying the rent and utilities," he said. His roommate was still working at Jackson and Ellery's former firm, but she'd told them, under no uncertain terms, that it was only until Ellery drummed up enough business to need his own computer and statistics expert on staff. Crystal was… well, freaky. Ellery wasn't sure what it was about Jackson that attracted the woo-woo, but Crystal was one of two psychics Ellery knew now. And while he didn't doubt either one of them possessed an ability of some sort, he was really, really, super not interested in knowing anything else about what that ability was.

But even Ellery couldn't deny that Crystal was kind to AJ, and given that AJ and Crystal were recovering addicts *without* the resources of a Galen Henderson, he and Jackson were grateful that the two had found each other.

"Yeah," Jade said knowingly, "but I know you're saving for a new car. That old one is parked outside the duplex often enough, I know you're not getting any use from it."

AJ bit his lip and looked sideways, and Ellery and Jade traded glances. The other half of the duplex Jade lived in *used* to be occupied by Jackson, but when Ellery had sort of… drafted Jackson to live together, Jackson had made it a refuge for people getting out of jail who had no way of getting on their feet. He monitored it, and he'd told social services that it was there—and he and Jade vetted all the residents. AJ had lived there for a short time before he and Crystal found each other. There was no reason Ellery could think of that he'd be returning there now, unless—

"Are you seeing that Jail kid?" Jade asked, concerned.

"Ja-*el*," AJ corrected her. He shrugged uncomfortably. "We, uh, play video games. He, uh, you know. I moved in with Crystal, and then he texted me and said he missed me. The last couple weeks, we've played video games. You know. When we're not working."

Jade looked at him.

"And Jackson said it's okay, so I could keep an eye on everybody. I've been doing that. Jael's mother has a job, and his two friends are staying clean. Not that they talk to me much. Or Jael. But, you know. We play games."

Jade said, "Hunh," and she kept looking at him.

AJ smiled greenly. "And sometimes, his mom cooks, which is nice, and Crystal bakes them cookies, which is nice, so they don't feel so alone. Crystal tells Jael what classes to take because he wants to be a computer tech like she is, and we look at college catalogs and...."

Jade was still looking, her round brown eyes fixed solidly on AJ's sweating, blushing face.

"And he's kissed me twice and says he wants to keep doing it." AJ's shoulders sagged as he spit out the confession.

Jade met Ellery's eyes. "Thoughts?"

Ellery's brain blanked out. "You need to talk to Jackson." Because Jackson did people, and Ellery did briefs and cases and courtrooms.

"I will. I just wondered if you wanted to weigh in on the care and feeding of our favorite unpaid intern."

Oh great. This was apparently one of those duties of parenthood—Ellery couldn't escape this conversation.

"Is Jael in the closet?" he asked, because he knew the boys Jackson had installed in the duplex were not the most educated bunch. This could be a sticking point.

"He told his friends he's got a crush on me." AJ grimaced. "I think they've been avoiding us both ever since."

"What about his mother?" The woman who had been arrested for distribution, along with her son and his friends.

"She's been really nice," AJ admitted.

"That's promising," Ellery said, considering. "And I like that it's a couple of kisses with the promise of more. That speaks of two young gentlemen and courtship—not just hooking up." Finally he had something constructive to say. "Just hooking up is hard," he said, thinking about Jackson's rootlessness when they'd first met. "You're doing really well in recovery, AJ. I don't want you to have to deal with anything hard." AJ had been on the cusp of dropping out of life permanently when he'd wandered into a house of death having a heroin free-for-all. His dedication to making his job work, to keeping the human connections that Jackson had established had been heartening to watch.

AJ nodded. "Thanks, Mr. Cramer. I appreciate—"

And at that moment, there was a knock on the door and the delivery men were there, and everybody had something to do.

Inside the Chocolate Factory

GALEN VERY gallantly offered to let Jackson sit in the front seat of the Buick LeSabre while Henry drove, and Jackson took him up on it, because as pleasant as Galen Henderson seemed to be, Henry was the one Jackson had to work on.

"So," Jackson said as they were making their way through traffic to J Street. "You were in the military?"

"Yessir." The snide little twist on "sir" was not lost on Jackson.

"When did you get out?"

"About two months ago."

"You came straight to Sacramento to see your brother?"

"No, sir. I went home first." Henry had donned military sunglasses in the knife-bladed sun, and Jackson had pulled on his own as well. Galen had pulled out a tablet from the satchel on his hip and was working industriously, offering nothing, so Jackson supposed he was on his own.

"And where is home, Henry?" Jackson asked, gritting his teeth.

"Montana," Henry replied smartly. "Outside of Billings."

"Wow. What made you decide not to stay there?"

Henry came to an abrupt stop at L, and they waited for the light. "I was not welcome there," he said, his voice gruff.

Jackson's eyes went wide. "A clean-cut charmer like you, Henry? What did you do?"

"I would rather not talk about it," Henry said with dignity.

"That's great," Jackson said, trying to keep things pleasant. Sort of. "Let's talk about how Martin Sampson was killed."

"I told you—he got his head bashed in."

"That's great. Was the weapon in the dumpster?"

Henry thought for a moment as the light turned green and he pulled forward. "No," he said. "And the dumpsters are fairly clean. There was no blood or hair on the corners either."

"Head wounds bleed a lot. Was there a lot of blood in the surrounding area?"

Henry bit his lip. "No," he said, thinking. "No, there wasn't. That means it's a secondary crime scene, doesn't it?"

"Mm-hm. It does indeed. And it means that there's a murder weapon somewhere and a car or rug or a tarp with lots of trace evidence floating around."

"The face was bloody," Henry said, as though this had just occurred to him. "The guy's face was bloody, but I didn't see a wound."

"So probably a tarp, but I wouldn't rule out a rug," Jackson murmured. "About the cops who showed up—was there a forensic team there?"

"Yessir," Henry said. "Isn't there always?"

"Not always. It depends on the budget and the DA's office and how thin everything is spread and which district the crime occurred in. Where's the flophouse?"

"Off of Howe Avenue, on Hurley. It's in one of those big apartment warrens with more residents than my hometown."

Jackson felt his mouth quirk, because that was the closest thing to humor Henry Worrall had offered him so far. He'd take it. "Lucky you. I grew up in Sacramento—not big enough to be impressive, not small enough to give a shit. Everybody's got some childhood damage to repair."

"I didn't," Henry muttered.

"No?" Somehow Jackson doubted that.

"Dad was a hard man, but only when he needed to be."

"So if you anticipated his every move, he didn't bruise your face," Jackson translated, and Henry gave him a sideways scowl.

"He just needed us to not be dumbasses."

"And your mom?"

"Did everything she could to make him happy."

"Hunh." It was Ellery's least favorite sound of Jackson's, but he couldn't help it. He could see the whole picture fairly clearly, he thought. He just couldn't see what a good little son-bot like Henry could have done to not be welcome there anymore.

"What the fuck does that mean?" Henry growled.

"It means we're getting off the subject," Jackson evaded, and pretended not to hear Galen's amused grunt behind them. "Exactly what drugs was Sampson trying to sell?"

"Pills," Henry said promptly, and at the same time Galen said, "Coke."

Jackson's eyes went wide. "So, Henry, that's *only* pills, or was it both?"

"No, it was just pills," Henry said. "Oxy, gabapentin, Vicodin. He was really fucking organized. Had little ten-pill bags going for thirty bucks a piece, all of them labeled and shit. No cocaine. Not even a little."

"How can you be so sure?"

"Well, when he first came around, one of the guys asked if he had… I guess he called it P-Top. When I asked him what the hell he was doing, he said, 'Cool your jets. It's a diet aid—supposed to curb your appetite.'"

Ugh. All the guys on the site were ripped and shredded with zero body fat. Jackson figured there had to be a lot of that going around. "Did Sampson have any of it?"

"No. But he *did* say that coke used to keep him skinny, but he didn't sell any of that anymore."

"Hunh," Jackson said thoughtfully.

And behind him he heard Galen go "Mm…."

"You knew for sure it was coke?" Jackson asked, pitching his voice to reach behind him.

"Yes," Galen said without hesitation. "John had picked up the habit in college. He stayed away from meth or crank because he thought he could control coke better."

Yeah, he'd heard that from other people. "It's as docile as a pony until it turns into a dragon," he said mildly.

"Yes, well, so is oxy." Galen let out a sigh. "Which I'd give my left nut for right now, but I shall valiantly make do with ibuprofen instead."

"Do you need a soda or water for that?" Jackson asked, as he heard the rattle of pills in plastic behind him.

"That would be great, thank you."

"Henry, take a right up on L. There's a teriyaki chicken place here, and I can run in and get us sodas."

"Think there will be parking?"

"If not, there's a bank nearby—they're not full often."

"Let us all go in and get some food," Galen said. "My treat. I'll bring John some takeout, and we can sit in the air-conditioning so Jackson can continue his fascinating discussion of why it's important that our friend Scott was no longer selling coke."

FIFTEEN MINUTES later, they were sitting at the I-<3-Teriyaki, and Galen was looking around the area with interest. "So there's a dance club and a pizza place," he said, checking out the block. "And is that a library?"

"It's an LGBTQ library," Jackson said. "Small but active. This is part of Sacramento's Rainbow District. We have a decent Pride parade every year and a couple events."

Henry's eyes widened, and a faint look of horror dawned on his face.

Jackson and Galen both breathed out of their noses in a very similar-sounding sigh.

"Problem there, Henry?" Jackson baited, watching Henry's reaction as two women in their forties came in, holding hands. They were both dressed semiprofessionally, and if Jackson had to guess, he'd say they worked nearby and were coming in for lunch.

"I'm sorry," Henry said, sounding unexpectedly sincere. "My whole life, I was supposed to think one way. It doesn't matter that it's my brother, or... or anyone I know. Thinking about it the other way is *hard*. I get that doesn't mean it shouldn't be done, but every time I hear you talk about my brother and his... his *husband* or a girl and her *wife*, I hear my father's voice in my head, and it's... it's not saying good shit."

"Well, yeah, Henry," Jackson said, keeping his voice as patient as he could. "I get your old man's voice in your head might be a giant fucking distraction from being a decent human being. But what does *your* voice say, and when do you get to listen to *it*?"

To Jackson's complete surprise and horror, Henry's lower lip wobbled. He got hold of it almost immediately, but it wobbled, and his entire tough asshole façade threatened to come crumbling down. Before Jackson could say anything, though, Henry took a deep breath and stood.

"I'm going to get more soda," he said, heading for the fountain. Jackson and Galen let him go.

"Well, knock me over with a feather," Galen said, whistling softly. "That was damned near a miracle. Nobody told me you walked on the side of the angels, Mr. Rivers. I am quite impressed."

Jackson chuffed out a breath. "Well, don't be. If I can't get him to crack and stop acting so fucking guilty, he's going to be tried and convicted before I can figure out what his damned secret is."

Henry stalked back before Galen could reply, but Jackson got the distinct impression that Galen had been going to spill. It was probably just as well he hadn't. Confession was good for the soul. If Galen had gossiped, Henry'd be pissed. If he told Jackson and realized the world didn't come to an end, well, that would be slightly better.

"We ready to go?" Henry asked bluntly.

Galen and Jackson traded glances. "I'm still finishing my chicken," Galen said calmly.

"I was thinking of getting some fro-yo from the place next door," Jackson said. It sold Hawaiian ice and ice cream bars too. "Galen, you want some?"

Galen smiled, catlike. "Of course."

They both looked at Henry, and Jackson saw the terrible conundrum. It was hot as *balls* outside, and frozen yogurt or Hawaiian ice would go down mighty sweetly. But it was hard to maintain a bitchier-than-thou front when you were eating fro-yo. No two ways about it.

"I'll go look," Henry muttered, obviously aware that anything else sounded childish and petulant, and he really had no place to pout.

"What shall I bring you back?" Jackson asked Galen.

"Mm… Hawaiian ice, cherry." He grinned, obviously delighted, and Jackson felt his liking for the man increase. "Too bad we're so far away from the shop, or I'd bring John some."

"I'll see if I can get them to package some on ice," Jackson told him.

"Frozen yogurt, chocolate and vanilla mixed," Galen replied promptly, and Jackson nodded, then took off.

He wondered if he'd know Ellery's order quite so promptly.

"Strawberry," he murmured on the way into the shop. "With strawberries, if they had them."

"Is that what you're getting?"

Jackson had almost forgotten about Henry. "No. That's what I'd get Ellery if we were heading that way. But we're not. It was like a test. I was just thinking that Galen knew John's order, that's all. It was cute."

Henry looked stricken, a sudden, unexpected pain twisting his handsome features. "Oreo," he whispered. "Chocolate topping."

He wasn't talking about his own order, obviously.

"Good for you," Jackson praised, hoping to get a smile. "You must be a good boyfriend."

And Henry's face closed down like a steel trap. "I'm not a good anything." He shook his head. "I'm not in the mood for this. I'll be waiting in the car."

"C'mon, Henry!" Jackson called to his retreating back. "If you don't tell me what you want, I'll get you something blue!"

Henry paused at the doorway and swore softly to himself. "Peach freezy," he growled, then turned around to stand next to Jackson in line. "But I don't want to fucking talk about it."

"Deal."

Ten minutes later, they were all back in the car. The rest of the drive was actually pleasant. Galen chatted a little about hopefully passing the bar exam and how excited he was to be practicing law again.

"Are you going to open a practice or just work for Johnnies on retainer?" Jackson asked.

"John actually has a semidecent lawyer on retainer," Galen told him. "Not that I haven't been called in a few times. But his first guy is a former model, and John, being John, feels responsible."

"Gotcha," Jackson said. "Well, I'm sure you'll find a place to land."

"Indeed," Galen said, sounding speculative. "Can you tell me something? Why did it matter what kind of drugs Mr. Sampson was selling?"

Oh, the guy was sharp.

"Well, coke is one supplier, pills are another. Coke is imported from down south, usually passing through a port, and gets distributed once it gets here. Of course, all of this was made easier by the US government, who started the process a few years ago. But since the Colombian government has started to pay their farmers to grow food and not cocaine, it's slowed down a little."

"What about all them illegals, hauling shit up in their assholes?" Henry asked crudely, and Galen let out a frustrated gasp.

"That's not really happening all that much," Jackson told him crisply. "I know the news likes to make it sound like every person crossing the border shits cocaine, but in reality, it's shipped in bulk through the ports. It has nothing to do with people fleeing from war. And I'm pretty sure the math bears me out on this."

He tried to keep his voice measured and not to have a kneejerk reaction to Henry's ignorance. How was this kid going to learn if Jackson jumped down his throat?

Henry grunted. "I did not know that," he said after a moment. "What do you think it means that he changed his product?"

"I think it means he got a different source. If he's selling pills, that's coming from a shady doctor or a stolen prescription book or a pharmacist with bad morals and a bad habit. The thing is, the violence is going to come from a different place too. Cocaine has a subterranean supply structure. There's always a dealer who gets his shit from a dealer who knows the actual people importing the product. It's a complete criminal network, and that's shady, but it's also traceable. Pills are different. Pills are a white-collar crime, which means somebody involved has a mantle of respectability on their shoulders. That's a whole different rock to turn over, and it's usually a rock that's got somebody standing on top of it shouting, 'Do you know who I am?'"

Galen chuckled. "You do know your scumbags, Mr. Rivers. How did you get into this business, may I ask?"

Jackson grimaced. "I was a policeman," he said. He felt comfortable with Galen, but Henry's derision was going to be a shitty cross to bear.

"Was?" Henry gave him the side-eye, sure, but it was a thoughtful side-eye, so Jackson went on.

"My trainer, the guy who put me through the academy, he was dirty. I was sort of a street rat. He thought he was training a partner in crime."

"You ratted him out?" Henry's disgust was exactly as bad as Jackson had anticipated.

"I wore a wire for months," Jackson said, his stomach clenching just saying those words. "As it turns out, IA was crooked, and so was the DA putting the wire on me. They hired a sniper to take me and my partner out. It only half worked."

"Oh dear God," Galen murmured. "That's... that's terrible, Mr. Rivers. I'm so very glad you survived. Does that explain the scars?"

Well, he had been shirtless when they'd walked in. "Some of them," he admitted.

"Yeah, I thought some of those looked recent," Henry observed. "You rat anybody else out?"

"You want more details, check the papers," Jackson snapped, done. "Does your apartment complex have a camera? Security? Anything that maybe has a recording that proves you didn't beat up the scumbag?"

"Well, I did," Henry reminded him. "Just not the fatal time, right?"

"Maybe just say you didn't kill him," Jackson advised. "And the camera, Henry, focus."

Henry grunted. "I don't know."

"I'll have Ellery ask." Jackson took out his phone and tapped in *Cameras?* Just so he'd have the connection to Ellery.

God, as eager as he was not to talk to the guy, he sure could use his reassurance sometimes. Reliving his past was *not* his favorite.

Which got him back to the questioning. "So, Henry, about the time you *did* beat him up… what was that like?"

"My fist hit his face, he hit the floor," Henry said promptly.

Ass. Hole. "Did he look good? Bad? He was scrawny, you said. Was he shirtless? Dressed in a suit? Did he have a trench coat that he kept his little baggies in? Give me some details."

"He was wearing nice jeans and a T-shirt," Henry conceded. "Nothing torn. He smelled like he'd had a shower, didn't look like miles of bad road. Not homeless… but skeezy."

"Skeezy how?"

Henry lifted a shoulder. "I don't know. Entitled, I guess. Like he could just come in and sell to my guys and grab their asses. I mean, I know what they do for a living, but… but some of them are just, like, bright-eyed kids, you know? I mean, most of them are. They're like hyperactive schoolkids who found out something really fun that they could do to keep out of trouble. It's… it's fucking weird."

"It's fucking human. Whatsamatter, Henry? You never get laid for the fuck of it?"

"Fuck off and fuck you!" Henry snarled.

"I guess not," Jackson muttered. "But you were protecting your guys, and I can respect that. Did any of them see the first altercation?"

"Yeah—Lance and Billy and… and their friends Bobby and Reg were there too. I think they were going out somewhere, like to swim or something, and I heard Kiefer and McCall yelling. I ran down the stairs, and Bobby was screaming at Sampson to get out of there, and Reg was…."

An odd expression crossed Henry's face. "Reg was in tears," he said.

"Now that's a damned shame." Galen didn't sound friendly or easygoing right now. "What did Scott say to him?"

"I'm not sure—something about Bobby, because I guess they all worked scenes together, and Bobby was standing between Scott and Reg, looking like he was going to take the guy out."

"He could have," Galen said. "In fact, it's a good thing he didn't. He's barely off probation."

"Who'd he hit?" Jackson asked. Maybe Bobby was another suspect?

"The cop who got in his face while he was getting his chest stitched up and his boyfriend was getting treated for a concussion. I can't say I blame him. But that kid grew up quick. Bobby doesn't fight anymore," Galen said, sounding confident. "He walked out of two weeks of jail like a man who knew what mattered. Did he lay a finger on Scott?"

"No, sir," Henry said promptly. "But he was standing in front of Reg, trying to protect him. That's when I grabbed the guy by the back of the neck and threw him at the dumpster."

Galen grunted. "Well done. I didn't know you were protecting Reg. Thank you."

Henry swallowed and looked uncomfortable. "Poor guy cried for ten minutes. It was all Bobby could do to calm him down."

"Reg is special to all of us," Galen said, and he was careful around the word *special*.

"How?"

"He's…." Henry cleared his throat. "He's got a…." He cleared his throat. "Dammit," he complained. "Every way I can think to say this sounds mean. But I like the guy, and I can't say something that sounds mean about him! Galen, help me out!"

"He's got some cognitive issues," Galen said, sounding matter-of-fact. "He's a fully functioning adult, but it takes a while for him to process things. When you meet him, he's just like a good ol' boy, right? But you realize you have to repeat things once or twice before they stick, and if he doesn't have a concrete task to do, he gets a little lost."

"Wait," Jackson said. "Reg? Like from the site?"

Galen nodded. "Yeah. His challenges are what made him so damned good at porn, actually. Every boy likes to do what feels good, and he's a sweetheart, so he did what felt good for everyone else. Like I said, concrete goals. But he's been helping John with promotions since last year. He's actually pretty good at it. He's just nice. Club owners, venues, the print guys—they all love him. They help him out when he forgets stuff, and his job gets done."

Jackson swallowed, feeling a little more of the porn fantasy slip away. Dex and Kane were married and raising a child? Reg was trying to make a living with a disability? It just wasn't as much fun when they were real people with real problems. But wait….

"So Bobby is the same guy…."

"Yes, I know them all by their porn names," Henry snapped. "It's what they call each other off set. It's fuckin' weird."

Jackson chuckled. "I'm just happy to know they date each other," he said, meaning it.

"It's very sweet." Galen's voice was a dry burn on Jackson's starry-eyed joy. "Now about Henry—what are the odds that he's going to get picked up for questioning?"

"Pretty good," Jackson told him. "You've got Ellery's number. Make sure Henry has it. And Henry, make sure your brother and his husband have it too. Now, Henry, I'm going to tell you what I told *my* brother last year, when he got arrested for a crime he didn't commit—don't say a fucking word. The minute they read you your rights, they'll say, 'Do you understand these rights as I have read them to you,' and you say, 'Lawyer. Right now. His number's in my phone.'"

"Won't that make me look guilty?" Henry asked. "That's what I don't get. I didn't *do anything*."

"Did I not tell you about my brother?" Jackson asked irritably. "He was working a late shift in his own gas station when two cops came in. He woke up with a headache, a gun by his hand, and a dead cop in front of him. The only reason the other cop didn't take him out was that he called in the officer-involved shooting before he took out Kaden, because he wasn't that fucking smart."

"Oh my God," Henry said, and Jackson felt like he'd punched the kid's pet bunny. "*Cops* tried to frame him? Why did they think they could get away with it?"

"Because Kaden is Jade's twin," Jackson said, and let that sink in for a second. He wasn't related by blood to Jade and Kaden, but they were the only two people from his childhood who had cared for him. He'd die for them. Ellery had made his peace with it from their very first case.

"You'd think that sort of thing only happens in the South," Galen said softly. "That is too bad."

"It happens everywhere." Jackson turned his shudder into a shrug. "That's why Ellery and I work on the defense side of things. People are people—cops and lawyers fuck up like everybody else."

"You ever defend the guilty?" Henry asked snidely.

"Yup," Jackson said cheerfully. "You ever seen a nineteen-year-old single mother go to jail for ten years for muling a vial of coke for the boss who writes her check?"

"No," Henry said, the attitude fading. "Have you?"

"Not on Ellery's watch," Jackson said proudly. "A month's probation, time served. If she hadn't been a friend of a friend, they would have put her in for the full sentence. Even the guilty deserve representation. Are you guilty, Henry?"

"No." Henry was scowling against the sun, and Jackson could tell it took a whole lot out of him to admit that. No matter what he felt he'd done in the past, he was not guilty of murder.

"Then what are you going to say when they pull you in for questioning?"

"Lawyer, Ellery Cramer, lawyer."

"Good. Boy. Wait a minute... is this it?" Henry was pulling Galen's—or maybe it was John's—cream-colored sedan up in front of a set of office buildings that Jackson and Ellery passed every day. Plain, wood-paneled, painted brown, it was one of those ugly structures designed in the '70s to look cutting edge and organic at the same time. Unless Jackson missed his guess, the offices extended in a rough hexagon, with a courtyard in the middle—he could see trees growing up from outside as Henry parked the car in the parking lot, next to a motley assortment of everything from big trucks to big SUVs to shitty little Toyotas.

It was the shitty little Toyotas that got Jackson. Those were young people's cars. Young like late teens, early twenties—the age of most of the guys Jackson saw in porn.

"This is it, indeed," Galen said, and Jackson could hear the pride in his voice. "Office sweet office. Please don't go beyond the reception area and the front office. Once you get back into the corridors, you're headed for the scene rooms and the lockers. And believe it or not, that's a comfort zone for the models. They expect the people in the room to be there. If a stranger suddenly shows up, well...."

"You get shitty porn," Jackson said. "I understand."

Henry turned off the ignition and sighed. Jackson and Galen—both conscious of the sun beating down on them—had their doors open and were out in the sweltering parking lot before Jackson even thought to ask.

"You coming?" Jackson asked.

Henry groaned and tilted his head back. "God."

"Ain't here," Jackson muttered. "C'mon, kid. Sex isn't evil unless you make it evil. I know you must have had some, at some point in your life, or you wouldn't be so hung up on it! Now get out of the car, and let's go interview John, and maybe a few more people, with Galen's permission."

"It's yours," Galen said. "John can take me home. Henry, just bring the car by tomorrow, and I'll drive it from here."

"Thank you, Galen," Henry said grudgingly. Then he got out of the car, looking like Jackson had made him do it and he'd never forgive him.

Jackson didn't see what the big deal was.

The offices were very professional, and the receptionist behind the counter—a middle-aged woman with blond-streaked hair, a worn face, and a warm smile—told them to make themselves at home and then offered them cookies. She was kind to Henry, respectful of Galen, and welcoming to Jackson. If Jade wouldn't have roasted Jackson's ass slowly on a bed of hot coals, Jackson might have asked her to come work for Ellery. Galen went into an adjacent office and brought out a guy a little older than Jackson, with shaggy red hair, green eyes, and a tan that had probably been made possible by a lot of running wearing SPF 3000. Right behind him was a sandy-haired man in his late twenties, average height, with solid stringy muscles, who looked like he worked out a lot but his frame just wasn't going to go gargantuan. He had friendly blue eyes and the sweet, puzzled smile of a Labrador retriever.

"Reg, John, this is Jackson Rivers. Jackson, this is John Carey, owner of Johnnies, and Reg Williams, our promotions director. Reg, Jackson wants to talk to you about what happened when you and Bobby ran into Scott a couple weeks ago."

Reg—the guy with the sweet blue eyes—swallowed and rubbed his stomach. "I hate that guy," he mumbled.

"Yeah," John said soberly. "You should. Not a nice guy. But...." He looked up at Galen for confirmation, and Galen nodded. "But Scott was killed last night, and they're worried that Henry might have done it. We need you to tell us what happened so we know before the cops ask."

Reg looked at Jackson, temporarily confused. "But isn't he a cop?"

"No, Reggie," Galen said. "He's a friend."

Reg's face lit up a little. "That's good. He looks like a cop—scared me a little. Henry scared me a little too, but that's 'cause he was a soldier." Reg gave Henry a shining look. "But he's the good kind. What do you want to know?"

Jackson looked up at Mrs. Roberts in reception and shrugged apologetically. "Is there any way we can go into one of the offices and talk?" he asked Galen.

Moments later, he was ushered into what was apparently John's private office, and it wasn't bad. Wood paneling and a cream-colored carpet made the place neutral and restful, but brightly colored photos on the wall kept it from being bland. Surprisingly enough, the pictures weren't porn—although some of them were shots of the guys who worked there, but with their clothes on. Mostly they were just cityscapes, pops of color—a flag against a heartbreak blue sky, Raley Field on a cloudy day, the construction above the Golden 1 Center, promising commerce and events.

It was a good place—one that saw the beauty of this city and not the crappy parts Jackson usually saw. He approved.

"So, Scott's dead," Reg repeated as they closed the door. He looked to John apologetically. "I'm not sad?"

John nodded like that was okay. "I'm not even sure his parents were sad," he said grimly.

Jackson cut a quick look to him, and John didn't make him wait.

"Scott's father is rich—he's a doctor, one of the ones who's on the board of everything and on every committee. It always makes you wonder who's taking care of his patients, right?"

Jackson nodded, and John looked away and sighed.

"Or who was looking after Martin Sampson when he was a kid," John added.

Galen rolled his eyes. "Don't tell me you fell for the 'poor little rich boy' routine!"

John cocked his head and raised his eyebrows. Galen narrowed his eyes back.

"*You* didn't become a blackmailing scumbag—"

"Just a drug addict," John said levelly. "Let's just say he used it as bait. We'd sit in this office and do lines and complain about our shitty childhoods until I almost lost my company." He looked Jackson in the eye. "He was very manipulative. That's not to say there wasn't a poor little lost boy in there. It's just that he knew how to get his way, and then how to fuck you for it."

"He'd fuck your earhole," Reg confirmed. "He had a nine-inch dick, and he'd put that thing anywhere he thought it would get him off." His expression grew sullen. "He didn't much care about *us* getting off, which was sort of stupid, right? 'Cause that was part of his job."

Jackson nodded—that would be part of the job—and tried hard not to imagine a guy with a nine-inch dick fucking Reg in the ear.

"So tell me about the day you saw him near the dumpster."

Reg nodded. "You should probably ask Bobby about this. He's way smarter, and he's got a better memory. He's at a job site across town, though. He works construction most of the time 'cause he's real good."

"Well, if we need any more details, I will. But how about you tell me first." Jackson smiled his most winning smile and got sunshine back in return.

"Bobby and I were there to get Lance—he's our friend. Anyway, we were going out on the river. Bobby worked on a houseboat for his boss, and his boss wanted us to come ride down river with him, 'cause it was a sunny day and everything."

"Did you make it to the boat?" Jackson asked, and more sunshine. *Gah!* Someone should try to bottle that smile. Reg was probably the plainest of the Johnnies models—his hair was receding a little, his almond-shaped eyes a little lost, his cheekbones a little low—but if he could have smiled like that in every scene, Jackson was pretty sure the world wouldn't need porn.

"It was a real good day, after Henry threw Scott in the dumpster," he said, then clapped his hand over his mouth.

Jackson shook his head. "It's okay, Reg. I already knew that part. Just tell me, what led up to it?"

Reg took a couple of deep breaths and tried to calm down. "Well, we'd pulled in—we were driving my shitty Camaro that day. It's orange, but it has AC—and Bobby threw his arm around my shoulders as we were walking and told me I had to remember sunblock 'cause otherwise I burn really bad." He nodded seriously at John. "Not like you do, Johnny, but my nose'll peel, and I'm not good with pain."

"You shouldn't have to be," John said, and Jackson heard it then. Love, like for a brother or a friend or a nephew. John loved this guy, and had probably watched over him for a lot of years. This was why John wanted to help the guys find life beyond porn, to help guys like Reg who couldn't always think with their words.

Reg smiled shyly and kept going. "So Scott calls my name from behind the dumpster. At the flophouse, they got those ones behind the walls, right? So you usually gotta have a key to open them. And I didn't know Scott was a real bad guy then. I guess there was lots John didn't tell me about 'cause I'm not bright, but I didn't really like Scott anyway. So he calls my name, and I sort of pull back so Bobby can protect me and say 'Hiya, Scott,' sort of quiet-like, and he laughs super mean. Then he asks me if I'm still screwin' for a living, which is sort of a shitty way to put it, you know?" He paused for a second. "You know I was a porn star, right?"

Jackson nodded. "You made real pretty porn," he said, hoping that wasn't going to get him kicked out but sensing Reg needed some approval.

Reg lit right up then, like someone had just told him he'd won a prize for being a nice guy. "Thank you! I thought so! So it wasn't like that was a real nice thing to say. Anyway, Bobby said, 'What're you doing here, Scott?' And I wondered that myself, and Scott gets this sort of nasty look on his face and says he's got the cure to all John's ills right there. He wanted to know if me or the other guys at the flophouse would buy from him, and I said no, 'cause John runs a clean house."

"What'd he say back?" Jackson prompted.

"He said that was John's problem, it wasn't necessarily the guys' problem. Then Bobby said he needed to leave, because nobody there wanted what he was selling." Reg swallowed and looked at John unhappily. "And then he got in my face and started yelling, saying he knew I needed to get high because my sister was crazy and anyone with my problems had probably done buckets full of drugs—which isn't true. I couldna taken care of my sister for as long as I did if I took drugs. She almost killed me, like, three times, and all I was doing was trying to sleep and live my life!"

Reg's voice pitched unevenly, and John wrapped an arm around his shoulders.

"We know that, Reg. You did real good with Veronica. That's not your fault. That was just Scott trying to fuck your earhole, right?"

Reg nodded. "Yeah, 'cause that was Scott, right? Anyway, so what he said upset me, and Bobby got between me and Scott, and he looked like he was gonna fight him. And he can't 'cause he went to jail for fighting once already. I know he said jail was fine, but I don't want him to go, even for a short time, right? So I started hollering, and then Henry came out of the apartment—we were real close. And he goes charging down the stairs, and the rest of the guys come out, except for Lance, who wasn't ready yet, which isn't like Lance. But Henry comes charging down the stairs, and he sort of… you know. Sizes up the situation, like a cop!" Reg beamed at Jackson. "Like you, really. And then before Bobby can even tell everybody to calm down, Henry just sort of runs across the parking lot and decks him."

Jackson looked at Henry with his eyebrows up. "Just decked him."

Henry swallowed. "Yessir."

"You didn't stop to ask any questions, did you?"

"He had packets of pills in his hand, and Reg was crying!"

Reg stared at his feet in tennis shoes. He was dressed casual—cargo shorts and a shirt with a collar—but Jackson got the impression of Reg taking this job seriously—and taking these questions seriously as well.

"I *was* crying," he confessed. "That's not wrong. But Henry yelled at him, called him Sampson, which was weird 'cause I knew his name was Scott, and then Henry decked him."

"He did, did he?" Jackson said, eyes on Henry.

Henry looked away. "I did."

"And he threw him in the dumpster after that. Was the dumpster open?"

"No, but Henry had the key in his pocket. He had to drop some trash as he ran down the stairs. Bobby told me later that he was probably on his way out anyway."

"That's true," Henry said hurriedly, as though to make up for the blatant lie hanging between them.

"What happened after that?" Jackson asked.

"Well, Lance came running down the stairs then. He was all dressed and ready to go out on the boat. It looked like he'd showered, so I figured that's where he was."

Jackson's eyes didn't leave Henry's. "Well, you're probably right," he said, a suspicion forming in his stomach. A couple of them, really, all vying for attention. "So Lance got in your car, and you took off?"

Reg nodded. "Yeah. Henry told us to go, and the rest of the Johnnies guys are sort of buff, and Scott's gotten a little thin. Henry said go, and Bobby said he thought everybody could take care of themselves. I guess none of us is real fond of cops, not after last summer."

Jackson nodded, curious, but needing some time in the car with Henry. "Someday, Reg, you and me can have a beer and you can tell me about last summer—how's that?"

Reg lit up again, and Jackson thought he would make that a promise. "Really? Like a friend? 'Cause Bobby's getting friends from construction, and I got friends in Johnnies, but I don't get a chance to make friends who don't work here, and…." He looked embarrassed. "That's a little weird."

Jackson made sure his smile was as close to radiant as he could make it. "Nothing weird about liking the people you work with. Here." He reached into his pocket and pulled out the plain business card Jade had made him. It had the not-yet-installed business line on it, but Jackson took a pen from John's desk and wrote his cell phone number. "You call me any time you want a friend. I can't promise I'll be able to come over, but it's never wrong to ask."

It was like he'd given the guy a Christmas present. "Really?"

"Sure. My boyfriend's got a big house with a pool. I'll try to have you over someday."

"Did you hear that, John? Someone's got a pool besides you!"

"That's pretty awesome, Reg," John said, eyeing Jackson with speculation. "Do you mind if I walk Mr. Rivers out? Assuming he's done, of course."

"No, that's fine. I got to put his number in my phone."

"Ellery has my numbers," Galen said, easing himself down into what looked like an orthopedic chair as they left.

"Good to meet you, Galen. Remember, let us know if anything goes down."

John practically had his hand on the small of Jackson's back, he was so hot to get out of there. As soon as they cleared the office, he said, voice hard, "You had better mean that."

"Be his friend? Of course. He's a sweet guy." Jackson shrugged. "He… he just seems like he could use as many people as possible on his side."

John nodded and swallowed. "As long as you're on his side."

"Reg's side? Absolutely." He gave Henry a dirty look. "Lying liars that lie? Not so fucking much."

Henry had the grace to look away, and John caught the byplay.

"What'd Henry lie about?"

"How'd you know him?" Jackson asked, voice hard. "Sampson. *Scott.*"

Henry gave John a surreptitious look tinged in shame. "Can we talk about this somewhere else?"

"Nope." Jackson got out his phone. "And I'm not getting in the car again with you until you tell me what's doing."

"But my case!" Henry cried, sounding genuinely panicked. "Man, Rivers, I will tell you anything you want—just don't…." He gave John a look that was half shame and half defiance. "Not here."

Jackson got sort of a sick feeling in his stomach. "Outside," he muttered. "In the car. Goddammit!"

Jackson gave John a nod, said a sweet goodbye to Mrs. Roberts, and stalked toward the car in the blistering heat. He got halfway there when his cell phone rang, and he swore under his breath and answered it because he'd promised Ellery he would.

"Yeah?"

"Look, I called Toe-Tag so you can get a look at the body. Do you need me down there?"

Jackson swallowed and tried not to throw up his lunch and frozen yogurt. "Naw. Fine. How's your end of things?"

"I got AJ to go bother the office of the apartment complex for the video from last night. He says the cops haven't gotten to it yet, and the manager is cooperating. He has it on a thumb drive and is running it back."

Oh. Smart. "The cops haven't asked for it?" That did not bode well. "Why in the hell not?"

"I have no idea, Jackson! Do you need me at the morgue or not?"

"Wait—they took him to the morgue? Wouldn't that mean they'd tried to resuscitate him?"

"Well, I guess the body was pretty fresh when Henry found it. He called 911, so an ambulance got the body, not the coroner's bus. I don't know what to tell you. It's at Toe-Tag's. He called me—"

"Why'd he call you?" Jackson asked suspiciously.

"Why do you think he called me? Because you haven't been down there to see him since…." Ellery's voice dropped. "November. His house, yes, but he knows. He wanted to give me a heads-up."

"I'm fine," Jackson said tightly. "I'll catch a Lyft."

What he really wanted to do was work off some energy, but he figured a Lyft would be fine.

"Okay, if you're sure—"

Jackson hung up on him, painfully aware it was a childish move and Ellery didn't deserve that, but he didn't want to talk about it anymore. He looked up at Henry and glowered.

"Go back to your apartment building or go visit your brother or whatever. I'm catching a Lyft to Med Center—"

"I thought you wanted to know the truth?"

Jackson scowled at the kid. "Of course I want to know the truth. But I'm in a shitty-assed mood right now, and it's not going to get better—"

"But what are the cops going to think if they talk to Reg?" Henry asked plaintively.

"They're going to think you're guilty as balls! But I gave you all fucking afternoon to talk, and you didn't because you thought Reg wasn't going to remember that you knew who Sampson was—by name—before you decked him. But he did. Which means his boyfriend will too. And that means you're fucked. And *now* you want to play nice?"

Henry glared at his feet. "Look, let me give you a ride to Med Center. I'll tell you… well, some of it—"

"All of it!" Jackson snapped.

"What you need to know!" Henry yelled back and then squeezed his eyes shut. "Just, not here. Not when everybody who knew what that guy was can hear."

Jackson's shoes were sticking to the parking lot, and sweat was rolling down his back. Ugh. Climate change sucked ass. "Turn on the fucking car!"

Henry did, but Jackson waited three deep breaths—and until the AC kicked on—before he hopped in.

"What's at the hospital?" Henry asked, turning back the way they came to get to Alhambra.

"The morgue. Your guy—I want to get a look at the body."

"You can *do* that?"

Well, the kid was right to be a little surprised. PI's did not just get access to a hospital morgue. "I got a friend there." He grimaced. "Got a lot of friends there. It helps."

"Why do you—"

"'Cause I go there a lot. Tell me about Scott, Henry. I'm in the mood to hit something."

"Yeah, well, so was he!" Henry snapped back. "As in 'hit that'—so we did. We hit that!"

Jackson almost swallowed his tongue. "What in the fucking hell?"

"The Army kicked me out, so I went to my parents' place. They kicked me out, so I came here because Dex was maybe the last person who'd talk to me. I showed up at the bus station at fuck-you o'clock and found a shitty hotel on my phone. As I'm walking there, this guy starts to chat me up. And...." His voice sank. "I was... you'd have to know everything else, and I just don't want to fucking talk about it, but I was as low as I've ever fucking been in my life, and he was talking real goddamned sweet. And... and I've only... the one person I've ever... he's back in that old life. Back the way I came and can't go back. And it was just really easy."

Jackson's brain was going to explode. "You're *gay?*"

"So are you!" Henry snarled.

"I'm bi, and I told you. But this is a plot twist I did not see coming! Jesus, wait until I tell Ellery—he's going to shit walnuts."

"So the fuck what? You just talked to a zillion goddamned gay men and it didn't bother you—"

"You know, Henry, your fuck-you-asshole force field is premium fucking quality. I can usually spot that shit a thousand miles away." Jackson tried to wrap his mind around it and couldn't. He was usually just... just spot-on. With a good-looking guy like Henry—even if Jackson didn't want to hit that, and he didn't—he'd know if it was an option.

God, Ellery was right. He really was off his game these last few weeks.

"I'm sorry!" Henry protested. "I… I looked Davy up the next day, and he was nice. He was…." Henry's voice dropped. "Considering what an asshole I'd been to him last time we saw each other, he was great. He gave me the number to the flophouse, made sure I had access to a car, has been helping me look for a job. I didn't… I mean, our older brother might have filled him in, 'cause they talk sometimes, but I haven't even told him how I ended up on his doorstep."

"How did you end up on his doorstep?" Jackson asked, appalled. He'd been kicked out of the military? Jesus fuck!

"I don't want to talk about it!" Henry shouted. "I haven't told Davy, and I'm an asshole. I get it! I know it! I don't make it easy! And then I saw Martin being shitty to Reg, and after I clocked him in the jaw and threw him in the dumpster, all the guys in the house gave me the backstory, right? About how they knew Sampson by another name, and how he'd been my brother's ex-boyfriend and a real bastard. But all I could think of was I'd slept with my brother's ex and Davy didn't even know I was gay. Do you understand how awful that is? And then Martin Sampson, who was Scott the evil ex, turned out to be a drug-dealing scumbag to boot. I was *embarrassed*. So I haven't told *anybody*—well, except Lance. But…." Henry shook his head.

"Wait, was that the guy who was coming down the stairs from the shower after you threw Sampson in the dumpster?"

Henry looked wary. "Yeah?"

"You're not hitting *that*, are you?" *Because Jesus!*

"No!" But Jackson heard the note of defensiveness in his voice.

"But would you like to?" he wheedled.

"I don't want to talk about it. He's a porn model—don't you get it? How am I going to have that relationship, particularly when nobody knows I'm gay!"

"Well first, sugar-booger, you tell people you're gay!"

"But…."

Oh God. And Jackson got it now. "So all this attitude is about what? Trying to hide the secret that apparently destroyed your life in the first place? Jesus, Henry, it's hard to have a learning curve on a plateau, isn't it?"

"Shut up," Henry muttered. "Just shut the fuck up. I'm sorry I told you."

Jackson rolled his eyes and pulled out his phone. *Henry slept with the vic when he got to town. Had no idea his brother did it first.*

There. Hopefully that would ease Ellery's mind just a tad—

Fucking fascinating, came the reply. *Are you going to be okay?*

Jackson took a deep breath. *I'll. Be. Fine.*

Of course he would.

He tucked his phone into his pocket and failed to keep a growl from escaping.

"What's your problem?" Henry demanded. *Surly fucker.*

"Ellery's getting in my face about something."

He heard the question in his head before Henry asked it.

"What?"

"None of your business."

"Aw, c'mon, man, that's not fair. I unburdened my *soul* to you. You can't just shine me on like that!"

Jackson ignored him for a few moments, trying to get his breathing under control. "I fucked a lot of people before I met Ellery," he said, knowing it sounded random when he said it. "Women, men, multiples thereof. Most of them were decent people, but there were a few I regret touching. I would rather give you a verbal breakdown of every sexual encounter I've ever had, complete with pictures and their notes on me as a lover, than tell you why I hate the morgue."

Henry blew out a low whistle. "Wow. That's bad."

"Yup. So I'll go visit your brother tomorrow. You can drop me off—"

"I'll park," Henry said, surprising him. "I can come in with you."

Ugh. No. "I don't need a babysitter," he said, trying not to sound bitchy.

"Obviously." Jackson could have scoured graffiti off a cinderblock wall with the sound of Henry's voice alone. "I would like to get a look at him again too," Henry continued. "Maybe if he's cleaned up, I can see something I missed. Something that would help."

"Your stomach that strong?"

"I was deployed twice," Henry said, voice measured. "I've seen bodies before."

"The morgue is different," Jackson said. "Just like killing someone in battle is one thing but killing someone up close is another."

"And you've done that?" Henry asked, and God, wasn't he a snide little shit.

"Yes," Jackson answered. "You?"

Henry swallowed and looked away. "Not up close and personal," he said softly. "How—"

"I am not sharing that information."

Henry pounded the steering wheel with his fist, hard and fast, startling Jackson so badly, he threw his elbow back and cracked it on the door.

"*What the fuck!*"

"I'm sorry!" Henry shouted back. "I'm sorry! I'm sorry! Is that what you want me to say? I'm sorry I'm an asshole and everything that comes out of my mouth is wrong! I'm sorry I don't know what to say and it all comes out fucked-up! I just wanted you to be fucking human is all! Jesus, you, acting like you got all the answers! I haven't had a friend I can talk to in ten goddamned years, and now the one person I'm supposed to tell my whole life to is so fucking closed off, I'm not sure when I'm gonna step on his toes!"

Jackson's elbow was singing a song of pain all the way up to his shoulder. "Pull over," he snarled.

"What?"

"Pull over!"

Henry was driving in front of a tiny strip mall that featured a taqueria on one half and a vintage clothing store on the other. The afternoon sun beat down on the broken tarmac like the jackhammer of the gods, and as Jackson threw open his door before the car was completely stopped, he had to ask himself if heat stroke was going to kill him or an actual stroke from dealing with Henry fucking Worrall.

Henry squealed to a halt and Jackson launched himself out of the car.

Henry followed him. "What the hell—"

"Don't do that shit!" Jackson snarled. "Don't pull that psycho tantrum bullshit on me. Pull it on your brother, on his friends, on whoever else puts up with that, but don't pull it on *me*. I've been a nice guy, I've been an honest guy, but I draw the line at spilling my guts for some numbnuts who doesn't know the truth from his own goddamned left toe. Now get the fuck out of my way and let me go. I need to cool off, and I need to move. And if I have to *walk* all the way to Med Center, that's what I'm gonna fuckin' do!"

"Come on, man," Henry cajoled, getting in front of Jackson and holding up his hands. "I'm sorry—"

Jackson knocked his hands away. "Are you insane? I said *get out of my way*! You fucking child—you don't know who you're dealing with! *You* may eat bullets and crap lead, but *I'm* still sitting up in bed screaming from the last time I did that! So bully for you! You win in the emotional health department! I don't care! I'm *done*!"

His heart was still hammering in his ears, and he couldn't get a handle on his panic breathing. God*damn* this kid for ripping him wide open like this. Like a slug to the gut, he wanted Ellery. He wanted Ellery's touch on the back of his neck, wanted his voice, irritated and persnickety and soothing, telling him he got to feel like this. Wanted Ellery, who would forgive him for not being able to do what needed to be done when Jackson couldn't forgive himself.

Jackson would walk inside that morgue if it killed him—but he needed to do it without this fucking kid.

"Look, you can't just walk off. It's five miles if it's a step, and it's hot as balls out here! Come on, Rivers, just get in the car and—"

"And nothing," Jackson muttered, putting his hands in his pockets and shoving past him. Yeah, he wanted Ellery, but he knew how to use a phone, and brother did he know how to catch a goddamned bus. He was two blocks from the next stop, and one transfer would take him down Alhambra until it turned into Stockton Boulevard. Would it take longer? Yes. But Jackson could calm himself down and get really fucking zen about going inside the hospital, which weighed on him like two-hundred tons of lead and concrete just thinking about it, and into the morgue, which added war gods tap dancing to Irish rap music on top of that weight.

He just had to get away from this kid, with his need and his anger and his hair-trigger temper and—

And his fucking hand on Jackson's shoulder!

Jackson grabbed his hand and yanked Henry forward until his face cracked into Jackson's skull.

Jackson threw his head back, wrapped his leg around Henry's, and shoved forward until Henry fell roughly to his knees on Jackson's side, sputtering blood from his nose.

"What in the hell—"

"Please, kid, could you just go?"

"No! Man, all day, you've been in my face about telling you the truth and talking and shit, and now you're just gonna walk into the sunset with all your bullshit—"

"Because my shit's my problem, kid! Your shit is your *case!*" Jackson kept walking, thinking, *Let it go, kid, let it go. Let it go, kid, let it go. Let it go—*

"Augh!"

Henry rushed him so fast, Jackson didn't have time to sidestep. Instead, he got thrown forward onto the gravel, his knees making contact first and then his elbows as he tried to protect his chin. He rolled, throwing Henry off so he could scramble to his feet, and he got there just in time to catch a haymaker in the ear.

He shook it off, his head ringing, and launched his own series of jabs—eye, nose, chin—roundhouse!

Henry caught him twice in the ribs, which were surprisingly sore from the fight with the guy who had hospitalized him six months ago, and Jackson howled, lifting his foot and scraping his shoe down Henry's shin.

It was a kid's move, designed to hurt not injure, but Jackson's vision was red, and he was one swing away from dislocating Henry's kneecap and leaving him writhing on the ground.

"What's your problem, Junior!" he taunted, stepping back when Henry tried to get close enough for another roundhouse. "I was trying to help you!"

"Sure!" Henry shouted. "Sure! You were trying to help me! It may have been just a job to you, but I told you shit that mattered! Shit that nobody else knows about me! And you were *fine* with it. And I'm like, if you knew *that* shit about me, maybe… maybe I could finally… I could finally…."

Henry's shoulders slumped forward, and Jackson held his hand to his ribs, breathing hard.

"Finally what, kid?" He blinked hard, getting the sweat and the blood out of his eyes, and tried to assess the damage.

"I could finally tell someone everything," he said pitifully, and the look he shot Jackson was so mournful, so lost, that Jackson stopped counting bruises. Fuck it. Everything hurt.

He took an unsteady breath and tried to decide if his ribs were cracked. "Kid, you really suck," he muttered.

"I'm twenty-seven," Henry said back, glaring at him defiantly.

"I'll be thirty-one in September, and I'm still way the fuck older than you." Oh God. That naked admission of wanting to talk—six months of trying to talk and Jackson wasn't sure he was strong enough. But this kid wanted to talk and that meant something. "Look. I don't want to talk about it now. I mean, I *really* don't want to talk about it now. But if you can get me to the morgue before Ellery starts freaking the fuck out, maybe we can try this again tomorrow. Same deal. You take me around, I ask questions, we talk. Can we try that?"

Henry nodded, his relief palpable. "Yeah. A do-over. I can deal with that."

Great. "But first, we need to get to the hospital. If I don't call Ellery in an hour, he's going to come looking for me."

Henry straightened and used his shirt to wipe the blood from his nose, wincing when it kept flowing. "You don't *look* like a guy who needs a leash."

"Ellery's spent a lot of time next to my hospital bed," Jackson told him. "I would just as soon we not spend any more. Can we go?"

"Sure. Shouldn't we clean up or something?" Henry wiped his nose again, and if Jackson's face had been any less achy, he would have rolled his eyes.

"We're *going* to a *hospital*," he muttered. "Now could you get your ass over here and start the car?"

Bruised Lovers and Slippery Fish

ELLERY PACED the confines of Toby's—aka Toe-Tag—small office one more time.

"Ellery, I can wait for him, you know." Toby Tagliare was a small round hobbit of a man with so much curly gray hair it overran his eyebrows, his mustache, and his ears. He had more kids than Ellery could keep track of, a bunch of grandkids, and a grown gay son who had—as far as Ellery could tell—a lifelong crush on Jackson that Jackson had never noticed.

He worked in the morgue because he liked the quiet and because he had compassion for the dead, but also because he enjoyed his life to the fullest and liked for it to have meaning.

Ellery never would have thought to look in a morgue for a good friend, until Jackson had introduced him to Toby.

"It's just that he hasn't been back here in... in a while," Ellery said lamely. Toby had called him, and Ellery had made the appointment before texting Jackson.

And then he'd looked at Jade, and she'd looked back, and she'd shaken her head and said, "I can deal with all this other shit. Just go."

Jackson should have beaten him here by about ten minutes, but he was ten minutes late.

"So maybe he's getting himself together," Toby said gently. "Not every guy wants to come apart in front of his significant other, you know."

"*No* guy wants to come apart in front of his significant other," Ellery snapped. "There are entire *books* written about the fact that men are socialized to communicate worse than twelve-year-old boys at a sock-hop. I don't give a shit. If he's coming apart, he's coming apart, and I want to be here, and *oh my fucking God, Jackson, what the hell?*"

Jackson—face and knuckles bloody, left cheek bruised, eye blackened, shirt torn, dust coating him like a fine mist, had just rounded the corner, looking shocked as hell to see Ellery standing there. He turned his head for a second, as if he was going to talk to someone behind him, and then Henry blundered into his back and bounced off.

Henry looked, if anything, worse than Jackson. His face and shirt were smeared with blood, his nose was swollen, and his eyes were blackened for good measure.

He too had bloody knuckles and was wearing dust like body spray, with a few streaks of grease on his T-shirt.

The two men looked a lot like... well, exactly like....

"You tried to kill each other, didn't you?" Ellery asked, horrified.

"No!" Jackson protested, while Henry said, "Yes," nodding emphatically.

Jackson glared at him like he could change Henry's answer by will alone. "No."

Henry looked vaguely uncomfortable. "No?"

"No."

"Fine." Henry gave Ellery a ghastly smile. "No."

Ellery took a deep breath. "Who started it?"

"Henry," Jackson muttered, and to his credit, the kid nodded.

"Yeah. That's fair."

Okay. That was promising. "Who finished it?"

Jackson laughed. "Heh heh heh heh heh...."

And Henry slumped, looking profoundly embarrassed. "Rivers. Definitely Rivers."

Ellery's eyebrows ratcheted up. "Not bad, old man." And then, before Jackson could preen, Ellery continued, "Are we still on the case?"

Jackson rolled his eyes. "Yes, we're still on the case! Jesus, we're not babies." He looked over Ellery's shoulder. "Sorry, Toby. I know I'm late, but is there any way I could get—"

Toby's office was very government official—the chairs were only as comfortable as they had to be, and the desk was a utilitarian monstrosity. Toby often had interns and attending doctors in there, students looking to see if learning from the dead was any more appealing than healing the living. This afternoon he'd been alone, but that didn't mean he didn't come prepared.

He rooted in the bottom drawer of the utilitarian desk and came up with two sets of scrubs. "Men's room is around the corner, Jackson—you know the drill. Young man, there's a small washroom here. I'm going to run you through the basics of making yourself contaminate-free there—and see if maybe we can stop that nosebleed while we're at it. Meet back here in ten."

Jackson grimaced. "Sorry to take your time like this, Toby."

But Toby just grinned fondly. "I've missed you here, Jackson. You liven the place up, you know what I mean?"

Jackson groaned at the pun while Ellery took the proffered scrubs and the small packet of antiseptic wash, gauze, and shoe and hair covers.

"I'm sorry I don't have enough for you, Ellery," Toby said, sweetly ignoring the fact that Ellery didn't really do the morgue, not after his first time when he'd tossed his cookies all over the floor. If Henry thought he had the fortitude, good for him.

"No, you're not." Ellery shrugged. "But I'm glad he's back too."

He followed Jackson down the hall and to the bathroom. Jackson stood, once again without his shirt, as he rinsed it out in the sink.

"So...," Ellery said, leaning against the wall. Jackson spared him a look in the mirror, his green eyes taking him in with a flicker of appreciation Ellery liked very much.

"So he got on my last nerve, like I thought he would," Jackson told him, wringing the shirt out. "And I made him let me out of the car so I could walk to the bus stop and cool down."

"And...?"

Jackson rested his weight on the sink, his head dropping for a moment in discouragement. "And he got out of the car and tackled me."

"Wow."

Jackson turned his head. "Ellery, I swear I was trying not to be an asshole."

"What did he want from you?" Ellery closed the distance, took the shirt from him, and wiped his face down first before rinsing it out. He could tell by the way Jackson's mouth worked that he was having trouble framing his answer.

"He'd told me something personal because, you know, *the case*, and I guess he wanted the same from me."

Ellery was standing so close to Jackson's overheated, sweaty body that he was starting to sweat in sympathy—but he didn't back away. "There's a lot of that going around," he said, wiping down Jackson's shoulders.

Jackson sighed and covered Ellery's hand with his own. "I'm sorry," he said softy.

"You were doing really well," Ellery said, pulling Jackson's battered knuckles to his lips for a kiss. "And suddenly we're back to... I don't know. November? Is that where we are?"

Jackson's faint smile was reassuring. "Christmas," he said throatily. "We're not back to November."

Ellery searched his brilliant green eyes. "Why aren't we in June?"

Jackson closed those eyes, and Ellery took a step back. "When do I get to stop?" he asked plaintively. "When do I not have to… I don't know… let the bad things that hurt me affect everybody else? Isn't it bad enough that you were hurt too? Isn't it bad enough I had to sit by your hospital bed and worry if you were going to live or die?" He rubbed his chest. "I just don't understand why I have to talk about stuff that…." He took a deep breath. "Give me the cloth and let me get my face some more. I need to put a butterfly on my cheek and my eyebrow and cover them before I go in there."

"Jackson," Ellery said softly, and Jackson concentrated on the cloth in his hand, scrubbing with what looked like unnecessary force.

"What?"

"You will *never* not have to talk to me. Especially if you're going to keep walking in to places bloody and pissed. I will *never* not expect you to unload your shit on my shoulders, and I swear to you, you're going to carry your fair share of my shit too, so get used to it. That shit's ours."

Jackson scowled at him, and Ellery stole the T-shirt and used it to wash his hands, then grabbed the sterile gloves from the kit Toby had given him to help clean Jackson up.

"Did you just tell me to suck it up, buttercup?" Jackson asked, and he sounded pissed off all over again, which was fine with Ellery.

"Yes," Ellery said crisply, snapping his glove. "Now stand still and tell me what you were going to tell me tonight."

"No!" Jackson argued—but he did stand still. "I'm not talking about that now, because I'm about to go in and look at a dead body, and I'm telling you, I've got enough of those on my conscience."

Ellery paused and then continued to dump disinfectant on a cotton ball. "Oh," he said softly. "I wondered when that would hit you."

"Oh my God. Stop reading my mind!"

"Then stop being a decent human being with perfectly predictable emotional reactions!" Ellery blew out an exasperated breath and moved the cotton ball to the cut on Jackson's cheek. His movements were as gentle as he could make them, because he knew Jackson had scrubbed excessively hard. "Jackson, of course you're having problems. What you had to do down south, that wasn't easy." Two men. Jackson had killed two men in Ellery's defense, one of them up close and personal. With him standing shirtless,

Ellery could have felt every scar on his body, the old and the new. For the new, he would trace the scar from left collarbone to right nipple, where Jackson had been sliced open and needed stitches. Below the nipple, Ellery could see the horrific network of scars where the scalpel had been turned on his vital organs, nicking his liver and sending him into emergency surgery. Ellery had been helpless, lying drugged after his own gunshot wound, and Jackson had killed a man in close quarters to protect him. Ellery had known, at the very least, that this would need to be dealt with.

Because Jackson could never give himself a break.

"Why do you think you keep ending up with bad guys and knives?" Ellery pondered, mostly to lighten the heavy silence.

"Because the ones with guns almost always win," Jackson muttered. They were standing close enough to feel each other's breath, and Ellery could tell by the hoarse note in Jackson's voice that he was not unaffected. But Jackson was going to go confront death at its grisliest in a few moments, and Ellery didn't want to strip him so emotionally naked he couldn't do that.

"I'm sure that's it." Ellery reached for the butterfly bandage he'd left on the shelf above the sink and turned back, wobbling a little from standing quite so close. Jackson's hands on his hips were intimate and reassuring.

"Careful, Counselor," Jackson said dryly.

"With you, Detective, always."

Neither of them said much as Ellery finished his doctoring, but after he rinsed off Jackson's neck and shoulders, just to get rid of the dust, Jackson turned around and gave him a short, hard kiss on the mouth.

"Thanks for the fixing up," he said, grabbing the shirt Toby had given him and pulling it overhead.

"Anytime." Ellery stepped back and let Jackson drop his cargo shorts, swearing when they both heard his keys and phone and wallet jingle. "Leave it—I'll get them. Get dressed and go look at what Toby has ready for you. Then I can take you home."

Jackson grimaced. "Really? That late?"

"Yup." Ellery grinned. "Aren't you glad to finally have a case?"

Jackson laughed throatily as he finished, and they walked out of the bathroom.

HALF AN hour later, as Ellery sat in Toby's office and clicked desultorily through Martin Sampson's financials, Jackson and Henry walked out of the cold room of the morgue in a less jovial mood.

"You swear," Jackson asked seriously, and Henry nodded.

"It wasn't an old puncture wound. I've seen addicts—there's a surprising number of them at the VA—"

"I'm not surprised," Toe-Tag interrupted. "Many doctors would rather prescribe opioids instead of rest or mental health measures. And many patients are less afraid of physical pain than emotional. You've seen the news. It's literally a crisis!"

Ellery watched with bland amusement as both Henry and Jackson shifted from foot to foot.

"Apparently that's because nobody's prescribed a good old-fashioned fistfight as therapy," Ellery said dryly. "Now are we going to share with the class?"

"He had an injection site on his hip. Brand-new—immediately perimortem," Jackson said without preamble, pulling off the plastic gown he'd put on over his scrubs and throwing it in a hamper in the corner of Toby's office. Henry did the same, and Ellery tried not to search Jackson's face too closely for signs of trauma or stress.

Jackson looked pale—but composed—and Ellery took a deep breath. Jackson was right. They weren't in November. They might even have been all the way to February. Either way, they were most definitely not at last August, when Jackson wouldn't even admit to needing any help at all, much less Ellery's.

"But I thought he sold drugs. Why are you surprised?" Ellery closed his laptop with a snap. He'd had Jade ask Crystal nicely for the financials, and right now they told the story of a rich kid who got regular installments of Daddy's money—and who knew how to spend accordingly. Ellery wasn't seeing any cash infusions from drug sales, but that kind of thing tended to get tucked under a mattress or put in a gun safe or something, and he wasn't seeing any debt either.

"He did!" Henry was excited, for once, and not defensive. "He tried to sell to my guys, like I told you!"

"And he definitely sold to John." Jackson frowned. "But he sold different drugs."

Ellery's eyebrows went up. "So…."

"He went from coke—by the rock, from what John was saying—to little packets of pills in plastic bags. But that's the thing. His liver was shot—"

"So. Bad." Toby confirmed it. "Fifty-year-old drinking-Jack-for-breakfast bad."

"So we know he'd been doing product. But he hadn't been *shooting* it."

"His septum was almost completely gone." Toby nodded. "But the damage looked as though it had been repaired and was healing. So doing lines was no longer his thing. Eating pills was."

Henry shuddered. "He... he didn't look that fucked-up when I met him," he said. "I mean, he must have been, if his liver and stuff.... It's just... he seemed so normal."

Jackson met Ellery's eyes grimly. "Kid," he said to Henry, "I get that you may not have had many of these, but ships passing in the night don't really know each other. And that's okay. His corroded liver and shitty life were not your fault. As long as you used a rubber—"

"And PrEP protocol." Henry nodded vigorously. "Yeah. Safety first."

"Good. You both got off—the end. That's all it needed to be."

"Or would have been," Henry said glumly. "If, you know...."

"If your luck hadn't been that shitty." Jackson rolled his eyes, and Ellery had to laugh. So this afternoon they'd been fighting, and now Jackson was trying to big brother their hostile little wildcat out of a tree. How very typical.

"Truth." Henry blew out a breath and pinched the bridge of his nose. "So he had a puncture wound—and we're pretty sure he didn't shoot up. What does that mean?"

Jackson looked at Toe-Tag. "It means we're going to need a copy of his tox screen, and one needs to be ready when the cops come in." Cops had many cases and a chain of command. Jackson and Ellery just had one client, so they got there first.

Toby nodded. "It does indeed. I should have the results tomorrow morning." He grimaced. "I was off tomorrow, but given that this is Robert Sampson's son...."

"Big shot gets big-shot treatment," Jackson said. "He's on the board of trustees here?"

"The very same." Toby's expression was as sour as a kid's candy. "But notice how he is not in the morgue even for his own son."

"I do now." Jackson gave a quiet little chin bob to Ellery, who took the handoff.

"Not a helicopter parent?" Ellery asked smoothly.

Toby raised an eyebrow. "When this kid was sixteen—still old enough to be saved, I'd wager—he threw one of those epic parties. You know, the ones that make the papers, where the damage done to the house is more than most people make in a year?"

"Aw, the childhood years," Jackson said cynically. "So what did Daddy do?"

"He blamed it on another kid. Martin's best buddy, Jimmy. And in spite of the fact that Martin told the cops—in no uncertain terms—that it was his fault, Jimmy did two years in juvenile hall."

Jackson grimaced. "I don't remember that. If he was twenty-nine now, I was barely out of high school myself."

"God, you're young," Toby chided. "But see? That's the complete lack of accountability we're talking about. So yeah, Martin was doing all the drugs with all the wrong people, but you won't see the grieving family here to ask about his tox screen. His mother's living somewhere back East, from what I hear, but there's been no word of her coming out. It's damned suspicious. The guy's liver was pretty seasoned. It would take a lot to put him under, but that's what it looks like happened. Someone drugged him and cracked his skull from the front *and* back and left him to bleed out and die, which he did."

"But the body was moved," Jackson said. "We established that."

"Yes. By the time he was found in the dumpster, rigor had come and gone. Given the heat, even at night, that could have taken four hours or so. But because of that, I'm not sure if he was moved perimortem or postmortem or even if he died during transit. But there were carpet fibers in the wound that I have to send to CSI. The point is, if he has the kind of drugs I'm thinking he did in his system, the head trauma would have done it."

"Was there any insect activity?" Ellery asked, because that was often a marker to help establish time of death.

"Not much," Toby said and then looked at Henry. "Unless someone scraped him for maggots, I saw relatively few eggs."

"There were flies gathering," Henry said thoughtfully, "but they weren't a swarm yet."

Jackson blew out a breath. "So he was killed, held or moved for we don't know how long, and dumped maybe half an hour before Henry would have been dumping trash. Henry, how much a creature of habit are you?"

"Clockwork," Henry replied reluctantly. "Trash out, eight thirty, every morning."

Jackson grunted. "I have no way of getting into the CSI lab," he muttered. "None. Ellery, can you subpoena the reports on what was in the trash can, as well as the carpet fibers in the vic's head? Henry doesn't remember a carpet—just the vic on top of the trash. If there were carpet fibers in the wound...."

"Somebody's running around with a bloody carpet that needs to be disposed of," Ellery said, surprised. "Why would they do that?"

Jackson cocked his head. "That is a very good question, Counselor. In fact, I think we've got a lot of questions here and no answers."

"So when can I expect the cops at my door?" Henry asked quietly.

"Mm...." Jackson looked at Ellery. "Two days, would you say?"

Ellery nodded. "Two days. Henry, given that we know the body was dumped about a half hour before you got out to the trash can, do you think you can come up with an alibi for that night?"

To Ellery's surprise—and Jackson's amusement—the kid turned a brilliant shade of magenta as they watched.

"No," he lied.

Jackson tagged him on the back of the head. "Try again, asshole!"

"Ouch!" Henry rubbed his head but didn't make eye contact either.

"Oh my God! Kid, were you getting laid again?"

"No!" Henry protested. "No, I was *not* getting laid! I was... I was talking to a... one of the guys at the flophouse. He's a... a friend, I guess. We were talking. All night—which was dumb because he had class in the morning, and I kept him up and...." He shook his head. "Just... it was private."

"Yeah, well, you're in the flophouse with what? Five other guys. How private could it be?"

Henry let out a small laugh. "Well, since we were in the living room on the couch and one of them was asleep on the air mattress on the floor in front of us, not very, I guess."

Ellery cocked his head. "Then why that spectacular flush?"

Henry's flush—which had been receding—heated up again to an even deeper purple at the question. "I don't know," he muttered, obviously mortified. "It's just... it just felt important, I guess. I don't know. I can give you his Johnnies name. I... I haven't asked his real name yet." He looked at his feet and all but twisted his toe against the tile. "I feel like I should know his real name."

"Intimate," Jackson said, and Ellery raised his eyebrows in surprise. Of course, that was it. God, for guys like Jackson and Henry, a conversation—a real one—would be considered more intimate than sex. "You had a moment of intimacy, and you don't want to make it public."

Henry covered his eyes with his hand. "None of this is making me feel less stupid."

"Henry, it's practically the most adult thing you've said today. Tell this guy that when the cops ask, you guys were bullshitting on the couch. Use that exact word. They'll know the truth, but they won't know what it means to you. Nobody needs to know but you and…?"

"Lance," Henry supplied, half-guiltily.

"The med student?" Jackson asked in surprise.

Henry nodded. "I…. Fuck. I'm…."

"Not obligated to talk about it now," Ellery said smoothly, putting his laptop away and standing up. "So Jackson and I will be at the office at nine tomorrow. Call us before you come pick Jackson up. I understand he has more interviews to do."

"Tomorrow's Wednesday," Henry said blankly, as though just realizing the world kept turning.

"Which means if we want to get a jump on the police, now's our chance." Ellery had hoped for Jackson's help at this phase, but he understood. And having Henry shuttle Jackson around would help them bypass the parking problem Jackson had so correctly predicted—without making him unlock the trunk for the goddamned skateboard.

Jackson shrugged. "We're really trying to get the office ready for next week," he explained. "It's…." Ellery saw the moment of softness in his jaw, the way his eyes lightened fractionally. "It's really Ellery's baby."

Ellery wanted to argue that Jackson had worked just as hard if not harder. Jackson had looked up property on property before calling a Realtor, and had run background checks on the Realtors as well. He'd painted the entire office suite, including the doorframe outside, and had collaborated with Jade for a wish list, a need list, and a "when we make our first million" list for the office.

He'd even picked out artwork for the walls.

But the fact that Jackson thought it was Ellery's baby, and was doing all that work for Ellery? That was as close as this man was ever going to get to a grand romantic gesture. Of course, on Valentine's Day, they'd both been recovering from their wounds and from the drive from down south to Sacramento. Jackson had made them soup and salad and made sure they'd both had their pain pills—it was as romantic as either of them could manage at the time. Ellery was perfectly aware that when the time came for a marriage proposal, he was completely in charge of delivery and execution, and even making sure the proposal was accepted when Jackson's lizard brain pushed him to run.

For a man who would work side by side with Ellery to build his dream, Ellery could do no less.

"I'll be there at ten," Henry said. He grimaced. "I…. God. I need to stop by my brother's house and talk to him." He swallowed. "I hope Kane doesn't pound me into the floor first."

"You look pretty pathetic," Jackson told him, cheering up. "Run with that."

"And fuck you back." Henry flipped him the bird and left, leaving Jackson and Ellery to say their goodbyes to Toby.

"When are we getting together for dinner again?" Jackson asked, grinning.

"I don't know—when are you asking me?" Toby grinned back. "I understand *somebody* has a yard with a pool!"

"A pool that didn't get nearly enough of a workout last year," Ellery said smoothly. "We should have people over in a couple of weeks. Sort of a celebrate the business thing."

"We should?" Jackson asked, looking surprised.

"Yes, Jackson. We should."

"Can I invite a few porn stars?"

Ellery blinked, but it appeared Jackson was completely serious. "As long as the trunks stay on during the party, I don't see why not. Galen and his significant other?"

Jackson grimaced. "Sure. They're nice. But Reg—Henry's witness? He's… well, he needs friends. I told him I'd be one."

"Sure. He can come too." Ellery started to put the guest list together in his head. AJ and Jade, Jade's boyfriend, Mike, AJ's friend, Jael, Toby, his family—

"I'll call you later with details," Jackson was saying to Toby. "But don't forget to let me know when you get the tox screens, deal?"

"Deal."

They left, and Jackson took a right when Ellery would have taken a left. "Where are we going now? The car's out here!"

"Yeah, but I want to talk to Dave and Alex before we leave." Jackson was scowling, his eyes intent on a far point in space, even as he navigated the corridors of the mostly empty basement.

"Why? We can call them." Jackson had been putting up a good front, but Ellery could see the strain around his eyes and the faint pulsing of his jaw as he ground his teeth. "Aren't you ready to go home?"

"I've been ready for a while," Jackson said with a humorless laugh. "But I've got...." He rubbed his stomach over the scrubs he'd kept on.

"Indigestion? Did you eat?"

"Yes, Counselor, I ate. Did you?"

"Yes." Ellery sniffed, offended. Jackson was the one who could pretty much wake up and go until midnight and then had to raid the fridge because he'd forgotten to eat. He might never know it, but *those* were the times Ellery was closest to breaking up with him. He'd claim he'd forgotten to eat. Fucking bullshit. Who did that? "But if you didn't forget to eat, what's the problem?"

"It's a hunch," Jackson said, clearly uncomfortable. "Look, I've just got to go with my gut... you know? I've followed hunches before. You've seen me. I've got one here."

"Oh." Ellery tilted his head. "Yes, you follow them. But you don't usually bring me along. This will be an adventure. Excellent!"

Jackson turned to look at him, almost running into the corner of the corridor where it turned. "You're insane," he announced before striding to the elevator.

"I must be," Ellery murmured to himself. "You get sexier with every goddamned bruise."

Jackson's eyes widened just as the elevator doors opened. Ellery put his hand on the small of Jackson's back and guided him in.

Old Friends, New Vices

WHEN JACKSON had been incarcerated—erm, recovering—at UCD Med Center the first time, he'd noticed that Dave, the handsome tall nurse with the pale brown skin, round face, and scalp-trimmed hair who gave Jackson his twelve-o'clock meds, seemed to time his breaks with Alex, the tiny, perky blond nurse who checked Jackson's vitals at three. It didn't take a genius to see the way they looked at each other and know they were probably banging like a drunk drummer on their breaks. Or that, in fact, Dave's old SUV held a place of romantic honor for both of them.

By now they'd been living together for ten years, and their sexual exploits were numerous and probably exaggerated, but their affection for each other—and for Jackson—was wholly 100 percent authentic.

And since Jackson hadn't been compelled to stay in the hospital for the last six months, they were even *more* excited to see him.

"Oh my God, look at this!" Dave wielded his cigarette like a conductor's baton. "This young man is here, voluntarily, with no blood in sight!"

Alex had switched to e-cigs in the last year, and he took a long puff. "Shocked, I am—shocked! When was the last time we saw you, like, four months ago, to check to make sure your stitches had all dissolved?"

"Late February," Jackson agreed. "Good times. God, you guys, you couldn't smoke in a kiddie pool or something? This place hasn't gotten any more comfortable in the last few years."

They indulged in their filthy habit in a little-used exit beyond the parking garage, where the sun hit in the late afternoon as if it was trying to cook them all like flounder.

"Well, we're holding out for the Lido deck, darling, but you know it's all booked up." Dave took a drag movie star style, and Jackson laughed.

"We'll have to get you a misting hose or something," he said sincerely.

"So, what do you need from us, baby," Dave asked, ever the leader between the two of them.

"Well, we *were* going to invite you to a pool-dinner thing," Jackson said, checking with Ellery as he said it. Ellery nodded, looking like that had been his intention all along, and Jackson plowed ahead. "We'll call you with particulars later," he said. "Sometime in the next two weeks— sort of to celebrate Ellery's new office, right?"

Alex grinned. "Fantastic! Wait, are we, like, the only ones besides Jade and Mike who will be there?"

Jackson snorted. "No. We've hired actors to pretend to be our friends, just to take away the awkwardness."

"Fantastic." Alex turned his cig off and tucked it in his pocket. "I'll bring the good shitty wine. So, I know that's not all. You always ask the most interesting questions, doesn't he, Dave? I mean, when our car's not catching on fire, you're pretty entertaining."

"That's a big if, sweetie," Dave said, both of them sharing a moment to mourn the car that had gotten blown up in one of Jackson's prior cases. "But yes." He snubbed his cigarette out in the sand top of a nearby trash can and pulled out some hand sanitizer. "Lay it on us, sweet stuff. We've got five minutes before we have to report to Nurse Ratched, who hates our gay asses with a passion."

"That woman doesn't do anything with a passion," Alex said sourly. "But whatsisface's kid was killed, and I guess she can't suck his dick when he's grieving, so yeah. Not a fun day."

"Robert Sampson has a mistress?" Jackson asked, not surprised, exactly. But usually a detective had to do a little digging before things like that fell into his lap.

"I'm not sure if they're knocking boots, because *eww*." Dave shuddered. "It's like looking at the mating habits of moray eels. Just why? But she sure does have her head far enough up his ass to polish his rims and wax his balls for good measure."

"Moray eels to classic cars and everybody's having gross sex," Ellery murmured unhappily.

Jackson flashed him an amused look but kept talking to his guys, because this—this was interesting. "So, Nurse Ratched's real name would be…?"

"Summer. Summer Frasier. She's a piece of work. She hates men. I mean, *hates* men. Gay, straight, purple—it doesn't matter. I've watched her ignore pain med requests because she thinks a guy is whining too much." Dave shuddered again, but Alex just snickered.

"What?" Dave arched an eyebrow at the love of his life. "Why is that funny?"

"Because I know something you don't know," he said smugly.

The corners of Dave's full mouth folded in, as if he was keeping the wicked secret that was Alex to himself. "Highly unlikely."

"Nope. Highly likely." Alex pulled out his phone and showed Dave two pictures.

Dave's eyes grew big and all of his playfulness evaporated. "What the hell?"

"Can we share with the class?" Jackson asked. Sweat was starting to saturate the back of his scrubs.

"Baby, this is serious. What were you going to do with this?" Dave's concern was almost cold water on the four of them.

"Well, I *was* going to share them with you later tonight," Alex confessed. "But Jackson showed interest. And remember what happened the last time we tried to keep paperwork?"

"I do. Our car blew up. So you're going to keep it on your phone?" Dave's voice rose, and Jackson held out his hand.

"What?" But Alex trusted him so he handed it over.

Jackson sent the two photos to his phone, to Ellery's, and to Jade's, before deleting them from Alex's phone.

"Our entire law firm has those now," he said soberly. "But you don't." He handed the phone back. "Now explain what they are."

"Thanks, Jackson," Dave said, shuddering. The look he sent Alex was pleading. "Baby, you know—"

"I do!" Alex looked at Jackson and sighed. "They were the same drug order," he said. "You can tell. We pull up the documents on our tablets now, and they're numbered. Even on the tablet. So this had the same number, it was for the same patient, for the same time and the same date. The first one was right after the doctor sent it. The second one was right after Nurse Fucking Ratched fucked with it and made a copy."

Jackson's eyebrows went up. "Why would she do that?"

Alex shrugged. "I don't know. She's using? She's selling? The doctor was drunk? It was Sheideman, and we all know how much he sucks, so take your pick. All I'm saying is that it was hinky, and I don't want any part of it. I was thinking of taking it to my union lawyer, but...." He grimaced.

"That would be her brother-in-law," Dave said, rubbing the back of his neck. "Gah! This is bad. I don't want any part of it!"

"What kind of pills did she mess with?" Jackson asked, his antennae perking up.

"Oxy," Alex said. "Oh-so-sellable oxy."

"How often would you have to do something like that?" Jackson pondered. "To have a business? How many pills would you need to score for something like that?"

"More than this," Dave said, grimacing. "But if she's doing it a lot and if it's giving her access to the drugs all the time, it's a start. But it's definitely not to use. A little oxy might make her bearable to work with. Not safe for other people, no, but fucking bearable."

"So, uptight?"

"Anal retentive, controlling, power-tripping—" Dave categorized, until Alex interrupted.

"She's just fuckin' mean!"

He and Dave both grimaced.

"And we don't want to be on the bad side of that, do we, baby?" Dave murmured. "C'mon."

"You guys call me later?" Jackson said, and then remembered they all had lives. "Tomorrow. Call me tomorrow."

Alex flashed him a brilliant smile. "Good move, Jackson. We all got better things to do after shift!"

Dave's look was more troubled, but Jackson wasn't fooled. Alex was smart, and in spite of his perky-adorable-look-at-me-ness, he was also aware of the world around him. After their car had been destroyed, neither of them was talking about what had just happened with anybody but Jackson and Ellery.

"Air-conditioning now?" Ellery asked, and Jackson nodded. It might have been full daylight, but it was also seven o'clock. It had been a long damned day.

"Can we check the parking lot on the way home?"

"AJ already got the thumb drive—"

"Yeah, we can look at that later. I just want to get a look at the layout. We don't even have to go in. There's stuff you can't see from a fish-eye lens."

Ellery grunted. "That should be a metaphor for something."

Jackson eyed him to make sure he wasn't mad. "Like...?"

"I don't know," Ellery replied mildly. "I'm working on it. Poetry isn't my strong suit."

Jackson shrugged and waited for Ellery to press the button for the elevator. "This I knew." Ellery still looked crisp and professional, even at seven o'clock on a 105-degree day, while Jackson felt like ten miles of shitty road. "Up for a swim after we get home?"

"Dinner?" Ellery complained. "Some of us need food to survive."

"You eat, I'll swim."

Ellery grunted. "No. You swim, I'll put something together. God, you'd seriously skip dinner if you could, wouldn't you?"

Jackson not eating was a point of contention between them. He'd gotten better since February, but sometimes, when things were eating at him, Jackson just couldn't eat.

"Morgue," he said briefly, because he'd been fine until after lunch. But it wasn't just the morgue. It was also the hospital and Henry, although Henry was slightly less of a weight on his chest than the other two.

"Yeah, well, fuck the morgue. Fuck the hospital. We'll check out the goddamned parking lot tomorrow before work and you can swim when we get home. Jesus Christ, Jackson—balance. Is it so much to ask?"

"We can drive by the parking lot on the way home," Jackson said, feeling the urgency building. "It's Tuesday, Ellery. The cops will bring him in Thursday or Monday—who wants to put money on Monday?"

Jackson wouldn't. You had a guy living with a bunch of porn stars accused of killing the son of a prominent citizen. Besides being juicy, it was also, they probably figured, a slam dunk. Wednesday or Thursday. They'd bring Henry in on Wednesday or Thursday, and if Ellery wasn't on his game and fully prepared, Henry would be spending a really uncomfortable, wholly unnecessary weekend in a place where one misplaced bout of temper could give him permanent scars.

Ellery's grunt told Jackson that he'd won, and the elevator door opened, beckoning them inside the sweaty maw of death. They both eyeballed the fetid, swampy little space before Ellery backed up and let the doors close. "Fourth floor," he said, heading for the stairs. "I'll drive us to the apartment complex, but you're right—we're not getting out."

"See, compromise."

The freedom of the walk up the stairs made it seem like it was only 101 instead of 105. Ah, choices.

THE SWIM felt amazing—Jackson could have done laps for hours, but Ellery turned the lights off in the pool after thirty minutes. Jackson pulled himself out and saw green salads with chicken breasts on the patio table, complete with napkins and silverware—and Ellery, who had showered before bringing everything out, apparently, and was wearing some sort of linen leisure pant and an expensive T-shirt.

Jackson wrapped a towel around his shoulders and looked down at his board shorts, which were so old the elastic was going out around the crotch net. Self-consciously he adjusted himself, wincing when the disintegrating rubber pulled at his pubes.

"This is nice," he said simply, scrubbing at his face. "Should I go in and put on a—"

Ellery held out one of his older, much laundered T's.

"Thanks," he said, sliding it over his head. "I didn't expect fancy."

"You would have been happy with nothing," Ellery told him. "I know it. Now sit down and eat like a human. Also, throw those shorts away."

"I'm *not* swimming naked!" Jackson protested.

"Not that I'd mind, but there should be two pairs on their way by mail. God, I can't believe it took me this long to order them. Those are so transparent I can pretty much see your entire package."

Jackson shifted again, losing another patch of hair, and tried to think of a reason not to comply. "You know, another couple of wears with these things and I'll be almost completely waxed. It's better than a kit."

Ellery's eyebrows hit his hairline. "Then, by all means, keep them on. There's nothing I like more than a fully adult lover with the privates of a prepubescent boy."

Jackson recoiled. "That's horrible!"

"So is waxing by board shorts! If you don't throw them away voluntarily, I'll put them in the garbage disposal while you sleep!"

Jackson straightened up in indignation and then yelped. "Oh my God! Too late! I'm bald!"

"Just take them off!" Ellery commanded, and Jackson stood up and did just that.

They both went completely still as they realized he was naked in the backyard. Jackson felt Ellery's eyes on him, heated, wanting, as the air grew thick around them. The flush started at his toes, and he took his discarded towel and wrapped it around his waist.

"Don't say it," he muttered.

"You still have a little hair left," Ellery observed in a quiet voice.

Jackson's flush grew worse. "You, uh, are welcome to do a detailed inspection anytime," he mumbled, and then sat down in front of his salad again. The towel around his waist didn't feel like any sort of barrier to the imagined intimacy of having Ellery's hands on his skin.

"I'm going to take you up on that," Ellery said calmly, but what Jackson heard was, "I'm going to take you apart."

"After we look at the video from the apartment," he mumbled, feeling virtuous.

"Maybe."

Ellery sounded incredibly smug, and Jackson's cock grew thick and fat against his thigh. He shifted in his seat again and caught Ellery's eyes.

"Feeling… ambitious, Counselor?"

They'd made love a lot as they'd recovered, and Jackson kept waiting for the sex to pall. No bad guys chasing them? No pressing need to be glad they were alive? But it had simply gotten comfortable—not routine, not boring, but comfortable.

Jackson was comfortable knowing Ellery wanted him.

It was such an enormous thing that they'd discovered during the last five months of peace—Ellery wanted him. Ellery wanted him in their bed every night, whether they had sex or not. And now, as they both became acutely aware that Jackson was naked under his towel, Ellery wanted Jackson in a way both carnal and intimate.

Jackson took a bite of salad in self-defense.

Comfortable did not mean you took that sort of thing for granted. It didn't mean you didn't get nervous.

It meant that when they came together, the stakes were even higher.

Ellery didn't want Jackson the sex god who had three lovers a week just to keep the monsters at bay.

Ellery wanted Jackson the vulnerable man who was beset by monsters almost nightly.

And that was the scariest person to be.

"Always," Ellery said, taking a sip of wine. He smiled and licked his bottom lip. "Feeling a bit drafty under that towel?"

Jackson swallowed, and the slight crispness of the breeze off the river was suddenly unbearably suggestive. "No. Not at all. Sweating like a pig."

Ellery's low chuckle told him exactly what that meant. "You lie for shit, Detective."

Jackson squirmed, and somehow the intimacy of Ellery knowing he was lying was even sexier than being naked under the towel. He took another bite of salad and chewed boldly.

"I'm supposed to be on the side of truth," he bantered. He was fully aroused now, the skin of his stomach tingling with anticipation.

"You want the truth?" Ellery asked mildly.

"I can handle it." Not really. In spite of the famous movie line, Jackson had been having trouble handling this truth since the two of them had gotten together last August—when Jackson had pretty much bullied Ellery into taking Kaden's defense case.

"No, you can't." Ellery took a bite of his own salad and swallowed. "Not tonight." He met Jackson's eyes with a thoughtful gaze. "The truth is difficult. I want something easy for you right now."

Jackson frowned, confused. "Wait, what about 'Bare your soul, Jackson,' or 'Tell me all your troubles, Jackson'? What happened to that?"

"Jackson?" Ellery purred.

"Yes?"

"Are you hard under that towel?"

Jackson fought against banging his head against the table. "Oh God, I really am."

"Because as soon as you're done with your dinner, I'm going to take you inside and ride that thing like a show pony. Do you have a problem with that?"

Jackson shoved the last bite of salad into his mouth and shook his head. "Nu-nuh!" He chewed and swallowed—twice—and washed everything down with a gulp of water, then stood and turned for the sliding glass door to the kitchen.

Ellery caught him before he could open it, pressing his body up against the glass and mouthing the back of his neck. "Maybe I'll just ride you here," he whispered, running his hands along Jackson's backside, his thighs, outlined under the towel.

"People can see," Jackson goaded. Ellery thrust up against him, neither of them naked, both of them exposed.

"Only if they look," he murmured.

But Jackson had an ace up his, erm, sleeve. "You're loud, Ellery," he almost sang. "Really loud. Especially when I'm inside you and you're losing your mind."

Ellery rutted up against his backside again, and Jackson shuddered. It wasn't always Jackson inside Ellery. Sometimes it was Ellery inside Jackson, and Jackson had learned to love that, crave it, especially when his head was a mess and having Ellery force him to be in the present, in their bed together, was exactly what he needed.

"You're louder," Ellery whispered. "Go inside and make yourself ready. I want to hear you scream."

Jackson almost melted against the door. Oh yes. This was one of those times. This was exactly what Jackson needed—to be owned. To be taken. To be possessed and cared for.

But he never went that way easy. "Make myself ready can mean a lot of things," he taunted. "I grease one thing, it means that. I grease the other—"

"It means I fuck you raw," Ellery growled, and even though he wouldn't do it, even though Ellery was meticulous about never taking more than Jackson could give, the threat of it, that he would want Jackson that much, was enough to make Jackson's knees go weak.

"You can try." He pushed back enough to slide the door open and then ran inside, clutching his towel around his waist as he ran. When he got to their bedroom—bed neatly made up—he pulled down the comforter, dropped his towel and his T-shirt, and scrambled underneath.

Ellery was outside, probably moving the dishes to the sink, and the thought of what Jackson was supposed to do in here sent pulses of desire down his spine, straight to his balls.

He took his equipment in hand for a moment, teasing it with light touches before he rolled to the nightstand for lubricant.

He paused in the act of dumping some on his fingers.

What Ellery was asking him to do would render him totally vulnerable. He'd done it before for Ellery—no regrets—but as a spasm of want washed over him, making him helpless, he remembered for the umpteenth time how hard he'd worked to be strong enough to face his monsters on his own.

Then he purposefully reminded himself that he didn't have to do that anymore. Very deliberately he rolled to his side and teased his crease, the slick gathering in his entrance as his overheated body shuddered. *Tease tease tease—thrust!*

One finger inside was really all he needed to prep himself, but he shuddered again because it felt good, because he was naked and finger-fucking himself and the rawness of the moment was annihilating him at the knees.

He heard Ellery's step in the bedroom and a choked sound of want.

"I need to see," Ellery demanded hoarsely. Jackson looked at him, eyes hooded, fingers working.

"Come look."

Ellery's linen rich-guy's summer sweats fluttered to the ground, and Jackson realized he hadn't had any underwear on while they'd been outside.

The thought made him groan.

"Don't you dare come," Ellery snarled. He ripped away the comforter, and Jackson tilted back his head, brazen and exposed as Ellery rolled him to his stomach and pulled his hand away.

Jackson had no more pride. He pulled his knees up to his chest and held himself still, shuddering, while Ellery positioned himself.

For a moment, the game disappeared. "You're ready, right?" Ellery asked, totally serious. All Jackson had to do—all he *ever* had to do—was say no.

"Please," he begged, arching his back, making his ass available.

Ellery thrust in, and they both cried out, because God, this was glorious. "Good?" Ellery demanded hoarsely.

"Don't stop now, Counselor, you've almost got me convinced."

"Ha!" Ellery slammed into him, hard, fast, powerfully, and Jackson thrust his ass back, amping up the intensity, throwing them both from zero to brutal climax in a couple of strokes.

For a few breathless moments, there was the sound of their flesh slapping together, Ellery's grunts as he fucked, Jackson's low moans as arousal twisted a hard knot of want in his stomach.

Then Ellery did the unthinkable.

He slowed it all down.

Jackson bit the palm of his hand in an effort not to beg.

"What?" Ellery baited, sliding out at a snail's pace. "There was something you wanted?"

Augh! The bell of his cock was right there! At Jackson's stretching point! Jackson's arms shook underneath him and sweat broke out along his spine.

"Not a thing," he groaned. "All good here!"

"God, you're stubborn." Ellery paused interminably, Jackson as stretched as he could possibly get, and then rocked forward. Slowly. So slowly. Stopping an inch or two before the very bottom.

Staying there.

A whine escaped Jackson's throat, and sweat stung his eyes. His arms gave and he was mashed facedown against the sheets, helpless, his plundered ass in the air. "About what?" he almost wept.

Ellery started to pull out again, slow. Slow. Slow. The thought flashed through Jackson's brain that Ellery needed his surrender as much as Jackson needed Ellery's when it was his turn, but not... yet....

Ellery paused again at his widest place, and Jackson's entire body began to shake uncontrollably.

"Comfy?" he gasped.

"No," Ellery admitted. "I want to fuck you so hard my cock blurs. What's it gonna take?"

"*Go!*" Jackson shouted, and oh God, Ellery gave it to him hard and fast and without mercy, huge, swollen in Jackson's ass, his fingers gripping Jackson's hips hard enough to leave bruises. Oh Jesus, oh God, oh hell. "Oh *fuck*, I'm gonna come!" Jackson screamed it, not caring who heard, not caring what they thought, because his entire body was rocketing toward white light, toward orgasm, toward peace.

Ellery beat him to it, giving a surprised little "Oh?" as he came. Jackson could feel him—he shot hard, pouring everything he had into Jackson's body. It felt hot, boiling, searing, steaming its way through Jackson, branding him as irrevocably on the inside as he was on the outside.

As Ellery collapsed across his back and Jackson's legs went out from underneath him, he had a moment to admit that he was happy that way, Ellery permeating his flesh, his soul, his heart.

They took a moment, panting, their hearts thundering in their ears.

"Am I squashing you?" Ellery asked finally.

"Yes. Don't care. Squash away."

Ellery's breath brushed Jackson's ear when he chuckled. "So, swim or shower to wash off?"

"Shower. I feel round two coming on."

"You on top?" Ellery sounded *very* excited about this, and Jackson gave a lazy smile.

"'Course."

"Don't say of course when my dick is still in your ass!" He got indignant and pushed up on Jackson's shoulders and fell out in a gush. Jackson guffawed, rolling over and pinning Ellery to the bed.

"Not anymore," he teased and then kissed Ellery, hard, openly carnal, enjoying the way Ellery went boneless and pliant underneath him. Ellery could top when he felt like Jackson needed it, but sometimes Jackson's persnickety little control freak really just loved to turn the reins over to somebody else.

Ellery moaned and wrapped his legs around Jackson's hips, grinding their cocks together. Jackson began to swell again, but they had time. He immersed himself in the kiss, learning Ellery's taste and texture again, because every day was brand-new.

"Mmm…." Again and again, a slow build grew, with time off for Jackson to nuzzle Ellery's neck, nibble on his ear, lick his lightly defined chest.

He wiggled a little so he could take Ellery's nipple into his mouth, and Ellery arched up into his body, gasping as Jackson teased with his teeth.

"Yeah?" Ellery asked, as they rocked against each other, steering toward round two in earnest.

"Oh ye—shit, who's that?"

They both heard it. Jackson's phone—which he'd left on the charger when he'd gone swimming—was suddenly buzzing urgently. It wasn't Jade's ringtone or her brother's or any of the other people he'd programmed special ringtones, and he grimaced unhappily at Ellery, who was blinking hard, trying to think. Probably, like Jackson, all his blood was bringing oxygen to an entirely different head.

"Henry?" Ellery mumbled as Jackson rolled over to grab his phone. "No, 'cause he would have called me or Galen—"

"Rivers," Jackson said crisply, and the voice on the other end was panicky and tearful—and a little familiar.

"Jackson, this is Reg. You remember me? I just didn't want to call the cops because last time we called the cops, Bobby went to jail. But there's a guy here, and Bobby's sitting on him, and… could you help? 'Cause you're helping Henry, and this is about Henry, and the guy just broke in and started hitting, and he told me to change what I'd said about the video. I don't know anything about the video but he said I had to change my words and—"

"Reg, calm down," Jackson soothed. He was already standing up and scrambling for a clean pair of underwear and cargo shorts. He put them on one-handed as he talked. "What's your address? Tell me and I'll be there as soon as possible!"

"You sure? 'Cause I… I can call Galen, but Bobby's got the guy tied up and is sitting on him, and I don't know what Galen would do, and—"

"We'll be there," Jackson said firmly. "But call John anyway and tell him we're coming. Now, where are you?"

Reg gave him an address in Carmichael, maybe twenty minutes away at this time of night, and Jackson signed off, grabbing the T-shirt he'd worn at dinner off the floor.

When he looked around for Ellery, he was surprised to find him pulling on his clothes from that afternoon—and not the slinky linen things from that evening.

"You're coming with me?" he said, not sure he liked this idea.

"Yes. You expected me not to?"

"Well, just, there's a porn star sitting on a housebreaker in Carmichael, and I'm not sure what you'll do there."

"Obviously I'll keep the porn star out of jail if we need to call the police," Ellery said, as though that was a foregone conclusion. "I'll just add it to Galen's bill. His deposit on this case was *very* generous."

"Okay…." Jackson bit his lip. "I'm not sure if I like you coming out to calls with me," he said, but he was striding through the house like he knew there was no choice. He hit the living room to grab his keys from the bowl on the table and was confronted by two very indignant crossed blue eyes.

"Aw, buddy," he said, stroking Billy Bob's whiskers back. "I'm sorry. I know. You were expecting the noise to die down so you could go in for the snuggle. We'll be back soon, I promise."

Billy Bob bit his thumb, then licked it and told him it wasn't a problem. Jackson took the moment to look at Ellery.

"Did you hear me?" he asked.

Ellery pretended to be searching the cosmos for answers. "Well yes, but I didn't really think you expected me to respond."

Jackson chuffed out a breath and shifted his feet. "You… I mean, last time we went out together, it…." He swallowed, not wanting to say it, too superstitious even to think it.

Ellery managed to look bored. "Remember the first time I saw you shot?"

Jackson shifted from foot to foot again. "My kitchen?"

Ellery nodded, as though extravagantly praising an unruly child. "Yes. Very good. And the second time you ended up in the hospital on my watch—remember that?"

Jackson bit his lip. "It was a bunch of things, really...." A killing fever, stab wounds, exhaustion, an infection....

"Mm. Then there was the planter that fell on your head."

"That was not my fault."

"Mm. And *then* I was shot. And *then* you were scalpeled—*in the hospital.*" Ellery glared at him.

"I was saving your life!" Jackson protested.

"I didn't say you weren't! But what about those stitches across your knuckles? Nobody will tell me how you got those!"

Jackson swallowed, not sure how this argument had blown up over his concern. "Those were... necessary," he said with dignity. Even though they hadn't been.

Ellery moved toe to toe with him and took his hand, the left one, the one he'd injured throwing a punch to a mirror, because seeing Ellery shot, praying for his life, was the worst moment of his life.

Gently, he pulled Jackson's knuckles to his lips. "Let's go help our client, Jackson," he said throatily. "We can get hurt anywhere we go— you in particular have a talent for it. But us, together, is like the business. It only works if it's *us*, together. Okay?"

Jackson had so much more to say. So much more to argue. But Reg—Reg who seemed to need protection, Reg who didn't like pain— had been in tears because some random stranger had broken into his house and told him to change his words.

Words about what?

Jackson narrowed his eyes, a hunch building. "Fine. But bring your computer and AJ's thumb drive. I want to see what the video says."

Two Bettas in a Bowl

ELLERY COULD see why Jackson—and Henry, for that matter—had been so protective of Reg Williams.

Sure, he was built, as, apparently, all the guys on the website were, but he was also… young in a way that had nothing to do with his birthday, and curiously fragile.

By the time Jackson had pulled his gargantuan car up to the house—which looked to be in a state of recent repair, judging by the new porch with the old siding and the new kitchen flooring inside with the battered walls—Ellery had looked at the footage on his computer twice. And he'd seen exactly what he'd been expecting to see: Henry, coming down the stairs shirtless, wearing a pair of basketball shorts, lifting up the lid of the dumpster and recoiling in horror.

The end.

Everything that had followed—guys on the stairs, cops in the parking lot, ambulance, forensics team, all of it—was exactly what Henry had said.

No surprises.

But when Ellery told Jackson that, he'd merely nodded and said, "Good!" Then he stepped on the accelerator.

When they got to the house, Jackson had flown out of the car, Ellery hot on his heels, and had burst in without any preamble. What they saw there was, well, chaos, but also pretty much what Reg had promised.

A giant of a young man in his boxer shorts, over six feet tall and built like a tank *brigade*, with sandy-brown hair and hazel eyes, was sitting on a much smaller, wiry man, holding both of his prisoner's wrists in a one-handed grip with a little help from a twisted dishtowel.

A slightly built man with his receding hairline cut close to his scalp was practically dancing around them in his boxer shorts, fussing.

"Bobby, they're here. Should we let him up now?" said the man who *must* have been Reg.

"Nope," Bobby said, eyeballing Jackson and Ellery with no excitement whatsoever. "Not happening."

"Man...," the prisoner panted. "You've got to let me up. I can't... fuckin'... breathe...."

"*You* broke in here," Bobby said, his voice obdurate. "You held a knife to my boyfriend's throat when he went to take a leak, and he broke a perfectly new mirror with your head. You think I'm letting you go?"

"So turn me over to the cops!" the guy whined. "Something! My shoulders are fucking killing me."

Bobby did what looked like a sitting crunch—something that forced his ass to bounce up and down on the guy's spine. The guy whimpered.

"I'm sorry!" he cried. "Jesus, I'm sorry! I'll tell them this was a wash! You weren't home! Anything! Jesus, man, I'm just trying not to get killed by my boss...." The would-be attacker burst out sobbing then, weak, snuffling sounds against the clean tile.

Bobby looked at Jackson with a lazy up-and-down motion of his eyes. "Reg said you could help," he said laconically. "I'm not seeing it."

Jackson reached into the pocket of his loaded cargo shorts and pulled out a packet of large zip ties, the ones used as restraints, that Ellery didn't even know he had.

"Got these," Jackson told the young skeptic. "You ready for a break?"

Bobby brightened. "I'll be honest. My ass is sort of cramping." He bounced up and down on the unfortunate housebreaker's back again, and more sobbing ensued.

"Then, here." Jackson crouched down and zip-tied the guy's wrists together, then gave Bobby a hand up. The housebreaker didn't move, just stayed on the floor sobbing and sort of flopping around like a fish.

"So," Jackson said, prodding the guy's shoulder with his toe. "You, uh, feel like telling us why this trip's necessary?"

"My boss," the guy snuffled, "is going to kill me."

"Is that like, 'My boyfriend's gonna kill me if I forget milk' kind of kill?" Jackson asked, prodding him again. "Or my drug-snorting, psychopathic, criminal, douchebag boss is going to stick a gun in my mouth and twitch?"

"The second one," the guy mewled. "He's an animal. Fucking psycho. His brain's more meth than brain!"

"Seriously?" Jackson looked at Ellery, who arched his eyebrows.

"Now there's meth?" Ellery was as surprised as he was.

"What the hell are all these drugs doing in the same fucking case?" Jackson muttered. He prodded their guy with a toe again. "You got any ideas?"

"All I know," their soon-to-be-dead guy whined, "is that I was supposed to make the retard change his statement. My boss told me to make sure he told the cops that the video was right. The new one, not the old one."

Ellery blinked. "All my faculties are right on point," he said, coming to stand shoulder to shoulder with Jackson. "And I have no idea what you mean."

"Man, all I know is that. Please let me up."

"No." Jackson aimed a kick at the guy's side, and he howled when it landed. "Watch your mouth around my friends." He pulled the packet of zip ties out again and linked the guy's ankles together, then stood and turned to Bobby and Reg.

Bobby—the tank—had his arm around his smaller, more frightened boyfriend in a gesture of protectiveness that made Ellery like him even more.

"Reg," Jackson said softly, "this is Ellery. He's Henry's lawyer, like Galen is John's. He's my boss, and we're trying to keep Henry out of jail. He's going to show you and Bobby a video, and I want you to tell me if you've seen any part of it before, okay?"

Reg nodded, and Ellery pulled his laptop out from the briefcase he'd brought with him out of sheer stinking habit. He had a sudden suspicion where this was going.

The two guys—apparently comfy and casual in their underwear in front of strangers—watched the film of Henry finding the body in silence, and then Reg looked up. "I guess that's this morning. Why are we looking at it again?"

Jackson scowled at the housebreaker. "Because I think what *he* was trying to convince you to do was verify another tape." He prodded the guy with his toe. "Am I right?"

"I replaced it at the apartment building before I came over here," the guy muttered. "The cops'll ask for it tomorrow."

"Why not today?" Ellery wanted to know.

"I don't know. We just got tipped off today that we needed to change it. My boss figured the guy was a junkie. Nobody would look too hard for whoever killed him. But there's an investigation and shit. How were we supposed to know a doctor's kid would get that much attention!"

"I got no idea," Jackson muttered, and then looked at Bobby and Reg. "Guys, look. I think we're absolutely going to have to turn this guy over to the cops. But let Ellery call them, okay?"

Jackson bent down and rolled the guy onto his back and then helped him up and into a chair while Ellery watched. Ellery had pulled out his cell phone and stood staring at the criminal with ill-concealed distaste.

Their guy was a weasel.

Small—maybe five feet five inches at the tallest, he probably weighed around one twenty—and most of that was what looked like a beer belly. His nose was lit like a Christmas tree, and he had the broken blood vessels around his face that indicated alcohol was his longtime companion.

"What's your name?" Ellery asked, pulling out his legal pad.

"Herbert," he said miserably.

"No, seriously, really?" Jackson asked, pulled from his conversation with Bobby and Reg.

Ellery's mouth twitched. "You have a problem with Herberts?"

They made the mistake of meeting eyes, and both of them burst into inappropriate giggles.

"Only when they look up my skirt!" Jackson snorted.

Ellery glared at him and settled into questioning mode. "So, Herbert, what's your last name, and who's your boss?"

"Herbert Dalton," he said defensively. "And my boss is Candy. Candy Cormier. And he's going to kill me. He's got guys in the prisons, guys in the cop's office, guys in the DA's office...." Herbert trailed off, giving Ellery big limpid green eyes and a professional whine, but Ellery had heard guys like this every day of his professional life.

"I'm not taking any clients right now," he lied, "but I can refer you to another outfit." Without any qualms, he rooted through his wallet and pulled out a card from his old firm—he kept a couple of them for just such emergencies. Given that they'd cut him loose after he and Jackson had been wounded solving a national conspiracy because they'd pissed off someone in Washington, it was really the least he could do.

After he'd tucked the card between the guy's fingers, he set about calling 911.

By the time the police arrived, Jackson had convinced the guys to go put on some clothes and Herbert had managed to tell Ellery very, very little.

"So Candy Cormier—are you sure that's a guy?" Jackson asked, puzzled.

"Yes, Jackson. Male pronoun was used."

Jackson grunted. "He's this guy's boss. He didn't *kill* Martin Sampson—"

"Not that Herbert said," Ellery told him, just as puzzled. "But you know what we *didn't* see on that footage?"

Jackson grunted. "I was waiting for you to notice that," Jackson said grimly.

Ellery smacked his forehead. "Oh my God!" Because what wasn't on the video was the body dump. The computer had shown a perfectly calm parking lot for at least three hours before Henry found the body. "I was *so* distracted!" And mortified.

Jackson's filthy chuckle didn't help. Well, yes, they'd just come from sex, so Ellery's prized sense of observation and reason was a little bit pickled. "Herbert here was told to change out the video and then to intimidate Reg into saying this was the right one."

"I don't understand!" Ellery muttered. He'd been in the top of his law school class, literally Harvard Law. He'd seen his first courtroom as an intern and hadn't looked back. But this? This game of switch-the-tape and intimidate-the-porn-star was *not* making any sense.

Jackson took a breath, frowning like he did when he was trying to break something down.

"Here's the thing. This video? This video has been doctored by somebody who didn't want us to see the body dumped, right?"

"Right." Ellery nodded. "AJ said it was easy to get. He asked the apartment manager, who went into the security room and came back with a thumb drive."

"So this footage was prepared," Jackson said. "Now, I would bet— just bet—that tomorrow, when the cops ask for a video, they're going to find a *different* section of footage, all prepared like this one. The manager will go back into his security room, grab a thumb drive, and say, 'I have it all right here, officers!' Then hand it over."

Ellery thought about it. "And it will have Henry throwing Sampson in the dumpster, with Reg and Bobby and the other guys as witnesses."

"Yes!" Jackson punched fist to palm. "Exactly! And they were trying to get Reg to say *that* tape was from yesterday. There would be no question."

Reg was standing by the refrigerator, opening and closing it fitfully until Bobby told him to pour everybody some lemonade, probably just to give him something to do.

"So we need to assume two things," Ellery said, hoping the cops could wait to arrive just two more minutes. He almost had this.

"One," Jackson said, "is that there's more than one outfit here. Martin Sampson was selling pills—probably procured from the hospital because he had connections. He *used* to sell coke, and then he went to jail for a little while and lost that connection."

"Two outfits," Ellery said, trying to think like Jackson. "But this guy sells meth, so that's a whole other subculture."

"Manufactured in your own backyard," Jackson said bitterly. "Oh my God, this is *huge*."

Ellery nodded and resisted whining about "Why us?" because seriously, couldn't they just get the guy who didn't do it? No, instead they got the guy who didn't do it and was *framed* by three different drug lords.

But maybe that wasn't the question he should be asking.

"Why Martin Sampson?" he asked, at the same time Jackson said, "Why Henry?"

They looked at each other, and Jackson said slowly, "Martin Sampson was shitting in someone else's pond. And he was also shitting in his own. He pissed off the coke dealers he used to work for. He got *caught* by Henry a couple of weeks ago when he was selling pills, so he probably pissed off the outfit he works for now. I'm not sure what he did to Candy Cormier and the Meth Monsters, but somehow he stepped on their toes too."

"Henry was an easy scapegoat," Ellery said, pacing a few steps toward the refrigerator and turning around to pace back. "Henry's altercation with Sampson was well known. So whoever took him out altered the tape the first time—they just took out the part where somebody dumped the body."

"And Candy Cormier wanted Henry pegged for the crime, so they had another tape made by whoever is in the backroom of the manager's office. And they sent Herbert here to intimidate Reg and make him agree the doctored tape was the real one."

"Why not Bobby?" Jackson asked, and then he looked over at Herbert. "Why Reg? Why not Bobby?"

"We didn't know they lived together!" Herbert wailed. "We knew the big guy defended the little guy, but we didn't know they were sleeping together! Jesus, Sampson slept with all of them—we didn't know they got attached."

Jackson frowned thoughtfully. "They did porn scenes with Sampson," he said, nodding at Reg and Bobby, and they nodded back. "That's not a relationship. Who told you it was a relationship?"

Herbert got a crafty look on his face, and Ellery was even more glad he'd given the guy his old firm's card. "I got no idea what you're talking about."

"Somebody told you they were all humping like bunnies, didn't they? Was it Sampson?"

Herbert shook his head. "It was general knowledge," he said firmly. "And that's exactly what I'll tell the cops."

Who picked that exact moment to pull up.

THE NEXT hour was a blur. Jackson explained six times what he was doing there, while Ellery stood in front of Bobby and Reg and forced the police to address *him* and not his new clients. By the time they were done and Herbert Dalton had been taken into custody, Ellery's brain was buzzing with more questions than answers.

The cops pulled away, and Ellery raked his fingers through his hair.

"Why was Martin Sampson the lynchpin of a drug war?" he asked into the sudden silence.

"Why is it so important that Henry Worrall is blamed for his murder?" Jackson asked in return.

"We know how Sampson's old dealer got his supply, and Candy Cormier probably makes his own," Jackson said. "Where did Sampson get his happy hospital meds?"

"Who in the hell is in the manager's office of that apartment making all the goddamned director's cuts!" Ellery demanded, furious all over again.

"And how am I gonna sleep here when any idiot can just break in through my front door?" Reg demanded, sounding frightened.

Jackson and Ellery exchanged a look.

"You'll sleep in our guest bedroom tonight," Ellery said smoothly. "Tomorrow, I'll have AJ come over if he's got time and help Bobby install some locks and an alarm system."

Bobby grunted. "It was on the list," he said apologetically. "Jesus, you should have seen this place before I got here!"

Ellery knew his mouth twisted as he looked at the changes wrought by home improvement. Every time there was new paint or a new appliance or new flooring, it showed up against the old stuff like a bloody wound. Fixing this place up had to be an act of love, because Ellery couldn't imagine even the most dedicated house flipper doing it for money.

"I'm going to call Henry," Jackson said. "He needs a heads-up."

He wandered into the living room, which had a threadbare rug that looked thin enough to use as a flour sifter, and Ellery was stuck in the kitchen, trying and failing to guess which case was going to take his attention first.

"Can we really stay at your house?" Reg asked, with a little bit of awe. "'Cause that's... I mean, he said he'd be my friend, but that's like something John would do."

Ellery nodded. "Well, Jackson's that kind of guy," he said, not even wanting to think about these two vulnerable guys alone in the world. The tenor of the police questioning had been decidedly unfriendly, particularly toward Bobby, but that kid—barely twenty-one, judging by his driver's license—had been as calm as Ellery had seen *anybody* on the stand.

If that young man was any more grounded, his toes would be tree roots.

That impression of Bobby didn't change after they locked up the house and left, Reg following in a bright orange car that Jackson seemed to approve of, and Bobby following *him* in a truck that looked like it should have fallen apart before Bobby had been born.

The kid had apologized about the truck before they'd even left. "I'm sorry, man. I hate to park this anywhere near your house, but it's got my tools in the back, and we can't replace that shit."

Jackson had chuckled and pointed to his SUV. Once upon a time, it had been an Infiniti QX30. But that was before it had been blown up and reconstituted as an urban assault vehicle with a translucent oyster-gray paint job.

"What in the fuck is that?" Bobby asked, entranced.

"That is a tricked-out rich-man's car," Jackson told him proudly. "And everything is bulletproof. Ellery's neighbors have actually filed complaints about it because they think it's military issue."

Ellery sighed. "We usually keep it in the garage," he confirmed. "But, you know, we didn't know what we were driving into tonight."

"Aw, man," Reg said, tapping the hood of the Camero he apparently loved. "If I wasn't afraid for my car here, I'd totally want a ride in that thing."

"Rides like shit," Jackson consoled him. "It's loud and it rattles your teeth from your head. But the glass is bulletproof, and it sounds like a herd of gas-drinking elephants, so there's that."

"Awesome," Bobby crooned. "Wow. That's some car."

He got into his battered truck, and Jackson and Ellery got into the urban assault vehicle, Jackson chuckling all the way.

"What's so funny?" Ellery asked, once they were belted in.

"That kid, Bobby."

Ellery knew who he was—he'd spent a half an hour skimming through the Johnnies website. "Technically Vern Roberts," because that was the name the kid had given the police.

"Yeah, but I've seen him naked. He's got a ten-inch—"

"I know what he's got," Ellery muttered. He'd actually forgotten what those two kids—tender as bunnies—did for a living. Or had done. Reg, he knew, was working promotions now, and Bobby seemed to be getting most of his income from working construction. He remembered his outrage that Jackson had been watching porn, but he'd done it too, particularly when he was younger and single and driven. You didn't always think about the people behind the bodies. But having watched Vern Roberts defending his boyfriend and facing down the police with that laconic, steady-eyed patience, Ellery had completely forgotten about the kids on film and had only seen the adults trying to live their lives. "Who cares how big his… equipment is?"

Jackson shook his head and steered the vehicle formerly known as an SUV through the quiet streets. "I actually don't," he said. "It's just… just all the bullshit guys talk about. All a guy's accomplishments are boiled down to his dick size. But that kid didn't give a shit. He was just a kid who liked the big shiny toy car. They both were. And after the way the cops went after him tonight—and, hell, having some guy break into his house and assault his boyfriend? To see him light up and be sweet like that. It just proves people are much bigger than that thing between their legs."

Ellery swallowed. His thoughts were so damned similar, it almost hurt.

Jackson pulled up to a light, and Ellery cursed the specialized webbing and the triple-release seat belts that held them in—not to mention the thing's size. He wanted to lean over and kiss Jackson's cheek in the worst way.

"You've always been able to see beyond the obvious," he said mildly, and he didn't have to even look to see Jackson roll his eyes.

He looked anyway. Just like those years before they'd dated, when Jackson had seemed aloof and disdainful and unobtainable, Ellery found it impossible to look away.

BILLY BOB was thrilled to have company, and he seemed to have a real fondness for Reg, who just melted when the cat rubbed against his ankles.

"We should get a cat, don't you think, Bobby?" he asked, holding Billy Bob up to his chest and letting the cat rub noses.

"Sure, Reg," Bobby said patiently, hauling a single duffel with both their clothes into the bedroom Ellery indicated. He looked around unhappily. "This place is… really nice," he said, his discomfort obvious. "I… I'll have us out of your hair tomorrow, I promise. If your friend can give me some pointers on security and shit, I'll take the day off."

Reg looked around and smiled uncertainly. "It's a real nice place," he said to Jackson. He didn't really talk much to Ellery, but then, Ellery did that to people. "I can't believe you said we could hang out."

"We've got video games," Jackson said, and Reg lost some of his discomfort.

"Well, maybe someday," he said, and then yawned. "But now, God, I could sleep anywhere. Even on that nice bed that smells like dead grandmas."

Jackson choked, and Ellery's eyes got really big, and they both watched the younger men disappear into the guest bedroom.

"Who told them your mother stayed there in April?" Jackson asked, smirking.

"Nobody." Ellery grunted. "It's that rose-and-vanilla perfume you gave her for Christmas, you know that, right?"

"It's dead grandmas," Jackson said, "and nobody can tell me any different! Lucy Satan smells like dead grandmas!" He giggled his way into *their* bedroom, and Ellery followed him grimly.

"My *mother's* name is *Taylor*," he said, but it wouldn't matter. Ellery wasn't sure what had prompted Jackson to start calling Taylor Cramer "Lucy Satan," but he had the feeling it had something to do with a big dose of morphine Jackson had been given when he'd been laid up in the hospital—and Taylor Cramer's inimitable Machiavellian style. All he knew was that Jackson and his mother seemed to have an agreement that he call her nothing *but* Lucy Satan. And since Ellery had the feeling Jackson sort of *liked* his mother, he wasn't sure what to do about it.

His mother might have been positively diabolical, but she was *not* the devil.

Although, when she'd flown out to stay with them for the week of Passover, Ellery had been sorely tempted to agree with Jackson that she was.

After Ellery did the rounds, double-checked the doors, set the alarm system, and made sure the cat had water and food—because if he didn't, Billy Bob had been known to wake them up by standing on the nearest face and meowing pitifully—he followed Jackson to bed and found him stretched out under the summer-weight comforter, staring sleepily at his phone.

"Whatcha doing?"

"I texted Galen to let him know what was up. And I texted Henry to remind him that he'd probably be taken in first thing in the morning and his only words had better fuckin' be 'Talk to my lawyer.' Then I texted Jade to tell her we might not be in immediately, so she's on for bossing the workmen around, and finally, I texted AJ to tell him to meet Bobby at his house tomorrow at ten."

"Is that all?" Ellery asked, stripping off his clothes and throwing them in the hamper. The night had been sticky, and he was grateful for the air-conditioning, but that didn't mean the clothes were good for one more wear.

"And I texted AJ *and* Bobby so they'd have each other's numbers and could communicate without me," Jackson finished up, yawning. He waited for Ellery to crawl under the comforter before turning off the lamp.

For a moment, the room was quiet, but Ellery could see Jackson's eyes, still gleaming in the light from the window.

"What's wrong?" Ellery asked. But he knew.

"Nothing," Jackson said softly. He turned over to his side, away from Ellery so Ellery wouldn't worry.

Ellery always worried.

He rubbed Jackson's back softly, the spot between his shoulder blades, which was so tense the muscles felt like a knot.

"Nice," Jackson mumbled.

"Tell me when they come," Ellery instructed.

"Sure."

Sometimes he didn't. Sometimes Ellery would wake up at four in the morning and Jackson would be huddled in the far corner of the bed, shaking from whatever dream had ripped apart his sleep. Sometimes he got up and said he was going to the bathroom, and Ellery would find him dozing on the couch, a video remote in his hand, because he'd played games to calm his nerves.

And sometimes he'd scream in his sleep and neither of them could pretend it didn't happen.

For a while, after they'd come home from the hospital in February and he'd started talking to Ellery's rabbi, who—like every other human being on earth—seemed to have taken a shine to Jackson, the dreams had eased up. Jackson would tell Ellery when they hit. They could breathe through them together.

But the last couple of weeks, well, Jackson's impatience with himself had been palpable.

Ellery couldn't seem to find the words to tell him that healing all of the myriad wounds Jackson had survived, both physically and emotionally, wasn't going to happen overnight. As much as Ellery liked to think he'd made a positive difference in Jackson's life, he couldn't fool himself into believing that by the power of his mighty wang and some really rocking sex, *poof*! Jackson was cured.

People with Jackson's damage didn't *get* cured. They got better. And people with Jackson's strength soldiered on through the bad times and celebrated the good.

And people with Jackson's conscience didn't want to inflict any of the bad times on the one person they loved most of all.

Ellery scooted closer, not minding the heat Jackson's body threw out naturally. He placed a very precise, very tender kiss on the back of Jackson's neck.

"Tell me, *please*," he begged.

Jackson let out a sigh. "Counselor, the way this one's brewing, I'm not going to need to tell you a damned thing."

Ellery wrapped his arm around Jackson's middle and held him tight, any thought of the heat, of discomfort, evaporating into the humid night. "I'll keep you safe," he promised, hating that he couldn't.

Jackson laced his fingers with Ellery's as they lay over his chest.

"You always do," he lied.

Murky Waters

DEAD PEOPLE. Jackson was surrounded by dead people—overdosed junkies, noses bleeding, vomit-stained, lips blue, eyes open and staring. His mother was there, although it hadn't been the drugs that killed her because serial killers work for free. Jade, her brother, Kaden, his wife and his kids, although none of them had ever touched that shit. Jade's boyfriend, Mike, was particularly gruesome, face purple, tongue black, rangy body distended with bloat.

Henry, John, Galen, Bobby, Reg—all the new people he'd met that day, including Herbert the housebreaker—they were all facedown in the gutter, needles in their arms.

Martin Sampson, aka Scott the porn model, but younger, his face softer as a teenager, lying face-up, dick hard, iced in coke and meth like a dead-flesh cake.

And he knew it wasn't Ellery, facedown at his feet, knew it wasn't Ellery, knew it wasn't Ellery. But he had to crouch anyway, had to touch the pallid flesh, had to roll him over, see the brown eyes wide and staring, the pale skin practically green, see him as he almost had been, dead, the drugs gone now, his stomach opened up by a gunshot, bleeding, bleeding, bleeding—

"*Ellery!*"

He was trying to sit up in bed, his throat raw, and Ellery was practically lying on top of him, hands on his shoulders, pinning him to the mattress so he couldn't flail.

Footsteps from the hallway startled him enough to roll out from under Ellery's pinning body to land crouching on the floor, staring wildly at the bedroom door as two vaguely familiar guys in their boxer shorts burst through.

"Mr. Rivers, you okay?"

Jackson glared blearily at them, relieved when Ellery turned on the lamp behind him. "Peachy," he said through a rough throat. "Sorry to bother you."

Bobby—the big one was Bobby, right?—tilted his head to the side. "Bad dreams?" he asked, not with sympathy, really, just assessing the situation.

"I get them sometimes," Jackson muttered. "Sorry. Should be done now. Go back to sleep."

Bobby nodded slowly. "Okay. We're sorry, Mr. Rivers. For whatever did that to you. Don't worry—me and Reg'll keep you safe. We're just in the other room."

Behind him, he heard a weak laugh from Ellery, and he fell onto the bed in a puddle of dream-aftermath and mortification.

"Thanks, Bobby. Reg. Sorry about that. Go back to sleep. It's all good."

They disappeared, closing the door behind them, and Jackson collapsed on the bed unhappily. "That was embarrassing."

"You managed not to do that when my mother was staying here," Ellery muttered in agreement.

"Sorry." Jackson went back to his side, burying his face in his pillow, freezing from the dream's aftereffects, wanting nothing more than to be by himself so he could cry. "So sorry. Seriously. God, Ellery, I didn't mean to do that to—"

Ellery was suddenly plastered along his back, holding him tight. "You're shaking."

"Cold," Jackson mumbled. Oh, he hated it when it got this bad. "So cold."

"Shh, baby. You're all right."

Jackson squeezed his eyes shut tightly. "You know it's not me I'm worried about," he said, stupid tears of reaction trickling down the corners of his eyes.

"*We're* all right," Ellery said. "We're all right. We're all fine."

"Thanks," Jackson murmured. What he really wanted to say was *I hate this. I hate being this weak. I hate being this broken. I hate that I shatter your sleep as well as mine. I hate that you have to love me with all my bullshit baggage!*

"Can you talk about it?"

"Please. God. No." Jackson shuddered really hard, clutching Ellery's hand tighter to his chest, and Ellery's sigh practically rocked the bed.

"You need to talk it—"

"No."

"God, you're stubborn."

"Ellery, do you really want to have this fight right now after what I just did in front of two practical strangers?"

"Sure," Ellery said, letting go of his chest and sitting up. "Yes. Let's have this fight now. Let's have it in front of strangers. Let's have it in front of friends. Let's have it in front of *anybody*, because you're certainly not talking about it to *me*!"

Jackson shushed him, placing two fingers on his mouth and pushing at his shoulder. "Look, it's jus.... It's dumb. It's obvious. It's stupid to even say—"

"Well, apparently *not*, if not talking about it is doing this to you!" Ellery hissed. But at least he'd lowered his voice. Gently—so damned gently—he cupped Jackson's cheek, the heat from his hand welcome. "You're right. I *do* know what this is about. I *do* know why they got worse again. But I need you to say it, and so do you, so you can build up your defenses again."

Jackson grunted and dropped his chin to his chest, rubbing the back of his neck with his hand. "You were shot," he said grimly.

"I was." Ellery took his hand and held it to the scar. The bullet had hit soft tissue and gone straight through, blessedly missing his heart and his spine. But it had hit plenty of other things—a lung, kidneys, an intestine, a rib. The worst thing about bullets wasn't the blood loss, but the way they bounced around and turned a person's perfectly ordered insides to mushy goo. Ellery had needed a lot of blood units and stitching up before his mushy goo was intact—and it still wasn't as much as Jackson had needed nine years ago, when he'd been almost blown apart by a sniper's bullet.

But the hole it made in Jackson's well-being seemed to be twice as big.

He held Jackson's hand against his scarring—the bullet wound, the incision scars from the surgery. Jackson had spent long hours mapping his flesh in the past five months, relearning the new Ellery after their last adventure. No matter how much Ellery told Jackson he wasn't at fault for that moment, for Ellery stepping in the line of fire in a fit of uncharacteristic rage, that wasn't what Jackson believed.

Jackson closed his eyes, fingers stroking the skin unconsciously. "I was so lucky," he whispered. "A little higher, a little lower, a little to the left...."

Ellery's mouth twisted, and for once Jackson couldn't make the joke.

"Don't," he said. "Don't make fun. Your job isn't supposed to be dangerous. Don't you think that's what helps me sleep? Knowing it's not supposed to be dangerous for you?"

"Baby—"

Jackson held his fingers to his lips. "It is never going to be okay that you were hurt," he said. "I am never going to be fine with you lying in the hospital while some guy tried to poison you." And the deaths of the two men he killed, the ones who'd hurt Ellery in the first place, were weighing heavy on his soul. He shuddered. "And I hate myself for dragging you down with me."

"I hate you for not letting me help!" Ellery snapped, then looked appalled. "I mean, I don't hate you—I hate *the fact* that you won't let me help. And you're not talking about the other thing—not at all. You did right afterwards—going to the rabbi, at least. But it's like, the more you thought about it, the deeper it burrowed."

Jackson pressed the heels of his hands into his eyes, because hearing Ellery talk about it brought back the dream, the fear, all of it. "Later," he said hoarsely. "It's bumfuck in the morning—"

"Baby," Ellery begged. "Baby, you can't torture yourself. Not for what happened to me and not for what you did because of it and not for the people you couldn't save. Those two guys who just ran in here to protect us are sleeping and feeling safe because you offered them a place to stay. I could have done it, but they would have picked a hotel instead. They agreed because you're their friend, and I'm okay with that. You... you have chosen this role, this vocation, of protecting people, sometimes the most unlikely people. You look at them and see human beings and not sex workers or drug addicts or ex-cons. And it's this gift—this *amazing* gift. I'm not sure if I've ever told you how wonderful it is that you do that. But the downside is, you hurt for them. You saw the Dirty/ Pretty victims when nobody else did, but you hurt for them. The serial killers trained up in Karl Lacey's compound—you saw how they'd been violated and you hurt for them. And when you had to kill them, you still hurt. You saw who they could have been. You saw our friends in them, not the people who tried to kill us both."

Jackson swallowed, so acutely uncomfortable in his own skin he wanted to scream. "They hurt you," he snarled.

"And you killed them, and that hurt you," Ellery told him, not wavering. "And you need to face that—that you don't kill like an automaton. You're *not* a soldier or a killer or a bad cop. You need to be okay with how you feel, or… or it's going to tear you apart." Ellery let out a twisted laugh. "I was getting used to getting a full night's sleep once in a while," he said. "I'd really like to go back to that. I mean, it's not a deal breaker, but…." He shook his head. "One case. This is only our first case back. And you are already so knotted up, you can barely breathe. You need to learn to breathe."

Jackson took a deep breath. "Breathing," he croaked. His throat was swollen tight, and his ears hurt, and he knew the signs of needing a good long cry, but God, he didn't want to do it in front of Ellery. He wanted to go play video games or go running or go swimming—he'd done them all in the middle of the night to keep Ellery from knowing how bad it had gotten in the past couple weeks. But he couldn't leave. Their houseguests didn't deserve to have him wandering around the house, and they certainly didn't deserve Ellery's promised fit if he did.

Ellery closed his eyes and leaned forward until their foreheads were touching. "Again."

Deep breath. Any toddler could do it.

"Again."

This one wobbled, in and out, the pain in his ears, his throat, his eyes receding ever so slightly.

"Again."

Jackson lost himself in Ellery—his touch on his face, the feel of his breath, the quiet of the house. Billy Bob jumped on the bed, purring, and Ellery took Jackson's hand that was still pressed against Ellery's stomach and put it on the cat.

Meditation by cat—Jackson had perfected it.

"Jackson?"

His eyes were closing easily now, the brightness of the lamp an unwelcome intrusion.

"Yeah?"

"You're going to have to let it out sometime."

"It's so awful," he whispered. "Ellery, why would you want to stay with me when everything inside me is awful?"

"What's inside you is beautiful. Don't ever forget that." He believed that—Jackson knew it. Just the fact that Ellery Cramer believed that meant there might be a God.

Ellery pushed on his shoulder, and Jackson let him, lying down facing him and not turning away. Ellery reached over Jackson's shoulder to switch off the light.

"I still worry," Ellery said when he was done. "That my scars will turn you off."

"That's stupid," Jackson muttered thickly. "You're the most beautiful man I know."

Ellery's soft chuckle reassured him. "You believe that. That's amazing." Jackson felt the kiss on the forehead and allowed the blessing to seep through. For tonight, he was going to be comforted. For Ellery's sake, he'd let them have peace.

Old Enemies

ELLERY LOOKED at his opponent across the beat-up interview table in the police station and tried not to yawn. His usual nemesis—Arizona Brooks—had been promoted, mostly because of the work Ellery and Jackson had done on the Dirty/Pretty case, he was sure. This time, Arizona had sent in a green recruit. Young, fresh out of college, shiny faced and scrubbed clean, ADA Siren Herrera had razored her tight ebony ringlets close to her head and wore two-inch gold hoops in her ears to accent bone structure so clean and fine, she looked to be carved out of a stunning cut of onyx.

The brilliant red lipstick was just the kicker to show she had no fear.

Ellery approved, actually. Herrera had a sleepy-eyed gaze that was probably meant to lull her opponents into somnolence before she gutted them like a trout, and Ellery had to admit that if he and Jade Cameron hadn't been sniping at each other for the past six years, he might have been a bit intimidated.

But he was starting to see what made Jade Cameron tick—she wanted no more and no less than to be treated as an equal for her strength, intelligence, and perseverance in what could be a damned hard world.

Ellery was willing to give Siren the same consideration, but that didn't mean he was going to let her win.

"You look exceptionally pleased with yourself," she said, eyeing Ellery and Henry warily. "I've offered your client ten years on involuntary manslaughter if he pleads guilty right now and we don't have to take this to court. Shouldn't you at least conference with Mr. Worrall to see if he'd like to do that?"

"He doesn't," Henry said, and then looked at Ellery anxiously. "I don't, do I?"

"You do not," Ellery said firmly. "You haven't even been arraigned yet, and I don't think Ms. Herrera wants this to get that far."

Henry had been brought in at eight o'clock, on the dot. One of his roommates had called Ellery's cell at eight ten, after they'd called John in a panic, and John called Ellery from there.

Ellery had been dressed and showered and in his courtroom suit when the call had come in, and he and Jackson had been getting into the car to drive downtown.

They just turned onto 7th Street toward L instead of going down to 10th and F—that was the only way this news had impacted their morning.

He had literally made it to the processing room in time to see Henry get his prints taken, and that was all the time he'd needed to tell Henry the deal with the tape.

Siren might have *thought* she knew what her case was, but Ellery was about to explain what they were *really* doing there.

"We have witnesses that saw the defendant attacking the victim. We have video that backs that up, time-stamped yesterday—we practically have the murder on tape!"

"Do you?" Ellery smiled, catlike, and pulled out the thumb drive. "Does it have the time and date stamp and a little watermark in the corner with the address on it?"

Siren's sleepy eyes widened. "It might."

"Mm... those witnesses. Did you ask them *when* they saw the altercation between Mr. Worrall and the victim?"

"No—"

"Did you happen to look at the time stamp of the supposed murder and put that together with the forensics information that said the vic had only been in the dumpster for about an hour? Because it's my understanding, the original altercation happened midmorning, and Henry reported that body in the early a.m. There would have been flies for miles, and yet *my* forensics information says there was hardly any fly activity at all. There was some building—but the body couldn't have been there more than an hour. Do you even have a motive?"

"He was protecting his boyfriend," Siren said confidently. Henry made a face and shook his head no, and some of her confidence faded. "He was not protecting his boyfriend?"

"Reg is a friend," Henry said. "His boyfriend was protecting him. I was just... protecting the guys."

Siren's eyebrows knitted together, and she swallowed, much of her "I got this" expression fading. "Are you going to tell me what it is that I don't know?" she said. "Because I got this folder and was told it was a slam dunk. The father of the victim has pretty much been calling my office on the hour for the last day, insisting that the killer be brought in for questioning. How are you so sure your guy isn't the one?"

"What if I told you that *neither* of us has the right tape," Ellery said, and watched her finely plucked eyebrows arch up.

"Wait, yours is doctored too?"

"What if I told you that the police have a man in custody who broke into the witnesses' house and tried to intimidate our witness into saying that *yours* is the right one."

Siren sat straight up. "They do? Why wouldn't they *tell* me that?"

Ellery gave a thin smile. "Can I make a guess here? Was this case supposed to belong to ADA Brooks, but she took one look at my name on the docket and handed it off to you?"

Siren looked a little sick. "I had about four minutes warning," she said dully. "What does that mean?"

"Well, for starters, it means Arizona has learned that I do not take the easy way out—no plea bargains unless my client is guilty. Now you know. It means that there are two doctored videos out there—both of them easily disproven, but that's not the bad part."

"I'm on the edge of my seat," she said, resting her chin on her palm.

"The bad part is, the real footage is nowhere to be seen. *Our* video shows the dumpster for three hours—a couple people come and go, but there's nothing happening until Henry here goes out to find the body."

"But if there was no forensics...."

Ellery nodded. "That's how we know it was fake. That body was dumped sometime in there. Your forensics will tell you this was the secondary crime scene, even if your doctored footage tries to say it's the primary."

Siren's eyes narrowed. "Four minutes warning," she muttered. "So you're telling me I have no case."

"You have no case. Not yet."

"Yet?" Henry sputtered at the same time Siren raised those stunning eyebrows.

"Yet?"

Ellery grimaced. He was supposed to be a professional.

"Ms. Herrera, I would not be surprised if new information comes across your desk very soon. And when it does, I would be very suspicious of it. Somebody wants Mr. Worrall to take credit for this crime, and my office would very much like to see credit go where it is rightfully due."

Siren's scowl grew. "I don't like the implication that the DA's office is that easily influenced."

"Then you need to be the ADA that changes it," Ellery told her. "My client is innocent, and I've got enough evidence to torpedo anything you bring to the table. If I were you, I'd refrain from charging him again until you figure out why it's so imperative that *he's* the one who did it."

Siren narrowed her eyes. "Again, I resent the implication—"

Ellery held up his hand. "Ms. Herrera, *are* you going to charge my client?"

"May I see your evidence?"

Ellery waved at the mirrored window, and the door was opened by the arresting officer.

"Ms. Herrera would like to view this in a private place," Ellery said, and she snorted.

"I don't think it's going to be that exciting," she said before standing up and taking Ellery's copy of the video. Ellery had the original in the hidden safe in the back of his closet, because no amount of paranoia was too much.

"I don't know, ma'am," Henry drawled. "I live with porn stars, and I'm telling you, if that thing gets me off, it's going to be the sexiest movie I've ever seen."

Ellery snorted, and Siren rolled her eyes—but Ellery saw the corners of her mouth pinch in, like she was holding back a smile. She disappeared, and Henry turned to Ellery, all traces of the hostile young man they'd seen the day before gone.

"She's a tough cookie," he said nervously.

"You should meet her boss. Arizona would be picking her teeth with your bones right now."

"But I didn't do it!"

Ellery let out a breath. "I know that. You know that. But it would help if we had a more specific crime theory to put in her lap. Right now, what we have is a drug cartel train wreck. Figuring out who wanted Sampson dead—and why—is like sorting snakes in a sack."

Henry studied his hands—callused from what looked to be hard work—and picked fitfully at a nail. "He...." Suddenly Henry looked at Ellery hard. "Did Rivers tell you? About... you know?"

Ellery slow blinked. "Yes," he said guardedly. "He did tell me about Sampson's past with drugs. Do you know anything about that?"

Henry straightened his shoulders, obviously remembering it was possible they were being observed. Their meeting with Siren had not been confidential.

"I might," he said.

Ellery nodded and looked up at the green light by the clock. "Sound off," he said, and watched as it turned red.

"We're confidential now. I know you and Sampson had a ships-passing thing. Did he tell you anything?"

Henry shrugged. "We weren't about conversation, really." He looked embarrassed for a moment. "I'd, uh, never done that, really. Someone I didn't know, didn't care about. It was—" He swallowed. "—empty."

Ellery felt a reluctant tug of grief for Henry Worrall. Hard lessons didn't get any easier when they came with a price tag like a possible jail sentence.

"It's not always the most emotionally healthy thing you can do," Ellery agreed. He'd had one or two flings, but Jackson... Jackson had been having nonromantic one-night hookups with friends for *years*, just so he didn't have to sleep alone. The desolation on Henry's face brought the night before back in startling clarity, and Ellery had to forcibly separate his heart from his head.

Jackson was strong—stronger than he'd ever given himself credit for.

Henry needed them both.

"No. And... the thing is, my face was bruised up. I'd... I'd just gone home to tell my folks about my discharge...."

Henry's next breath was unsteady, and Ellery knew that the paperwork *he'd* gotten when he'd come to get Henry had said "Dishonorable Discharge" on it. He was itching with curiosity—he couldn't deny it—but he knew that Don't Ask/Don't Tell had been repealed. Legally it couldn't be because Henry was gay, but what Henry's CO thought about that and what the US Army thought weren't always the same thing.

"You'd planned on a career there," Ellery prompted gently.

Henry nodded. "Let's just say that... that the circumstances that led to my discharge outed me rather spectacularly. My face was all banged up because... I went home. And when Sampson asked me about it, I said... I don't know, something like, 'A parting gift from Daddy Dearest.'"

Ellery's eyes popped open, and his spine straightened.

"And what did he say back?"

"He dug in his pocket and took out a pill bottle—he'd sharpied it up a lot, like it was his very own special recipe. He pulled out a couple of God knows what and popped them in his mouth and swallowed dry." They both shuddered. "And he said, 'Was it wrapped up in a bow, like mine was?'"

Ellery sucked in a breath, and he and Henry locked gazes. Why *had* Martin Sampson switched sides in the drug war?

At that moment, the door opened, and the light above them switched to green. Siren Herrera bustled back in, her high-heeled black pumps clicking purposefully on the tile.

"Well, that was an education," she muttered, glaring at Ellery.

"It was just a video."

"Well, it didn't exactly clear your client, but it did nullify the evidence we were using to hold him. You're free to go. Get Mr. Worrall's things from processing on your way out, and Mr. Worrall?"

"Yes, ma'am?"

"Don't leave town."

Henry leveled one of those flat glares at her that reminded Ellery that he'd served nine years in the infantry, deployed more than half the time. "Don't worry about it, Ms. Herrera. I don't have anywhere else to be."

JACKSON WAS waiting for them when they emerged, having secured a slightly illegal loading-unloading parking space right outside the white cinder-block building.

Ellery was grateful. Henry had been checked in wearing cargo shorts and a tank top, which was almost exactly what Jackson was wearing, but Ellery was in a summer-weight suit. Walking the ten blocks to the office in the already sweltering heat was not his idea of fun.

They loaded into the Lexus, Ellery in the front, Henry in the back, and Jackson pointed to the icy bottles of water sitting in the cup holders. Both of them drank blissfully as Jackson pulled into traffic.

When Ellery felt like he could speak again, he briefed Jackson on what had gone on, finishing up with Henry's revelation about Martin Sampson's "gift" from dear old Dad. Ellery left out the part about what had prompted the confidence—he felt like that was something Henry should share on his own.

Jackson came to a stop at a light and raised an eyebrow at him, and Ellery shook his head. Jackson nodded and hit the gas when the light turned green.

From the back of the car, Henry spoke, his voice sounding faraway and a little sad. "My brother and his husband do that. Have eyeball conversations with no words. I went there last night, and… and… and told them. Everything. Even the shit I haven't told you. The shit I've only told one person since I got here. And they had one of those eyeball conversations, and then my brother… just hugged me. Kissed my temple. Like I haven't been the most outrageous asshole to the two of them for the last year and a half. And his husband rolled his eyes, like he was being really put upon, and then he came and held us both. Like… like all was forgiven. And… that's not the way we were raised. That's not how it works in our family. You fuck up like I did, you get what's coming to you, boy." His voice wavered, then broke a little.

"I'd almost rather go to jail and get what's coming to me than deal with people saving my ass and having eyeball wars about me and…. Fuck."

His voice broke, and Ellery sent Jackson a frantic message in eyeball semaphore, because he just did not *do* tears, and Jackson knew it.

Jackson let out a breath through his nose. "Henry, what you got doing today?"

"Nothing."

"You still got the scrubs from yesterday? I washed mine."

"Yeah, me too. They… didn't smell too friendly. Why?"

"Wanna go break some rules and raise some hell?"

Henry let out a long breath. "God, yes."

"Too bad. Our goal here is not to get caught. I want to do some snooping at the independent outpatient offices of Carver, Sampson, Warburton, and Patel."

"Sampson?" Henry's voice held a note of hope, as though he'd caught on to something.

"I take it you tracked him down?" Ellery asked, feeling optimistic.

"Indeed." Jackson smiled and patted the tablet at his side, which was probably what he'd been doing when Ellery had been getting Henry released.

The car was flooded with oxygen and hope and the promise of adrenaline for the two junkies who needed something—*anything*—to do.

Ellery smiled. "Is one of the partners really named Carver?"

"Yes."

"In a co-op of surgeons?"

"Indeed."

Henry let out a chuckle from the back of the car. "That's sort of sick."

Jackson's smirk went nuclear. "Indeed."

HE PULLED up on the street side of the office and put the Lexus into Park so Ellery could get out and Henry could move to the front. Ellery paused, though, before undoing his belt.

"You'll be careful?" he asked, scowling.

Jackson rolled his eyes. "We'll be safe as kittens. I'll only get him a little dusty, I promise."

He still had the bruise on his cheek, his shoulder, and the torn knuckles from the day before. "Like you got dusty yesterday?" Ellery inquired sweetly.

"Yesterday was sort of getting to know you." Jackson cast a hard grin over the seat to where Henry was getting out. "Right? Don't you feel like we know each other better?"

"It's a friendship bound in cement," Henry replied, that flatness in his voice telling Ellery everything he needed to know about how soft and squishy Henry Worrall was *not* going to get around Jackson.

"Don't go swimming," Ellery snapped, rubbing the bridge of his nose. "You need to come in and see everything," he said, feeling plaintive. Jackson had helped choose the furniture, design the layout. It only seemed fair that he got to see it before the inevitable wear and tear.

"I'll come in later today," he promised, and Ellery saw his eyes softening. "I'm just as excited as you are."

Ellery leaned forward, half expecting Jackson to pull back, but he didn't. He met halfway for a quick kiss on the lips.

"I'll text you when we're done at the clinic," Jackson promised. "Let you know where it leads. I'd like to see who's playing film school at Henry's apartment complex while we're there getting his costume."

Ellery nodded. "I'll be in the office all day, so feel free. Be careful!" he admonished again.

"Always!" Jackson winked, and there was nothing else Ellery could do. He backed out of the car and let Henry take his place. As Jackson pulled away from the curb and Ellery took his briefcase to the office, he had to admit he felt a lot better knowing there was somebody *with* Jackson this time out, somebody who could hold his own in a fight, by the looks of things.

He remembered Henry's voice from the back of the car—wobbly, broken, the anger and the bravado washed out of him by the very real possibility of going to jail.

Whatever had damaged that kid—and Ellery would put money on there being damage—the person left behind was still sound, still a good soul.

Ellery hoped he was good enough to have Jackson's back.

To Hell, With a Shovel

THE SILENCE in the car was stifling, and at first, Jackson wasn't sure how to break it.

"So, did you meet Arizona Brooks?" he asked. Ellery's usual opponent at the DA's office rubbed Jackson the wrong way, but Ellery insisted she was a decent person with a mostly functioning moral compass.

Jackson would believe that when they got some help for the good-faith work they did to make sure justice was done.

"No. She passed us off to someone new," Henry said, staring off into space. "Siren Herrera." He made a noise. "If I swung that way, I'd say she was smoking hot."

Jackson chuckled. "I *do* swing that way. Sorry I missed the show."

Henry grunted, and Jackson felt Henry's cold blue eyes searching his face. "I thought you and… I mean, you and Mr. Cramer seem to be…. Don't you live together?"

"Well, I didn't say I'd hit on her *now*!" Jackson snorted. "I just said I appreciate a pretty girl."

"Oh, yeah." Henry's voice sank again. "Bi. You said it yesterday. I was like, 'Yeah, sure, buddy, you're bi. That's an excuse for being gay.' But it's not. Not for you. Weird how you never think of that as an option."

"*You* may not!" Jackson somehow managed to keep the scorn out of his voice. Homeboy was obviously going through something. "I would wager there are more bi people than strictly straight people or strictly gay people. I mean… pretty people are pretty. It just seems… odd to not be attracted to *the person* who turns your key." Of course, Jackson had spent eight years being as responsibly promiscuous as humanly possible—he'd been exercising his sexuality more than most.

"So like good and bad," Henry mused. "Not always black or white."

"Nope."

Henry nodded for a moment, and the silence grew oppressive.

"So your brother was okay?"

"He was just so happy," Henry said. "He wanted his family. Sure, he's sort of built his own—but I realized he really *hadn't* wanted to leave us behind. Dad just wanted him to choose between Kane and us."

"That usually doesn't end the way people think it will," Jackson said. He wasn't sure when people would learn that, actually.

"And watching them together, raising that little girl, with fifty-dozen creatures in their house—like, they have a six-foot iguana, man!"

Jackson was enchanted. "That is totally cool. I *must* meet them!"

Henry's laugh had a strained edge to it, but it was still a laugh. "They have turtles too. They built an outdoor terrarium for the summer, with a little swimming pool and running water and shade and a rock in the sun. It's... I mean, it's like the perfect place to grow up. If I could have picked a house as a kid, I would have picked theirs. Except I wouldn't have. I was too brainwashed, trying too hard to be Daddy's little soldier." His snort held all the bitterness, and Jackson hurt for him.

"Kids want so badly to please you," Jackson said. "My brother—Jade's twin—has a wife, and they have three kids and a house. One of the kids, the oldest, a girl, is named after me. I was in the hospital when she was born. They didn't know if I was going to live or die, and they wanted a piece of me to carry on. But River, she's her own person. She's as girly as they come—Jade was never like that. Her mom was never like that. But River is all pink and purple and sparkles, and it drives Kaden batshit, you know? But he will buy her bright rainbow skirts and a thousand rainbow Barbies and those weird dolls with the detachable feet that look like baby Frankenstein and shit, because that's his baby, and he loves her. And they took in a foster kid. This kid, his life was one long blur of home after home after home. For the last six months, he's been the perfect kid, because he was afraid if he screwed up even a little—like forgetting to brush his teeth—he'd be sent back to another house. His first report card was a mess, too much time wondering where he was going to live to pay attention in school, right? And he was so scared they'd kick him out, he ran away for a day."

"Poor kid," Henry said softly.

"Yeah. Freaked us all out. Ellery and I had to drive up to Foresthill to try to find him. He was up in a tree—he'd never climbed a tree in his life. He just wanted to be near the house. It was the only real family he'd known."

"Aw, man, you really gonna tell me this story now?" Henry complained.

"All I'm saying is kids want a family. I'm saying a good family needs to understand that kids are going to be themselves. None of that changes when you grow up. You are not going to stop wanting the family you grew up with—that was safe for you. And they are going to need to accept you as you are, good and bad, gay or straight, if they're going to claim they've done their jobs."

Henry let out a shaky breath. "I've done some really shitty things," he whispered. "In the name of hiding who I am from my family."

"How'd they take it when you came out?"

"Same way they took it with Davy. Cracked me across the face and told me to get off their property." Henry let out a little laugh. "My oldest brother, Travis, said Kane only let Dad hit Davy once, 'cause it took him by surprise."

"And you?"

"More than once," Henry said softly. "I don't know why I just let him keep hitting me."

"Because you thought you deserved it," Jackson said, pulling into the guest parking lot of the flophouse complex.

"Maybe I did."

"No. Nobody deserves that from their father, Henry."

Henry let out a half-hysterical laugh. "You know why I got kicked out of the military?"

"Nope." Oh God, Jackson was *dying* to know.

"Because I got a promotion."

Jackson widened his eyes. "Ooookay...."

"I got a promotion, and my brother-in-law didn't. We'd kept ourselves at the same rank our entire careers. I'd passed up promotion three times, and I just couldn't do it anymore. Because if I outranked him, that meant the affair we'd been having for nine goddamned years was suddenly coercion. I tried to break it off with him, but he wouldn't let go. That's why I took the promotion finally. He... he's married to my sister, and she just had a baby, and I just couldn't... couldn't do that to her family anymore. But he got... got furious. So he told our CO he'd been coerced, just for spite. I'd spent nine years in the military, and suddenly it was all gone."

"Dayum, son." Jackson let the engine idle, because Henry wasn't done, and he didn't want to kill the air-conditioning.

"And I could take the dishonorable discharge or me and Malachi could pull out all the bullshit during the court-martial. But that... that would kill my sister. That would kill her little boy. So I took it. I lost my career. Because *I fucking deserved it*!"

Henry's shriek rent the air inside the car, and Jackson watched him with compassionate eyes.

"What?" Henry mumbled, obviously embarrassed.

"How old were you when you started the affair?" he asked.

"We started sneaking around in high school." Henry closed his eyes.

"That must have hurt like a sonuvabitch."

Henry dug the heels of his hands into his eyes, like he was trying to stop the burning. "Not so's you'd notice."

Right.

"That's a hard thing to stop once it gets going," Jackson said softly.

"I was fucking my sister's husband!" Henry snarled. "Don't you get it? I'm the bad guy!"

"You made some shitty decisions," Jackson said. "I won't lie. But so did he. Did he give you excuses? For keeping it up?"

"What she didn't know wouldn't hurt her," Henry mumbled. "What me and Mal had was different. Just guys fucking around. It didn't matter, so why quit?"

"You've got a pretty solid moral center, Henry Worrall. I bet keeping that shit up hurt you more every fucking day."

Henry leaned his head against the window and nodded. "I didn't know how bad, though, until this week. It's like I've been flailing, looking for something to hold me down. Because that weight on my heart—that used to be the only thing that kept me here on earth."

Jackson turned off the car. Henry needed to back away, to regroup, and he needed to do it without Jackson there. "So think of this as a chance to find your purpose," Jackson told him. "I spent a year in the hospital thinking about mine."

"And you came up with private investigator?" And *there* was the judgy snarky bastard Jackson had wanted to put in the ground all yesterday.

"For the innocent, Henry. Think about that. I spent the first part of my life as a street kid, until Jade and Kaden's mom took me in. Then I wanted to become a cop—because I thought that meant having power. Then cops tried to *kill* me, and I didn't want any part of that. So I became the guy who helps stand up for the guys who didn't do it. Yeah, sometimes they did—I won't lie. Me and Ellery have defended some dirtbags in our time. But we've also taken some dirtbags down, because we didn't just stop looking when the system said 'They did it.' So you may not think much of me, but you damned well better think something of Ellery. Because his job is what keeps assholes like you out of jail."

Jackson opened the door and stepped out into the inferno, and Henry followed suit. The heat rolled off the newly laid blacktop, hitting their lungs in a palpable blow.

"You go inside and grab your scrubs," Jackson said. "There's some decent gas stations around the corner from the clinic. We can change there."

"What are you going to do?"

Jackson had picked guest parking for a reason. In an apartment warren like this, the spots marked guest were usually by the office.

"I'm going to go check out the film school," he murmured. Then he made eye contact. "Seriously, I'll be right back."

"Me too," Henry said, and he started trotting down the sidewalk. From what Jackson could tell from the video, the flophouse was about four buildings in, on the second floor, so he didn't have far to go.

Jackson made his way to the manager's office, purposefully not knocking as he burst in.

The guy standing behind the counter jerked upright as Jackson walked in, and a thump echoed in the chamber underneath the counter itself.

"Jesus, buddy," the guy choked. "Could you knock?"

Sallow, as if he'd replaced sunlight with nicotine, and in his fifties, with washed-out hazel eyes and sandy-gray receding hair, the guy looked like a favorite uncle. Then the tension on his face suddenly increased, his eyes closed, and he shuddered.

A favorite uncle on the john.

He let out a breath that whimpered down his throat and rested his head on the countertop in front of him. Underneath the counter, Jackson heard a muffled grunt.

Nope. Not on the john.

Jackson's eyes got really wide, but he knew an advantage when he had one. "Look, buddy, your audiovisual room is in the back, right? I'm just going to run back there and give you a second to pull yourself together."

Jackson started moving before the guy could object, pushing past the lift-up of the counter with only a sideways glance at the guy pulling up his pants and someone crawling out from underneath the counter.

Then he saw the someone.

The kid was young—maybe nineteen, but definitely eighteen, because the Johnnies website said so—and cute, African American with a gentle brown complexion and a military haircut. He climbed out of the recess under the counter with no attempt at subtlety. He was wearing high-end cargo shorts and a Steven Universe T-shirt, and Jackson's heart hurt a little. Babies. All of the Johnnies guys were babies—even Henry, who was old enough to know better.

"So that's the last time, right? You said you'd keep the rent down for three blowjobs—that's the last one."

"It was interrupted!" the manager whined, and a look of profound distaste crossed the kid's face.

"That is not my fault! Look, we're all saving money until our FAFSA kicks in, and some of us don't have cars! You told me you were upping the rent, and I told you I'd take a couple for the team, but buddy, I usually get paid a *lot more* for a blowjob, and my other guys *wash*!"

Oh Jesus. With Reg and Bobby fresh in his mind, Jackson felt compelled to intervene.

"You might want to ask him how many of your other roommates are giving him blowies for rent," Jackson said, raking the apartment manager with unfriendly eyes.

Sure enough, everybody's least favorite uncle shifted from foot to foot. "Well, you know, there's, like, six of them living in there, and it's only a two bedroom—"

"How much are you charging them—without the blowjobs?"

The look on the guy's face went crafty, and the kid—Curtis? That had been his name on the website—had the freshly enlightened look of someone who realized he'd been had.

The manager named a rent price that almost popped Jackson's eyes out of his head. "In what fucking city?" he asked, and Curtis rounded on the manager.

"I *knew* it! You're overcharging us for rent and blackmailing us for blowjobs. And *Jesus*, asshole, would it kill you to fucking *wash*?"

The apartment supervisor twisted his mouth derisively. "I thought your profession *liked* to dine on cock cheese!"

The kid might have been able to give a champion blowjob, but he could also telegraph a punch. Jackson grabbed his arm gently. "Hey, hey, hey—look. If you hit him, the cops side with him. You go tell Henry and have him tell Galen. We'll get a lawyer on this guy's ass so quick, he won't have time to wipe."

Curtis stopped struggling—and in spite of his muscles, it was clear he'd never been in a fight in his life—and looked at Jackson with a little bit of worship.

"You know Henry, John, and Galen?" he asked, and from the tremble in his voice, it was clear he'd been feeling a little bit out of his league.

"Yeah. Galen and John are great."

"Henry's a bit of an asshole," Curtis said, nodding. "But he wouldn't let anything bad happen to us. Are you sure he'll help us out?" He frowned. "Is he back?"

"Yeah, he's up in the apartment right now. Go talk to him." Jackson narrowed his eyes. "What's Cock Cheese's name?"

"Mr. Sternberg." Curtis spat it like a curse, and then he brightened. "But I may just call him Mr. Cock Cheese for the rest of his life."

Jackson dug into his pocket for some gum and handed it over. "Here. Knock yourself out. Go talk to Henry. Tell him I'll be up in five." Curtis took off, and Jackson turned to Sternberg Cock Cheese. "And I'm going back to the audio-visual room."

"Hey, man, no, you don't want to do tha—"

But Jackson had spotted the little door—a one-inch gap indicating either it wasn't locked or that somebody was in there—and went barreling toward it, his gut telling him that he was close to something big.

"No—no, man, don't go back there! I'm telling you, there's nothing interesting in there, just some monitors and—"

Jackson hit the door hard and was ready for it to rebound back in his face. He dodged out of the way as the room's previous inhabitant launched himself forward, waving a two-inch fixed blade like he knew how to use it.

The small knife flashed down, and Jackson jerked back and then charged before the guy had a chance to reset. Jackson wrapped his arms around his assailant's shoulders and threw him against the doorframe, where his head cracked with a thud. The guy didn't let it slow him down, raising his hands around Jackson's back, and Jackson felt a rip and a burn as the fixed blade sliced the skin over his shoulder blade, glancing off the bone.

"Sonuva—"

Jackson broke out of the hold and kicked forward, his foot rebounding off his attacker's thigh and coming damned close to his balls. With a yelp the guy rushed out, barreling into Cock Cheese Sternberg and knocking him on his ass before darting out from behind the counter and out the door.

Jackson followed, cursing when his attacker turned right into the small apartment complex, but following him anyway.

God, he hated chasing people in places like this. He saw a tennis shoe to his right and took off that way, heart hammering in his throat. The November before, he and Ellery had cornered a serial killer in a vacant apartment complex like this one, and when Jackson saw his attacker round another corner to go left, he had to fight a very real compulsion to haul ass out of the apartment complex and breathe.

He didn't, though. A guy with a knife was running loose in a place with innocent civilians. Henry, Curtis, any of the other guys in the flophouse, much less the children he heard playing nearby in the apartment pool, could be hurt.

Jackson kept running, following the sound of retreating footsteps, left, right, left—but this guy knew where he was going, and Jackson was lost, turning where he thought he heard footsteps, and confused by the echoes, his heart thundering with every blind corner.

Running balls out until this moment in the heat stretched long and hot, like tar, his shoulder aching fiercely, lungs burning like a crucible, and a left and a right—

Right into a solid wall masquerading as a human being.

Jackson pulled back and took a swing, only to have Henry block it, shouting, "Whoa, whoa, whoa. I thought we were past this!"

"Fuck!" Jackson panted. "Motherfucker got away!" Oh, he should not be this out of breath. He ran every morning, but God, he was short on wind.

"Who? Who got away?" Henry got a good look at him, and then at his own hand, which was coated in Jackson's blood. "Jesus, Rivers, you were just supposed to go into the AV room. What the hell hap— Where you going?"

Jackson took off running for the manager's office, a sick feeling in his stomach. *Goddammit and motherfucker, no. No. No no no no no no....*

He ran, Henry hot on his heels, back to the apartment manager's office, swearing as the door threw inward without any resistance whatsoever.

Jackson hurried back behind the counter, muttering under his breath until he saw the body, stretched out on the floor. Sternberg Cock Cheese was clutching his hand to his throat as he gasped, his blood pooling on the ground.

"He's still alive," Jackson muttered, and then looked Henry in the eye. "He's still alive. Call 911, tell them we've got a stabbing victim here. And give me your goddamned shirt!"

Henry pulled his shirt over his head without question, and Jackson took it and bent down to apply pressure to the neck of the scumbag who might not have completely deserved this.

They were in a nexus of four different hospitals, so an ambulance arrived while Sternberg was still kicking. The medics started working on him, one of them giving Jackson a bemused glance. "Oh, look. You're not on the ground this time."

Jackson gave a tired grin. "Surprised?"

"Pleasantly." The guy was in his forties, with a ruddy face and faded blue eyes. He'd seen Jackson in some of his... less mobile moments. "But you're not off the hook entirely. You need another unit for that?"

Jackson's shoulder felt nuclear, and blood was still dripping down his elbow. "Christ, no."

"Wrong answer," the guy said mildly, but Henry gave Jackson a glare.

"Don't worry. I'll get him treated," Henry muttered.

"By the time the cops get done with me, the wound'll be closed," Jackson told him. Yup. Here they came.

"Rivers."

"Kryzynski." Jackson nodded at the young detective who had ridden his and Ellery's coattails right into a promotion. They'd done some good work together, actually—but Jackson wasn't going to forget that Sean Kryzynski had only listened to Ellery because he'd wanted to hit that. And he'd been an asshole to Jackson about the wore-a-wire thing, because hey, the whole rest of the department did, so why wouldn't Kryzynski?

"You look like shit." Kryzynski looked over at one of the patrolmen marking off the crime scene. "Evans, can we get a water over here? And is there another ambulance outside?"

"I don't need another ambulance!" Jackson protested. Then his shoulders slumped. "I wouldn't mind another water, though."

"Don't worry about the ambulance," Henry muttered. He looked at Kryzynski. "Hey, I'm going to run to my apartment and come right back. One of the guys I room with might be able to help."

Without waiting for an answer, Henry disappeared, leaving Jackson alone with Kryzynski's irritation.

"You just can't go to the goddamned hospital, can you?"

"Hey, don't you have any questions for me?" Jackson asked, not wanting to talk about the hospital or his wound, or how really unexcited he was to let Ellery know he'd been hurt again.

"Yeah," Kryzynski said, gesturing to the office, which was actually still neat and tidy except for the guy getting loaded onto a gurney, leaving behind about two pints of blood. "What the fuck happened?"

Jackson nodded in Henry's direction. "That guy going to fetch his roommate was wrongly accused of murdering the guy who got found in the dumpster. He was brought in for questioning this morning, but they sent him home because not only did he not do it, but two different videos from the same perspective emerged, both of them doctored to incriminate him."

Kryzynski's eyes widened. "That's... not convenient."

"Right? So I thought I'd check out the film school here, and that guy was behind the counter doing shit you don't want to know about. I came behind the counter, headed for the little room where the video footage is processed—you can see it there, with the wide-open door."

"And what looks like your blood spraying the wall. Well done."

"I was proud. Anyway, I busted in, and an asshole with a Schrade dagger busted out, and I lost him in this goddamned apartment complex." Jackson shuddered, remembering the panic of not catching his wind. "I *hate* these fucking places."

To his dismay, the look on Kryzynski's face grew unutterably compassionate. "I was there the last time you took one on," he said softly.

Fuck. "I don't remember. Once I hit the pool, it's all a blur." He'd been consumed by fever—the cold of the pool had induced a heart attack. Ellery had bailed him out and saved his life, but that didn't mean he remembered much except the ambulance ride after that. And the doctor's orders that he keep an eye out for symptoms of the murmur he'd picked up from the damage to his most vital organ.

"Well, good for you, trying to get this guy here."

"Bad for me, because I lost the motherfucker and he doubled back and tried to tie up Cock Cheese Sternberg here."

He and Kryzynski watched as the paramedics loaded the gurney into the ambulance and took off, sirens belting, because they had a patient who might live or die.

"Well, if he lives, it's because you got here soon enough," Kryzynski said. "And if he dies, it's probably because he let the wrong people use his video room. We'll dust it for prints and check it out."

Jackson looked at it yearningly. "I could always have my friend check it out," he said, thinking about Crystal or AJ, both of whom could take a look at the equipment in there and maybe figure out what the original image had looked like.

"Could you just trust us a little," Kryzynski begged. "Just a little. Just maybe this once, trust us to have your back in a timely fashion. I promise, Jackson, I've got an expert coming in, and I'll have the results to you by tomorrow."

Jackson scowled at him. "Who are you and what did you do with the SACPD detective who keeps hitting on my boyfriend?"

"I'm the guy dating a fireman right now who would like to be your friend!"

Jackson gaped at him.

"What?" Kryzynski muttered, all irritation. "We've worked together before."

"Why a fireman?"

"He was, uhm… well, older. And sort of bossy. But not an asshole. And he pointed out that people trusted firemen because they didn't judge. And I realized I'd judged you without ever meeting you, because of ancient history. And you'd been a better man than all the bullshit. So anyway, can we start again?"

Jackson was supremely aware of how much his shoulder hurt, and of what an act of will it took to hold a grudge. "Fine," he muttered. "Call us tomorrow with the results, or an update, or something."

"I will, but you have to get your shoulder looked at."

"Didn't you hear my client? He's got it covered. Don't you even want to know what this guy looked like?"

The look Kryzynski sent him was decidedly unfriendly, and he pulled out a notebook. "What did he look like?"

"Taller than me, rangy, a white guy with tanned skin, hazel eyes, dark blond hair, bucked teeth, bad breath." Jackson shuddered as he remembered the stench of his breath. "Brown teeth and sores on his face."

He heard the sound of Kryzynski sucking on his teeth, which was good, because it meant Sean Kryzynski knew his street shit. "Meth?"

"Yeah. The guy we busted last night—the one who was trying to convince a couple of witnesses that the doctored video was the right one—"

"Which one?"

Jackson blinked at him, his mind blank. "Which what?"

"Which doctored video?"

"Jesus God. The fuck with this case. The second one—the one given to the DA and not the one that our assistant got when he asked. The guy who broke into Reg Williams's house—Herbert something. Anyway, *that* guy, with *that* footage, said he worked for Candy Cormier."

Kryzynski's eyes grew huge. "Jesus God. The fuck with you guys. You can't lift up a single goddamned rock and *not* find a goddamned fire-breathing dragon, can you?"

Jackson had the perfect retort on the tip of his tongue when his shoulder gave a vicious throb. All he could manage was a wince and a grunt.

Kryzynski took a deep breath. "You'd rather have a mechanic stitch it up with dental floss and gasoline than actually accept help, wouldn't you."

Jackson let out his own breath. "Ellery worries all the time," he said, thinking about the night before. "It would just be wonderful if this could not be a thing."

"Maybe if you get it treated like a big boy and don't try to pretend it doesn't hurt, it will be less of a thing."

Jackson glared at him. "And I hate you again."

At that moment, Henry called his name, jumping up and down behind the yellow tape that the forensics team had put up. "C'mon, man, you come out or we go in, what's it gonna be?"

Kryzynski jerked his chin in Henry's direction. "I'll be out to ask some more questions. All you've managed to do now is give me a headache."

Jackson grimaced. Between the heat and the pain in his shoulder and the near panic attack in the apartment warren—God, his heart was pounding threadily in his temples still…. "Join the fuckin' club."

He turned reluctantly and headed for Henry and his med-student friend.

Who was so beautiful, Jackson almost held his breath.

About five feet ten inches tall, the kid had high cheekbones and almond-shaped eyes, with a rectangular face and a slight point to his chin. His skin was a tawny gold, and his smile was so sweet, so charmingly at odds with Henry's surly irritation, that Jackson knew—it only took an instant—that this could be true fucking love.

Between Henry and the kid doing porn through med school.

Jackson stepped out of the office and into the shade under the awning. "Nice to meet you. I'm Jackson Rivers. You must be...?" He glared at Henry, who had the grace—and the manners—to flush.

"Uh...." He looked at the kid. "Lance?"

Lance shrugged. "Sure. Beats the shit out of Merlin."

Jackson's eyes widened. "Your parents named you Merlin?"

Lance had wicked eyebrows and a sort of laser-pointer gaze. "My parents named me Galahad. I'm not joking. When I picked a name for Johnnies, I went with another knight from the Round Table."

Jackson's headache lifted by virtue of pure fucking magic. "That's amazing. So, Galahad, what can I do for you?"

Lance smiled winsomely. "I'd say it's more what I can do for *you*, sir. Would you like me to stitch you here or stitch you in the apartment? The apartment has running water and air-conditioning, and as long as you don't use a black light in there, it'll at least *feel* cleaner."

Jackson's headache returned, taking his breath away. "I'll take the AC," he admitted, hating himself a little. He looked into the room, which probably had another hour of processing in it. "Kryzynski!"

"Idiot!"

"I'm gonna be up in one of the apartments."

"Room number—" Lance offered, but Jackson shook his head.

"Which room number?" Kryzynski huffed.

"The one that's none of your business. Text me if you need me. I'll be done in twenty."

Jackson nodded for Lance to lead the way.

"Why'd you do that?" Henry asked lowly.

"Because you guys don't need the cops to know where you are," Jackson muttered. "Consider that my favor to you."

"God, you're paranoid."

Jackson sent Henry a sour glance. "God, you're a Boy Scout."

Ahead of them, Lance snorted.

"What?" Jackson heard the defensiveness in Henry's voice and the need to be liked. "What's so funny?"

"You're just awfully law-abiding for a guy under suspicion," Jackson told him mildly, and Henry groaned.

"God, this is not how I thought my life would look!"

"And yet," Lance said, "here we are."

Henry groaned again, and Jackson chuckled, enjoying his discomfort immensely. Lance continued to lead the way, around a corner and up a flight of stairs, and Jackson was forcibly reminded of their errand when he put weight on his shoulder to grab the stair rail. *Goddammit. God-fucking-dammit.* At least he wasn't going to the hospital, right?

The apartment was much as Jackson had imagined it. Plain white walls and beige carpet in the living room, with white tile in the bathrooms and kitchen. The best thing about it was the air-conditioning. There were two bedrooms down the hall, and Jackson got a glimpse of two twin beds in the closest one, and probably the same setup in the other one. The living room had a well-worn couch with a pile of sheets and blankets on the end, and a full air mattress leaning against the wall in the corner. There were posters on the walls of movies, rock groups, and Sacramento during the seasons, and the blankets on the couch looked homemade.

It was a dormitory, plain and simple, whether the guys got paid for sex or just had all the free stuff college would allow.

"In here," Lance called, and Jackson followed him to the bathroom. He disappeared for a second and showed up with an honest-to-God little black bag. He pulled out gloves, antiseptic, cotton balls, and a stitching kit that he set up on a tray on the back of the toilet before running the water hot in the sink.

After a few minutes of extremely competent, conscientious preparation, he sighed, like it wasn't up to his standards, and had Jackson turn around and take off his shirt.

Jackson had forgotten what a nightmare his body was until he heard the low whistle.

"Damn, son."

"Yeah."

"What blew up your shoulder?"

"Sniper round. Wait. Which scar?"

"The newer one."

"Uzi."

"The older one is the sniper round?" With cool, impersonal hands, Lance pulled Jackson to face him so he could trace the damage paths. Bored, Jackson let him explore for a moment before turning back around.

"There's been some things," he said vaguely, wishing for Ellery's tender irritation instead of Lance's clinical concern.

"I can see that. I'm going to be sewing through some scar tissue here. It's going to hurt. Are you sure you don't want a hos—"

"Positive," Jackson said shortly. "But I wouldn't mind some Novocain."

"I can do that," Lance said with a sigh. "Sit on the toilet, would you? I'm only so tall." Jackson felt the bite of the needle, and gave a sigh of relief as the chemical blanket washed the entire area in a soothing numbness. His opinion of Henry's pretty roommate doubled when Lance grabbed a scrub brush and went to town with some elbow grease to clean the wound. Better a good scrubbing now when it was numb than an infection later. He was just relaxing into the procedure when his pocket rang. He held up a hand and picked it up when Lance paused.

"Ellery?" Behind him, Lance started moving again.

"Have you gotten to Sampson's medical practice yet?"

Lance plied the needle, and Jackson felt pressure as the silk pulled at the edges of his wound. "Not yet. I checked the manager's office for whoever was doctoring the vids. He got away, but he left the apartment manager—" Lance made another stitch, the needle sticking, apparently on the scar tissue, and Jackson suppressed a gasp. "—in a pool of blood. Last I heard, he was still kicking, but it means the cops have the crime scene. Kryzynski promised us an update tomorrow."

"Are you okay?" Ellery asked, because dammit, he'd never been stupid.

"I gave chase," Jackson said. "It's hot outside." Both of which were true. He heard a subtle shifting of feet and looked over his shoulder in time to see Henry glare.

Jackson stuck out his tongue and turned back around. "Give us an hour. I was going to swing by your place and get my scrubs in a few. Why? Was there something you needed?"

"Our place," Ellery corrected automatically, "and I just wanted to give you a heads-up. One of the partners—Carver, actually—"

Jackson snorted, and Ellery kept going right over him.

"—has moved to… where was it? Bumfuck, Arkansas."

"Is that a real town?" Because that would be *awesome*.

"No, it's not a real town! I just can't find my notes! But he moved, so the place is going to be a little emptier than you might think."

"Moved…," Jackson said quietly, wondering. "Hey, is there any way to find out whether or not he's prescribed any drugs in the last year?"

Ellery grunted. "I'd thought of that. I need to call some people. Medical law is *not* my specialty. I'll get back to you."

"I'll let you know what we—" *Ouch!* Jackson looked over his shoulder at Lance and glared, and Lance grimaced in apology. "—find out."

"When you get home," Ellery said, voice mild, "you are going to have to explain to me, very carefully, exactly what you did today."

"I found a victim. Chased a bad guy. Same ol', same ol—" Sudden, sharp inhale. "But we're running late. You may have to get Jade to take you home." Jackson made a mental note to borrow a towel so he didn't get blood on Ellery's car.

"I know what the same ol' is, Jackson. Same ol' is what happened last night. Let's go for different, shall we?"

"Hey, the body was still kicking this ti-*ime!*" Mother*fucker*, that hurt! "I was hoping to get to the clinic after lunch, when the doctors are mostly out, so we gotta motor. Later!"

"Later."

Jackson hung up on the suspicious funk that was his boyfriend and let loose. "Son of a whore's jizzy tits, Lance, what in the hell was that?"

"That was pulling scar tissue over your exposed bone," Lance snapped back. "Jesus fuck, Rivers—no wonder you hate hospitals!"

Jackson took a few deep pulls of oxygen and tried to calm his temper. "Yeah. I'm starting to wonder if they're giving me an extra spiffy drug cocktail," he admitted. "Seriously, I'd rather just belt out a good scream and get it over with." Inside he shuddered. Addiction was his greatest fear.

"Well, suck it up for two more stitches and I'll have this done," Lance muttered. "Jesus, how you think you're going to hide this from your boyfriend, I have no idea."

Jackson felt the needle go in this time, because the Novocain was wearing off, and he grunted. "Forgiveness, permission, I'm sure I'll think of something. Do I have to keep it dry? Because I gotta tell you, I'm getting used to his pool."

"If I tell you yes, for at least twenty-four hours, will that matter to you?"

Jackson grimaced. "Mmmaybe?"

"Then don't sweat it. Just don't come crying to me when your stitches rip out because your skin gets soft."

"It's a deal!" Jackson figured he could shower instead of swim that night—and deliberately *didn't* think about needing help taking the bandage off or putting plastic over it.

"God, you're a shitty patient. I'm glad I'm not your doctor!" Lance finished up, the relief of pressure telling Jackson that he'd knotted the silk and snipped the thread. A few more passes with antiseptic and a bandage, and Jackson was good to go. But Lance wasn't done with him yet.

"So you're not planning to take care of your wound, and you're not going to tell your boyfriend—do I have that correct?"

Jackson shrugged, then winced. "He'll figure it out eventually, and I'm not going to rub dirt in it. Henry and I just have things to do."

"I get it," Lance said, carefully packing up his supplies. Jackson imagined his little black bag was as neatly organized as the sock drawer of God. "I get the He-Man tough-guy thing, and I get the hating hospitals thing. But I need you to think of something before you walk out of here and go look for a way to get Henry out of the hot seat."

"Yeah, sure—oh! Do I need to pay you for suppl—"

"No, but thank you for asking. I want you to think about Curtis, the guy who'd been blowing the super to give us a break on rent."

"I remember him." Jackson frowned. "Is he here?"

"He's in the bedroom with the closed door, chewing an entire pack of gum. He was super embarrassed, by the way, but I think he's texting the other guys to see who else got caught up in that scam. Anyway, you stood up for him."

Jackson wrinkled his nose. "Your super is—maybe was—an asshole," he said bluntly. "Curtis was trying to give honest trade."

Lance nodded, not taking those amazing amber eyes from Jackson's. "You treated him like a person. And he's embarrassed because he got taken, but he's not ashamed. And he's not dead, like he might have been if you hadn't warned him off—"

Jackson's eyes got big. "Wait, did he remember anything? Seriously, was he there when the guy went into the back room?"

Lance's eyes got big too. "Shit! Dammit. Here I am trying to give the grown-up speech—"

"It was a real nice speech." Jackson patted Lance's arm. "You're gonna be a great doc. But right now, can I talk to your roommate?"

"Sure, but let me get you a shirt. We've got some shit in the community laundry pile nobody will miss."

Jackson grimaced. "That's a good idea." He looked at the T-shirt he'd put on that morning—one of his newer ones that said "My Favorite Color is No Pants" on it—and sighed. "Yeah. Thanks. Do you want this one to wash your car or something?"

"Oh my God. We're starving students, and even *we* throw bloodstained clothing away."

"Or not. Get me the shirt. I need to talk to Curtis."

Curtis, as it turned out, had heard a great deal.

"Yeah, I'd just gotten down there when whoever it was came in to use the back room—not sure if you noticed, but there's a little dust-cover curtain thingie that hides the space behind the counter." He was sitting on a twin bed, chewing his gum, listening to music, and Jackson got a look inside the other bedroom.

One of the beds was a queen-sized bed and the other a twin, but the covers on both mattresses were personal, and there were two dressers, one of them very clearly marked "Rick and Skylar" with masking tape, and the other "Curtis and Billy." Jackson wondered if Billy slept with Curtis or if he got the air bed or the couch.

"I did," Jackson responded, tabling his curiosity. The curtain and supplies seemed to indicate that Cock Cheese Sternberg had been getting enough blowjobs to add a few office modifications for convenience. "Were you down there?"

Curtis nodded. "There's a little portable fan, some Kleenex, condoms, a bottle of water, lube, disinfectant wipes—all the amenities."

Jackson blinked suddenly dry eyes. "That's... well...."

"Prepared. Yeah." Curtis tipped his head back and sighed. "I should have known. I just... we're all saving money, and it seemed easier than all of us coughing up more cash."

Jackson resisted the temptation to ruffle his tightly cut hair. "Your heart was in the right place, kid. You're a sex worker; it's a skill. Just remember it's not the only one you have."

Curtis shrugged and managed a small smile. "Thanks. So you want to know what they said?"

"I'll buy you lunch!"

Curtis shook his head. "Naw, I've got a scene in four days. I'm all veggies for the next two days and then fasting."

Yikes! "Well, hit me up after your scene. I'll spring for a buffet or something."

Curtis's face lit up. "That there is a deal. So, I'd just gotten situated and was waiting for him to drop his drawers when Sternberg yanks the curtain shut and says, 'Gordon! I thought we were all done with that shit!'"

"Gordon?" Oh, hey—a *clue*. "And then?"

"And Gordon says, 'Dude, Candy's losing his shit. Who made the other fuckin' tape?'"

So Gordon worked for Candy Cormier. Holy crap. This kid was a *wealth* of information. "What did Sternberg say?"

"He said *he* did. He got a call before the cops even got there. Someone asked him to loop the night feed, right up until Henry found the body."

Jackson closed his eyes. "So Candy wanted Henry pinned for the body, but the first tape was just supposed to erase the actual dumping of it."

Curtis looked surprised. "Yeah, I guess that's right."

"What did this Gordon with the fucking Schrade blade say afterwards?"

"He said he was going to go erase *all* the tapes so nobody could figure out which one was which. Sternberg said go ahead, but I don't think he thought much of the guy's competence."

"Why not?"

"Because the door clicked, not completely shut, but you know, enough, and Sternberg muttered, 'Good luck, ya fuckin' psycho,' before unzipping like it was business as usual."

Jackson frowned. "Uh, how long before he came?"

"Twelve interminable minutes," Curtis said grimly. "And thirty-two seconds."

"So Sternberg was right—a guy who knew what he was doing would be a lot quicker." Jackson grimaced. "I think. I've got a friend I can ask to make sure. So Gordon—our scumbag with meth mouth and twitchy eyes and the Schrade—had twelve minutes. And tomorrow, we should see what he did with them. Curtis, this is really important. Are you sure he didn't know you were down there? Nobody saw you?"

Curtis nodded. "Man, do you think I wanted anybody to know what I was doing? I mean, as a matter of professional pride, that asshole was a step *down*." He gave his gum a particularly vicious gnash of his teeth and wrapped his arms around his knees as he sat on his bed. "And do I have to explain about the taste?"

"No, no, I would rather you didn't. Just, you know, be safe."

"Always," Curtis said sourly.

Jackson nodded, trusting him, and called out, "Look, Henry, Lance, come here."

They both showed up, and Jackson looked Curtis in the eyes. "Curtis was here all morning. He hasn't left the apartment, do you understand?"

"But don't you need him to tell the cops what he heard?" Henry asked, scowling.

"No. We know what he heard. We can tell the cops. He's not a source. We don't mention his name. We've already had somebody break into Reg and Bobby's place. I don't want you guys at risk."

Curtis nodded. "Thanks, man. I appreciate it. But, you know, if it's a choice between me telling my story and Henry going to jail—"

"It won't be," Jackson said grimly. "Not if I'm any good at my job at all. Thanks, Curtis. And don't worry. I'm pretty sure Henry will keep you in the loop."

"Yeah, well, he's a grumpy bastard, but we're used to him," Curtis said, nodding earnestly.

"I'm right here!"

Curtis's smile at Henry was all saccharine. "I know, sweetie. Go you!"

Jackson smirked. "All right, then. I'm out. I'm going to shut this door here, and Lance, I don't think the cops will stop by, but if they do, Henry's out and Curtis—"

"Has been here all day," Lance repeated dutifully.

"I knew you understood." Jackson extended his hand, and Lance shook it, hard and with purpose. "And thanks for the stitch job. I appreciate it."

"Please keep it dry for at least a day. The bandage is waterproof, so a shower should be okay. Oh, and get someone to take the stitches out in a week."

Jackson nodded, thinking Jade might do it for him. Or AJ.

Or Ellery. Because Ellery wasn't stupid, and he might have forgiven Jackson by then.

"Will do. Thanks again."

"And keep Henry safe." Lance slid a sideways glance toward Henry, and Jackson watched everybody's favorite military asshole turn a dull red. "He *is* a grumpy bastard, but Curtis was right. We do like him here."

"I'll protect him like it's my job," Jackson said dryly. "Because it is."

Lance's laugh was a soft surprise. "You take your job seriously. I just gave you the stitches that prove it. That's good enough for me."

They left, waving goodbye to Kryzynski as he hovered over the crime scene. As they slid into the car, Henry asked, "Aren't you going to tell him what Curtis told you?"

"That depends," Jackson said, backing Ellery's baby out with the finesse of a neurosurgeon, "on whether he shares the forensics with us. If he plays nice with me, I'll play nice with him."

"But... I mean, he's the *police*!"

"Yeah, he's the policeman we told about a serial killer for months, and who didn't believe us until I was half dead and the asshole had a knife to Ellery's throat. I'm not giving him any dots to connect about Curtis. That kid doesn't need the fucking harassment."

"Why would he be harassed?" Henry asked, completely puzzled, and Jackson blew out a breath, remembering that Ellery had been that naïve.

"Because he's really, really tanned. Did you not hear what I told you about my brother?"

"But he wasn't charged. He was let go, right?"

"Sure, he was. After my house got shot up and Ellery risked his life to bring in the guy who did it. Let's just say we won't start nothing so there won't be nothing and leave it at that."

Henry let out an irritated sigh. "Is there anybody you *do* trust, Rivers?"

"Ellery," Jackson replied promptly. "Jade, Kaden, and AJ. And a couple of people you don't know. So yes. Yes, there *are* people I trust."

"Good to know."

"Hey, I don't feel the trust rolling off *you* in waves. As far as I can tell, you've been like every other client who lies to us to make themselves feel better."

"There's a reason for that!" Henry snapped.

"Yeah, well, ditto."

Henry huffed out a breath. "I just don't get how you can go through life without believing in anything. You don't trust the cops. You don't trust the military.... You're working for a system you think is going to let you down!"

"I'm working for a system that *did* let me down," Jackson argued. "That's why I'm working where I'm working. Systems let you down. *People* don't always, so I keep my faith in a few of those. Why's it so important to you?"

"Because…." Henry sagged against his seat. "Because people already let me down. All I have left is the system. And it's trying to put me in jail."

Augh! "Your brother sounds like a standup guy," Jackson said reluctantly. "John and Galen don't suck." And then, delicately, because Henry might or might not have noticed that he and his roommate seemed to have been destined for each other since birth, Jackson added, "And, uh, there's a guy actually named Galahad who looks like he'd throw himself in traffic for you."

"He's a porn model," Henry said, as though that somehow prevented a guy from falling in love.

"If that's how you're going to be about it, you deserve to die sad and alone."

"I'm sorry?"

Jackson shook his head. "Nope. Not gonna talk to you anymore. You're too stupid to live. Make sure Galen pays us when you forget to breathe, that's all I ask."

They drove in silence for a while until they passed a little nest of fast food chains and Jackson turned into it, craving a soda in the worst way.

"Want anything?" he asked, forgetting his earlier resolve.

"I thought I was too stupid to live," Henry said sullenly.

"Yeah, but not feeding you before you choke on your own stupidity is inhumane."

"I could use a burger," Henry muttered. "Here, let me—" He reached into his pocket for his wallet, and Jackson waved him off.

"Ellery lets me pay for very little," he said. "I can handle a sandwich."

"Why does he do that?" Henry asked, frowning. "Pay for everything?"

Jackson shrugged. "He likes to… I dunno. Take care of me. Seems to think I don't do a wonderful job on my own. He's not half wrong." He stopped at the intercom and ordered two sodas and a burger, but before he was done, Henry shouted for a second burger.

"Hungry?" Jackson asked, pulling forward.

"It's for you. You forgot."

"I did not. I wasn't hungry."

Henry grunted. "I can officially see Cramer's point. Look, can we make a deal?"

"I don't see why."

"Because you're *dying* to tell me why I'm a dumbass. I promise I'll listen if you fucking eat."

Jackson let out a sigh and reminded himself that he'd managed to get himself doctored in an apartment bathroom, and that he was a big boy and could feed himself.

"Sure. Fine. Would you like to know why you're a dumbass?"

"I'm on the edge of my seat."

"Because that porn model you just dismissed is a nice guy. He stitched me up, didn't give me shit, and tried really hard to get me to take care of myself. He was obviously the den mother there before you got hired as the daddy—"

"I think Bobby was the daddy first," Henry said, not surprising Jackson much. "They still call him to fix the plumbing like I've never seen a goddamned sink before."

"Well, maybe you need to relax your plunger about other people's plumbing," Jackson said sourly, pulling up to the drive-thru. He rolled down his window, bracing himself for the furnace blast, and handed the clerk his card. The kid—a sweet-eyed boy with a long face and a complexion that reminded Jackson of his own acne years—gave him a tentative smile that Jackson returned full bore. The kid lit up like a Christmas tree, his voice getting extra animated as he handed Jackson his receipt, and Jackson told him yes, it was hot and to stay cool himself before he winked and pulled forward.

"Do you think that kid knows he's gay?" Henry asked, almost to himself.

"Maybe, maybe not," Jackson said. "Some kids don't know it until somebody special grabs their hand and says, 'Hey, I want to kiss you above all others,' and they go, 'Wow, I want that too!'"

"You know, for a guy who doesn't trust anybody, you have an awfully rosy view of the world."

"I don't trust authority," Jackson corrected. "Why is it bad that Lancelot is a porn model?"

"He's sleeping with other people," Henry explained, as though Jackson was stupid.

"He's performing a mechanical function with colleagues that leads to orgasm," Jackson corrected. "He has no more attachment to the guys he has sex with at Johnnies than you do to your favorite dildo."

"How do you know that?" The desperation in Henry's voice to believe him was almost a palpable thing.

Jackson waited until he'd gotten their food and sodas from the second window before he answered.

"Because I've had sex for sex and I've had sex because I cared about someone, and they're two totally different things. It's like comparing a cat to a llama. The fact that you don't know this tells me that your asshole brother-in-law kept you on a very short leash."

Henry let out a sad little grunt.

"How short?" Jackson wanted to know.

"Well, I just found my second lover dead in a dumpster. How short is that?"

"Just long enough to think things through," Jackson told him. "What hurt more? Finding Sampson dead in a dumpster or finding out your brother-in-law would take you down to keep you doing something you felt was wrong?"

The silence from Henry's side of the car wasn't encouraging.

"That?" Jackson said. "That way you're thinking about your actual lover versus a one-night stand? That's the difference between how Lance feels about the guys he fucks on camera versus... I don't know. The grumpy bastard who just refused to consider him as a person because he's got an unusual job."

Henry sighed, and Jackson let up.

"Eat your burger, Henry. It's been a week of life lessons. Allow them to soak in."

Henry opened the bag and pulled out a burger, then wrapped the bottom half in a napkin and handed it to Jackson. "I will if you will."

"Fine."

Jackson bit into the burger and chewed steadily. He wondered if he was going to have to add another person to his list of people he trusted.

His stomach rumbled, displeased by the intrusion when he'd so carefully avoided breakfast that morning.

Maybe not.

HENRY WAS mildly impressed by Ellery's house—as any sane person should be—but he gave Billy Bob the side-eye, and Jackson hoped he tripped and cracked his head open on general principle.

"What in the hell is that?" Henry stared at Billy Bob, who was eating on his mat on the table, next to a giant paperweight that Ellery's mother had bought them after she'd gone shopping at an artisan fair that spring.

"That's two pounds of blown glass and some dye, in bronze and magenta. Don't knock it until it keeps your mail from blowing off the table."

"I'm talking about the growling thing next to it!"

"Man, you dis my cat and I'll break your face. Now stay here and apologize while I go get my scrubs!"

He also had to change. He could feel the blood seeping through the bandage and onto the shirt. He put on another T-shirt—this one said "I'm a llama-corn!" on it—and a new pair of cargo shorts, making sure to bury the ones with the blood drops on them under that morning's towels and underwear. He came out of the bedroom with the scrubs and a towel neatly rolled under his arm and got to the living room just in time to watch Billy Bob execute a three-legged leap from the table to Henry's head.

"Oh my God! Get it off! Get it off!"

Henry flailed around the dining room, the cat digging into his shoulders and biting his scalp, while Jackson doubled up laughing.

"Rivers, help me!"

"Okay, fine! Fine! Stand still, moron!" Jackson took two quick steps to where Henry had ended up, in the living room by Ellery's leather couches, and put a steadying hand on Henry's shoulder. "Hold on a second."

Gently, because Billy Bob was his friend, Jackson lifted him off Henry's shoulders, detaching his claws one razor at a time.

"Aw, buddy! What'd he do to you?" Jackson soothed his beloved kitty with full-body pets while Billy trembled up against his chest, letting out the occasional hiss in Henry's direction.

"I petted him!" Henry defended, wiping at the blood on his shoulders. "I swear! I put out my hand and scratched him on the ass!"

"Oh my God, man! Slow down! You don't even know this cat! You start with a finger on the forehead and then take liberties if they let you. Has nobody taught you about cats?"

"My dad let them sleep in the barn and live on mice!" Henry retorted. "And they still looked better than that asshole you're treating like a victim!"

"Shh…," Jackson soothed. "He didn't mean it. He's just being a prick because he was raised by wolves."

Billy Bob meowed pitifully, and Jackson went to the drawer in the living room that held the brush Ellery had bought him. "Here, brother. Let's chill you out, okay? I know—he's a bad guy. Next time, maybe just hide in my room when he's here, okay?"

Jackson took the cat to his and Ellery's bed and brushed him for about five minutes, until his fur stopped standing on end and he wasn't growling anymore. He cleaned up the fur, grabbed another clean T-shirt, and went to find Henry in the guest bathroom, wiping the blood off his head and shoulders.

"Here," he muttered, throwing the shirt.

"Thanks." Henry changed shirts, and Jackson turned to leave. Henry's voice stopped him. "You weren't wrong, you know."

"About what?"

"I might have been raised by wolves."

Augh! Every goddamned time Jackson thought Henry was beyond redemption, he said something honest.

"Well, I was raised by a junkie. Wolves at least feed their young. Clean up. We've got places to go."

A HALF hour later, Jackson was parking Ellery's car behind a small cluster of doctors' offices next to the Kaiser outpatient clinic on Fair Oaks. Across the street sat a Shell station, but Jackson had parked in a corner by a neatly kept stand of oleander bushes that hid him from view. Without talking to a mostly silent Henry, he opened the car door and executed a quick change right there in the parking lot, and looked up to see Henry doing the same.

"What's the plan, hoss?" Henry asked when they were done.

"There's a transport bay to the side," Jackson said. "It's for patients who need to be driven in for consult, and right now, it looks to be empty. I say we enter through there and snoop around. We're checking for the drug cabinets and holes in their security. Something made Martin Sampson turn from dealing coke to dealing oxy, and somewhere in there, he pissed off the meth dealers. I'm pretty sure if we follow the drugs, we'll find the guy who killed him. We need to split up and follow our noses, understand?"

"What if we're caught?"

"Say, 'Oh my God! I was here for the last transport. I got so lost!'" Jackson handed him a small packet of forensic gloves. "And put these on before you touch anything."

"I'm not dumb!" Henry denied hotly, and Jackson wished he had something to throw at him.

"Do you really care what these strangers think? Jesus, dumbass, better to play stupid than get caught! Now Carver is supposed to be out of state, but I've got an idea about that. I'll take Sampson's office. You take Carver's. Look for anything out of the ordinary. You have your phone—take a picture if you need to. Remember, don't lift any drugs even if the labels are incriminating. That's a handy way to get arrested. We take twenty minutes, maximum, after we split up, and we meet back here. Are you ready?"

"Yessir." Henry stood straight and proud, the Army grunt any CO would ask for.

"Henry?"

"Rivers?"

"Learn to slouch."

"Goddammit."

Henry adjusted his posture, and Jackson led the way.

The op went smooth as silk.

The practice was a big one. Jackson had gotten a look at the total number of employees, and while the four surgeons made up the medical group, there were a number of general practitioners and physicians' assistants using the building and generally beefing up the co-op. Jackson and Henry slid in through the loading bay and scanned the site map, both of them acting like they had a reason to be there. They went down the central hallway, Henry peeling off to the left toward Carver's office, Jackson heading toward Sampson's.

The offices themselves were standard—beige carpet, beige walls— but there was a navy-and-burgundy stripe around waist level, apparently meant to instill confidence or something. Jackson just thought it made the hallway look longer. Sampson's office was easy to identify—it had a name plate on the wall with all the accompanying letters of the alphabet that spelled out "Very Educated Man." But the door was locked.

Well, sort of.

Jackson slid a slim, flexible blade of metal out of his wallet and wiggled it around a bit, and suddenly, the office wasn't locked anymore. He hadn't always walked on the side of angels.

Also, he'd taken a PI class the last time he'd been laid up. Amazing what you could learn online.

He slid into the office and looked around, thinking he should add Very Rich Man to Very Educated Man. The rug wasn't beige in here, and the desk wasn't Formica and metal. The room was decorated with solid oak furniture with nice tapestry cushions, and photos with matching frames. Some were of Robert *Scott* Sampson getting awards and shaking hands with the mayor and various celebrities, and some were of his family.

The realization of where Martin Sampson got his porn name left a taste in Jackson's mouth like sour come. If that wasn't a fuck-you to dear old Dad, Jackson didn't know what was. So much of this case was cock cheese, he didn't know where to start.

The pictures didn't make it any better. Martin Sampson had been a cute kid once, with an infectious smile. Jackson looked at a grade school montage and tried to decide when that smile had become a cynical smirk. Was it grade school? Seventh grade, when he grew tall but his jaw still sported that softness of young adolescence? Was it his freshman year, when his father's hand on his shoulder looked like a manacle of doom?

Jackson squinted at that picture, frowning. There was something off about Sampson Senior's expression. It wasn't… paternal. It wasn't avuncular. Jackson shuddered, having recognized that look from some of his mother's boyfriends—including the one who'd woken him up with a hand on Jackson's dick and his tongue down his throat.

He looked at Martin Sampson in later photos—cynical, lips pulled back in a sneer that passed as a smile, his eyes narrowed in pure venom.

Not a nice guy, no.

But he'd hung with nice guys—John, Henry's brother—and then he'd screwed them over. Maybe it was the only way he knew how to be. Jackson had seen firsthand that monsters were more often made than born.

Jackson's suspicions for what made *this* one, found dead and discarded like trash, made his stomach churn.

He had no qualms grabbing a couple of sterile gloves from his pocket and looking through Robert Scott Sampson's mail after that.

Drug advert, drug advert, several of them, actually, for oxy or an oxy-like substitute. Interesting. Jackson laid them all flat and took a picture, then stacked them as he'd found them. QuadCeption rental properties, a receipt. Very interesting. Jackson took that out of the opened envelope, took a picture, then replaced it. He searched some more but saw nothing of interest—no receipts to Bad-Guys-Are-Us or You-Sell-It-We-Snort-It— but that was standard. Most people kept their legitimate stuff online these days, and there was a solid desk unit front and center.

The desk done, Jackson rifled through the trash, unsurprised when it yielded very little—but stunned when he heard the doorknob jiggle.

Shit.

He set down the trash can, shucked his gloves into his pockets, and sprawled on the visitor's chair like he owned the place.

He barely moved his head when the door flew open and the tall, distinguished man in his fifties, with Martin Sampson's brown eyes and dimples, barged in.

"What in the hell—"

"Wait…," Jackson muttered, holding up a finger but continuing to tap on his phone. "I'm almost at the next level…." He finished his text to Henry—the one that read, *Come knock on Sampson's door and tell me to get my ass in gear!* And then he concentrated diligently on Simon's Cat, the newest phone game he and Ellery were trying to best each other at this month.

"Who are you, and what are you doing in my office?" Robert Sampson sounded pissed and baffled, which was about perfect.

"Waiting for my transport patient," Jackson said, sounding bored. "Dude, if you didn't want me to chill in here, you should have locked your door!"

"I *did* lock my door!" Sampson raged.

Jackson rolled his eyes. "Sure you did. That's why I'm sitting here, because the door was locked." He tapped a few more times, then stood up and shoved his phone into his pocket. "But whatever. I'll leave your precious office—"

"What is your name? You have violated protocol, and you need to be disciplined."

Jackson pulled a name out of his hat—the name of his least favorite doctor and one of Dave and Alex's most hated bosses. "Scheideman," he said, smiling. "Junior Scheideman."

Sampson's eyes got really, really big. "Any relation to—"

And Henry, bless him, pounded on the door. "Dammit, move it! We need to get going, *now!*"

And Jackson sauntered past Robert Sampson, phone in pocket, and out the door with Henry.

He didn't even break a sweat.

They broke into a run once they cleared the door, though, the early evening heat hitting them like a hammer after the air-conditioning inside. Jackson had the car gassed up and was peeling out of the parking lot before they said another word.

"What did you find?" he asked tersely.

"You know those drug prescription pads?" Henry replied. "You know, the ones that are numbered so they can't be duplicated?"

"Yeah?"

"Well, Carver's office was empty, but there were, like, cases upon cases of those stacked up on his desk."

Jackson whistled. "That's subtle."

"Not so much, no."

"Did you get pictures?"

"Oh yeah—you?"

"I got some other shit that will be very useful. Send your stuff to me and Ellery, and I'll take a look at it after I drop you off. Where to, by the way?"

Henry thought about it for a minute. "The flophouse," he said softly. "I… I don't know. I feel like the guys might… need a little reassurance, you think?"

Well, shit. Again with the totally human Henry. "Yeah. I think that's decent of you."

"What about you? What are you going to tell Ellery about your shoulder?"

Which was currently on fire and stiff as a porn-star's prick. "I've got a plan," Jackson said. "Right after you hand me the ibuprofen in the glove compartment."

Shattered

ELLERY LEANED over the kitchen table and reexamined the pictures Jackson had just sent him. Interesting—both sets—and they tied into what Ellery had discovered about Sampson's financials that afternoon. They'd have to discuss his findings when Jackson got home, right after he found out what it was Jackson was trying to hide from him.

He hadn't liked the sound of Jackson's voice—not one bit—and he was tired and cranky. And he and Jackson *still* hadn't had a good chance to talk about Jackson goddammit *talking* about what was eating at him.

Ellery had the feeling this was some sort of a test.

He was not great at emotion, really. Had always approached things from a place of reason. But once he and Jackson had gotten together, reason had been taking more and more of a back seat. On the one hand, being in love with Jackson was sort of an amazing experience—totally worth changing for. On the other hand, it left him emotionally raw in a way he'd never imagined. It was like those crimes of passion he'd defended. Now he understood why they were committed.

When you felt so strongly about another human being that their happiness was yours, it left you profoundly vulnerable.

He tried very hard to be patient with Jackson, given what Jackson had grown up with, but he didn't like being vulnerable to a man who had a problem with communication and possessed an uncomfortable relationship with the truth as it applied to people who cared about him.

Jackson lied cheerfully about his state of being. The word *fine* graced his lips so often, Ellery had been tempted to buy him a T-shirt that said nothing *but* "I'm fine."

And he was so obviously not fine. The night before had not been fine. The sound of his voice that afternoon had not been fine.

And Ellery needed to know Jackson was fine before they went any further.

Still… those pictures…. Ellery had gotten the photos right before Jade left the office. Jackson had asked Ellery to compare the numbers on the narcotic prescription sheets to the one on Summer Frasier's tablet, but the codes had been completely different in the electronic prescription. Jackson had included pictures of the family—Robert, Martin, and Martin's mother, Hadley. In a way, they reminded Ellery of his own family—well-heeled, everybody wearing the right thing for the right occasion, almost professional smiles on everybody's faces. But Robert's face was missing the warmth of Ellery's own father, and Hadley's eyes didn't have Taylor Cramer's wicked intelligence or dry humor.

And Martin Sampson looked fucking miserable from the minute he hit junior high onward.

Resolutely, Ellery tried to make a list of things to do. He'd run Martin Sampson's financials and had found some interesting things, but he wanted a deep dive of Martin *and* Robert Sampson's money paths, as well as Summer Frasier's. And the name Candy Cormier was starting to niggle at the edges of his brain, like there was something important there he needed to see. He added *Ask Kryzynski about Cormier* to his list of things to do.

He was still pondering the pictures, the evidence, the things he'd discovered and the things Jackson had told him, when he heard the garage door open. Jackson was home, but Ellery was still leaning over the table, studying the files and his phone, when Jackson's hands, ripe with the heat of the furnace-like day, circled his waist.

"Mmm…," he murmured, thrusting back a little, finding Jackson's thighs as strong as they'd always been, in spite of the lack of meat on his frame. Jackson bent over him, rucking up his shirt and kissing up his spine. Ellery melted into the table, fully aware he was being used for sex and was okay with that.

"You look thoughtful, Counselor," Jackson said, draping himself over Ellery's back and whispering in his ear.

"Lots of info to process," Ellery mumbled. Jackson slid his hands up along his back and his ribs, pulling his polo over his head and peppering his back with kisses. "Should we move to the bed?"

"Nope."

Ellery squirmed, feeling wanton and a little dirty. For the most part, they'd stuck to the bed in the past few months, because both of them had been healing and things got stiff—and not the good things either—when you had sex on the floor or the table.

But here, with his weight on his elbows, he was acutely aware that he was thrusting his ass out in what could be a blatant invitation.

He'd been *so* ready to have Jackson take him the night before. Jackson didn't let him down.

He kissed down Ellery's naked spine again, then dipped his lips below the belt line, tugging at Ellery's slacks. They didn't yield, so his hands went to the belt holding them up, and Ellery whimpered with impatience. He wanted Jackson's naked body against his.

The slacks fell to his feet, and Jackson shoved his boxers down, then, oh my God, squatted behind Ellery, his hot, callused palms parting Ellery's cheeks.

"Really?" Ellery breathed. "We're going right th—*ere?*"

Jackson didn't just go there—Jackson went to *town* there—tongue extended, whisker stubble abrading the soft inside of Ellery's cheeks. Ellery moaned, naked and spread out on the kitchen table, needing more, harder, needing penetration, fast and dirty and now. He reached behind him, trying to grab Jackson's hair, but he ended up pushing on his head, demanding more.

And Jackson gave him more. He reached between Ellery's legs and grabbed his balls—firm, but still gentle as he rolled them softly between his fingers. Ellery's knees threatened to buckle, just that quickly.

"Lube?" he squeaked, needing it all *right now*!

Jackson pulled away, giving Ellery a quick bite on the soft part of his bottom, and his face was replaced by—oh thank God—his well-oiled cock.

Sometimes, stretching was a good thing, but right now, he welcomed the bite of pain that came with Jackson's sudden intrusion. With a quick thrust, Ellery's confusion, his vulnerability, was washed away, and he was filled with Jackson, filled with power. He felt desirable and hot and needed.

And Jackson was skillful—Ellery had never doubted it. With long, full, fast strokes, Jackson dominated him, hands on his waist, hips rocking. Ellery was incoherent, a sweaty mass of desire sticking to his kitchen table.

Jackson slowed down long enough to pull him upright, weight on his hands, so he could nibble on Ellery's neck, his shoulders, trail gentle fingers down his flanks. His rhythm turned languorous, drugging, and Ellery dropped his hand to his cock shamelessly, needing more.

Jackson pulled it away and chuckled, right in his ear. "You're that ready?"

"Zero to fifty, one good lick," Ellery panted, and Jackson's laugh rumbled through his stomach, to where their bodies were touching.

His next thrust was brutally hard, and then he stopped, leaving Ellery quivering, waiting for the next blow.

"Please," Ellery begged. "Please, baby, finish me—*ahh*...."

This flurry of fucking was it. He could feel it, the violent tingle that started at his taint and rushed his thighs, his stomach, his balls. No touching necessary. Just Jackson's furnace-like body throwing heat into Ellery's ass.

Ellery cried out, collapsing on the table, pushing hard to keep from overbalancing, and Jackson let out a soft little moan of completion behind him. Jackson fell heavily over his back, as though he'd suddenly run out of strength, and Ellery felt the table rock.

"We're gonna break it," he mumbled, and Jackson chuckled and stood heavily upright, hefting Ellery up against his front and nuzzling his temple as though suddenly weary.

"Hey," he whispered, "I love you."

Ellery felt the first stirrings of suspicion. "I love you too," he murmured, leaning into Jackson's cheek. "What's up?"

Jackson shook his head and bent over enough to capture Ellery's lips briefly. "I'm gonna go shower," he said. "I'll be out in ten—we can go over stuff then." He held Ellery tight again and slid out in a wash of come before pulling his underwear and scrubs up his thighs.

"I might as well shower with you," Ellery said, crouching to get his pants up from around his ankles so he could walk into the bathroom.

Then he saw it. Jackson had turned around as he'd reached the door to the hallway and their bedroom, and the patch of blood seeping through Jackson's white scrubs stood out like a red flag to a bull.

"Jackson, what happened to your back?"

Jackson didn't even bother to look at him. "Doesn't matter—I'm fine, right? We had sex, it's all good, I'm fine."

Fine?

Ellery had never lost his temper like this in his life.

He'd heard of people seeing red—had defended clients who had looked at him helplessly and said, "I don't know what happened then. I just... snapped."

But until the glass paperweight his mother had bought them went sailing past Jackson's head to *thunk* and shatter on the wall, he had never thought it would happen to him.

Jackson went very still.

"Ell...." His voice wobbled. "Ellery?"

"Tell me," Ellery said, his own voice shaking. "Tell me we didn't just have sex on the kitchen table so you could hide whatever the hell *happened to your back*!"

Jackson's shoulders rolled forward, stretching the scrubs tight enough that Ellery could see the outline of the bandage. "We had sex because you were hot," he said, sounding lost.

"Jackson, look at me."

Jackson crouched instead, picking up glass shards with fingers that shook. "I really liked this."

"I did too." Ellery's eyes were hot, and he couldn't seem to find his center. "I liked the sex. But... but did you really just come home and seduce me so I wouldn't see you'd been hurt?"

"I just wanted you not to worry," Jackson said, looking at him for the first time. His green eyes were wide and shiny and scared, and Ellery's chest went cold. In their entire relationship, Jackson had never looked at him with the eyes of the victim he must have been as a child.

Until now.

"I'm sorry," Ellery told him thickly. "I shouldn't have lost my temper like that. My emotions were... were just too close to the surface. Man, I've been worried about you since that phone call." He walked toward where Jackson crouched, but Jackson held out his hand, so he stopped.

"You're barefoot," he said, because Ellery had kicked off his loafers by the rack in the kitchen.

"I don't care!" Oh God. Ellery had done this. That haunted look on his lover's face—*Ellery* had done it.

"I do," Jackson rasped, collecting the shards in his hand. "This was really pretty—"

"And I broke it because I'm worried about you!"

Jackson recoiled from Ellery's raised voice in a way he never had before, and Ellery felt the helplessness of knowing he'd violated Jackson's safety when he'd been the only security Jackson had ever known.

"I… I gotta shower," Jackson mumbled, gathering the pieces together in the front of his scrubs. "Just let me shower." He disappeared down the hallway, and Ellery heard the tinkle of glass from the guest bathroom a moment later, while he stood, pants clutched around his waist, still in a state of shock.

The guest bathroom.

Oh God.

Jackson was bathing in the guest bathroom.

Like he didn't belong in the house.

Like they hadn't lived together, slept together, showered together since September when he'd gotten home from the hospital.

Ten months—ten months they'd been in each other's back pockets, and Jackson was putting distance between them again.

Ellery looked at the hand that he'd used to dash their future against the wall and fought the temptation to cry.

TWO HOURS later, he stopped fighting.

Jackson had showered and done a load of laundry, then sat in the guest bedroom and worked on his laptop.

He'd closed the door, but Ellery had peeked in to ask him if he wanted some dinner.

Ellery had gotten a shake of Jackson's head and eyes that skated away from an actual meeting. That's when he'd gone to their bedroom to cry.

What had he done?

He didn't even realize he was texting his mother until he pressed Send.

Mom, I did something awful.

His phone buzzed. "Do I need to hire you a lawyer or buy you tickets to a nonextradition country?"

She was completely serious.

Ellery smiled in spite of the ache in his chest. "Not quite that awful," he said, sighing and wishing for Billy Bob. The cat had ended up in the guest bedroom with Jackson. Of course he had.

"What's wrong, honey?"

Oh, he must sound worse than he thought. Honey. His mother never used endearments, but her voice had dropped softly, and he realized that the last time he'd cried had been when Jackson's heart had stopped.

"I… I got mad enough to throw something," he said. "And I did. And I broke the thing, and I might have broken us, and I don't know how to make it right."

"If you didn't like the paperweight, Ellery, all you had to do was say so."

"I didn't," Ellery told her. "But Jackson loved it. And I broke it when I missed his head."

"On purpose?" Like this meant something.

Ellery thought about it. "Yeah. I was really just trying to get his attention."

"About what?" she asked, delicate and direct at the same time, because that was Taylor Cramer.

"He… he came home with a big… wound on his back, and he didn't tell me. And he evaded me. And he…." Oh God. This was his *mother*!

"Used sex to distract you?"

"How did you know that?" If his mother had bugged his house, he'd jump off a cliff.

"It wasn't hard to figure out. It's worked so well with all of his past lovers, I don't see why he'd quit now, do you?"

"But I'm different!" he argued, affronted.

"Of course you are! You're the only real relationship he's ever had. And he was trying to keep you from worrying about him. Why would you be doing that, by the way? I thought things were going well between you?"

"These last couple weeks he's been… been slipping. He stopped talking to Rabbi Watson, stopped eating, stopped sleeping. He skipped his cardiologist appointment—" He took a deep breath because he didn't like to think about Jackson doing all that running around with a chronic condition, so he mostly just didn't. But he'd been the one to make the monthly appointment, so he'd gotten the call that it had slipped Jackson's mind. That's when he'd seen it—how much Jackson *wasn't* taking care of himself. "And this case we're working on—"

"You have a case?"

Ellery had discussed his cases with his mother since law school, and he wasn't going to stop now. He came to a close and heard her fascinated hum.

"Give him some space tonight," she said after a moment. "Maybe let him talk to his new partner—"

"Henry? Henry's a client."

"Sure he is. But give him some space. Talk to him tomorrow. Don't give up on him, son. He's hurt, but so are you. He loves you very much. He'll see that."

"I just took away the only security he's ever had."

"Because he was slipping away from you. Maybe he's never had a lover who cared enough about him to break a hand-blown glass paperweight."

"I'm sorry," he said, feeling like crap.

"No worries. I found another one on Etsy from that same vendor—different colors, but still, it will do nicely. But this one's Jackson's. He gets to open it, and you get to not touch it. Ever again."

Ellery dropped his chin to his chest and rubbed the back of his neck. "Sorry, Mother."

She let out a sigh. "You're a good man, Ellery. And like I said, he loves you. He loves you so much that maybe your worry is the problem."

"I can't stop worrying!"

"And you shouldn't. But maybe… maybe take the weight of it from his shoulders a little. He's not broken to vex you, you know."

"Sometimes I'm not so sure about that," Ellery said darkly.

"Ellery…."

Sigh. "Yeah. No, you're right, Mother. You are. I just… sex should be off-limits," he said, not caring suddenly that she was the one he was confiding in.

"It should be." She was agreeing with him? He looked outside the window quickly to see if the sky had turned to blood. No, the sun hadn't even set, because it was damned close to summer solstice.

"But so should breaking things," Ellery said with a sigh. He slid down his bed, hating himself all over again.

"You'll figure it out, son," she told him softly. "You said he hasn't been sleeping well?"

"Yeah."

"So tonight?"

Whether Jackson wanted him to be or not, Ellery wasn't going to leave him alone to his demons.

"I'll be exactly where he needs me," Ellery said, his voice steely with resolve.

"Good boy."

His mother rang off soon after that, and Ellery went out to the kitchen table—freshly cleaned—to run Sampson's financials, and Carver's as well. When he was done with that, he went over the bills and the specs for the office, because it was coming together nicely. By the end of the week, they could welcome a new client in there with the same amount of grace his old firm had provided, without quite the same strong smell of paint the place had sported this past week.

He paused for a moment, yawning and stretching and wondering if he should just go to sleep, when Jackson's scream ripped the house—and his heart—wide open.

"*Ellery!*"

Ellery was through the door to the guest room before the last syllable died.

Jackson was thrashing on top of the covers, wearing a pair of sleep shorts and nothing else, and the lamp was still on next to the bed. Billy Bob leaped down and ran toward the open door as Ellery rushed to the bedside, and Ellery let him.

He'd chosen this job—Billy Bob got nights off.

"Baby, I'm here!"

"Ellery, don't go," Jackson whimpered.

Oh, baby. "I'm right here."

"Don't go. I'm sorry. I'm sorry. Don't go."

Ellery slid next to him and wrapped his arms and legs around Jackson's shoulders and hips, binding him as tightly as possible. "I've got you."

"I'm sorry. I'm sorry. I don't know what I did—I'm sorry—"

Ellery's eyes, hot and swollen from his little pity party before he talked to his mom, began to sting. "I'm sorry too," he whispered, holding Jackson as tight as possible and still not keeping him from shaking. "I'm so sorry. I won't go. I'm sorry. Don't leave me. Come back. Wherever you went, come back. I'll stay if you will. God, baby, you're shaking so hard."

"I lost you."

"No, no, baby. Never."

"I don't even know what I did…."

Ellery let out a broken laugh. "We'll have a talk about that in the morning," he murmured. "Come on. Get up." He shoved gently at Jackson's hips until he rolled out of bed and stood.

"Where we going?" His eyes were at half-mast, and Ellery realized that no matter what his day had been like, Jackson was exhausted.

"To our bed, Jackson. You're not sleeping in the guest bed ever again."

His lips parted and wobbled, and he palmed his eyes. Ellery nudged him gently until they were out of the guest bedroom and back in their own. He turned off the lights on the way, glad he'd locked everything down before he'd sat down to work. When they got to the bed, he paused and took off his pajama bottoms and T-shirt, then helped Jackson out of his sleep shorts.

Skin to skin. He needed as much of Jackson's skin touching his as possible tonight, no matter how hot it was outside.

He turned off the light and crawled into bed, pulling Jackson so tightly against him that for a moment, Jackson struggled.

"Not letting you go," Ellery murmured.

"Okay." Jackson went still in his arms, which was almost as bad.

"I loved the sex," Ellery said. The sandwich method, right? The good, the bad, the good? Well, the sex had been great. "I always like sex with you."

Jackson melted a little—active acceptance instead of passive, at least Ellery hoped so.

"But... but you weren't honest with me. You didn't tell me you were hurt. It felt... manipulative. You wanted me to leave you alone about something you didn't want to talk about, so you had sex with me." Ellery grunted. "It's not flattering to think that's the only reason you want me, Jackson."

"I want you all the time," Jackson rumbled, and Ellery smiled a little. He meant it. Ellery had never fooled himself that he was in the same sexual league with Jackson Rivers, but Jackson had never seemed to think otherwise.

"That's good. Because I want you, and that makes me an easy mark."

"I don't... I get banged up," Jackson muttered, sounding irritated. That was a good sign too. "You freak out over every damned bruise!"

"Because I don't want you hurt at all!" Ellery snapped, and then he took a deep breath. "But... but let's do a rewind. Let's go back to that phone conversation—you remember that?"

"Hunh."

Never Ellery's favorite word. "What?"

"You're hella fucking smart, do you know that, Counselor?"

Ellery grunted, remembering the way that paperweight shattered. "No. Not tonight I'm not. Let's try that convo again. 'Jackson, you sound out of breath? What happened?'"

Jackson grunted back. "I chased a guy out of the manager's office, and he got me with a Schrade dagger across my back. Henry's buddy is stitching me up so I don't have to go to the hospital."

Ellery took a deep breath, keeping the retroactive panic at bay. "That's nice of him. Is he qualified?"

Jackson let out something that might have been a laugh but was muffled against Ellery's chest. "He's a med student, but he was good. I mean, my back could look like a crazy quilt, but at this point, it would be an improvement."

Ellery shuddered hard in what might have been a laugh, and kissed the crown of Jackson's head. "I'll look later," he promised. "Is there anything else?"

Jackson grunted. "Fucking apartment complex. Got lost in it, like... like November. Almost shit my pants. Panicked. Couldn't breathe."

Ellery closed his eyes. "Oh." He took a deep breath. And another. "Is that why you didn't tell me?"

Jackson pulled back, and Ellery got a look at Jackson's face, still haunted but without that air of victim that had so gutted Ellery after his stupid-ass temper tantrum. "I gotta function, Ellery. Sometimes I just need to put the bad shit in the box."

Ellery nodded and kissed his forehead. "Understood. How about, 'Is there anything else?' and you say—"

"I'll tell you later?" Jackson swallowed as he offered it.

"Good." Ellery closed his eyes. "That would be... be a lot better than... you know, finding out you just tried to fuck me as a distraction."

"I didn't try," Jackson said with a hint of a smirk. "I *did*."

Ellery *tried* to laugh then, and it came out broken and a little hysterical. "And I lost my temper," he added. "And I'm sorry."

"I always want you, but I... I hurt your feelings. And I'm sorry."

They both took a collective breath.

"Remember November?" Ellery asked. "When... when you had one foot out the door?"

Jackson nodded, and Ellery's heart wrenched. He'd known it then, but to hear it confirmed, to know how close they'd come to losing each other, to him losing Jackson forever, was hard just the same.

"You were afraid I'd kick you out," Ellery said. "You wanted to leave before I... I made you go."

"Yeah."

"Conversations like this—they make sure that never happens."

"Okay," Jackson whispered, and Ellery could sense the doneness in him. "Okay."

Ellery kissed him, a salty, stinging messy benediction of everything they'd just said, and then he pulled away. "Don't, uh... don't go anywhere tonight? Don't... don't go play video games? Don't go running or swimming or whatever? Just... even if you dream some more, just stay."

"Ellery, no—"

"Just stay," he begged.

"It is all bad in my head right now," Jackson said, his voice raw. "I... I may not sleep at all. I...."

"Just stay," he begged again, voice breaking. "Please. Nothing inside you is so bad I'll run away. I mean, I know I fucked up. I know. I should know not to lose my temper like that, but—"

"Hey, hey...," Jackson soothed him. "You have the right to lose your temper. I... I don't make it easy on you. You shouldn't have to worry about not getting mad—"

"Lose my temper, yes," Ellery said bitterly. "But throw shit? No. You... you didn't know what to do with that. I made things worse."

Jackson gave a fractured laugh. "I didn't know you had that in you," he said, a little wonder tinting his voice. "I was... surprised."

He'd been terrified. Frightened. Hurt beyond words. Ellery would never forget the lost look on his face.

"I took away some of your... your faith in me—"

"Never."

"No. I did. And I need to own it. I can't do that again. I depend on that, you know."

"On what?"

"On you believing in me."

Jackson was quiet, and for a glorious, hopeful moment, Ellery hoped he'd fallen asleep. "You're.... It was good, you did that," he said at last. "I... you, loving me. It didn't seem quite real. But you're not perfect. And that makes it real."

Ellery almost smacked him. "Oh my God, that's warped," he muttered. "Are you ever going to trust me again?"

"No, no—it makes total sense." Jackson nodded at him, as earnest as a child. "It's hard to trust someone who's perfect. But I trust that you'll try."

Ellery supposed he could take it as a win. "Only to you." Ellery kissed his temple, and almost like that was a signal, they relaxed enough to let some oxygen between them. "So now that I know the guy in the manager's office had a knife, is there anything else you want to tell me about him?"

Jackson chuckled and then told Ellery—*really* told him—about his day. For a few minutes, Ellery lost himself in Jackson's story of Cock Cheese Sternberg and the dormitory full of porn models who were not fully grown.

And in all of the repercussions this new information might have for the case.

"Okay, so we know a little more now," he pondered, sitting up in bed as Jackson had been for the past few minutes. "That's good."

"If Kryzynski calls us with new information tomorrow, that would be better. But we've got a name for the second round of tapes, and an organization—that's important."

"Yeah. Now if we could only figure out what it all means." Ellery chewed his lower lip for a moment, until Jackson's stomach broke the silence—loudly. "You didn't eat," he said softly, and Jackson shrugged his good shoulder. "Come on, I'll make you a sandwich. You can do dinner theater for me, and we can talk about what you learned in Sampson's office."

He expected to have to argue fiercely about this, but Jackson got out of bed almost immediately. Maybe it was because he wasn't ready to sleep yet, or maybe he just wanted them to get along.

Or maybe he had relaxed enough to be hungry.

Small steps. Ellery celebrated small steps.

A few minutes later, Jackson sat shirtless at the kitchen table with a peanut butter sandwich—his request—and a glass of milk. Comfort food for the child Jackson never got to be. While he ate, Ellery doctored the wound on his shoulder.

"This is neatly done," he appraised. "But you tore it a little. Here, I'll go get some more gauze to suck up the blood."

"Thanks," Jackson murmured, head down.

"You didn't really expect me not to notice this, did you?" Ellery kept his fingertips on Jackson's skin so Jackson would know he wasn't mad.

"No. I knew you'd see it. I know you're not stupid, Ellery."

"Then what? Why wouldn't you even tell me about it?"

Jackson reached behind him and laced his fingers over his shoulder. "I just wanted to skip to the part it was old news," he confessed. "Yeah, that? Happened a few days ago. No big deal."

Ellery squeezed his hand and bent down until he was whispering in Jackson's ear. "You are *always* my big deal. Understand? You may not like it—not all the time. But if I have to live with worrying about you, you have to live with the fact that I'm worried. That would be *great* if it inspired you to take fewer chances, but I'll take what I can get. Understood?"

Jackson squeezed back. "Understood."

Ellery went for gauze, and when he came back, Jackson was feeding a corner of his sandwich to an imperious Billy Bob, who was standing up on his haunches—missing back leg and all—and batting Jackson's fingers with his paws. Jackson took a bite of the sandwich and pulled off another corner for Billy Bob and then took a swig of milk, and Ellery's heart thudded hard in his chest.

His man. This was his man. All of the worry, all of the damage, and Ellery had a superhero who would split his meal with a three-legged alley cat and swear playfully at him at the same time.

"You want that? You can't have it. Nope. No bread for you—oh! Nice try, no-thumbs-having motherfucker. Nice fucking try. You want some more? Why would I give you more? You're lazy. Go kill something for me. Go fucking kill me a possum to cook for food, motherfucker. Go do that, maybe I'll give you more peanut butter. Oooh… nibbles? You're gonna nibble me? Sure. You go ahead and nibble me. I'll take what's left of your teeth, asshole, oh yes, I will. Fine, fine—more. That's fine. You eat all my sandwich and see if he yells at you. No, no he doesn't yell at you, because you're a big cheesy motherfucker with no thumbs. He doesn't love you, he *pities* you, so don't get ideas. Nobody loves you. Fine, I'll scratch your ass. Don't think that means anything. Yeah, you drool on me tonight, I'll lock you in the bathroom. Hot, sweaty, and covered in cat fur—what kind of nightmares you think I'll have *then*?"

Ellery walked up behind him, much like Jackson had come up behind Ellery earlier, and dragged his lips down the back of Jackson's ear.

"What?" Jackson muttered, surprised.

"Want another sandwich?"

"No, this one's good."

"Detective?"

"Yeah?"

"I love you."

Jackson turned his head, and Ellery found his mouth for the awkward over-the-shoulder kiss. "Love you too, Counselor. Now do you want to hear about the rest of my day?"

Ellery grinned and pulled away. "Oh, I do. I really, really do. You still have milk left. Want cookies?"

Jackson smiled then, holding his hand palm out over his mouth, as though to hide any food left in there. "Oh, I do. I really, really do." His green eyes crinkled at the corners, and his dark blond hair was messily attractive over his brow, and Ellery thought that he would lie down and die for this man, a thousand times over, just to see him mangle a smile over a peanut butter sandwich and milk.

"Then let's make that happen."

They talked about the case for another hour, until Jackson rested his chin on his hands and closed his eyes—seemingly in thought.

Ellery yawned and nudged him to bed, making sure their phones were in the chargers this time but not setting an alarm.

Jackson slid bonelessly into bed, and Ellery followed, the air-conditioning zealous enough—and the night outside cool enough—that some of the stickiness in the air faded.

This time, they both slept until morning.

Jigsaw and Duct Tape

JACKSON'S PHONE was buzzing, but not with an alarm.

"What the… fucking… mother*fucker.* Ellery, did we oversleep?"

"No." Ellery yawned delicately—like the cat. "We can't oversleep. We're the bosses. I turned off your alarm."

"But I set that on purpose—fuck!" He said that last part right into the phone.

"Thank you, no," Kryzynski said dryly. "You are not my type."

Jackson's head ached, and his fucking back felt like a big throbbing inflatable raft. "I wouldn't bang you in the dark on Viagra. Why are you here in my bed at fuck-all in the morning?"

"It's nine, Rivers. Must be nice to keep your own hours."

Oh Jesus. The night before—Jackson looked at Ellery, who was arching a singularly unrepentant eyebrow. The night before had been an emotional meat grinder.

"It is when your boyfriend doesn't keep them for you," he muttered. "I'm sorry about that—my bad. Why are we talking again?"

"Because I know who your guy with the blade was. First name Ralph, last name—"

"Gordon," Jackson said, and yes, a little bit smugly. "He works for Candy Cormier."

"Jesus," Kryzynski swore. "I did not know that last part. How did you?"

"Gnomes. What can you tell me about Cormier?"

Kryzynski gave a sigh. "Newcomer. Last few months or so—word is he's up from down south. Meth, manufacture, distribution, and sales. He's sort of…." Jackson could hear the gears turning and respected that. "He's organized," Kryzynski said thoughtfully. "Like, since February, he's infiltrated all the mini-markets in the area and taken over. I think he even refined the product. I know we've had half the poisonings in the last six months."

"Does he use?" Jackson asked, remembering Herbert's claim that he was more meth than brains at this point.

"From what I've heard? No. But he *is* certifiable. We've got a couple of butchered bodies that were his errand boys who got greedy. Can't pin it on him—can't pin him down—but we've heard his name whispered often enough, you know?"

"February," Jackson said, looking sideways at Ellery. Ellery paused from reading his phone long enough to raise his eyebrows.

"Interesting," he mouthed, and Jackson nodded.

"Very." Then he tuned back in to Kryzynski. "So, Candy Cormier—meth, militarized, douchebag. Sent Ralph Gordon in to erase the original footage. Did he succeed?"

"Yes and no," Kryzynski said. "We've got a car and a partial plate driving up near the dumpster about twenty minutes before Henry Worrall did his chores, but nothing beyond that. Not even a shadow."

Jackson grunted. "Did you run the partial?"

"Yeah—the car's decent. A Buick Encore, big enough to hide the body, not big enough to be noticed. But our list is about two hundred possibilities long. Do you have any names you want me to run it against?"

Jackson sighed. It was time to put up or shut up. "Got three possibilities," he said. "Summer Frasier, Ash Carver, or Robert Sampson."

"The vic's father?" Kryzynski said, obviously impressed. "On what evidence?"

"A hunch," Jackson said. "We're working on evidence."

"Well, let me know when you get something. I mean, I know Martin wasn't a model son, but his dad's a—"

"Drug-dealing douchebag. And we *will* get evidence of that, I promise you. Anyway, I think the drug dealer Sampson pissed off was his father—or in his father's little ring. Dad cracks him over the head, knows about the altercation with the porn kids, drugs him so he dies, and plants the body. Cormier realizes Dad is *not* a master criminal and tries to doctor the tapes. What we don't know is how exactly the drug ring operates and what evidence we can gather to nail Sampson Senior—or why Cormier wanted to keep Daddy Sampson in the clear. And that shit's important if we want to keep Henry out of jail."

Kryzynski grunted. "I will run that partial against those names," he said, obviously unconvinced. "And thank you. See? Did that hurt? Don't you want to cooperate with me again? We can be a team! Hooray!"

"I am a-jizz with excitement. Really. So a-jizz I need to hang up now. Get back to me on those plates."

"Roger that."

And Jackson was free to listen to the purring of the cat between his knees and the buzzing in his own skull.

"You unset my alarm," he said, keeping his voice even.

"I did."

"So we talked about *my* faults. Are we going to talk about *yours* now?"

He sent a sideways glance to Ellery, who looked back at him and smiled without guilt. "No. I don't think so."

"*What*?"

"Did I lie to you?"

"No, but—"

"Did I lose my temper?"

"No, but that's not the—"

"Did anything *bad* happen because I let us sleep in?"

Beyond the thundering headache and the wound, Jackson felt more refreshed than he had in weeks. "You suck," he muttered.

"Not last night, because you seduced me from behind."

"Bite me."

"Later. I want you to see the office first, and then we can discuss our game plan."

Jackson growled, and then Ellery leaned against him, dropping a kiss on his bare shoulder.

"And maybe," Ellery continued, "we can try the sex thing again tonight."

Jackson side-eyed him again. "I might be tired tonight."

"I might lie next to you and touch myself while you listen."

"Augh!" Jackson rolled out of bed and was about to stalk to the shower—with full expectation that Ellery would join him and maybe make it up to him—when his phone buzzed again. He stalked back to the dresser and answered it. "Henry?"

"Yeah. Uh...."

"Did I miss an appointment? Were we supposed to do anything today?"

There was an awkward pause. "No. But, uh, I'm bored. I... I mean, I don't have anything to do today. I.... Sometimes I run errands for John and Galen or Davy, but, uh. Do you need any help on the case?"

Jackson blinked and looked at Ellery helplessly. "We're gonna be at the office in two hours. Meet us there—and bring your scrubs."

"Two hours?" Henry asked, sounding puzzled. "Where are you now?"

"About to have really aggressive sex. You want a part of that?"

"Two hours it is!" Henry hung up, and Ellery smiled.

"How aggressive?" he asked, hope lacing his voice.

"Come to the shower and find out."

Ellery's filthy chuckle followed him to the bathroom, and his cock started to throb.

TWO HOURS later, laden with iced coffee and takeout, they pulled up to the office. Jade had beaten them to it, and she and her boyfriend, Mike, were busy bringing in books from Jade's car. Jackson hopped out to help them but was stopped by Mike's critical look.

Mike was actually Jackson's tenant. After Jackson had taken his golden handshaft from SACPD, he'd bought a duplex and rented out the other half. Mike had been living in that other half for a while now, the self-professed redneck from Virginia, the cranky conservative whose heart was as open as the sky and who was constantly trying to figure out how to live a humane and kind life in a world so very different from the one he'd grown up in.

He'd appeared to be the last person in the world Jade would want to be with—until you saw the quiet worship in his farm-boy blue eyes when he looked at her.

"Did you bring some of that for me?" Mike asked as Jackson got out of the car.

"I did, indeed. Here, let me take this up, and I'll be down to help."

"Don't you dare. You look like hell."

Jackson frowned. Mike hadn't said that to him since February. "Hey, I got to sleep in."

"Whatever. Go upstairs and chill. I'm afraid you'll fall over."

"But…," he floundered, looking helplessly at Ellery. "What did you say to him?"

Ellery rolled his eyes. "You've got luggage under your eyes I could ship to Europe, Jackson. One decent night's sleep in a month isn't going to fix that."

Jackson grunted, and for the first time in the last month, he *felt* tired. Not manic, not edgy, just… exhausted. Like banging Ellery over the bathroom sink should have been the climax that led to a nap, not to a full day.

He trudged up the stairs, wondering how he could not have known he was hurting that bad. That moment—that breathless still—of the beautiful thing exploding right by his head and the silence that followed, hit him hard in the gut. He set the coffee on the desk throughway that separated Jade's office space from the reception area and all but ran to Ellery's office.

It was a lovely space, the corner office, with two windows, one toward the street and one toward the great fruitless mulberry tree that grew between this building and the one next to it. The day was slightly less brutal than the previous week, and the sunlight through the green of the leaves looked tranquil and nonthreatening.

Jackson had painted one wall in this room a sort of sea blue—some gray, some green but enough blue that people didn't walk away thinking "What color *was* that wall?" He'd picked out the artwork—an oceanscape done by an artist in San Francisco, and two pictures of the nearby river, with a brilliant sky beyond.

He closed the door behind him and looked at the framed pictures, which had been hung in the past two days, and slowly he sank into the guest chair, which Ellery had chosen to be the most comfortable thing on the planet. There was another one, not so soft, for clients who needed to lean over the desk and didn't want to feel coddled, but this one was the comfort chair, designed to soothe and calm so Ellery's clients felt safe.

If nothing else, Jackson liked to think this chair made it harder to lie.

Jackson's own space—a smaller desk with a chair and a computer—had been set up in the corner, because that's how they'd worked in their last few months at the old firm, and they'd both liked it. They thought well together, when they weren't fucking or fighting, and Jackson loved the way Ellery's mind worked.

Jackson heard a clatter of people coming into the office but stayed put. He and Ellery needed to move the rest of Ellery's law books in, and hang his degrees on the wall too. Ellery had put pictures on the desk already, though—him and his family, and one, reluctantly taken, of him and Jackson in front of his parents' house when Jackson looked like death warmed over, mostly because he *had* been.

"Hey, Riv—" Henry's voice dropped as he stuck his head in and saw Jackson just sitting. "What's up?"

Jackson shook himself slightly. "Nothing. Mike told me I looked like death, and suddenly I felt tired. Weird how that happens."

"Is Mike the guy with the young face and the white hair and beard?"

Jackson smiled. Mike was, in fact, not quite forty-five. Older than him and Jade, but not so much. "Yeah. From Virginia."

"Nice guy," Henry said, and Jackson turned toward him, not seeing a trace of sarcasm.

Well, of course. Mike was learning, Henry was learning—rednecks riding the learning curve. Jackson sort of loved that people could do that. Change and grow and learn, become different people by fixing their own damage.

"He is. He and Jade are good people."

"Yeah. In a million years, I wouldn't have seen her with someone like that, but now you can't unsee it, right?"

Jackson laughed and started to push himself up. "Here, they're going to need some help—"

"They need nothing," Henry said, coming to sit on the smaller straight-backed chair. "AJ got here while we were coming up the stairs, and now everybody's falling on top of each other trying to unpack boxes. I feel sort of bad. We walked in here two days ago and sat on camp stools in your reception area, and I've sort of monopolized your time. You were supposed to be opening a business."

Jackson shrugged. "Yeah, well, you *are* the business."

Henry laughed. "The thing is—I mean aside from the trip to the police department and the finding the dead body—it's been sort of a fun two days."

"Yeah?" Jackson couldn't contain his grin. "Adrenaline junkie."

"Well, *yeah*! I mean I *liked* being in the military, you know? No offices, lots to do, PT was always an option." He let out a sigh. "I was going to get my degree in computers before I got out and found something else to do. I thought I had time, you know? But these last two months, I've been cleaning up the plumbing in the flophouse and giving the guys rides and helping them with their FAFSA.... I'm not saying I haven't been busy but...."

"You're used to having a purpose," Jackson said intuitively.

"Yeah."

Jackson pulled out his phone and started pulling up websites. "You got a laptop at home?"

"Yeah, why?"

"Give me your email. I'm sending you a couple of links."

"To what?" Henry rattled off his email, and Jackson fiddled around a bit.

"To places you can get a criminal justice AA and your PI's license. I mean, the money's okay but not great, and you may find something else you want to do, but in the meantime, you know. It's a thing."

"Yeah," Henry said, his voice full of wonder. "It *is* a thing."

"Sometimes it's a fucking boring thing," Jackson warned. "Stakeouts are the suck. And you started out as a person under suspicion who knows *me*, so that's no good for contacts. Unless you find yourself at a law firm—a good one—you're going to be eyeballs deep in guys banging their mistress or their rent boy or wearing a diaper and a clown suit and getting fed a bottle or whatever—"

"Ew!"

"True story." Jackson shuddered. "Talk about shit you can't unsee. But, you know. Sometimes it's pretty fucking cool. And sometimes it's dangerous, and sometimes it'll break your heart. But nobody said you have to do it, and nobody said forever."

"And right now," Henry said slowly, perusing the website on his phone, "it's a thing that interests me that may eventually get me out of the flophouse and into an apartment of my own."

"Word, brother. Also? If the flophouse ever gets too… hormonal for you? I've got sort of a halfway house for young guys just getting out of jail. I worry about them—I don't oversee them as much as I should, and they need everything from rides to their parole officer's office to help with their student loans. Anyway, I have no money to pay you with, but if you're looking for a place to spend your time where there's not twenty-four-seven man-titty, there's worse ways to go."

"I'd be happy to volunteer some time," Henry said, sounding surprised. "It turns out that babysitting mostly grown young men is sort of a talent of mine."

Jackson chuckled and was going to stand up and go join the living when Ellery came in. "Oh, here you are. Henry, can you give us a minute? Jackson has some plans for you today, but I wanted to talk to him first."

Henry rolled his eyes because Ellery sounded like a supercilious asshole when he asked people to leave, but he hopped up and vacated. "I'll go help…." He waved his hand vaguely. "Whatever they need help with." And then he disappeared.

Jackson went to push himself up—again—when Ellery waved him down. "Mike's right," he said softly. "You look tired."

Jackson let out a sigh. "Last night... last night was a long time coming, wasn't it?"

"It's been the last couple of weeks, yeah. You stopped talking to Rabbi Watson, and... you know. The dreams got worse. We talked about this."

"Yeah. But it didn't hit me—I mean, *really* hit me—about how bad I felt until Mike said something. Then I realized, you know, for a while there, I felt better. We were sleeping through the night a couple of times a week. Every bite wasn't a struggle. I didn't feel triggered by every stupid thing I'd ever run into in the past."

Ellery stood behind him, putting warm hands on his shoulders and dropping a kiss on the top of Jackson's head. "Yeah."

"I owe you that guy."

"You owe me noth—"

"No. I do. I owe you the best guy I can be. I... I guess I wanted things to be easier. For me to get better. For me and you to be together. But... but ignoring shit when it was sliding south only made things worse."

"Last night was not fun," Ellery admitted. "But I saw it coming a mile away. You're not that subtle, you know?"

Jackson closed his eyes. "I'll get up in a minute," he murmured. "We have so much to do."

Ellery wrapped his arms around Jackson's shoulders and brushed soft lips against his ear. "You and I will always have so much to do."

But for this moment, looking at the office he and Ellery had chosen, knowing they were going to do something they both felt was important, it felt like they *were* doing something, indulging in a moment of silence, appreciating the solid world they were trying to build in what they knew to be mostly chaos.

His life was worth something. The man at his back was worth something. The heart to enjoy it—his peace of mind—was worth fighting for.

These were good things to remember when he was running around fighting the good fight. He needed to remember what he was fighting *for*.

EVENTUALLY HE got up and went out to drink his coffee and eat his marzipan pastry (*oh my God, yes!*) and to get a look at the rest of the office. AJ had finished painting the day before, and Jade and Mike were putting the finishing touches on the books Jade used for reference on the shelf behind her. Jade served people from behind the throughway, and her computer, her office supplies, even the office refrigerator, were all her domain, and she had organized it as thoroughly as God's pantry. The furniture—a couch, a love seat, and three end tables—was comfortable, upholstered in navy-and-cream tapestry, and hopefully impervious to stains.

The lamps on the pine end tables had charging stations on them.

It looked… comfy. Not homey, but professional and designed to put people at ease who might not deal with lawyers a lot. Jackson had advocated for the charging stations in the waiting area and the changing station in the bathroom, for the pine furniture and not the oak, for the stain-resistant couches and the navy area rug on top of the deep brown carpet. Warm. Solid. Safe. Jade's office space had a wall done in a playful magenta, and a picture of hers and Jackson's resignation letter from Pfeist, Harrelson, Langdon, and Cooper, Ellery's old firm. The letter featured brightly colored sharpies and their bare asses, so she'd set it up out of sight of the customers—and she had a small tub of toys behind the throughway, including a cheap tablet loaded with kids' games. Sure, the tablet might be the first thing to go—but it might also be the first thing to save the life of a mother who was losing her mind because her oldest had been taken into custody, or the emotional security of the younger sibling whose older brother had gotten popped for drugs.

This was a safe space. This was a space that took people's lives seriously and gave second chances, and Jackson had helped make it that way.

He looked around with appreciative eyes. "Great place," he said. "Too bad Henry and I gotta motor in a few."

"Where you going?" Ellery asked, and Jackson smiled at AJ, who had just walked in the door.

"AJ, do you have hours at Pfinger, Hamster, Whomazoo, and Clopper?"

Ellery snorted. "That's not actually the name of our old firm."

"Is now. So how about it, AJ?"

AJ nodded. "Yeah, I do. I need to be there after lunch, actually."

"Excellent. Ellery is going to provide you with preliminary financials for Robert Sampson and Ash Carver. I need you to have Crystal do a deep dive—in particular, I want to know when Robert Sampson gets his house cleaned and by whom. In the meantime, Henry's going to go get my scrubs out of the car, and we're going to go back to the hospital. Sound good?"

"What are you going to do while I'm stepping and fetching?" Henry asked irritably.

"I'm going to be making a phone call nobody here needs to know about."

There was a collective intake of breath.

Everybody knew who that meant—everybody except Henry, but Henry wasn't stupid.

"I'll just go down to the car," he said. "Keys?"

Ellery threw him the keys to the Lexus, and Henry disappeared.

Everybody in the room took a deep breath because they were all remembering why Jackson and Ellery had spent the last five months in recovery.

In January, they'd gone to San Diego to find the training ground of the monster who had almost killed them both. What they'd discovered was a nest of assassins—and assassins in training—being led by a megalomaniac.

Big stuff for two hometown boys, it was true, and they'd almost lost their lives. Lee Burton—and his psychic boyfriend, Ernie—had been part of the reason they hadn't.

Just knowing a Lee Burton existed was scary shit—shit that they didn't let keep them up at night—because they held on to the fairy-tale hope that guys like Burton were watching out for guys like them.

It was time to put that to the test.

Jackson turned back toward the office, and Jade said, "Jackson, are we in danger?" She and Mike had stopped an assassin in their backyard the last time—in spite of the black ops guys in their living room telling them it would be okay.

Jackson shook his head. "I don't think so. Right now, this guy doesn't know our names. I'm going on a hunch that this is related to what happened down in San Diego—not Sampson, but the cover-up. There were two things going on with that video disaster. One of them is related to Sacramento's newest meth lord, who showed up in February and organized the entire trade."

Everybody nodded soberly.

"I'll let you know what Burton says," he told them, and went back to Ellery's office, Ellery at his heels.

"We didn't agree to this," Ellery said as soon as the door closed.

"You didn't see it coming?"

Ellery paused, thinking. "I had the same suspicions you did. But why not the police?"

Jackson let out a sigh. "Because if this Candy Cormier guy is one of Lacey's trainees, he's out of their league. This will be just like before—we'll stand around waving a flag going, 'Serial killer! Serial killer!' and they'll look at us blankly and go, 'Where?' In the meantime, the meth business is booming, this guy is butchering his errand boys, and if Henry doesn't get charged, Cormier may take business into his own hands and try to kill him off, just to make the case die. And anybody Henry knows or hangs out with will also be in danger."

"Including us," Ellery said.

Honestly, Jackson hadn't thought about that. "Well, I was going to say, including his brother's family and all the porn kids he's trying to take care of, and yeah, Jade and Mike and AJ and us. It's worth it to at least ask, don't you think?"

Jackson had memorized Burton's number and deleted it from his phone because he *was* that paranoid. It picked up on the first ring.

"Rivers?"

"You busy?"

"Not so's you'd notice."

Jackson rolled his eyes. That could mean anything from getting a pedicure to sighting a bad guy down a scope.

"Tell him you're at home, Cruller!" came a voice from somewhere near the phone. "He's trying to be polite."

Jackson heard the chuff of air that meant Burton—one of the toughest badasses Jackson had ever met—had just totally melted under his boyfriend's charm.

"Day off," Burton rasped. "Sorry. Being an asshole comes second nature."

"First nature," Jackson retorted dryly. "Don't let Ernie tell you any different. I've got a name for you—a drug dealer who popped up in our area around February and has organized the meth trade with, and I quote, 'military precision.' And he likes to butcher his errand boys when they let him down."

Burton grunted. "Charming. Give me a name and I'll run it."

"Candy Cormier."

Another grunt. "Fuck. Don't have to run that one. He went rogue when I was behind the scenes. Cormier was his alias—don't worry about his real name. You'll never hear it again."

"Understood. We're trying to get a guy off a murder charge, and Cormier's trying to pin it on him."

"Fuck. Seriously, Rivers, your city is not that awesome. Where did you get the motherfucker magnet? *That's* what I want to know."

Jackson rolled his eyes at Ellery, who was listening in.

"Well, you know, the Kings started winning, and that activated the bad-guy signal. Don't know what to tell you—blame Xander Karcek." Karcek had been forced to retire two years earlier when he'd come out, and his absence had cost their beloved basketball team the championship.

Burton made a hurt sound. "I like Xander Karcek. Him coming out of retirement was the best thing on the planet. I'd rather blame you."

"Sure, you do that. But in the meantime, should we tell the cops about this guy—"

"No," Burton muttered. "I'll take care of it. Give me a couple of days—forgiveness/permission, whatever—and then stay the fuck away from him. Unless he's chasing you, and then feel free to kill him for me, because I was enjoying my weekend."

"I'd really rather leave the killing to you," Jackson said sourly. The two assholes he'd taken out in January were eating at his stomach lining daily.

"Which is why I trust you with it if you have to do it," Burton said, all of the irritation gone from his voice. "Just… you know. Do what you have to do to clear your guy. Did Cormier kill your vic?"

"Maybe? We're trying to figure out who, but Cormier wanted our client framed for it. We've run into two of his goons so far, trying to pin shit on our guy."

"You, uh, may want to check your local morgue to see if those guys got an emergency relocation shiv through their guts. I'm just saying."

Jackson growled. "Oh Jesus—can't you keep these assholes in a cage?"

"I'm doing my best here!" But Burton was laughing as he said it, and yes, Jackson felt marginally better.

"Well, we do appreciate your service. Like, personally. We appreciate all your help."

"Ugh. No sincerity, Rivers. Ernie just made me my favorite donut, and I'm about to enjoy the shit out of it before I plan me a little day trip."

"Sounds amazing—"

"Tell him to fucking eat something," Ernie said, and Jackson grimaced. Psychics. Wonderful people. Irritating as friends.

"I had a pastry," Jackson said with dignity. "And now it's time for me to sign off before my client starts getting antsy."

"Let him wait," Burton told him through a full mouth. "I mean, what? The victim's going to get more dead?"

"Tell him I'll send him donuts!" Ernie said again. "You can bring him a dozen, right?"

Burton groaned. "Baby, there's transpo and—"

"And I'll wrap them super good. Please, Cruller?"

Jackson smiled fondly. Ernie was not, in fact, a feckless child, as his conversation might imply. He was mostly an open nerve, and the people he cared about played about his psyche like a wind chime. For some reason, he'd decided Jackson was one of those people, and he delighted in doing things for him.

The last time Ellery's mother had stayed for a while, a pastry box had appeared at their door, with the words *Don't throw it away, I'll know* written on top.

The box had contained apple fritters—Ellery's mother's favorite.

"Sure, baby. The things I do for you."

"After you eat your donut, Cruller," Ernie replied smugly, and Jackson figured it was time to get off the phone.

"Thanks, guys," he said, meaning it. "I'll keep the investigation away from Cormier, and, uh, keep an eye out for a pink pastry box."

"We won't let you down!" Ernie practically sang.

"I may or may not warn you when I'm in town," Burton told him gruffly. "Try not to get dead."

He hung up, and Jackson and Ellery both gave a big sigh.

"You okay with that?" Jackson asked him quietly.

Ellery shrugged. "If it means we have a better chance of surviving this case with our skin intact? Sure. I'm great."

Jackson scowled. "Ellery...."

Ellery gave him a shaky smile. "Look, I know you're torturing yourself over what happened down south, but I'll be honest. It all feels... like fantasy to me. I don't *feel* like what's probably going to happen is going to happen. I *feel* like I want to see what kind of donuts Ernie makes for us this time. Everything else makes my head explode. Literally, the call to Burton is *your* call, and I stand by that decision. Is that okay?"

Jackson thought about the last guy they'd tracked down that Lacey had trained, and shuddered.

"It's good to have help," he said softly. "You know?"

Ellery nodded. "I'll hold you to that. Go meet up with Henry. By the way, why do you need to know who cleans Sampson's house?"

Jackson gave a wolfish grin. "Because nobody knows you like the people who clean your house, Ellery. Don't you think?"

Their last cleaning service had planted a bug in their bedroom. Both of them shuddered, and Ellery waved him off. "You know what? I don't want to know."

"You will if it gets us evidence," Jackson told him. And then, because Ellery was right there, because they were still standing close because of the phone call, and because he felt like they'd cleared a tremendous hurdle together and come down true on the other side, Jackson kissed him.

Ellery responded immediately, open mouth, hands grabbing Jackson's backside, body lined up, groin to groin and chest to chest.

Jackson moaned a little and squeezed Ellery's ass back before he pulled away.

"You are such a tease," he muttered, and Ellery laughed.

"Go have fun and play nice with the other kids," he said, but Jackson caught the hint of worry behind the smile.

"Ellery, you know that you're worth coming home to, right?"

Ellery kissed him briefly, then stepped back. "Glad to hear it. Go. Believe it or not, I've got an appointment for another case at two o'clock."

"Oh wow! Hustle, hustle, hustle!"

Ellery shook his head. "A referral from Pf—"

"Pfinger, Hamster, Whatwhazit, and Clopper?"

Ellery snorted, then waved his hand. "Go!"

"Seriously," Jackson said, moving toward the door. "Be wary of anything they throw you, Ellery. You know they had that policy of only taking cases they could win."

Ellery nodded grimly. "Yeah. Yeah, I know. It's a prelim. I'll brief you tonight."

Jackson winked. "I'll be there. And, uh, the place looks great, Ellery. You, uh, should be proud to greet people here."

Ellery didn't smile back. "I had a great decorator."

"Yeah, your mother!"

"Hey, Jackson—"

But Jackson was out the door.

Fish of Darkness

ELLERY WONDERED whether or not he should smile at the man sitting in the overstuffed chair across from him, and decided against it.

Charlie Cabot was wearing a gold-colored wool suit, with a plum waistcoat and matching fedora, with the brightest, shiniest wingtips Ellery had ever seen. His dark blond hair was oiled back, and his face—a mostly white complexion with green eyes, a decisive nose, high cheekbones, and full lips—was as expressionless as Ellery had ever seen in the courtroom.

Only Charlie's eyes gave him away.

He was terrified, but not for himself.

"Please, Mr. Cramer, the other place wouldn't do this for me. I need your help."

Ellery gnawed his lip and wished Jackson was here. "This is a highly unusual request, Mr. Cabot," he said delicately. "You say you didn't do the crime?"

"My nephew, Andre, see, he's sort of… well, innocent. A real sweetheart of a kid. And, uh, well, gay. Which is why I picked you, after the other place recommended you, because, well, word is you're gay, and you'd understand. Andre, he's… he's picked on a lot. And this kid—punk asshole of a kid—gave him a brick of meth to carry. 'Just carry it, Andre. I got a buddy who'll get it from you!' But the buddy was a cop, and the punk asshole knew it, and this was a way for him not to get caught. So Andre, who just turned eighteen and graduated from high school and is going to college and who's got no idea that his Uncle Charlie's a gangster, right? He's suddenly up the creek while the DA tries to shake him down for who gave him the fuckin' drugs. But I know the punk asshole who gave them to him, and he works for Candy Cormier, and if Andre squeals on him, he's…."

Ellery nodded. Well, he and Jackson had been out of the game for a few months—they would have heard of Cormier before now, apparently, if they'd been involved.

"I've heard of him," Ellery said, his throat dry. What was he going to do? Advise his client to hold on to his wad and hope the wheels of justice turned more slowly than the government assassin who was just waiting for donuts? "But why pin it on you? Why not let me try to get him off?"

"'Cause any jail time is too much for him," Charlie said, voice cracking. "We sprung him on bail, and his face was bruised, and... and he wasn't walking right, and his mom had to take him to the hospital. He wasn't raped—not this time—but you know it's coming if he goes back. He's not cut out for the joint, and I don't want him to be. Now me? I already got five years under my belt, but it was my first strike. Possession with intent to distribute. If you could talk that down to five years, I'd serve it with a fuckin' smile, as long as we could keep that kid out of jail for one more goddamned day, okay?"

Ellery nodded. "I'll take the case," he said thoughtfully. "But give me a couple of days. I'm going to stall the arraignment for a week while I dig up some dirt on Cormier—"

"He's a butcher," Cabot said grimly. "Now me, I got my little setup, I got my street corners, and I ain't got no excuse and no apologies. But this guy—I've seen his people when he gets through with them. I... I'm not a good man. But this kid, he's the one good thing in my family. If you can keep him out of jail, I'll keep him off the fuckin' street, you understand?"

Ugh. And *this* was probably why Carlyle Langdon had turned him down. Because Charlie Cabot was a drug dealer, pure and simple, and there was no way to make that better.

"I'll do it for half the fee," Ellery said, because who needed to work in the black, right? "On one condition."

Cabot raised his eyebrows. "Anything."

"If I keep you and your nephew out of jail, you have to spend one day a week volunteering at the local rehab clinic—"

"How long I gotta do *that*?"

"Six months."

"I'd rather do it for the full goddamned fee! What, do I look like Mother Teresa?"

Ellery narrowed his eyes. "No, you look like a guy who said you'd do anything to keep his nephew out of jail. This is anything, Mr. Cabot. Take it or leave it."

The internal struggle was epic and painful to watch. Ellery took a sip of his iced tea as he waited. Finally, Cabot grunted.

"Can you guarantee you'll keep the kid out of jail?"

"Can you guarantee he won't end up on the streets knowing what his uncle does for a living?"

Cabot grunted again. "Hunh."

Ellery hated that fucking word—but usually only when Jackson was using it. "And?"

"Deal."

"I'll have my paralegal draw up some papers—"

"Hey, speaking of her. Is she single?"

Ellery widened his eyes. "No, and she's out of your league."

"Yeah, I know, but a guy can ask." Cabot looked crestfallen, but Ellery had no pity.

"She's my boyfriend's sister. I suggest you don't."

He swore. "Dammit. So where do I sign?"

AN HOUR later—after Jade had amended their usual payment agreement to Ellery's specifications—Cabot was gone and Jade was sitting in the comfortable chair.

"So that was new," she said, sounding skeptical.

"Well, he offered to go to prison for his nephew. I know he's a scumbag, but I thought this would be a good compromise." Ellery was still not sure he'd done the right thing. Being the boss was harder than he'd thought.

"Well, I thought it was pretty damned clever," Jade said, with a sip of her own iced tea. "And not a bad way to start the business."

"I thought Henry was the start of the business."

She snorted. "No. Henry was the start of Jackson having a partner. That's what Henry was the start of. Not that I object. I think he's been knocking around on his own for way too long, but I don't care what we're making on Henry's case—"

"Enough to pay our first two month's rent, plus a retainer for any Johnnies' criminal cases in the future," Ellery said dryly.

"Oh. Well. In that case, I *do* care what we're making on Henry's case because money is good and rent is also good and I'm kind of partial to food. But I'm saying Jackson was supposed to be partnered up on the force, and we both know how well *that* turned out."

"I thought I was his partner," Ellery said, absurdly hurt.

Jade gave him a fond look. "Oh, baby, you and Jackson are going to be solving cases together for the rest of your lives. But you're needed on the paper end of things, because what you just did with that Cabot guy was pretty cool, and Jackson would be the first to tell you that drawing up all that paperwork would make him stupid with boredom. What Jackson's doing, getting all dressed up like medical personnel to try to save Henry's stupid ass and fix the world, isn't for you. You would just get the two of you shot, and you know that."

Ellery let out a sigh. "Last time I had a gun in my hand, it didn't end well," he admitted.

Jade grimaced. "It's not like Jackson carries one much anyway. But you understand what I'm saying."

"He's like a cop," Ellery said, getting it, all hurt aside.

"Yes. And now he's not alone and you're not worried."

Ellery poked that idea with a careful finger, surprised when it didn't ache like he thought it would. "We don't have enough money to pay Henry, you know."

"Well, to get his license, he needs to get an AA in criminal justice anyway. And yeah, we need to pay AJ first. But at this point, I think Henry's along for the ride. He'll probably help Jackson out on the exciting stuff just for the experience. Once you pick up another partner—"

"What do you mean *another* partner?" Ellery frowned at her, and she rolled her eyes.

"Oh, honey, do you really not see where this is going?"

Ellery stared back, and Jade snorted. "Let me know when it hits you. I'm going to go get you some cookies, because obviously you're low on blood sugar."

She left, and Ellery tried to figure out what she meant and couldn't. Restlessly, because he was used to balancing thirty cases a week, he picked up his phone and texted Jackson.

Are you dead or in prison yet?

Nope. Want me to be?

Nope. Just curious. What are you doing?

Hiding in a broom closet. May need to bail soon.

Ellery stared. *You're kidding, right?*

Jackson sent him a picture of a dark and cluttered space that looked very much like a broom closet.

Where's Henry?

Employee bathroom. Don't get your panties in a knot, Counselor— no bad guys with guns, just listening.

To what?

Robert Sampson assfucking Summer Frasier against the adjoining wall.

Ellery sat completely up in his seat and gave his phone a double take. *No, seriously.*

Seriously.

How do you know it's assfucking? Because women had another orifice for that sort of thing.

Because she was in the middle of "Oh baby," when she suddenly went, "Lube, Robbie—please?"

What an asshole! Because seriously!

I haven't seen hers, but I'm thinking he's a walking sphincter myself.

Did you learn anything other than he's cheating on his wife?

There was a pause, and Ellery got up and started to pace restlessly. He *should* be putting the final signatures on his commercial paperwork for running a business or setting up computer ads to run in the local law journals, but he could do that stuff when Jackson was no longer in a broom closet.

Suddenly his phone blew up with pictures.

There was the picture he'd sent before—the screenshot from the medical tablet with the medication that should have gone to the patient but had ended up in Summer's pocket. There was a picture of cases of medical prescription forms with different numbers on the corner than the medical tablet, and there was a picture taken inside the broom closet of boxes upon boxes of brown bottles, unmarked, with what looked like a variety of pills inside.

We THINK that they're going at it from both ends. She's stealing from the patients, and he's writing prescriptions from his partner's script pads, then they're putting them in bottles and distributing. Martin was one point of distribution, but Robert has others. Still don't know who offed Martin, but we have enough evidence to have Daddy arrested on drugs.

Ellery caught his breath as he saw the evidence, and then realized why Jackson was still in the broom closet.

But that won't get Henry off.

Nope. Won't even get him hard.

Ellery rolled his eyes. *I don't want to know what gets him hard, do you?*

Already know. A med student with a gym-bred chest—it's revolting. I like my meat stringier and meaner. Wanna bite me tonight?

Dear Lord. *Always, but you need to get out of the broom closet.*

"Oh baby. Oh baby. Harder. Harder. Harder, you prick, I'm getting dry! Jesus, can you fucking come already? Yes! Yes! Yes! Thank you, do you have a wipe?"

Ellery snickered, feeling about fourteen years old. *She's not really saying that, is she?*

No, but if she's happy about what they're doing, I'm not feeling it.

If she's not happy about it, why are they doing it?

For a moment, his phone was still except for the little bubbles indicating texting.

I get the feeling she was manipulated into it. She's not conventionally attractive—she had the keys to the drug cabinet and the means to fuck with the orders. He played on that.

Ellery grimaced. Well, Jackson had told him Dave and Alex thought she hated men. Maybe there was a reason for that.

Nice. But why? Ellery frowned. *His reported income seems decent. Nothing he's doing seems to be outside of that. He's got the nice house in uptown, and he only had the one kid who didn't seem like too much of a drain. What's his problem?*

Not sure. Waiting for Crystal's deep dive.

Do you have any idea who else is in distribution? Ellery was curious. One did not build a drug empire around one guy on the streets.

I'm wondering. It's not the porn kids—they all have to pee in a cup before they fuck. It's not the nurses, for the same reason. Does our doctor have any hobbies that put him in touch with people who might want to distribute? Does he check out pill bottles to "patients" and take a cut? These are things I'd very much like to know.

Ellery was going to speculate some more, when his phone flashed again.

GTG

Gotta go. Apparently the break in the closet was over and Jackson's work was back on track again. Ellery was ever so curious as to what he might find.

JACKSON AND Henry showed up at the office around six o'clock, both of them thoughtful and talking quietly as though chewing something over. They came through the door, and Jackson greeted Ellery with an unselfconscious kiss, and then pulled back, frowning.

"Wait, I can't do that when you're open for real, right? I mean, that's unprofessional. Wives don't do that to their husbands and all that—"

He was still dressed in his scrubs, and he smelled like heat and sweat and the wind that had sprung up that afternoon, pushing away some of the humidity. Ellery took his chin and pulled him into a harder, longer, more body-intensive kiss, and practically purred in satisfaction when the kiss ended and Jackson looked a little dazed.

"If they want me to represent them, they need to be okay with it," Ellery said, unruffled. "Now you guys are here early—what happened?"

"I finally got out of the broom closet," Jackson muttered, and Ellery noted the secondary smell of dust and pine-scented cleaner. Henry chortled, and Jackson sent him a sour look. "Just because some of us were literally taking a leak when the fun stuff went down—"

"That was not my fault!" Henry said, holding up his hands. "Oh my God, and it wasn't my fault they took an *hour* having sex either. That's not a quickie! Who taught them how to have an affair!"

Jackson snorted. "Well, if you didn't write a manual, you can't complain when people do it wrong."

Henry rolled his eyes, but his cheeks pinkened, and Ellery got the feeling he actually needed to be poked about this. Sometimes getting the worst thing you'd ever done out in the air made it not quite the worst thing in the world. "I was supposed to write a manual? Now you tell me, after I force flushed all the really important things."

"You can't do that!" Jackson complained. "You can't just *erase* your... twenties... like they never ex... shit."

"What?" Ellery, Jade, and Henry all looked at him excitedly, because it was obvious Jackson had had sort of a breakthrough.

"We've been trying to figure out Sampson's father, and we've had a glimpse of what Martin was like before he died, but we don't know what he was like, really, before prison. What was he like before he got John strung out? I mean, he dated your brother, right?"

Henry nodded. "Yeah."

"How long?"

Henry frowned thoughtfully. "I'm not sure—long enough to make an impression, I guess. Kane *hates* the guy, but Davy, he mostly feels bad. He feels like he should have seen who he was sooner."

"But maybe…." Jackson let out a breath. "Maybe he saw the good parts. Everybody has them. Maybe in order to know how he ended up in the trash can, we need to know who he was before he was headed there. Think your brother will talk to us?"

Henry grimaced. "I can call him," he said reluctantly. "I mean, I hate to drag up past history and—"

"And he's your brother," Jade said, flickering a look at Jackson. "He'll do it, for no other reason than you asked."

"Fine." He nodded toward Ellery's office. "Is it okay if I use your office?"

Ellery nodded, his heart going out to the kid. "Sure."

HENRY GAVE them the address, and Ellery and Jackson followed him in Ellery's Lexus.

"Looks a douche move to me," Jackson muttered. "His brother's just finishing dinner, settling down for the evening, and we pull up in a Lexus?"

"Whine, whine, whine—crank up the air-conditioning, your hot air is heating up my car."

Jackson grinned. "You must have had a good day!"

Ellery told him about Andre and Charlie Cabot, and Jackson blew out a whistle.

"That's rough. I like the way you handled it, but maybe next time, let me do some running before you make that deal."

"Did you hear what I told you?" Ellery asked, remembering the description of the kid getting out of jail.

"Yeah, I heard. And I'm not saying you shouldn't try to keep the kid out of jail, but let me do some legwork on Cabot to make sure he's not going to come back and murder you if this goes south. I get you want to do good work, Ellery, but sometimes the bad guys really *are* bad."

Ellery grimaced. Yeah, it was tempting to think Jackson was the only one who tried to rescue kittens out of trees. "Sorry. I'm still getting used to not having you hand me a folder of information before I'm even assigned the case."

"Well, that really only happened with you, you know."

"No!" Jackson's efficiency was legendary—Ellery hadn't been the only one clamoring for his skills at their old firm, even before Ellery had sort of co-opted him into his life.

"Well, not everybody wanted the same thing. Langdon liked to give me an annotated list. Pfeist used to expect me to tell him how to win the case. Harrelson, Cooper, and that little upstart hired after you—"

"Morgan?"

"Yeah—that guy? They used to assess the case as a plea bargain before they even knew if they could win it."

"Lots of lawyers do that," Ellery defended. He hadn't liked to.

"But not you. You wanted a complete file, so a complete file you got."

Ellery smiled a little. "I was sort of hoping it was because you liked me a little."

"I thought you were a persnickety asshole, but you did rock the power suit, and I was not immune."

"Oh yeah." Ellery nodded. "You liked me." He sobered before Jackson could respond. "How about from now on, I give you two days to research before I meet with a client. How's that?"

"That's fair. Tell Jade. She's good at that."

He sounded so confident—like it was so easy to just nail down office policy on a drive to work on a case. "Do you know anything about Cabot?"

"Yeah—actually yeah. He's a drug dealer, but so far there are no bodies at his doorstep, and his boys stay away from schools, which is a rare thing and a point in his favor. I mean, he's a criminal, but I think your assessment was sound. He wants to do the right thing for this particular person. You want him to do the right thing for everybody. Let's keep his boy out of jail, and we'll see how the rest washes out."

Ellery let out a breath, surprised at how much he'd needed to hear Jackson agree with what he'd done. Funny how Jackson thought he owed it to be the best person possible for *him*, when Ellery was working hard to be a better person for *Jackson*. A year ago, Ellery wouldn't have made that deal with Cabot. A year ago, he'd have taken Cabot's money, gotten the kid out of jail, and looked the other way.

"We can hope," Ellery said, because wasn't that why they did what they did?

"'Course we can. Uh...." Jackson gave that particularly uncomfortable grimace that indicated he was thinking about money. "You, uh, never talk about how long we have to make this little business work. I mean, I get you got a two-year settlement from your firm, and you're not exactly hurting, but—"

"Theoretically, if it was just you and me, my trust fund could keep us afloat until retirement," Ellery said. "But besides wanting someone like Jade on my staff, or wanting to hire AJ or Henry and be able to pay them, I'd be really embarrassed if that happened. I mean, my sister just figured out a new way to operate on cancer patients that doesn't rip a person's body open quite so badly. So it would be *great* if I could, you know, be that sort of genius."

For a moment he couldn't identify the sound coming out of Jackson's mouth. Then it hit him.

Laughter.

DAVID WORRALL and Carlos Ramirez's place was a nice little two-bedroom house, close enough to the college to not cost a fortune, but near enough to midtown not to be in a crappy neighborhood either. The outside was tan stucco, and the lawn in front was watered and neatly kept, with new paving stones and a new driveway showing that the place was maintained fairly regularly.

A giant black Navigator was parked in front of the garage, as well as the newer, more subdued sedan Henry had driven in to the office. Ellery wondered if his own home had ever looked quite as normal.

They got out, and Henry cocked his head, smiling a little. "They're in the backyard," he said. "Playing with the turtles."

Jackson's eyes got big. "We get to see the turtles? Do you think we can see the iguana?"

Henry just laughed. "God, yes. You can see through the glass wall in the house!"

"Cool!" He sounded just like a little kid, which charmed Ellery to no end. Meeting all of the reptiles did not fill Ellery with nearly so much glee.

They followed Henry through a six-foot-tall wooden gate into a medium-sized backyard dominated by a giant shade tree. Dug out between the roots and lined with brick sat an outdoor terrarium, with running water, plenty of shade, and a rock in the middle where an indulgent turtle might sun himself.

As one was doing as they entered. And Jackson was not the only one to notice.

"He's sunning!" said a little girl, who was maybe six, and tiny. She had pointed features with a hint of bronze in her skin and enormous brown eyes, and she crouched over the terrarium in a bright pink bathing suit, with her brown hair in a bobbing little ponytail at the back of her head.

"Is he sunning?" Henry asked, and it was like watching a theater performer drop his mask. "Frances, this is my friend Jackson and his friend Ellery. Can you tell us the turtles' names?"

"This one is Flower," she said, pointing to the one on the rock.

"What's the other one?" Jackson asked, squatting down next to her.

"That one's Flower too. All the turtles are Flowers because they all try to give flowers to each other."

"Heh heh heh... Bunny, you know we don't like to talk about the turtle flowers."

Ellery looked up to see one of the most beautiful men in the world. His hair was a wheat gold, his eyes wide and blue and innocent, and he had a mouth like a little cupid's bow. He was built rangy and lean, but his biceps and chest bulged through his T-shirt like someone who really cared for his body, and his thighs under his cargo shorts were works of art. As he set down the ice chest he was carrying and held out his arms for the little girl to hop into, Ellery had the wholly inappropriate thought that he'd like to do the same.

Next to him, Jackson cleared his throat. "You're drooling, Counselor."

Oh, how embarrassing. "I'm so sorry," he said, trying to hold on to the social niceties. "We didn't mean to barge in. I'm Ellery Cramer and—"

"And he was totally boning on you, Dexter." If David Worrall—because that must have been Henry's brother who had just emerged from the house—was the most beautiful man Ellery had ever seen, Carlos Ramirez was the biggest ball of testosterone he'd ever been subjected to.

Dark-haired, dark-eyed, with a jaw carved from granite and shoulders as wide as a car, Carlos Ramirez looked like he could crush a man into the ground with one casual swing of his fist. But as it was, he took the little girl from his husband and rubbed noses with her, making her giggle.

"He totally was," Jackson said, smirking. "You'll have to forgive him, guys. He's usually better trained than that." Jackson extended his hand. "Jackson Rivers—pleased to meet you."

David and Carlos shook hands with them while Henry took the little girl from Carlos and crouched down and talked to her about the two turtles named Flower.

"So, Flower?" Jackson said, one eyebrow arched, and to Ellery's surprise, both men—men who had probably been front and center, naked and fucking, on the Johnnies website in their younger years—turned a dull red.

"It's a… thing," Carlos said. "It's… it's a thing they do. When they're, uh… mating."

David squeezed his eyes shut. "Oh my God." He cast a quick look at Frances to make sure she was engaged with his brother, then dropped his voice conspiratorially. "Turtle dicks look like giant black flowers. It's *totally gross*. And we've been trying to explain this to her teachers for the last two years. That's two teacher conferences so far where we're giving turtle anatomy lessons, and teachers are patting us on the head because why would two men think they could raise a little girl anyway!"

Jackson covered his mouth, palm out, and smothered his laugh, and suddenly Ellery wasn't looking at David Worrall anymore.

"That's hysterical," Jackson sputtered. "Oh my God. I'm gonna be telling my brother that—he's got three kids and two giant dogs now. And he thinks *he's* got it rough."

"Dogs?" David said wistfully. "What kind of dogs?"

"They're American boxer-Labrador retriever mixes," Jackson said, and Ellery grimaced. Kaden and Rhonda had gotten the dogs for protection after bad guys had infiltrated their house last winter. Each one was roughly the size of a Honda Accord. "They're not fully grown yet," Jackson continued, "but they might end up being hundred-and-fifty-pound dogs."

"Really?" Suddenly Carlos was interested. "I never knew dogs got that big! Dexter—"

David Worrall's shoulders slumped. "Baby, your turtles are gonna break our house. I wouldn't mind something furry besides the bunny either, but, you know…."

"Grown-up things." For the first time, Ellery realized that Carlos was maybe ten years younger than his husband, and something pulled inside him. These were young men, dealing with this very little girl and all her pets and their own porn-star past.

"How's the bunny do with all the other animals?" Jackson asked, and Carlos grimaced.

"We had to move him out of Frances's room," he said, and nudged Jackson to look into the big picture window that protruded from the outside of the house. "See? Mrs. Darcy the iguana and Tomas the snake get along pretty well together, but any furry thing we put in that room thinks they're gonna be dinner. Poor thing was going bald."

And then Jackson, who had been almost incandescent with joy at the turtles, practically exploded. "A snake! Oh my God! Ellery, they've got a snake! And the iguana! Look at that!"

"It's a big sleeping lizard," Ellery said, trying to contain his horror. The glass enclosure looked two ways. That little girl was apparently comfortable sleeping with a ginormous scaly lizard.

"Yeah," David muttered, giving his husband a covert glance. "And a snake that's got a thing for my balls."

Ellery stared at him, feeling his equipment shrivel at the thought.

David Worrall nodded as though it was exactly as awful as Ellery was picturing. "I'm saying."

Carlos looked up from the window, face alight with joy that he'd found someone to share his pets with, and David gave him sort of a besotted smile.

"So, uh, Mr. Rivers, you got any pets of your own?"

"We have a cat," Jackson said, staring at the iguana with pure lust in his eyes. "He's sort of a furry food vacuum. We like him."

David had been honest with Ellery, so he thought he'd return the favor. Sub voce, he murmured, "Three legs, missing teeth, and missing parts of both ears."

The naked gratitude on David's face was his reward. "You understand," he murmured, and Ellery nodded.

Yeah, he got men who loved things that other people might find unlovable. He knew what it was like to love that guy, and how you'd change the shape of the world, or the shape of your house, to make them light up like the sun.

After a moment of quiet, during which neither Jackson nor Carlos seemed to notice time passing, David looked at Ellery with regret on his face. "So, I understand you guys might need to ask some stuff?"

Damn. Ellery really had been enjoying himself.

"Yeah. Maybe have Henry take the little girl inside?"

David nodded. "Yeah. Henry—"

"On it!" Henry whirled with Frances in his arms. "C'mon, bunny. Want to help me make the fruit salad?"

"But Unca Kane already chopped up the fruit!" she protested.

"Yeah, but has he added the Cool Whip and yogurt?"

"You can *do* that?"

Henry called to his brother. "You *do* have Cool Whip and yogurt, right? I'm not going to have to make this up as I go along?"

David grimaced. "Yeah, yeah—don't get used to fake whipped cream in our refrigerator, though, okay?"

"I won't get used to it," Henry said to Frances. "I'll just bring it myself."

Frances erupted into giggles, and the two disappeared into the house.

"There's also sandwiches to make," David said. "I just bought us about twenty minutes, and then you're welcome to join us for dinner."

"That's not nece—" Jackson said, popping up from his animal trance to be his usual no-debt self.

"That would be great," Ellery said rashly. "As long as you still want us here after this super uncomfortable conversation, we'd be honored."

"Didja hear that, Dexter?" Carlos said, happy as a puppy. "We got company for dinner that's not just your stiff-necked brother."

David grimaced. "Carlos and Henry. Not great friends."

Jackson grew from enchanted kid to somber adult in less than a heartbeat. "They both have reason, I would imagine."

"How much has he told you?" David tilted his head carefully, and Ellery recognized the universal need not to tell tales on your brother.

"He told me why he left the military," Jackson said, "and what sort of shape he was in when he came knocking on your door."

Carlos shifted, looking uncomfortable. "Yeah, that was the only reason I didn't kick him out, I'll be honest." His jaw hardened. "Dexter's dad is a piece of fuckin' work."

"That's not what they're here to talk about, though, is it?" David said quietly. "You need to know about Scott."

Carlos shook his head. "Dexter, do I have to be here for this? I'd literally rather help your brother cook dinner, and you know that's fuckin' somethin'."

David nodded quietly. "Here, let's go get a drink." He paused, and as Ellery and Jackson were heading for the table, Ellery saw David put his hand on the small of his husband's back, talking softly. Carlos nodded and kissed his beloved on the cheek, the moment so pure, so honest, Ellery had to look away.

"Ellery," Jackson said, pulling his attention that direction, "we've got beer, water, and soda—preferences?"

"Water," he said primly, while Jackson dug out a root beer and two waters, one of which he handed to David as he walked up, then handed the other to Ellery.

"So," David said, sitting heavily at the table. "Scott."

"Yeah." Jackson looked at Ellery and then shrugged. "So, I have these nightmares," he said out of the blue, and Ellery stared at him, surprised by the change of subject. "Like, all sorts of shit. If you're interested in what, read the papers. I'm sure there's microfiche and a whole file on the internet. Anyway, for years—like eight years of my life—I'd find someone, anyone, male, female, whatever, to sleep with, because I knew if there was a body in my bed, I wouldn't scream. I'd still have shitty dreams, but nine times out of ten, I wouldn't wake my neighbor up, sounding like I was being gutted in my sleep."

David blinked slowly, but he didn't look surprised.

"How'd you make them stop?" he asked softly.

"I haven't yet," Jackson said, glancing at Ellery. "But now I only have one guy, and he knows what my demons are. And when I scream, he tackles me on the bed and keeps me from falling. It's not a perfect system—it might not ever be. But it's… better. It's better than all the different bodies, staying friends with a thousand different lovers, never getting close. We all have our damage, you know? And in our twenties, when we got more come than sense, we're not always great at trying to fix it."

David Worrall nodded, getting the hint. He took a swig of water and started to speak.

"I lost my first lover in a car wreck when we were eighteen and nobody knew about us. So I tried to pretend it never happened and I wasn't really gay, but a kinky girlfriend suggested porn, and that seemed like a great compromise. I took his name as my porn name, so it's always a part of me."

Ah, Ellery thought. Dexter.

"And for years, I kept having girlfriends and fucking guys on camera and wanting something more. And then this hot guy, a guy I'd fucked a couple of times, feeds me a line about how relationships are for suckers, and I buy it. I buy into it for a year, while he goes to school and tells me I can just keep fucking for a living. I buy into it while I break up with my girlfriend—which was a good thing—and he keeps me on a string. I buy into it until I'm staying home at night hoping he texts, and I realize that I'm *in* a relationship, and it's breaking my heart, because he's fucking his daddy's pick for mail-order bride and giving me a booty call now and then. So I break up with him—" David looked fondly in the direction of the house. "—with a little help from a friend. And it turned out the friend was the guy I'd been looking for all along. But in the meantime, this first guy, Scott, is suddenly acting like I've wrecked him. And he starts doing these really… *really* shitty things. John's coke habit was like once a month until Scott started giving him some every night, to hook him for real. He sleeps with the receptionist and knocks her up and then hands her money for an abortion. When she doesn't get it, he breaks all the windows in her house. He tells John he's going to take the business—the business I helped build on my knees, and I'm not ashamed to say it—if I don't fuck him on camera one last goddamned time. And the whole time I'm wondering where that guy I fell for was. That guy I loved, he could be kind, for no reason. He'd go to the college tutoring center to help kids who had trouble. He…."

David aimed a compassionate glance at Jackson, who had just spilled something really personal in order to make him feel like he wasn't alone… and finished the sentence.

"He had bad dreams. When he called me up after seeing his girlfriend, he'd come over in tears because he knew what we were doing was no good. He'd surprise me with flowers one minute and tell me that flowers were a crock the next. He'd tell me his father was a raging hypocrite one day and leave mid blowjob when the guy texted him to come home." He shook his head. "He'd wake up from a dead sleep screaming 'Daddy, stop.'"

Ellery made an *oolf* sound, but Jackson didn't look the least bit surprised. He waited a moment while David caught his breath.

"Did he ever say anything else about that?"

David shook his head. "No. No. But...." He grimaced. "Look, I know how this is going to sound. He was blackmailing John, threatening to take away the company. It's how Kane—Carlos—and I still make our living, just not in front of the camera. We had nearly two hundred employees working for us, and some of us were like Kane. He started doing porn to pay Frances's medical bills because his sister didn't have insurance. I don't care what you think about porn—"

"It's a service," Jackson said bluntly. "Just like any other product. You can cook in a shitty restaurant with giant cockroaches or you can cook cordon bleu. You can run a crappy porn shop full of drugs and disease and exploited employees, or you can take care of your people and put out a quality product."

David nodded soberly. "Everybody—*everybody*—has health and dental. The good plan. We're offering employee stock options. We've got a life-after program for the guys who aren't smart about going to school and finding a different living. It's a good place. I'm proud of it. And Scott was going to take it away and break it up if I didn't film another scene with him." He closed his eyes and swallowed. "But I was... I was out. I couldn't do it anymore. Everyone hits their out button, you know? And Kane was still in. He took my spot. And Kane—man, he didn't even fuck him. He just... dominated him. I can't explain it, except that there was a thing in Scott that needed a daddy that fucking bad."

Ellery let out a shaky breath. "His father...?"

"I'm almost sure of it," David said. "I've seen submissive guys before—healthy submissives, and they're strong and kind and all the good things in and out of the bedroom. But Scott wasn't healthy. He was cruel when he topped, in porn anyway. And he was... frightening when he bottomed. Creepy."

"Reg said he'd fuck your earhole if you didn't cover it up," Jackson said. Ellery was pleased to see that bring out a slight smile on David Worrall's beautiful face.

"Reg filmed a few scenes with him too." Suddenly he was right there in the present. "And I can't thank you guys enough for what you did for them two days ago. Bobby's gotten a raw deal from the cops before. Reg hasn't stopped singing your praises." He looked thoughtful. "And he told us about your nightmare that night too."

Jackson laughed, but it didn't sound natural. "Yeah, well, like I said, the system's not perfect. Is there anything else you can tell us about Scott? We know he switched from coke to pills—any take on that?"

David wrinkled his nose. "He said once that coke was a rich-boy's drug. If he was hurting, he'd hit up Daddy for oxy."

They were all quiet for a moment, and Ellery's stomach roiled. Apparently, Scott, aka Martin Sampson, had been hurting all his life.

"Is that all?" David cast a quick glance to the sliding glass door, where Henry and Carlos were trying to bring out plates full of food, but Frances was getting in the way. They saw her hands on the sliding glass door, and even through the glass could hear, "I want to do it!"

"No," Jackson said, surprising Ellery. "Did he have any other friends? Anyone outside of Johnnies?"

David snorted. "He had a very specific dividing line, you know? There were his friends to piss Daddy off—that was us—and his friends to appease Daddy. That was…. Okay. Let me think. Barnes Carver and Teddy Warburton. You know, his dad's business partners' kids."

Jackson nodded. More names. He tapped them into his phone while Frances finally conceded to let Carlos open the door for her. He gave the men walking toward them a covert glance. "I think that's about all, but David? About your brother."

"What about him?"

"Tell Carlos not to give up on him. He's got his good points."

David Worrall smiled. And while he might not have been as beautiful as Jackson Rivers, Ellery thought he came in a close second.

THEY ENJOYED dinner, which was a true banquet of sandwiches. Everything from avocado and tomatoes on whole wheat to peanut butter and jelly on enriched white, with ham and roast beef somewhere in the middle. Carlos and David told amusing kid stories involving everything from the turtles with the flowers to the time the snake escaped the house in Frances's backpack, to the time all their friends from Johnnies gathered together to make the school Christmas show a big success.

Jackson—always good with kids—used his butter knife to make shapes for Frances with the sandwiches. The turtle was a big hit, as was the heart and the smiley face. Ellery was surprised to see him eat a little, and was grateful.

All in all, there was peace in that backyard, hard-earned strength, and an amazing amount of joy. After a dessert of fruit salad—with Cool Whip and yogurt topping—David pulled Ellery aside quietly, while Henry and Carlos cleaned up.

"We really do appreciate all you're doing for Henry. Do you think you can get him off?"

"They haven't arrested him yet, but that doesn't mean they won't. What we're trying to do is find out who really did it. They have a mostly circumstantial case right now, but if Sampson's father keeps yelling at the cops—mostly to cover his own ass, we suspect—that might be all the DA needs to go to trial."

David nodded, grimacing. "It would be really great if, now that I finally got him back, we could not, you know, lose him to twenty-five to life."

"Jackson and I will do our best."

David's angel-blue eyes took in Jackson, who was playing a game of chase and tickle with Frances while Henry wiped down the table. "His nightmares—will they ever be gone?"

Ellery followed his gaze, seeing Jackson laughing, swooping, making bizarre noises that threw the little girl into fits of laughter. "Probably not forever. But believe it or not, this was a good day for us. He might sleep through the night tonight. That's always a plus."

"I'm sorry about that. He doesn't deserve that—any of it. Yeah, I read up on him after Henry told me he was going out to help with the investigation. Seems like he's always been one of the good guys."

"Count on it. And I'm sorry you and Henry both got pulled into Martin Sampson's life. None of that was your fault either."

David's smile twisted. "What was it he said? In your twenties, you're more come than sense? Best description I've ever fuckin' heard."

Ellery chuckled. "Hey, next Saturday, we're having a thing. I mean, as long as we can get Henry off, we're having a thing, because otherwise it would be sort of shitty to throw a party. But if your brother's not in jail, do you want to come? I was going to invite Galen and John and Reg and

Bobby as well. My office is almost set up, and I've got two cases. I think we need canapés and wine."

David gave a snort. "As long as you've got cheese and salami and beer with that, me and Carlos are in."

"Bring Frances's swimsuit—there's a pool, and she might enjoy herself."

"If you keep my brother out of jail, I'll bring anything you want. If you hadn't invited Frances, I could have had half of Johnnies lining up to blow you."

Ellery almost swallowed his tongue. By the time young Mr. Worrall was done pounding him on the back and Jackson had come over to make sure he wasn't going to die, it was time to leave.

Henry trotted up to walk them out, waiting until they'd cleared the fence to say, "Thanks for being nice to them. They got enough attitude from me, my first month or two here. I'm glad I could bring somebody decent over."

"They're sweet," Jackson said. "You still want in on the fun stuff tomorrow?"

Henry grunted. "I'm all for it. But can we meet around ten? Part of my job is plumbing. Between you and me, I think some of the guys are hella fucking bulimic, because this is the second time I've had to deal with corroded pipes, and that's not natural in a newer apartment building."

"Thanks, you asshole. I have enough trouble eating as it is. I'll never get that image out of my head." Jackson looked truly nauseated, and Ellery wasn't far behind.

Henry shrugged. "So, ten o'clock?"

"I'll pick you up. We may have to hit the thrift store for some maintenance worker's outfits. Usually brown polyester button-up shirts with names on the front."

Henry nodded. "I'll see if any of the guys have some. You never know who's worked what job to pay for their last tattoo."

Jackson rolled his eyes. "You know, it's a good thing I was over porn, because I don't even think I can watch it now. I mean, I just ate dinner with Dex and Kane, and they're daddies. And now the sex thing is just weird. Dude. You're ruining my life."

Henry chortled—as he was meant to, Ellery thought. "Yeah, well, that's what I planned to do when I hit town. Sleep with my brother's old boyfriend, get accused of murder, and ruin your fucking life. See you tomorrow."

"*Mañana.*"

Henry left and they got in the car as Ellery tried to put together everything they'd learned. He turned to ask Jackson what he thought of the day and was surprised when Jackson's quiet snores filled the car.

He was asleep. He barely woke up enough to move from the car to the bedroom, and he slept all the way through the night.

Ellery stayed awake for a good half an hour, lying next to him, reading, rubbing a quiet circle between his shoulder blades. Surprised—he was always surprised—at the ways Jackson found to heal himself by helping others.

It was one of the things that made him the most beautiful man in the world.

Fish on Cleanup

THE REASON Jackson was meeting Henry at ten was because he was meeting Crystal at eight. But because he was a good friend, he wasn't just sneaking into his old place of business and hitting her up for information. Instead, he was greeting her and AJ at her house with coffee and pastries—the super good kind from a nearby bakery, not just a chain.

"Hey, Jackson. Did you duck from that glass thing Ellery threw?"

Jackson didn't even blink. Like Ernie, Crystal just sort of knew things she probably wasn't supposed to. "Yup."

She blinked at him owlishly from behind big-framed glasses and pushed her flyaway hair out of her eyes. She wore long-sleeved shirts, even in the summer, to cover her track marks, and frequently looked lost even though she was the sharpest, fastest hacker Jackson had ever met.

Being super psychic wasn't easy on anyone.

She patted his cheek, though, because Jackson was a safe space for her to be strangely discordant with the world around her. "You were hurt. Not by the glass, though."

Jackson caught her hand and looked at her firmly. "Darlin', I really need that to stay between Ellery and me. We're all good now, and that's what's important."

She squeezed his fingers. "If you really believe that, you didn't learn anything. Did you?"

He almost whimpered. "Maybe. But I'm here to hit you up for information, and sit down and share breakfast, and I'm just... raw. And still processing. And me and Ellery really *are* good. Can that do for now?"

She nodded. "Sure. Come on in. AJ sliced us some fruit, so we can say this is healthy."

Awesome. "Sounds great!"

She rolled her eyes. "Don't lie to me. Just sit down and eat because you know we'll nag if you don't."

Ugh. "I really need to start meeting less perceptive people," he muttered.

"Sure. We'll say that's the problem." She smiled sweetly, the expression lighting up her plain features into something elfin and charming.

"Have you cut your hair?" he asked, because there was less of it than usual, and it was going in fewer directions.

"I did. I adore it. If I hadn't heard it itches, I'd shave it bald."

Jackson laughed and shook his own hair out of his eyes. "That's a good idea. I'll think about it."

"You will not," AJ said, putting the fruit on the table. Crystal's house was small—two bedrooms, one bath, a tiny hallway behind the miniscule living room/kitchen/breakfast nook space to connect everything together. But she'd put a series of silver-inked quotes on the wall, everything from poetry to song lyrics, and the air was always pleasantly scented with vanilla and jasmine. The walls were painted a soft variegation from pale faun to ecru to lavender, and the quilt on the battered brown couch matched. She had a rocking chair, a knitting nook, a computer desk, and two enormously fat cats that took up residence on whatever any passing human wanted to sit on next.

The kitchen/breakfast nook space was painted a gentle yellow, and the drapes over the window that overlooked her postage-stamp front lawn appeared to be hand-knitted lace.

The place had an air of quiet grace—not wealth—and Jackson felt himself relaxing into her and AJ's gentle presence effortlessly, as if he'd been waiting the last month to be here.

"You like my hair?" Jackson asked. "Because it's a pain in the ass now."

"You say that, but I know it's the one thing you're vain about." AJ grinned. His own hair was sunset orange, and sometimes he loved it because it was his natural shade and unusual, and sometimes he hated it because apparently, that was how all redheads felt about their hair before they defended it to the death.

"That's not true," Jackson said, removing the chunky calico from the kitchen chair and getting a disgusted hiss in return. "I'm vain about my cat."

Crystal laughed, like she was supposed to, and they dug into the pastry bag and fruit. For a moment, they talked about small things—the calico, for example, had just returned from a frightening foray around the neighborhood and was so freaked out, she'd apparently vowed never to escape the front door again. AJ talked enthusiastically about the new office, filling Crystal in on the things they'd planned for her when the place started getting more business. And then, more guardedly, he talked about Jael, his former roommate, and now, apparently, his date.

"What about Wyle E. and the Roadrunner," Jackson asked gently, referring to the two other kids who had been on probation in his old duplex. "They good with their buddy wanting to date you?"

AJ shrugged gamely. "They have to readjust," he said. "I get it. They know their friend one way, and this feels like a lie. But Jael has been really firm on them being nice to me."

Jackson looked at him levelly. "If it helps, tell him that their free rent depends on it. Also, how are they doing on jobs?"

AJ frowned thoughtfully. "Not bad. Both of them have part-time gigs in an auto parts store that might move to full-time, and the one guy with the tattoos has signed up for classes at Sac City. Besides the redneck homophobia, they're not bad kids. And Jael's working on that."

Jackson nodded. "Just remember—anything you're not comfortable with, I'm not comfortable with. I will kick their asses out if they hurt you or Jail... uhm, Ja*el*, so you can drop that into conversation if you need to."

"I won't," AJ said firmly, and Jackson read the subtext. *Stop it, Dad, I'm trying to look cool.* Well, if he had to be Dad to AJ's lost boy, that was fine. Better Jackson as Dad than AJ in another drug flop, too stoned to run away from a serial killer, as he'd been when Jackson had met him.

"Fair enough." Jackson ripped off a piece of danish and shoved it into his mouth for spite. Try to make him feel old—little punk.

"Are you ready to talk about those financials yet?" Crystal asked after a moment. "Because the next stop in the conversation is my love life—"

"Are you dating?" Jackson asked, for form.

"No. I don't feel like it. My house is tranquil, and AJ is a good roommate, and I don't even mind if he and Jael have noisy sex in his room, which they haven't yet. Too bad. Are we good yet?"

"Fine," Jackson said, stunned.

"Fine," AJ mumbled, clearly embarrassed but intrigued by the idea of bringing a lover overnight.

"Good. Because the two deep dives you had me do are bad. Very, very bad. And one of these people is a very wicked man. You have to stop him."

Jackson stared at her until his eyeballs dried out.

"Drink some coffee," she told him.

He took a sip and blinked.

"What's wrong? You wouldn't have asked me for a favor if you didn't think I'd find something." She waved her hand in agitation, and he shook himself.

"Well, yeah, but I usually have to pull teeth to have my hunches confirmed. That was just so refreshing. Tell me more, Crystal. I'm waiting for your guidance."

"You only say that because you want to solve the case," she said primly, a little smile escaping at the corners of her full mouth.

"Why yes, I do," Jackson said. "The guy I'm trying to get off for murder is going to be arrested any day now, and it would be great if we had someone else to say 'This guy! He is the one!' so I don't have to see our new friend go to jail."

"He *is* a new friend!" She clapped her hands delightedly. "I *knew* there was something positive about your aura. Of course!" She frowned for a moment and then squinted at him. "But there's red too. You're... hurt? Not well. Something."

"I've got stitches," he said easily, ignoring the breathlessness of the last week. He'd know if there was something wrong, right?

She nodded, troubled. "That might be it. But now you're impatient. Here." She reached behind her to the phone stand by the kitchen counter and produced a folder, then pulled out three stapled packets from it and handed one to each of them.

"Now we're going to start on page one of Robert Sampson's outgoing payments. Notice the highlighted parts? AJ, you have to pay attention because you're answering Ellery's questions once Jackson explains it and goes on his adventure, okay?"

AJ nodded soberly, and Crystal took them on an odyssey of money laundering, drugs, and murder.

It was all there, highlighted in yellow, between the fruit stains, the coffee, and three friends at breakfast.

"WAIT," HENRY said when Jackson picked him up from the flophouse. "Explain this to me again."

Jackson nodded, glad he'd practiced on Ellery instead of leaving AJ to do it, because Ellery stopped and asked clarifying questions so

Jackson didn't go "Ablagh, blorp, squandoo!" and expect someone else to understand him.

"Okay," Jackson said. "So twenty years ago, when Martin Sampson would have been about ten years old, his father and three friends joined together to create a medical partnership. And at first it was just them and a couple of nurses and a combination of both state and private insurance to fund them. But cutbacks were made to the state insurance, and the private insurance kept going HMO, and our partners were sort of left out in the cold."

Henry nodded. "I get that. Why didn't they join an HMO? I know a lot of doctors did."

"Well, a lot of doctors had more business sense than these guys. Apparently, Ash Carver lived his life on thirty-black, Calvin Warburton hadn't met a woman he hadn't wanted to fuck and then cheat on, and Jordan Patel's sole interest was research, and he had a tendency to forget he even *had* patients. So these four doctors were about to lose everything—including their licenses, because Warburton's womanizing was damned illegal and Patel had turned his patient care over to a nursing student out of her league who had made some serious errors—"

"Summer Frasier!" Henry said, and Jackson took his hand off the steering wheel of Ellery's car to touch his finger to his nose.

"Yahtzee! Yes, for the win. And now we know why she has to beg for lubricant. Anyway, their business was going under, and little Martin kept getting kicked out of private schools, and Robert Scott Sampson noticed that oh my God! These pamphlets from the drug companies asking if he wanted free samples were *everywhere*. Different companies, different drugs—all of them just giving away narcotics and Ritalin and all the shit that's regulated *now* but wasn't so much back *then*."

"Like a dog rolling in flowers because he could," Henry said in wonder. "Where are we going, by the way?"

"Did you bring your brown polyester shirt and your jeans?"

Henry held up a small reusable shopping bag. "I did, indeed."

"Baseball hat too?" Because it was hot outside and because a little anonymity never hurt.

"I'm wearing it! Duh!"

Jackson chuckled through the low-level headache that had settled in after his caffeine wore off. "USAF—I should have noticed that," he said after a deep breath. "I've got one too." Jackson's had Daffy Duck on it, just because. "Good. The company that Sampson uses to clean his house is off of Richards Boulevard. According to his records, they take the money out on Friday of every week, which would indicate that *Friday—*"

"Today," Henry said, nodding.

"Yes, *today*, is the day they wander through his precious possessions invisibly and vacuum. Which is what we're going to do, to see what we can see."

"You... you've seemed pretty determined to do this from the beginning," Henry observed. "Can I ask why?"

Jackson grimaced. "Because Martin Sampson wasn't a good guy. But he had help getting that way. Let's just say that, serial killers aside, most people know their killers, and everything about Sampson screamed daddy issues."

"Any other reason?"

"I think Robert Sampson was our OG, our original gangster, our big drug kahuna. I think he's been doing it for years."

"Why would he kill his son?"

Jackson thought about it, thought about his mother on the coroner's slab, thought about how sometimes, parenting didn't take.

"Did Martin ever find out your name?" he said after a moment. "Did he have any way of knowing you were related to your brother?"

Henry blinked. "I... well, I remember him looking at my driver's license," he said after a moment. "He said, 'Henry Worrall, Montana.'"

"And you said...?"

"I said, 'Yeah, I'm here to visit my brother.'"

"And the next time he sees you, you're defending the Johnnies guys, being an all-American hero?"

"Yeah. Why?"

"Because in his fucked-up, 'burn the fucking world down' way, Martin Sampson loved your brother. And I think getting called out for a worthless piece of shit by David Worrall's little brother was his last straw."

"So his father's a drug dealer.... Do you think that's why he started using?"

Jackson shook his head. "No. See, here's the thing. Up to about a year and a half ago, Robert was giving his son an allowance like you would with a spoiled college kid who was still working on his degree."

"What happened?"

"Martin got arrested for taking out his girlfriend's windows. And when he got arrested, he had a shitload of cocaine on him, because he was dealing."

"And he never went to jail?"

Jackson grunted. God, this was so unfair. "Yeah, but he wasn't there long. He was out in plenty of time to get dead. Isn't it great to be rich, white, and male in America?" Jesus fucking Christ—if AJ had been busted with that much product on him, he'd be an old man before he got out. Except AJ wasn't Martin Sampson, and AJ wouldn't have made it so much as a month. Hell, Crystal had served three years for having paraphernalia—no drugs included—and that didn't include the two years for hacking to fund her habit. It all depended on who was being held up as an example of a "bad citizen" and who was the pillar of the fucking community, right?

That was why he and Ellery did what they did.

"Two out of three still ain't bad," Henry admitted sourly. "A thing I never thought about until I met you, fuck you very much. So when did Martin get out of jail?"

"A year ago," Jackson confirmed.

"So he's clean for coke and…?"

"And Dad's drug business isn't doing so well. And here's the thing. When Martin was dealing someone else's coke, Dad's business was doing great! But Martin goes up the creek and Dad's business falls off—the same business that was giving his son the allowance that let him feed his addiction and the addictions of the people around him. Why do you think that is?"

"I got nothing," Henry confessed.

"I've got an idea," Jackson told him. "This is all pure fucking speculation, based on the fact that Daddy Sampson's business picked up pretty much the same month Martin got out of jail. Now, Martin said coke was a rich-man's drug and if he wanted pills he'd go to Daddy. What if—and, speculation, mind you—what if the guys he hung with weren't so rich."

"But he hung with Johnnies guys!" Henry protested.

Jackson frowned. "Yeah, but hear me out. John was doing drugs, but he was doing them outside of the house. Does your brother look like he'd be running a house built on cocaine?"

"No," Henry said, adamant. "I'd be surprised if he more than tried it, and he probably felt super guilty later, if he did. Davy—he was always the good boy, the one who looked after the younger kids. He couldn't do that if he was high. And I don't think he could *not* do it, you know?"

Jackson nodded. "I got that from him. And I got that if he'd been coked up, he would have been like John—he would have told us up front. Besides, the business is porn, and we all know coke makes your balls shrivel. I'm sure there's some stimulants out there that keep you super aroused, but you can't use them too long or it's going to fuck up your porn, you know?"

"Hard to look cute and clean-cut when your septum is gone or you've got yellow teeth from meth," Henry confirmed. "I see you."

"So young Martin isn't dealing to the Johnnies kids, and his dad's not either. I don't know if his dad even *knew* his son was in porn—although I'm sure he heard about it when Martin went to jail. But his dad's got nobody to distribute for him. He can't even breathe about it to patients; too many doctors get ruined that way. He may have his doctor friends on board, but nobody else he knows is going to buy in. But his son—his son is sitting on a gold mine of distribution. Robert isn't going to have his son deal, oh no. But imagine if his son brings home friends, guys Robert's trying to hook up as professional contacts. Can you see how this would play out?"

"Hey, kid," Henry said in a conspiratorial whisper. "You look tired. I can give you something for that. Still buzzed? Want something to bring you down? Got that too."

Jackson grunted and steered them down Richards, which had been recently remodeled. Yeah, some of the street still housed sex shops and homeless shelters, but beyond the freeway interchange was a whack of new businesses, and Jackson was a fan.

"Stop doing the voice," he muttered. "It's creeping me out. But yes. Martin Sampson went to school with Jordan Patel's daughter, Calvin Warburton's sons, and Ash Carver's son. Patel's daughter got out—like, way out, to the Ivy League and then to practice medicine in Chicago. But Ash Carver's son, Barnes, did not. He was killed in a car accident while Martin was in prison."

"DUI?" Henry hazarded.

"And give the boy a cigar. But not any *ordinary* influence. Nope. I called my buddy in the CHP, and Mack said the kid had been doing so many different pills that if he hadn't exploded his brain against a tree, it would have exploded on its own."

"That's awful," Henry muttered, all trace of banter gone. "Oh my God. That's… that's really awful. His *father* did that to him?"

"Or his father's buddy," Jackson said. "And that's when things get strange. That's when the financials and the police reports stop telling the story. Or they do, but the missing details are really fucking important."

"Why?" Henry asked. "What happened?"

"Well, about two weeks after Ash—who was long divorced from his wife, by the way—has paid out for a casket and flowers, a bunch of things happen to his finances. His house goes up for sale, and the money goes in, but nothing comes out. He sells his car, and again, money in for a car, but no bills. There's no hotel bills, no rental agreements, no nothing. Nothing but his standard monthly contribution to his partner's checking account to spring for his overhead, which he can do for another five years without depleting his savings. Now you went into his office, and what did you see?"

"Nothing. It was used as a warehouse," Henry said. "Shit stacked everywhere."

"That's what you said. And we both heard from different places that Carver was out on sabbatical. It's general fucking knowledge, right?"

"Yeah, but, I mean, the guy's gotta eat, right?"

"You'd think." Jackson's voice got grim. "I mean, he must be a walking corpse by now."

There was silence in Ellery's Lexus as that sank in. "Or maybe not walking around so much," Henry said thickly.

"Maybe not."

"Shit."

Jackson nodded. Sitting at Crystal's kitchen table that morning, the light coming in through the gauzy curtains, the pastry sweet on his tongue, he'd looked at Ash Carver's financials, at that lack of activity in a checking account that had been rife with activity—including an allowance to a now deceased son—and he'd smelled nothing but death.

"So," Henry said after they'd both taken a deep breath. "We're going to the cleaning service."

"Yup."

"Because…?"

"Because Toby found carpet fiber in the wound, but there was no carpet in the dumpster. And when Ellery gives the police the financials today, they're going to have enough to start an investigation, but not before the cleaning service gets rid of all the evidence. And because...." Jackson wasn't sure he should tell Henry this, but he thought he'd better. "Because it's Friday. And if they're going to issue a warrant for your arrest, it's going to be today. And it's not that I don't think you're tough enough for jail—it's that you're my friend and I don't want you there. I know enough people who had to wait a month or three for a trial. You're finally getting your shit together, Henry, and as good as Ellery is, and as much clout as he still wields in this town, I would very much not like to have to live with him for the next three months if he's battering down the walls of justice trying to get you a trial."

Henry grunted as though struck. "Wow. That was almost a love sonnet. Does Ellery know?"

"That if we keep you out of jail, I may kill you? Yes. Yes, I'm pretty sure he does."

Henry snickered. "Don't worry about it if we don't beat the clock," he said after a moment. "I think it's enough to know I've got people who don't want me in there. Is this it?"

Jackson had pulled up to a bank of warehouses, some with hand-lettered signs, some with banners from FedEx, and some with street art on a piece of plywood. This sign was well made, metal, bolted into the archway over the carport, and it said, River Breeze Cleaning, complete with a little logo that featured running water and a spray bottle full of pine cleaner.

"This is the place," Jackson said. "Let me find Joey."

It was easy for employers of unskilled labor to exploit their workforce—particularly migrant labor—but Joey Duarte was one of the good guys. Topping out at five feet five inches, with a mischievous smile, sloe eyes, and a BA in business, Joey had taken his mother's pride in a clean home and a stake left to him by his grandfather and turned it into a housecleaning co-op that was designed to help kids through college, struggling parents make extra money, and give people who just wanted to make an honest wage a steady, no-drama income. He also offered health and dental, and, Jackson remembered fondly, was sort of amazing in bed.

Right now, he was underneath one of six white service vans in his fleet, banging away at it with a wrench. Joey had a quick mind and an unrivaled resourcefulness, and one of the reasons he'd been able to build his business so far, so fast, was that he could pretty much fix anything that came his way.

"Joey, you're gonna beat that thing to death," Jackson said as they entered, and Joey's dolly shot out from under the van so fast, Jackson had to jump out of the way.

"Rivers!" he cried, hopping to his feet and going in for a hug. "Good to see you!" And then, in a fluid shifting of English to Spanish, he added, "Are you hitting me up for an encore? It's been two years, but I'm still single and you're still hot!"

Jackson shook his head. "Sadly, I'm taken," he said, "but it's nice of you to remember."

Joey shot Henry a hard look. "If this is the guy, you'll melt his brain in a week. Come back to me, baby. I am waiting for you and you alone!"

Jackson snorted. Joey had played the field as much as Jackson used to—it's what had made them so awesome in bed. It was easy to be adventurous when neither of you planned to stick around much longer than it took to peel the condom off and make toast.

"This kid? I've got better taste. He's still trying to find his ass with both hands. No—me and a guy from the law firm are living together. He puts up with my cat, I put up with his fussing—it's a match made in heaven. Anyway," he said, switching to English, "this is a business call, not a social one. I could really use a favor."

Joey looked at the youngster he'd been working with, a blond, blue-eyed twinkie with "Callum" on his name tag, who was listening to their conversation wistfully, with no indication at all that he could speak Spanish.

"Cal, could you take over working on Matilda here? Me and Jackson have to have some words."

Callum nodded, crestfallen, but he slid back under the van like a kid who knew what he was doing, and Jackson had a moment to wish the kid the best. He seemed to have it bad for Joey, but Joey wasn't great at being pinned down.

Joey led the way through neatly boxed kits containing cleaning supplies, including gloves and face masks and special chemicals for the really hard-to-get places, and into a small office in the back of the warehouse. Joey had outfitted it with its own swamp cooler and two giant fans, because he was a creature of comfort. Jackson respected that about him.

"So, what can I do you for?" Joey said with a leer.

Jackson rolled his eyes. "For starters, you can stop hitting on me. I'm taken, and that kid's heart is gonna explode if he has to watch you flirt with someone else for another second. Stop taunting him—that's cruel."

Joey blinked, surprised. "Callum? He's not even bi—"

Henry snorted, and Jackson sent him a hard look.

"And fuck," Joey muttered. "I *like* that kid. He's super smart, he works hard, and he's a college student so he's got flexible hours!"

"There's no law that says you can't keep him!" Jackson said with a laugh. "Just don't sleep with him! Or if you do, don't toy with him." Jackson's voice softened. "You were always the nicest guy in the world, Joey. Treat that kid like his heart's fragile. And teach him some Spanish—I think he'd like to know what you're saying."

Joey cocked his head. "Jesus, Rivers, I'd forgotten how spooky you were about that. You knew my sister was getting married before I did. It was weird."

Jackson shrugged. "How's she doing, by the way?" Sandra had been just as sweet as Joey—without the inclination to bang all the things.

"I can't decide what she's whining about more—turning thirty or being pregnant. It's her first, but you'd think she'd have popped out seven of them by now."

"Is she still teaching English?"

"You know it." Joey made a face. "For that alone I guess I should forgive her for whining, right?" He sobered. "So, this is a business call—let's talk business."

If only they could sit down with a beer and discuss the old days, when Jackson had been recovering from the sniper shot that ended his career and in school getting his BA in criminal justice. He and Joey had met in an English class, and in spite of Joey being about four years younger than he was, they'd hit it off. Joey had been one of the first people he'd bedded to keep the monsters at bay, and maybe if they'd made a habit of it, he wouldn't have needed quite so many other people. But you don't know what a real relationship looks like when you're young and pissed and hurting, and Joey hadn't been ready to stop fucking everything that moved.

But in the end, he'd found a good friend—and, yeah, a sometimes bedmate—but mostly, a good friend.

"Well, I'm investigating one of your clients, and I was hoping you could help."

Joey grimaced. "Aw, man, Jackson, we're bonded! I've got paperwork and shit, and we can't have evidence disappearing or anything like that. It'll ruin me!"

"Look, you can hire us, if you want, and put us on probation. And I swear, anything we find, we'll report to the police. This guy's a piece of work, Joey. We're looking for evidence that he killed his own son because the kid didn't want to distribute anymore for him. I'll take pictures and send them to the police. It'll all be above board."

"What if you get caught!" Joey asked, and then grimaced. "I'm sorry. That sounds selfish. But—"

"But this is your business. I get it." Jackson sighed. "Look, I've got the address here. If I just happen to see when you'll be in the guy's house, we can show up and sneak in. If anyone asks, you've never seen us and we were never there."

Joey let out a snort. "Sure. Never there. I hear you."

"I appreciate it, man. I'm looking for Robert Sampson—"

Joey rattled off the address that Jackson had read on Crystal's financial forms that morning, and Jackson was impressed. "Yeah, you know this because…?"

"Because *nobody* replaces a six-thousand-dollar area rug twice in the same year because they suddenly got tired of the same color blue."

Jackson held his hand to his chest, not sure if the murmur the doctor had assured him he'd picked up finally decided to appear, or if he was just excited. Because hey! They might actually have a break in this fucking case.

"So, uh, these rugs—do you know where they went?"

Joey nodded. "We're going there after we do our rounds. Why?"

"Because we need to see Sampson's house, man, but we *really* need to see that rug."

Joey blew out a breath. "I don't suppose you both have fingerprints on file?"

"I'm a PI, Joey—I know you know that. I'm actually bonded myself."

Joey perked up. "And your buddy?"

"Ex-military," Henry said hopefully, and Joey blew out a breath.

"I'll take it. It might at least help me keep my business if this all goes south. I don't suppose you brought work shirts with you?"

Jackson grinned. "Brown like yours?"

Joey was barely twenty-seven, but the way he rubbed the back of his neck made him look like a much older man. "Yes, Jackson. Brown, just like mine."

"We have some in the car." Jackson smiled with all his teeth to indicate this was not a coincidence.

"Augh!"

Jackson grabbed Henry and trotted toward the Lexus, wanting nothing more than to skip and cheer.

"So," Henry said dubiously, "we're going to clean houses?"

"Well, yeah! Do you think we'd get this chance to break and enter without doing some of the work?"

HALF AN hour later they were heading out in "Matilda," whose engine was now purring like a kitten. "My office assistant, Sylvie, she makes out a list and a map for us every day. I've got two stops on the way to Sampson's place. You guys are welcome to sit in the van and wank off if you like, but it's cooler in the house, and the more you work, the faster we go, right?"

"Funny thing about being monogamous," Jackson taunted. "Don't need to wank off as much."

"Has said no married man ever!" Joey chortled.

"'Cause he hasn't been married to me," Jackson returned, and his chest—still a little tight after the excitement of the lead—gave a throb. He'd fuck Ellery until his eyeballs bled. He'd march into the bedroom every night, cock erect like a good soldier, if he knew Ellery would be his until death-do-us-part. The irony, maybe the true irony, of the flight of the expensive paperweight was Ellery thinking Jackson had to "take one for the team." Imagining a happily ever after with Ellery was the most cherished dream Jackson had never given voice to. Not to Ellery, and barely to himself.

"You should be so lucky," Henry muttered. "If Ellery Cramer ever asks to marry you, I suggest you jump on that horse and ride it into the fucking sunset."

"Yeah, I know it. He's out of my league." Which was why it was a dream, right?

Joey snorted. "Shows how much you know, Major Mopey. Anyone who actually lands Jackson Rivers must have a genie in his lamp—or in his pocket. Either one is good."

"And that's a little personal—" Jackson protested, but Joey laughed and held up his hand.

"I'm just saying, Rivers. You're hot, you're funny, you're a decent guy. I'm not sure what makes Ellery Cramer walk on water, but you could at least meet him halfway. Did Jackson ever tell you how he kept my sister out of jail?" he asked Henry.

Jackson grunted. "Please don't. It's not even like that—"

"So, Sandra was at a party, right? And she wasn't doing anything, but she was passing the joint down the road. And the cops arrive, and suddenly she's arrested like every other kid at the rave, and they get the blanket 'Call your public defender's office, here's how you do cash bail' speech. I'm in tears, right, because she's my sister, and she's a by-the-book sort of woman, and she's freaking out because she's wanted to be a teacher her entire life and having a conviction on your record makes that hard. So this boy, he researches law firms, right? And then he takes half the money from the settlement he earned by almost dying and walks us into the law offices of—fuck. Like Pflooey, Hammerstein, Whoever-the-hell, and Languish, and he lays out the case for them. He starts with how she was never drug tested, she was never seen actually holding any pot, she has no prior history, and he's got statements—I didn't even know he did this—where he went to six of the kids at the party, even some of the ones who'd been arrested and copped a plea, who all said that Sandra didn't do that shit and were prepared to do extra time for it. And the douche—what was his name?"

Jackson smirked. "Carlyle Langdon," he said, remembering the guy who had been his main contact at the firm until Ellery had pretty much dragged Jackson into his office and said, "Here, he will be mine and nobody else shall use him as a PI unless they clear it through me."

"Anyway—that asshole. He looks at Rivers and says, 'We need a PI. Are you certified yet?' And Rivers goes, 'I got three more months.' And Languish, he says, 'We'll take the case if you take the job.'"

God. Not even Ellery knew that story. "Yeah. Well, your sister got off, and I got a job."

"You still working for them?"

Jackson shook his head. "No, uh, me and Jade turned in our resignation letters after they let Ellery go."

Henry chortled. "Oh my God! Now *I've* got a Rivers story, because I've *seen* their resignation letters, and it's the funniest goddamned thing I've ever seen in my life."

Henry launched into a lengthy, comic—and accurate—description of the picture of Jackson's and Jade's epic "I quit" notices, and Joey laughed like he was supposed to. But when he was done, he gave Jackson a sideways glance.

"So why did you do that again? And he keeps calling you scrawny. What in the hell, man. I saw you after a year in the hospital and you looked better than now."

"They let Ellery go because he did the right thing," Jackson said. "It wasn't fair. Langdon said me and Jade could stay, but we didn't want to."

"So who are you working for now?"

"My lawyer," Henry answered. "Ellery Cramer. But I get the impression it's more of a partnership."

Jackson shrugged. His name was on the business lease—but not on the doors, because he didn't want to work without Ellery. "We're good together," he said, taking a deep breath. He was suddenly tired, which was weird. He'd slept well, gotten up, gone running with Ellery. He'd even had breakfast. Another deep breath. It didn't matter. They had work to do, and Joey was right. The quicker they got done with the next house, the sooner they could move on to the "disposal" place Joey was using to clean and repurpose the rugs. Jackson had asked if Joey had noticed a giant bloodstain on the rug they'd taken to his cousin's place two days ago, and Joey had rolled his eyes.

"No, but somebody had done a shitty job cleaning it and had ruined the pattern. I didn't think blood—I thought wine. Until you, Rivers, until you."

Jackson was reasonably certain that a good forensic team could find blood on a badly cleaned rug—but he needed more than that.

He needed proof of motive. What had led to Martin Sampson being thrown in a dumpster, and why frame Henry Worrall for it?

If nothing else, he was curious as hell.

He'd sunk into a slightly brooding silence when his phone rang. "Rivers."

"Yeah, Jackson, this is Kryzynski. I got some shit for you. You got anything for me?"

Jackson grunted. "I might. Following a lead right now. I'll tell you if it pans out. What do you have?"

Kryzynski grunted back. "You are legitimately the most closed-mouth motherfucker I have ever met. Jesus God, grow a spine and a set of lungs and join the rest of us in the evolution, cave boy!"

For a moment, Jackson's mouth opened in shock, and then he let loose with a guffaw that filled the van. "Wow. Just… how long have you been sitting on that one, because it was fragrant and ripe when you let loose. I am impressed!"

"I live to flip your switch," Kryzynski muttered. "Seriously, what's it take?"

Jackson closed his eyes and realized that this time around, Kryzynski had been square with him. "Look, we don't have proof of anything, but you need to do a deep dive into Ash Carver's financials. Because all activity stops as of last year, and nobody's heard from the guy since his son died."

Kryzynski sucked in a breath. "And this has to do with Sampson's death how?"

"For one thing, it establishes a pattern by Daddy Dearest. For another, I think all the doctors were in on a drug scam to fund their practice, which was failing because they were all a bunch of boneheads. Sampson went up the creek for possession a year and a half ago. He got out, and Daddy no longer thinks he walks on water. Then suddenly he's dealing oxy and Ritalin—do you see where this is going?"

"Sort of. Anything else you've got that can make me want to throw up my dinner?"

"Yeah. Candy Cormier wanted Daddy's business—his product and his distribution. I'm not sure if that was impetus for the murder or maybe just for the cover-up. If Sampson is up the river, no candy for Candy, you know?"

Kryzynski made a sound. "Okay, that brings me to what I was calling for."

Jackson nodded as Joey turned right onto an absurdly small road off Fair Oaks Boulevard. He knew there were some nice houses back here, but he didn't expect to go from happy suburb land to riverfront property quite so quickly.

"You need to hurry, Kryzynski. I'm about to go clean someone's house."

"Sampson's?"

"Cool your jets. I'm helping a friend."

He rolled his eyes when Joey flipped him off.

"Look, whatever you're doing, be careful. Sternberg died in the hospital two nights ago...."

"Cock Cheese?" Jackson had been busy with flying paperweights. Yikes—busy week! "Couldn't have happened to sweeter smegma."

"Nice. But he died, and Ralph Gordon was found in a dumpster the next day. They *just* identified him this morning. Oh, and remember Herbert Dalton?"

Jackson had to close his eyes. "The guy who broke into the porn kids' house?"

"That's our scumbag. Anyway, he got shanked in jail last night. He's in the hospital, but it's touch and go."

Jackson closed his eyes hard and opened them and was disappointed when the view hadn't changed.

"Candy Cormier does *not* like botched operations," he muttered.

"Yeah, Rivers, and weirdly enough, your name has come up twice in those botchings. So half the department is getting ready to issue an arrest warrant on your guy, and the other half is scrambling to connect the dots between Martin Sampson and Candy Cormier. It's a great time to be alive, but not for long!"

Jackson took a deep breath and tried to order his thoughts. "Okay. Let me know if they get the arrest warrant out. And I'll let you know when we've got definitive proof that Robert Sampson is the missing link between Martin and Cormier. Are we good for trade here?"

"Yeah. We're good. Are you tired or something? You sound out of breath."

"I'm great," Jackson said shortly. "Oh!" And Jesus, how could this be the last thing he'd thought about? "Do you have a guard detail on

Ellery?" If Jackson's name came up as a thorn in Cormier's side, then Ellery's would have too.

"We do now. Do you want me to tell him?"

"I'll text him. But let us both know the minute that warrant is issued."

"Will you tell us where you are then, so we can come get him?"

"Ouch!"

"What!" To his credit, Kryzynski sounded legitimately worried.

"I just rolled my eyes so hard, they popped out of my head!"

"Rivers...."

"Look, if we're a heartbeat away from finding the goddamned proof that he's innocent, I'm gonna find the proof that he's innocent. Otherwise, we'll talk. He's innocent. You know it. I know it. Putting him in jail with the same guy who shanked Herbert the Pervert is not justice. Let's do what we can to keep him out."

This time Kryzynski let out the deep breath. "Roger that. Happy hunting."

"You too."

Jackson signed off just as Joey pulled up into one of those weird driveways you often found in Fair Oaks, with the 6 percent gradient. As the car tilted up at an angle, he heard Henry swear and looked back in time to see him sliding sideways off the jump seat he'd been using in the supply van very much *not* meant for public transport.

Jackson snickered and got out, surprised to find himself wobbling a little in the heat. God*dammit*, he needed to get his shit together.

"Let me text Ellery," he said as they gathered around the back of the van to get cleaning supplies. "If nobody tells him he's got a detail, he's going to be pissed."

"Why's *he* get a detail, and *we've* got to clean houses?" Henry griped, and Jackson flashed him a quick sympathetic smile.

"Because when *you* get a detail, it's going to come with handcuffs and a metal table, suspect."

"Pass the pine cleaner, and let's get this bitch done!"

Joey handed him a basket instead. "You gotta listen to me when we're inside, you understand? There's three spray bottles in there, and if you use the wrong one on the wrong thing, I'm out a customer and I get sued to boot. Capiche?"

"Capiche," Henry returned soberly. "Hey, purple gloves!"

"You're going to want those—that shit in the green bottle will eat your fingerprints if you're not careful. You only use that on places that look like the germs will eat you first, understand?"

Henry regarded him with a fair bit of horror. "You really earn your money, don't you?"

"I've built an empire on knowing which stuff you wipe and which stuff you beat off with a broom. You can worship at my feet later, but for now, we're running late!"

Jackson watched them go, his own basket of goodies at his feet, and allowed himself to sag against the back of the van. His heart thudded in his throat, and in a clear voice in his head, he heard Dr. Keller, who'd attended him after he'd checked out of the hospital that November.

You have a heart murmur. All this means is that every now and then, your heart remembers it stopped and gets confused. Dizziness, exhaustion, light-headedness are all very much a part of the package. I'll want to see you in a few weeks, and if that goes well, in a few more. We might not need the heavy medication yet, but you need to eat well, eat more, and take care of yourself. Your body did you a favor by coming back this time. It won't always.

Good words—and Jackson had taken them, well, to heart. But after he and Ellery had gotten back from down south, Jackson had managed a couple of appointments. Right up until this last one, which he'd just sort of... forgotten. He'd been recovering, right? He'd been eating right—mostly. He'd put some weight back on.

Even so, before Ellery had thrown a paperweight at his head, he hadn't been sleeping well, and some of that weight had slid right back off again. And goddammit, Henry was depending on him right now, and he needed to get oxygen in and out of his body if it killed him.

Hey, Counselor—you there?

Yeah. What's up?

He frowned. Goddammit, he couldn't remember how to spell "Kryzynski"! *Officer Sean is putting a security detail on you. All of Cormier's former thugs are turning up with holes in them. I've been one of the people to see them last, so you get a tail.*

There was a silence, and his phone rang.

"What about you?" Ellery snapped.

"I won't tell him where I am, and you shouldn't either. I've got Henry with me, and we're about two hours from evidence that will clear him. If we can get to it first, we can keep him out of jail. And since that's where one of Cormier's people got his holes, I'm all for that, you know?"

Ellery grunted. "You sound funny."

Shit. Shit balls fuck. "My breathing's not great," he admitted, only because it felt like God had a steel-toed boot aimed at his balls. "You know what I skipped last month—"

"Your cardiologist appointment," Ellery said, his voice cracking. "God*dammit,* Jackson!"

"Look. I'll take it easy—"

"And I'll make you an appointment for this afternoon."

Jackson kept hearing that paperweight shattering by his ear. "Fine. Get me in if you can. After Joey takes us back to his warehouse, I'll drive—"

"Where are you now?"

"On Joey's housecleaning route. He's got two stops, Sampson's house, and then we're going to go see where Sampson's rugs went to be cleaned and resold—Joey's cousin's place out in Rio Linda. Joey got called in to pick it up three days ago. Joey thought it had been ruined by a bad cleaning, but—"

"But you think it was ruined by a pool of blood," Ellery finished. Jackson had sent him pictures of the documents Crystal had provided before he'd left her house. "Who's Joey?"

Jackson had to laugh. "He runs the cleaning service Sampson uses. I told you that's where I was going, right?"

"Yeah, but you didn't tell me you knew someone there!"

"I know lots of people in the city. Me and Joey used to hang after I was shot—the first time."

"You slept with him, didn't you?" Ellery's voice had a particular note when he made that deduction. It wasn't anger, wasn't jealousy, wasn't hurt.

But it wasn't ecstasy either.

"Way back before I even met Langdon," Jackson soothed, and Ellery snorted.

"Tell me which was harder," he said. "Talking to me about your health or telling me you slept with a source in the dark ages?"

"The first one," Jackson said gruffly. "Joey's a friend. The heart thing—that could hurt you."

"Love you, Jackson. Take care of what's mine. If things get any worse, call me. Henry's a big boy. He can take care of himself."

"Yeah, but we promised to take care of him when he needed us." Breaking that promise would hurt, Jackson couldn't lie.

"Jackson...." Ellery's voice broke, and Jackson realized how truly worried he was.

"I'll take care. And that's a promise too."

He heard Ellery's deep breath. "Good."

"Gotta go. I'll text you when we get to Sampson's."

"Deal."

The dizziness faded, and Jackson grabbed his basket of spray cleaners and headed for the house.

BY THE time they were done with the second house, Joey was willing to offer them both a job, and Jackson reminded Henry that he might have to take him up on that.

"Remember, you still have to get your degree before you do this for anything more than save your own ass," he cautioned.

"I could always use someone part-time," Joey chimed in. "You're a hard worker." He leered. "And you got a great ass!"

"He's taken," Jackson told him, before Henry could blush and sputter and generally string Joey along. "He just doesn't know it yet."

"I'm...." Henry flailed with the hand not shoving the cleaning basket in the back of the van.

Jackson took pity on him. "He's generally trying to pull his life together. He doesn't need Hurricane Joey and his nine-inch dick making things any more exciting."

Joey smirked, and Henry's eyes got really big.

"That really is about two inches more excitement than I need," Henry finally said after the shocked silence. "But I may take you up on the job offer."

"Well, I won't say I'm not disappointed." Joey pretended to pout, and they finished loading up the van. "You guys ready to see the bad-guy's house?"

"I'm on the edge of my seat," Jackson told him with a wink. But as they were getting into the van, Henry showed him, in no uncertain terms, that he wasn't fooling anyone.

"You look tired," he said quietly. "And pale. What'd Ellery say?"

"About having a detail watching him? He wanted to know why he was so special. Why?"

"Did you tell him you don't feel well?"

A faint headache throbbed at Jackson's temples, and he was done with the game. He'd conceded. He felt like crap, and it was time to do something about it. "He's meeting us at Joey's business to take me to a doc appointment." His phone had buzzed while he'd been scrubbing baseboards in the last house. All Ellery had put was the doctor's name and the time of the appointment, but it had been enough.

"What's wrong?"

"Just some residuals from treating my body like shit for thirty years," Jackson admitted. "Crap. Thirty-one years in September."

"We don't have to do this right now."

Jackson glared at him. "We do. Henry, you are on the fucking clock. Don't make this a deal, okay?"

Henry nodded. "Okay, fine. But how about you investigate and Joey and I clean at the next house." Henry raised his voice. "That okay with you, Joey? If Jackson sits this next one out? He's not looking so hot."

"Well, he always looks hot," Joey placated, "but he doesn't look *well*."

Jackson laughed, like he was supposed to, then leaned against the door and closed his eyes. "Thanks, guys. I appreciate it."

IF JACKSON had never been to Ellery's house, had never visited Ellery's parents, he would have said Sampson's house was classy.

The color schemes were actually similar, with lots of navy in the trim, lots of cream carpets and hardwood floors. But Ellery had odd touches—a deep red comforter or a throw his sister had made on the couch—that made the place a home. His parents' house had seen two kids and two grandkids, and the flowers were sometimes massacred, and there were dents in the doorframes where furniture had been moved, and Jackson had actually seen an entire room painted blushing pink. It had been Lucy Satan's office, so Jackson's mind had officially been blown.

The point was, people lived in those homes. Dust gathered in the corners sometimes, and the rooms were arranged for comfort, not for aesthetics. Ellery hired a cleaning company usually, although they were between cleaners at the moment. Still, not even a once-a-week dust and vacuum could combat Billy Bob's shedding problem or the fact that sometimes the cat thought the couch was a better place to sharpen his claws than the convenient scratching post scented with catnip. Even before Jackson had moved in, there had been slightly wilting flowers on the table and closet doors that weren't always closed.

Ellery had pictures on the walls that he liked—subtle colors, happy moments, watercolor prints. His mother liked pictures of flowers.

Robert Sampson had blocks of navy-blue canvas, carelessly splashed with white and black.

It made Jackson's head hurt, as did the rest of the house.

He haunted the place, stealthy as a cat, as Joey and Henry rushed around, conducting the most useless housecleaning ever.

"Fuck house-*cleaning*," Jackson muttered. "This place needs to be *cleansed*."

Because there wasn't a speck of dust in the place. But there weren't any good feelings either.

"Hey, Joey!" Jackson called. "Do you know what happened to *Mrs.* Sampson?"

"Hadley?" Joey called back from the kitchen, where he was sterilizing the trash can with whatever was in the green bottle. "Yeah. She moved to her sister's place in New Hampshire a year and a half ago. She discontinued housecleaning and let Mr. Sampson pick his own after that."

Jackson grunted. "Lucky for me he picked you."

"So, what were you going to do if he hadn't?" Joey asked, coming in from the kitchen to join Jackson as he—gloves on—checked all available drawers for incriminating information.

"My original plan was to slip in when the cleaners came by. And by the way, I knew this would work because that's how somebody used Ellery's cleaning service to bug his house last fall. We've been tidying up after ourselves since we found out, but if you've got room for another house on your roster—"

"Yeah, sure. You send me his address, I'll give you a once-a-week wipe job." Joey chuckled at the double entendre, and Jackson rolled his eyes.

And kept looking.

"Hey, the kitchen's done, and your boy's doing the bathroom," Joey told him.

"Because you're a sadistic punk who's taking advantage of a rookie," Jackson said, and Joey's chuckle picked up the evil.

"Well, *yeah*. But besides that. Do you want to see the office?"

Jackson's eyes popped open. "So could we look for bloodstains first?" he begged.

"Oh yeah. I'm all over that. Do you have a sample kit?"

Jackson pulled a Ziploc bag out of one of the pockets of his cargo shorts. It had thin nonlatex gloves, five small sample bottles, a sterile pack of Q-tips, and a little spritz bottle of luminol.

"Never leave home without it," he muttered. He had another Ziploc bag with scissors, tweezers, and small evidence bags in his other cargo pocket, for when only physical evidence would do.

"Good. Let's go find some blood spatter."

At first, it seemed impossible. The office was darkly paneled and oppressive as hell, with oxblood chairs and a desk topped with black marble. Joey started turning on lights, but Jackson stopped him and reached into his pocket again. This time, he came out with his keychain and a small-sized black light, which he switched on near the doorway and moved methodically from floor to ceiling along the walls as he moved.

"Look for dark spots," he said. "Like black holes. I don't want to hit the whole room with luminol—this will give us an idea of where to start."

Joey looked around and frowned. "Okay, so I know this is totally cliché, but there used to be a big chunky paperweight on the desk, and it's gone now."

"With square edges on the base?" Jackson asked, because could it really be that easy?

"You know it!"

"Turn on the light and look to see if it got moved," Jackson told him. "And show me where the rug went."

Joey looked at him funny. "How'd you know the rug was from the study? He's replaced it already."

"Hunh." Jackson had never really thought about it. "I guess, you know, bad guy kills his enemies in the study. It's a time-honored trope among bad guys."

"Does that really work? I mean, do bad guys honor the rules?"

"No," Jackson said definitively. "Our last bad guy was training assassins for the military—and he took good guys and broke them and made them bad guys. I'd say that's the opposite of honoring the rules."

"You broke my tiny brain, Rivers. I think that's why you and I never worked. I'd be all, 'Let's fuck!' and you'd be all, 'Are either of us ready for the relationship that another fuck would give us?' And by the time I answered that question in my head, my boner had disappeared."

Jackson snorted. "As if *that's* an option. Now show me where the rug used to be, and look around for that paperweight!"

"Come here and help me shift the rug that's down there now. It's bigger than the one he moved."

"Is the desk in the same place?" Jackson asked, because the rug was actually under the desk.

"Yeah, why?"

"Because he couldn't have done this by himself without fucking up his floor," Jackson noted, grabbing his end of the desk. "And I don't see any drag marks. So someone else must have been here. And I think I know who."

"Care to share with the class—*oof*! This thing is heavier than it looks!"

"No, because I want you to have plausible deniability," Jackson panted. Fucking desk—Jesus, his back would never be the same. He set it down with a thump, and both of them went after the rug. "Oh my God! This is two rugs—not even a rug and a pad. What in the hell?"

They both stared at the mess on the floor. What should have been super expensive lacquered ebony was scrubbed so hard, the finish had gone white and rough. A spot the size of a car seat had been completely sanded out of the black floor. "That's not blood," Joey said grimly.

"But it used to be." Jackson took a breath. "And on wood this color, it still might be. Kill the lights for me, okay?"

Joey did as he asked, and Jackson wielded the black light. Sure enough…. "See those drops right there?" Jackson asked, pulling out the Q-tips and luminol.

"Wow—in the black light they look… blacker."

"Yeah. I think it's the shiny lacquer. It works as a foil."

"Doesn't hurt that the bleach spot is glowing like the crab nebula," Joey said, awe in his voice.

"Right? Now here." Jackson tossed Joey his camera. "Film it."

For the sake of the video, he said, "I'm taking a swab here, from Robert Sampson's floor. First, I hit it with the luminol, and…."

And like magic under the black light, the blood drops appeared.

"And you've got yourself a crime scene," Joey said. "Damn! I learned how to crunch numbers, you learned how to solve stuff. Well done!"

And at that moment, three things happened.

Henry walked in carrying a big glass bad-guy paperweight, complete with blood and brain matter, secure in a Ziploc bag, at the same time the front door opened.

"Hey, River Breeze people!" called a familiar voice from the front door. "I need you to get the fuck out of here! Goddammit, I forgot this was your fucking day!"

They all met eyes, and Jackson swore, hopping up from the ground and kicking the rug over.

"He's seen me and Henry," Jackson muttered, settling the rug and grabbing one end of the desk. "Henry, put the murder weapon in Joey's basket. Joey, grab the basket and get out first. Get in the van, head for the rug, take my cell and call Kryzynski. He's 'Dickhead' on the contacts list."

Henry started moving before he was done talking. "What do we do?" he asked, grabbing the other end of the desk while Joey balanced the basket. Jackson's chest tightened all over again, and he saw stars, but they couldn't afford to slow down now.

"Get captured and follow him," Jackson said, taking a deep breath. "Joey, go!"

They heard him in the hallway a minute later. It sounded like he was stalling. "Sure, Mr. Sampson. Sorry—just you asked for an extra vacuum because of the new rug, right?"

"Did you get to it?" Sampson asked, a thread of panic in his voice.

"My boys were just moving the desk, right? But we didn't get to the rug. We got everything else done, almost. We were in the middle of the guest bathroom, I mean, and we haven't vacuumed the bedrooms, but the kitchen is *spotless*."

"I don't give a shit about the goddamned kitchen. And I changed my mind about the other rug. I want it back. Where did you send it?"

"My cousin's place. You know. Out in Levee Oaks?"

They set the desk down gently, but Jackson had a moment to smile. *Way to sound like an idiot, Joey—keep it up.*

"Okay, what now?"

"Ball caps on?" His was tucked in his back pocket, and so was Henry's. They replaced their ball caps, shucked their gloves, and Henry grabbed his cleaning basket.

Jackson called out in Spanish, "Get in the car and start it. We'll try to follow!"

"Hurry up. He's glaring at me as I walk, and I think there's a gun safe in the living room!"

Jackson kept walking, chatting conversationally with Henry, as though Henry knew what he was saying. "Just say *sí*," he muttered. "We might be able to fake our way out of here." Then, a little louder to Joey, "If he stops us, take off for your cousin's place and get the rug. Call Dickhead and tell him you have evidence, and have him meet us there!"

"*Sí!*" Joey called, and then the front door closed.

Jackson rounded the corner out of the study, leading the way, Henry behind him. He was waylaid by a heavy hand on his shoulder.

"You didn't take anything, did you?" Robert Sampson demanded, and Jackson shook his head, smiling guilelessly.

"Just your murder weapon and a blood drop," he said in Spanish, watching the suspicion in Sampson's tanned, handsome, middle-aged face deepen.

"Wait a minute, do I know you?"

Jackson turned to Henry and nodded decisively, relieved when Henry's military training kicked in and he took off.

"What in the hell—" Sampson had turned toward his left to see where Henry had gone, so Jackson cut to the right, hauling ass after him. The front door slammed, and his heart gave a giant throb in his chest, but he pushed on, thinking if only he could make it to the front door, he'd be clear. He could hop in the van, he could call Kryzynski, and he'd never skip his doctor's appointment again.

He rounded the hallway corner, Sampson hot on his heels, when the front door opened again, this time in an explosion of light.

"Cormier! Stop him!" Sampson yelled, and Jackson skidded to a halt, trying to sidestep the massive figure who'd just walked in.

Jackson couldn't make out the guy's features beyond his general size and build, but as he scrambled backward and into Sampson, Cormier said, "Wait, do I know you?"

And then Sampson clocked him on the back of the head with something, and he crumpled to the floor.

Panic Fish

ELLERY! THIS is Henry! Bad shit happened!

Ellery stared at Jackson's name on the phone and tried to keep his cool. He was just about to take a Lyft to River Breeze Cleaning, and goddammit if he wouldn't be early. The cardiologist's office hadn't just agreed to make an appointment. They'd asked if Mr. Rivers needed an ambulance. And Ellery was so goddamned done at this point, he almost said yes. To see "Bad shit happened!" coming up on Jackson's phone was about the last thing he thought he could bear.

"Henry?" he said after hitting Call. "Is he conscious?"

"He's *captured*!" Henry told him, sounding pissed off. "Sampson got back early, and Joey and I got out. But as I was getting in the van, this big Navigator pulled up and a guy the size of a mountain got out. Before we left the house, Jackson told us that we were supposed to go get the rug from Joey's cousin's place and call the cops and make sure they met us there."

Oh God. Oh God, oh God. "Well, did you call them?" Ellery demanded. "Where are you now?"

"We're about a mile from Sampson's place, heading—fuck. Joey, where the fuck are we going?"

Another voice answered him, and Henry got back on.

"We're on Fair Oaks," he said dutifully. "We're taking Fair Oaks to Watt, then Watt to 80, then we're getting off at Marysville. I have no idea where any of that is, but here's the address."

Henry rattled off the address, and Ellery wrote it down. "I can find it, and I'm pretty sure your buddy in the van can get you there quickly. Don't do anything until the cops get—"

"Fuck that!" Henry snarled. "They've got Jackson, and his lips were almost goddamned blue. Fucking Jesus, if he's not okay, I'll kill him myself."

"There's a lot of that going around," Ellery muttered, hauling ass through the office and ignoring Jade's surprised look. "I've got to go. Kryzynski's texting me—*fuck*!"

"What?" Henry demanded.

"Nothing. I'll see you there!"

"What's up?" Jade asked, stopping him at the door.

"They've got Jackson. He's not doing well, and *he's got the fucking car!*"

"Oh. Is that all." Jade turned and grabbed her purse from its perch on the counter and hauled ass past him as he held the door open. "And by the way? You can explain what all of that means as we go. Where the fuck are we going?"

Ellery rattled off directions as they pounded down the stairs and got into her car. The office only had one parking spot. Jackson had told him it would be a problem, and now he knew he was right. God*dammit.* It wasn't until Jade was peeling out of the parking lot that he answered Kryzynski's insistent buzzing on his phone.

"Stay put," Kryzynski ordered. "We've got this under con—"

Ellery hung up and blocked his call.

"Now," Jade said, as he threw his head back against the headrest, "you will explain 'they've got him' and 'not doing well.'"

"Jackson was searching Robert Sampson's home with the housekeeping service—someone he knew from the old days—"

"Joey?" Jade said with a twist of the lips, and for the umpteenth time, Ellery cursed the fact that he was late to the party. "Nice guy. He has the maturity of a twelve-year-old."

"I'm surprised they're not married, then," Ellery muttered.

"Jackson didn't take him seriously. You shouldn't either. Now what happened?"

"Sampson got home. Joey and Henry managed to get out, but Sampson had seen Jackson before, and before he could just bolt out the door, someone else got there." Ellery shuddered. "We think it might be Candy Cormier."

"Oh dear God!" Jade muttered. "And they just left him?"

"The plan was to lure them out to an industrial cleaning place, where the rug is waiting to be repurposed."

"What rug?"

"The rug with all the bloodstains on it that prove Sampson killed his son," Ellery said. Which apparently he had, given the financials he'd looked at that morning.

"So that's why we're going out past Marysville Boulevard?" she asked, and Ellery nodded.

"It's halfway to Levee Oaks," he said. As far as he knew, the only thing off Marysville and Elkhorn in that direction was sparse housing tracts and the occasional warehouse. That close to Watt, the depression caused when McClellan AFB had closed down had hit the area hard.

"So how do they know he wasn't doing good?" she asked, her voice sinking.

Ellery closed his eyes and then opened them quickly. Jade had taken 80, and they were almost to Watt, but behind them, he saw five police cars, lights flashing, closing in on them fast.

"Jade, I think that's Kryzynski and the cavalry. Do me a favor and gun it like you own the road?"

Jade's chuckle reminded him of Jackson, and the Celica practically lifted off the pavement and flew.

"So," she said, like they weren't breaking several speed laws with the full fury of SACPD flying, lights blazing, behind them. "Jackson."

"Remember November, when his heart stopped?" God. He even recognized the breathing. In through the nose, out through the mouth.

"Wasn't he seeing a doctor for that? Every month?"

"Yeah, but, well, after we got back from down south, he missed one and made one and missed one…. That last one was in May."

"And…?"

"And he got hurt two days ago, and he sounded out of breath, but we both assumed it was just adrenaline and panic. But today, he called me up, and he sounded breathy again, and he said, 'Hey, remember that thing that's wrong with my heart—'"

"He *said* that?" And for the first time, some of *her* panic slipped through.

"I *know*!" His throat was raw with the force of his shout, and she didn't even blink.

"Oh dear God. Unblock Kryzynski and tell him to have an ambulance ready!"

Ellery stared at her. "I can't believe I didn't think of that," he said after a moment.

"Well, that's why there's more than one of us looking after him," she muttered. "That man needs a team effort to keep him alive."

But Ellery was already calling a reluctant teammate.

"*Now* you decide to talk to me? Is that you ahead? Because the guys are fifty-fifty on whether to arrest you or pay you to drive *for* them—"

"It's Jackson's sister. He's got a heart murmur."

"Sampson?"

"No, idiot. *Jackson.* He was having trouble catching his breath. I don't know if Henry told you that. I figured you'd have a quick line to an ambulance and could have one on standby."

"Fuck. Yeah. I'll call that in." There was a tense silence while Jade took the Watt exit so fast, she almost ran into the rail. "You should have her pull back and let us go first," he said.

"I don't even know what's waiting there. For all we know, Robert Sampson is still back at his house carving Jackson into pieces with Candy Cormier," Ellery said bitterly.

"That occurred to me, but Henry seemed certain Sampson would show—"

"Then maybe *you* should be the ones to hold back!" Ellery told him. "If I get there, I'm only the freaked-out boyfriend. They'll still go after the rug—it's not as if I'm a threat—and we might get Jackson back. But if *you* go in there with the whole fucking SACPD, he's going to get his head blown off."

As if by magic, all of the lights in the rearview went dark, and the sirens cooled too.

"Are we on speaker?" Ellery asked belatedly.

"I've got a uniform in the car with me, relaying orders," Kryzynski confirmed. "Fine. Go in your way. We're right behind you."

There was a pause, and Ellery almost pressed the End Call button, when Kryzynski spoke up. "He didn't look good."

"When?"

"Two days ago, when he got sliced by Ralph Gordon. He looked clammy and out of breath—and he's fit. I thought it was panic. I mean, I was there the last time he did one of those apartment places. But his lips were pale. He didn't...." This was hard, Ellery realized. Sean Kryzynski didn't like admitting he was wrong. "Didn't look good."

"We'll get him back," Ellery reassured him, because somebody needed to say it.

"Of course."

Ellery hung up then so he didn't have to hear pity over the phone, but he unblocked Kryzynski and then held on to the Jesus bar as Jade cut off a delivery truck in order to jump two spaces ahead on the traffic over the bridge.

He didn't complain, though. He just closed his eyes and prayed.

THE TRAFFIC on the overpass seemed interminable, and when it thinned out, what was left was an uneven section of stoplights before Watt hit Elkhorn. Jade turned left toward Marysville, and then right toward Levee Oaks. She slowed down through town, but once she passed the railroad tracks, when things stretched out toward cow country, she gunned it until the first set of warehouses appeared.

"What's your program say?" she muttered. Once the car had stopped jumping around, Ellery had programmed the address into his phone.

"It says we're here, but it doesn't say which one."

The warehouses, painted yellow, were lined up facing the road, with a long, naked paved road leading up to the parking lot. Only two of the businesses appeared to be occupied—a pottery warehouse and Noel's Industrial Cleaning Solutions, the warehouse on the end.

"I don't see Joey's work van," Jade said thoughtfully as they drove up. "I'm going to swing around the back. Text Bozo the Cop and tell him where we're going."

The police had backed off, but Ellery figured the whole line of them would be finding a sly way to approach this naked building in the middle of scorched farmland soon enough. As Jade pulled into the parking lot and around to the back of the warehouses, Ellery spotted a copse of oak trees lining a drainage ditch about a hundred yards away, and suddenly felt better. The copse wasn't that big—maybe the size of a football field—but it served to break up the scorched straw that landmarked the area and basically surrounded the businesses sitting in the middle of the sweltering blacktop.

Closer to the rug-cleaning service, he saw a big vat of something sitting by a steam hose, both of them powered by what was probably a generator inside the warehouse. There were a series of pallets laid out neatly and a guy with brown hair pulled up in a ponytail, wearing a plastic apron and shoulder-length plastic gloves, holding a rolled rug upright next to him, and arguing with a younger, smaller man wearing a brown service shirt. And then he saw Henry, standing there, watching them. Beyond the pallets sat a big white service van with River Breeze Cleaning on the side.

"Must be the right place," Ellery said. "Henry's here, but no Jackson."

Jade peeled into a parking spot on the driver's side of the van, and they both hopped out into the blistering heat.

"Cramer!" Henry called. "Get over here and tell this asshole how important this is!"

"I could give a shit about important!" the guy sweating it out in the vinyl overcoat complained. "I've got six rugs—*six*—and it's already twelve o'clock. By two o'clock, it's going to be a fucking inferno out here, and I'll be dying of goddamned heat stroke!"

"Half of SACPD is about to show up to tell you how much they don't care," Ellery said. "Is that the rug from Robert Sampson?"

"Uh...."

The smaller man in the brown service shirt grinned up at Ellery. "You must be Jackson's boy," he said gleefully. "You don't look like his type, but that's probably his type totally, you know?"

Ellery smiled weakly. "Yeah, we make it work." Then, to the guy with the rug, "So—Sampson's rug?"

"Yeah, that's what it says on the tag."

"So how about you let Joey here take the damned rug before the bad guys get here. Then you're free to clean whatever the hell you want!"

"Oh!" Joey—it must have been Joey—was looking at Ellery with awe. "That's way better than my plan! Big brains," he said, turning to Henry. "Him and Jackson got big brains. Leaves me in the dust."

"Give them the rug," Ellery commanded, searching Levee Oaks Boulevard with anxious eyes. "And holy shit, that must be the bad guys."

"Yeah, that's the SUV we saw in front of Sampson's house," Henry muttered.

"Get Joey and the rug and go!" Ellery snapped, then turned to the guy with the ponytail. "And you just gave them somebody else's rug. Tell them that. Tell them you gave them Smith's rug or Kryzynski's rug or whoever's!" He turned to Jade and grabbed her hand. "Come on! I'm not sure if they've spotted us yet! Henry, get a move on!"

Henry and Joey hustled to the van, shoved the rug in, and slammed the doors, while Ellery pulled Jade into the shade of the stifling warehouse and looked for places to hide.

"Office," he hissed, nodding in the direction of a small cubicle with a roller chair, a computer, and a lot of loose files.

"That's the first place they'd look. Back here!" It was her turn to grab *his* hand and drag him back behind a service van much like Joey's, but this one was dark brown and less well-maintained. His deck shoes slid on the sealed concrete awkwardly as he tried to find a place to hide in the dim light. In the corner behind the van was a nook and a sink where someone might keep a mop bucket and cleaning supplies, but Ellery had spotted those in the corner by the office. He and Jade squeezed in and then crouched, one on either side of the sink. Jade's back was to the warehouse door, but Ellery could see a twenty-by-fourteen panorama of what happened next, including Joey's cousin Raymond still working in the shade of the warehouse, standing another rug on its end.

Joey's van peeled out, and Ellery swore as another shadow slipped into the warehouse to position itself behind the van.

"Henry!" he growled.

"Sh!" the shadow hissed back. "Joey's going to the station off Richards Boulevard."

Ellery pulled out his phone to alert Kryzynski. *Hiding. Rug is coming to station on Richards. Don't arrest Joey—please be nice.*

Hiding?

Cormier and Sampson pulling up. Sh!

He hid the phone in his pocket and met Jade's eyes over their small dark semicloset. The Navigator pulled up to the entrance of the warehouse, blocking the sunlight, and Ellery took another moment to pray.

Gasping for Breath

JACKSON SQUINTED against the pain in his head and tried to focus on breathing, in and out, and trying not to panic.

He was getting shoved in a car. *Oh God. Never get in the car.* He told people that all the time, but they were shoving him in a car, and he had to go.

Didn't he?

"Who the hell is this guy?" Robert Sampson—that was who was speaking, right? He was getting in the driver's seat, and the enormous refrigerator-sized white boy was belting Jackson in the passenger's seat next to him.

Wasn't that nice.

"You care," Jackson said woozily as the guy snapped the seat belt.

"You're awake," came the gruff reply. "Are you awake enough to remember me?"

Jackson squeezed his eyes tight. "Lacey's compound." Wait, this didn't make sense. "You weren't Lacey's guy. You were… what's his face. The German guy who just wanted mercs, not monsters. Hamblin. You were Hamblin's guy."

"Yeah, well, Hamblin took off, and we were left in the wind."

But not too long in the wind, if Burton knew Candy Cormier's name.

"Sorry he left you," Jackson said sincerely. Because if Hamblin, the mercenary king, had grabbed this guy, he wouldn't be there turning drug-dealing-pedophile doctors into murderers and ordinary bad guys into hamburger. "So you came to Sacramento to sell drugs?"

Cormier shrugged. "Bear market, what can I say?"

"Well, fancy meeting you here," Jackson mumbled. "Can I roll down the window? I'm gonna throw up."

Sampson and Cormier shouted, but Jackson would have rather they shot him than just let him puke on himself. Instead, he hung his head out of the side of the car in the slow suburban traffic and let loose. And again. *And… oh… there we go. All done.*

"Jesus God," Sampson muttered. "Could you roll up the window? The stench!"

"If you had some water, I could wash it off," Jackson said, spots still in front of his eyes. "You know, maybe next time think twice about how you incapacitate someone. Head blows make me woozy, ask me how I know."

Cormier shoved a water bottle into his hand that he must have gotten from the little amenities island in the middle of the back seat. A nicely stocked bad guy—Jackson approved. He rinsed and spat and drank a few swallows, then used the rest of it to wash the side of the car before partially rolling up the window.

When he was done, he leaned back against his seat, exhausted.

"So tell me when we get to the rug place," he mumbled. "I should gather my strength."

"You're not even curious?" Cormier asked. "Why I'm involved? I mean, last time we met, you couldn't help sticking your nose into everything." He grimaced. "That's why you and me met. I have screws in my arm, you know, from that fight. Can't wait to return the favor."

Well, with any luck, Jackson would have a heart attack and die before he got to do that. The tightness in his chest hadn't lessened one bit.

"You moved up to Sacramento, set up base, and you took over all the in-home meth operations with stupid ease. I hate to burst your bubble, but I met a bunch of those guys—they're not that bright. Anyway, well done."

"Thanks a lot."

"Wasn't a compliment."

"I'll break your arm twice," Cormier ground out.

"Looking forward to dying first." He wasn't really, though. He really wanted to live. He and Ellery had things to do—wasn't that what Ellery had said? They'd *always* have things to do? Jackson wanted to work in the little office with the shitty parking. He wanted to see Jade and Mike reproduce and have bossy and tactless children. He wanted to see Kaden's kids grow up.

He wanted to touch Ellery Cramer every day for the rest of his life.

"You should be so lucky."

Jackson barely refrained from chuckling as his heart pounded threadily in his throat. *Nuh-nuh*—no one was torturing *Jackson* to death. He had an *ace* up his sleeve.

"Good luck with that. Anyway, so you take over operations and realize—surprise! That meth isn't the only cottage industry in town. Poppies and coca plants are imports, but you're a domestic kind of criminal, and Sampson here has a corner on the opioid-crisis platform, and you want in. How'm I doing?"

"I should have made you my lieutenant," Cormier said, sounding impressed. "Tell me what happened next!"

"Mm…. How about I tell you what happened first, since I think you might have missed out on it. What do you think, Sampson? Should I tell him all the ways you made this happen?"

"Shut him up!" Sampson snarled, and Jackson gave Cormier the side-eye.

Cormier was listening very carefully. "You know, if you tell me something worthwhile, I might just make it quick," he said, thoughtful-like.

"I'll go you one better. I'll give you a reason to get rid of your competition," Jackson said. "On account of general assholery."

"Is that a word?" Cormier pondered. "Or did you just make that up?"

"I think you need to hear the story first," Jackson told him, closing his eyes and fighting nausea again. *Deep breath. Relax.* Open the chest and pretend his head didn't feel like an exploding water balloon. "Once upon a time, a man had a son."

"You leave my son out of this!" Yeah, he sounded mean, but the Navigator wasn't driving off the road, so Jackson was going to assume it was for fun.

"If only you had," Jackson said. "I bet he told you his son would get you a distribution network, didn't he?"

"He did," Cormier said, voice uninflected. "Only his son seemed… uncooperative."

"Well, let's look at that, shall we? Because little Martin Eugene Sampson spent his life being uncooperative—pretty much from… when was it, Robert? When did he start telling you no?"

"He never told me no." There was a nasty edge to Sampson's voice that said he was probably telling the truth.

"So how long *did* you molest your son? How old was he? From ten, I'd bet, maybe a little younger, looking at the family photos. If I looked back at his school history, is that when he started acting out? Did you stop when he got arrested? Or did you just pick up when he came back? Because by then, you knew about his history. You stopped treating him like Daddy's precious little angel—started treating him like a whore, right?"

"He's going to have a heart attack," Cormier said in detached wonder. "You're telling the truth."

Sampson just kept sputtering, choking sounds coming from his throat, spittle flying from his lips—but he kept his hands on the wheel, so Jackson kept going.

"So here's the thing. Sampson told you his son could bring you distributors—but he *lied*. Because until Martin got popped for coke eighteen months ago, he had no idea his son was into drugs and porn. Sure, he'd seduce his *friends'* kids into the business—and maybe even into his bed. He had no problem doing that. But see, that source of distribution was drying up. I mean, I only know of the three—but I'm betting you gave talks at college, talked to Martin's RA when he was at school, internships, graduation parties—I'm betting he had a whole little network, didn't he?"

"My guess there was twenty kids working for him," Cormier confirmed, like a businessman used to dealing with numbers.

"But his son—his precious only offspring—was never part of his network until he got out of prison, isn't that right?"

Jackson heard the click of the safety lock of a 9mm Beretta and gave thanks that it was aimed at Sampson's head and not his own.

Suddenly Robert Scott Sampson sounded very, very lucid indeed.

"No," he said. "I tried to keep him out of it."

"You failed," Jackson said cruelly. He *felt* cruel. God—Martin Sampson had been the bad guy—a piece of fucking work, and that was the truth. But he'd had help getting there. He'd had the best help that drug money could buy. "And in the meantime, Ash Carver's son was killed in a wreck, and suddenly people are bailing from your network left and right, because dumb drug-dealing college kids grow up, don't they?"

"I loved that kid!"

"Biblically, like you loved your own?" Jackson shouted back.

"Whoa!" Cormier murmured. "Getting heated here, Rivers. You jealous of that kid?"

"I feel *bad* for him," Jackson snapped. "Because his father was getting desperate. He still had drugs coming in—more, in fact, after he killed Ash Carver. What happened there, by the way? I'm curious.

Because Cormier wasn't there to help you move the desk or hide the murder weapon. How did Ash Carver rate the full-course-dead-monty?"

"He panicked," Sampson said gruffly. "Twenty years of getting his money the same way I was getting mine, and he started freaking out. We... we wrestled, I pushed him backwards—"

"And he cracked his head open on that massive marble desk of yours, and you had to get another rug."

"My wife... suspected. I got rid of the rug, and she moved out. She'd... she'd been hit pretty bad by Marty going to jail."

"So what'd she say when she found out you killed him?" Jackson taunted.

"Oh, we both did that," Cormier said casually. "He was freaking out. Big Sampson promised me his boy would deliver on more distributors, and suddenly Little Sampson's sobbing and telling his dad that he can't hit them up to be drug dealers, that he's not going to drag Davy's little brother down the same shitty road the Carver brat died on, and he'd rather go to rehab and live poor than get one more fucking day of allowance from someone who made their money like his old man."

"Why frame Henry Worrall?" Jackson asked, curious.

"He was there," Cormier said, with no passion whatsoever.

Then Sampson yelled, "Because it was his fucking fault. My kid had his flaws, but goddammit, he did what I told him. Then he sees... what? Some fucking grunt come out of the woodwork and tell him no, and he can't help his old man out? He talked about the guy like he was Captain America, and dammit, I wanted that guy to fucking pay."

A part of Jackson wept. He'd suspected that. Suspected that seeing Henry as a hero and himself as a pathetic dealer, feared by the guys he used to fuck, would do a number on Martin Sampson. Suspected that there was still that kid—the happy one, before Daddy started paying special attention to him—who thought that the world was safe and he had a special place in it.

He just hadn't realized that his special place was dead in a dumpster, which was apparently Jackson's special place too.

"So your son finally gets an attack of conscience, and your new business partner kills him," Jackson said.

"I said we both did it." Oddly enough, Cormier sounded wounded. "The kid was losing his shit, and Daddy gave him a sedative, to put him under. I said, 'What's going to happen when he wakes up?' Then this asshole goes, 'I'll figure it out later.' So I grabbed a big block thing and figured it out right then."

Jackson was tempted to throw up again. "Is that right?" he asked Sampson. "Wow. You must be so proud. Is this how you imagined your life turning out?"

"Is this how you imagined *yours*?" Sampson sneered.

"Believe it or not, this is better than I ever planned," Jackson told him, nodding. "I mean, people are going to miss me. I'm going to leave behind a pissed-off boyfriend and a psychotic cat and a brother and sister who might figure out how to bring me back from the dead so they can kill me themselves. I've got a partner in the business and friends who like donuts. Honestly—" He pulled in a deep breath and tried not to wheeze. "—that's way better than I ever thought I'd have it. And *so* much better than what you've got going on right now. *Hey!*"

Sampson jerked the wheel, and the Navigator almost spun off the road as they neared the big crossing sculpture that marked Levee Oaks.

"What!" Sampson shouted, just as Cormier yelled, "So help me, I will blow your brains out in this fucking car. And I *like* this fucking car!"

"Is that the rug place?" Jackson said, like he hadn't shouted loudly on purpose to distract them. Joey had been peeling out of the long road to the warehouses as they'd neared, and Jackson didn't want them to mark Joey, or his van, as they approached.

It worked—it must have, because Cormier tapped Jackson's delicate skull with the end of his pistol, and Jackson had to work not to throw up again.

"I just didn't want you to miss it," he mumbled, sagging into the seat. God, two concussions in a year. Ellery was going to make him wear a helmet to go to the bathroom, and Jackson would totally deserve it.

"You want to know who I'm not going to fucking miss!" Cormier yelled. "Oh my God—can we just kill him here?"

"The rug guy hasn't done anything," Jackson said. "Besides, you may need him to get rid of evidence for you someday. His cousin says he's the best at his job. I don't know why you're even trying to get the rug back now!"

"He's got a point," Sampson muttered. "I mean, if he just cleans it like they cleaned the old one—"

"I don't like loose ends!" Cormier snarled.

"Yeah, well, you didn't trust me to take care of the video either!" Sampson was pouting. Oh my God—he was having a big-dick throwdown to see who was the best criminal. "My idea was simple, elegant, and Henry Worrall would be in jail right now if you'd just left one doctored copy out there for the police to find."

"I do have to give it to him there," Jackson said, like he was weighing scumbag pros and cons. "It was the extra tape that got Henry off. You know, so you can live and learn."

"I just don't trust him."

"Well, Sampson *has* been running drugs for twenty years. I mean, let's hear it for experience. He's managed to hide the fact that he killed his partner off for more than a year—he does have some skills there." Jackson was getting some of his breath back. Maybe it was because he quit fighting, and maybe it was because talking the crimes out, even with the bad guys, relaxed him enough to breathe a little. "But then, he's a guy who would fuck his own son—and then fuck him over—so I can see your point."

"You're disgusting." Sampson curled his lip at Jackson, and Jackson's temper spilled over.

"He was a baby, and you betrayed him. You *betrayed your own goddamned son*!" Jackson didn't care if they *did* shoot him. "He could have been anything—he was beautiful, he was smart. Man, he could have gotten a boyfriend, gotten married, been happy. But you had to touch him with all your filth and think, 'Hey, I'm not having *him* sell drugs, so *he's* going to be okay!' You're like this... this fucking juggernaut of destroyed lives, and you're looking down on *me* because I figured it out? *You're* the one who deserves to be dead in a fucking dumpster, man. You should have held the funeral for your kid the first day you touched him."

"Wow," Cormier said. "Like, seriously. When you put it that way, I might do the world a favor and kill him after all. It's not like we've solved the distribution problem yet. He's got all this high-end oxy product sitting on his shelves, and I've had to kill two goons in the last week because they disappointed me!"

Jackson closed his eyes as Sampson gunned the motor in anger, taking the right-hand turn down the side road to the warehouse businesses at top speed.

"Maybe you want to wait until after he's gotten us there alive, brother," Jackson murmured to Cormier. "That would be great, you think?"

"This is why you beat me when we fought," Cormier said glumly. "You're fuckin' smart. Man, are you sure you won't work for me? I could really use someone fuckin' smart. This guy's a doctor—you'd think he wouldn't be this stupid."

The car hit a pothole at top speed, and Jackson was grateful his window was still down a little, the hot wind blasting his face. At least he didn't rattle his sore head off the glass. Cormier shut up, and Sampson spun the Navigator around the back of the warehouses and gunned it, then slammed on the brakes just in time to slide to a halt in front of the open back dock of the rug cleaner's unit.

Sampson slid out first and then Cormier, who muttered, "Stay here," to Jackson as they went to talk to a guy wearing a brown ponytail, plastic coveralls, and a really shocked expression.

Jackson watched as they approached and started to engage with the guy—who appeared to be stalling, his eyes flickering left, then right, then forward again.

Oh shit. This must be Joey's cousin, Raymond—and he looked terrified.

Jackson put his hand on the door latch and slowly opened the door, slid down under the window line, and hugged the side of the Navigator.

"Uh, yeah," Cousin Raymond was saying. "Here's your rug—see? It's got your name on it. Sampson, right?"

"That's not my rug!" Sampson snapped. "Jesus, how stoned are you?"

"Whoa, dude. I may have to go see if it's in the warehouse. Hang out here a sec!"

"I'm coming back there with you," Cormier said, and as they walked into the dark, Jackson peered into the warehouse and saw a brown service van parked a little back from the entrance. And, very badly hidden in a little alcove, he spotted movement—a flash of magenta, and beyond that, a pale face and big brown eyes squinting into the sunlight behind him.

Oh Jesus. Ellery and Jade were in the warehouse.

Jackson had nowhere to run. The warehouses stood isolated in the middle of the blacktop in the middle of a field that had been cleared for more development—development that had never materialized.

Cormier had the guns, and Sampson was pacing outside the warehouse. Jackson needed to go somewhere that *wasn't* the warehouse to get their attention, and he couldn't run.

Fast.

Couldn't run fast.

Restlessly he peered over the hood of the Navigator again, and saw—*oh, thank God*—six SACPD cruisers, no lights or sirens, pulling up the long road. But Sampson was peering into the warehouse, and inside, he heard Cormier say, "Hey, did you see that? You got rats or something?" And suddenly, he knew Jade and Ellery would be dead by the time those placidly moving cruisers got there.

Deep breath—the outside corner of the warehouse was what? Forty feet? Who couldn't sprint forty feet? He and Ellery ran miles every morning, and shit, if his heart gave out before he got there, Cormier and Sampson would at least be distracted, right?

He stood up straight and banged twice on the hood of the Navigator, loud enough to wake the dead. He looked Robert Scott Sampson right in the eyes. "Come and get me, fucker."

Then he turned and sprinted for the corner of the warehouse.

"He's getting away!" Sampson yelled, and Jackson had a blissful moment to think the bad guy sounded like every cop movie ever before his chest tightened like a rubber band and he had to fight for every breath.

Breathe Fishy, Breathe

ELLERY COULD see him, crouching by the side of the car, but mostly he was just a form. The big guy—Cormier? He'd followed Raymond into the warehouse, on the other side of the van, and Ellery and Jade locked eyes.

They were going to be found, and they were going to be killed, and Jackson would never forgive either of them.

And then Jackson cut Ellery's lifespan in half.

He stood up, banged on the Navigator, and yelled, then turned around and took off for the side of the complex, leaving Ellery and Jade to gape.

"Do you think he saw us?" Jade asked, but Ellery was too busy trying to run on the slippery concrete in his dress shoes. He slid once, balanced on his fingertips, caught his weight on the van, and still wouldn't have gotten any traction if Jade hadn't shoved him from behind.

In the meantime, Cormier barreled out of the warehouse, with Joey's cousin nowhere to be seen. Just as Ellery and Jade were getting clear of the sealed concrete, he passed them, unholstering his gun as he ran.

And then Henry rocketed past both of them, heading for the same corner of the warehouse Jackson had disappeared behind, his tennis shoes having no problem at all on the goddamned floor.

By the time they got to the outside corner of the warehouse, Ellery was thinking enough to slow down.

Neither he nor Jade were armed. If they ran into a situation without looking, he could get Jade killed.

"Wait," he breathed, grabbing Jade's arm and hoping she wouldn't deck him. But Jade was smart, and together they hugged the shady side of the warehouse, peering around the corner to the last scene of a Quentin Tarantino movie.

Henry was about two feet in front of them, and Robert Sampson had a gun trained on his head.

"Don't move," he muttered. "Jesus, you little pissant. Come out of nowhere on me? For fucking real?"

Henry slowly raised his hands behind his head and kept his eyes squarely on Jackson and the guy built like a tank in a suit that he was facing.

Jackson's face was turned toward Ellery, and he had a look of triumph in his eyes, like he'd accomplished something. His knees were slightly bent, his hands out, as if he was getting ready to move, but his chest was heaving in and out and his face was a waxy grayish color that had Ellery biting his lip so he wouldn't moan—or nag.

"You look like shit," the big guy said. "You sure you're up to this, or would you rather just roll over and die?"

Jackson's face—pale as it was—assumed that "fuck you to the balls" look that Ellery was so familiar with.

"If I roll over and die, I'm gonna have your throat in my teeth," he said, giving a feral grin. "You couldn't beat me on my best day, Cormier. Let's see if you can get me on my worst."

"Back up," Cormier barked.

"Why should I? You gonna shoot me, shoot me here!"

"Couple of feet. It'll make it last longer." Cormier gave a wolfish smile, and Jackson's eyes flicked up, just long enough to see Ellery peering around the corner.

"Get away!" he mouthed before looking back at Cormier and backing up one step at a time. After about ten feet, Cormier walked forward and very carefully set his gun down between them, then backed up. When he was done, the gun was in the middle, and they were eyeing each other like nobody else existed.

"See?" Cormier said, like he had something to prove. "I can be smart too. First guy to the gun in the middle wins, and the other guy's dead." Ellery ducked back as Cormier gave a quick look over his shoulder. "And so's his buddy," he said.

"You know," Henry spoke up conversationally, "you could always let me tag in. I mean, you seem to want a fight here, and I gotta say, I'm in better shape than Rivers there."

Ellery and Jade met eyes, and she shook her head. "Not gonna work," she mouthed, but Ellery shrugged. The kid had tried—Ellery gave him full points for it.

"I took you down four days ago," Jackson said, like every breath wasn't costing him. "Don't forget it."

"You bastard." Henry didn't sound mad, just resigned.

"So you still think you can beat me?" Cormier sounded pleased, and Ellery risked a look around the corner.

They'd each taken a step or two in, both of them had their weight balanced on the balls of their feet, their shoulders loose, their posture screaming *Fight! Fight! Fight!*

"Tell me this," Jackson panted. "What happens if you lose?"

Cormier shrugged and took another step in. "You threaten me and only shoot if I charge."

"You hope."

"You coulda killed me when we fought down at Lacey's compound, Rivers. Don't fuck with me."

"Fine." Jackson moved in a little, and this time, Cormier didn't match him. "What happens if *I* lose?"

Cormier let out an ugly laugh. "I kill you. I kill your little golden boy. I go after your butt-buddy lawyer guy. I get your receptionist and anyone you guys ever talked to about this case ever."

Jackson nodded and moved in just a little again. "So who's got a better chance to win? The guy with nothing to lose or the guy with everything to lose?"

Cormier frowned and looked sideways, like he was doing complicated math in his head. "Which one of those guys am I—mother*fucker*!"

Ellery's heart stopped in his chest as Jackson darted in to grab the gun. He made it first, but Cormier was right on top of him, hauling his foot back. Jackson took the kick on the shoulder and tumbled backward, his hands still on the gun, scrambling to get up before Cormier could round on him again.

In the meantime, Sampson had dropped his weapon, pointing it toward the ground while he waited to see the outcome of the fight, and Ellery took the opportunity to charge him. He knocked Sampson to the ground and kicked him hard in the back. Sampson's gun skittered across the ground.

Henry lunged for the gun at the same time Jade jumped on Sampson's back, putting her knee in the small of it and wrestling one arm behind him. "Hold this!" Henry commanded, handing the gun to Ellery. Ellery stood on the opposite shoulder and pointed the gun at Sampson's head.

"Don't move," he muttered. "Jade honey, do you want to take the gun or get off his back?"

"Hand me the gun," she growled.

Ellery handed it over without question, and as Henry moved closer to the fight, they all looked to where Cormier and Jackson were struggling for the other gun. Oddly enough, Ellery's pocket buzzed, but he sure wasn't going to check his phone now!

Jackson was still quick and still hit hard.

Cormier grunted as a chamber kick to the upper thigh landed, and Jackson managed to move his foot before Cormier could grab it. Cormier closed in tighter, though, moving faster than Jackson, and Jackson clocked him across the ear with the gun.

Blood fountained from his ear, and it stunned Cormier for a minute, but as Jackson danced backward, hopefully to find enough space to actually aim the damned gun and shoot the bastard, Cormier closed in again and backhanded him hard to the ground.

Jackson went flying into a crumpled heap, the gun falling from his hand.

Henry rushed around Cormier, obviously trying to neutralize the gun. And from far away, Ellery heard a shout.

"Everybody get down!"

Ellery dropped without question, at the same time Henry dove for the gun and Cormier stood, leveling a kick at Jackson's head that would have snapped his neck.

Except Cormier's head exploded, and the world held its breath.

Henry rolled over to his back, gun in hand, and aimed it at this new threat—which was too far away to see.

Ellery and Jade just stared, stunned, as Cormier's body dropped to the ground, still twitching, the remnants of his skull and brains draining blood into the dusty gravel that surrounded the warehouse.

Sampson started screaming, and Jade clocked him in the head with the butt of the gun. He went limp, and they all breathed a sigh of relief.

Ellery's pocket buzzed again as a thousand police cars turned on their lights and sirens, and Kryzynski screamed, "Everybody drop your weapons!" through a bullhorn.

Jade and Henry set their weapons down and raised their hands, and Ellery ignored everything else on the planet and ran to Jackson's side.

His lips were blue, his face shock white, but he still managed a smile. *"That,"* he wheezed, "was a surprise."

"You look like hell," Ellery said, his throat swelling. "You couldn't make it one day without scaring the shit out of me?"

Jackson gave a tight smile. "My life's mission is to know you care."

"I care. Now do me a favor and don't give the paramedic guy grief this time. He's going to think you don't like him."

Jackson nodded, blood streaming from his nose and a split above his eye. "You coming with me this time, Counselor?"

"They couldn't rip me away," he said. He grabbed Jackson's cold hand, knowing his was shaking but not able to stop it. His phone buzzed in his pocket again, and he was pretty sure he knew who it was, but Jackson's eyes were closed, and he was clinging so tightly Ellery wasn't sure the cops could separate them if they had to.

Kryzynski didn't even try.

THEY GAVE him oxygen and nitroglycerin in the ambulance, and then went about setting his nose and irrigating the cut above his eye. All things considered, he looked pretty good when they got to the hospital—but that didn't stop the doctors from admitting him and running a battery of tests.

Ellery sat with him, holding his hand and helping him breathe, because now that his heart was beating regularly, the anxiety of being in the hospital really might do him in.

"You going to nag at me, Counselor?" Jackson asked, his voice muffled by the oxygen mask.

Ellery looked up from his phone and shook his head. "No," he said, swallowing hard. "You called me. You told me you felt like crap. We're good."

Jackson's smile was as pure as a kid's. "Really? Good?"

Ellery chuckled brokenly. "I'm giving you points for a good try," he said. "But when you're all better, I'm taking points away for skipping your goddamned appointment."

"I know now," Jackson said, closing his eyes. "Can't let things slide."

"No."

"Who's on the phone?"

Ellery held it up so he could see, and he let out a bark of laughter.

Get the fuck down! was the first text from Burton's unregistered number. The second text read, *Goddammit, after all that, he'd better live.* It was followed by, *Don't mention me, okay?*

The last one was so uncharacteristically needy that even Jackson had a moment to be amused.

"What did you tell Kryzynski?"

"I don't know what happened, Mr. Officer. One minute he was standing there, and the next, he was missing his head."

Jackson gaped, and Ellery remembered that moment right before the ambulance doors closed, when Kryzynski had worn that same expression. Jade had been standing next to him, looking anxiously at Jackson, and when she heard what Ellery said, she blinked.

And then she'd repeated it. "That's exactly what happened," she confirmed. "Right, Henry?"

Henry had been eyeballing the body as the first responders swarmed, the missing half of the head obviously not taken off by a 9mm from forty feet away. "Uh, sure," he said, eyes darting toward the trees, where the mysterious cry of "Everyone get down!" had come from. "Yup, that's what happened. Mysterious shot. No warning. Missing a head."

He looked toward the trees again, and Jade kicked his ankle.

Behind them, Sampson made a retching sound as he stood, facing the body, getting cuffed.

"You'd think that guy would have a stronger stomach," Henry muttered. "I mean, wasn't he a *doctor*?"

And that's when the medic had slammed the ambulance doors and Jackson's living body had become the focus of everybody's attention.

"You might want to tell Burton I'll live," Jackson rasped now, in the chaotic peace of aftermath.

"No," Ellery said, his voice breaking again. "I'm unconvinced."

Jackson squeezed his hand tighter. "Oh, come on. I literally had an intervention from God, right?"

"Yeah, well, God's spoken to you before, and you've refused to listen!" Ellery's calm was melting. He'd managed calm in the ambulance. He'd done that shit before, right? And he'd meant it. Jackson was forgiven for skipping his appointment, because the truth—the hard truth—was that this could have happened even if he'd gone. He'd been living on borrowed time since November, when he'd been told his murmur might get worse. But the last few days had been stressful, and Jackson... Jackson was just this guy.

"I'm listening now," Jackson said. "I'm listening to you falling apart. Come here, Counselor. I need you."

And Ellery laid his head on Jackson's chest and cried.

JACKSON'S CARDIOLOGIST was unamused at his condition.

"Wasn't I supposed to see you last month?" she asked. A tiny, wizened woman with snow-white hair and ebony wrinkles, she took absolutely no bullshit from her patients, which was why Ellery had chosen her in the first place.

Jackson responded well to terrifying women. Ellery approved.

"You were," Jackson wheezed. "My bad. I thought I was fine."

Dr. Keller gave Jackson a stern eyeballing from top to bottom. "You look like hell," she assessed. "Your blood stats are shit. And given your oxygen levels and the way your heart was beating when the paramedics got you, I'd say you were about thirty seconds away from a full-blown heart attack and open-heart surgery on the fly."

Jackson gave a weak smile behind the oxygen mask. "Lucky me, you were on time."

"Oh no. I am not a believer in luck, Mr. Rivers. Now, don't get me wrong. You *will* need to have surgery to correct this murmur. It might not need to be open heart, but we need to clean out some of the scar tissue left behind from your heart attack in November, and we may need a pacemaker as well. I'm going to schedule the surgery in the next few weeks, and by then, you know what you need to make happen?"

Jackson sighed. "I need to gain ten pounds?"

"You need to gain ten pounds, and you need to gain it by eating chicken and vegetables and not crap. Your husband tells me you eat like a teenager, but that *will* kill you. Do you understand me?"

Ellery stiffened and leveled a quick look to see if Jackson objected, but he didn't. Ellery had used the word *husband* to preclude the inevitable discussion of who the next of kin was. But Jackson didn't twitch. He didn't even look surprised.

"I understand," he said softly.

"And you need to take your medication. I gave you something mild in November, and I see you've renewed the prescription a couple of times. Are you still taking it regularly?"

"Yes," Jackson said, surprising Ellery a little. "Every day."

"It's like a present, just for me," Dr. Keller muttered. "So I'm also giving you nitro, in case you have another episode of shortness of breath, and I'm giving you a multivitamin heavy on the iron so you can shore up your heart while we plan your surgery." She paused and scowled. "It will stop you up like a wrecked freight train if you don't take the fish oil I'm prescribing with it and eat the vegetables your husband will serve you, do you understand?"

Ellery expected some fight, some snark, some self-deprecating excuse to get out of it—but there was none.

"Understood."

"You are too quiet," Dr. Keller said. "I don't trust you. Why are you agreeing so easily? You are the worst patient I've ever had."

Jackson swallowed and breathed deeply through the oxygen mask before looking at Ellery. "I've got everything to lose," he said after a moment. "I'd like to keep it, if you don't mind."

Dr. Keller's eyebrows went up. "I'll believe this miracle when I see you again in two days, and then again two days after that, and then again in a week for surgery prep. In the meantime—" Her voice softened. "In the meantime, I know you don't like hospitals. I know they make your pulse rate spike, and that's not helping things. I'm going to cut you loose after your husband gets you your meds. And you are going to figure shit out so you can take care of yourself. Are we clear?"

Jackson nodded. "Yes, ma'am."

"Good."

She left, and Jackson turned to Ellery. "You lied," he said dryly.

"I don't know what you're talking about," Ellery lied again.

"You told that nice woman I was your husband."

Ellery looked away. "It made things easier," he said, using the tone of voice he'd learned at his mother's knee.

Jackson tugged at his hand. "Counselor?"

"Yeah?"

"It's okay. I don't mind pretending on this one."

Ellery searched his face. *I want it to be real.* "No?"

"It's a good dream."

Ellery started to relax against him, thinking that maybe he could convince Jackson that someday it didn't have to be a dream.

Then Jackson added, "You Machiavellian bastard."

Ellery sat up straighter. "Before they operate on you, you need to put me on your insurance papers," he said. "I don't want to have to ask Jade for permission to let you live."

Jackson chuckled weakly. "Kaden," he said. "You'd have to ask Kaden—he's on my paperwork now. Jade might let me die, just for spite."

"But—"

Jackson closed his eyes, obviously ready for the resting portion of his afternoon. "Sure, Ellery. I'll change it. God forbid you have to ask permission to let me live."

Resizing the Fish Bowl

KRYZYNSKI, JADE, and Henry were waiting for them when they got home that evening, standing in front of the house with a pink pastry box of donuts that had apparently been sitting on the porch in a cooler. Kryzynski was on the clock with a tape recorder for Jackson's statement, and Jade was there to make sure Jackson was okay.

Henry was there because, Jackson honestly believed, he was excited to be a part of the gang.

Kryzynski took Jackson's statement about six times before he finally told them what had happened.

"Your friend Joey showed up with a rug in his van," Kryzynski said. He grimaced. "He hit on half my department, by the way. He hit on guys who'd never thought of being bi before, and I think he got some numbers. Color me impressed."

Jackson grinned. "I taught him everything I know."

"I'm relieved to know you passed the torch to someone worthy," Ellery muttered.

"Well, it's a skill," Jackson returned modestly. "You guys didn't give him shit, did you?"

"No, I just said we gave him numbers." Kryzynski smirked, making his already boyish face regress back to the teen years. "And seriously, who gives that guy shit? It rolls off his back, right?"

"Like water off a duck," Jackson confirmed. It was good to know Joey could still make friends—and potential lovers—at the drop of a hat. Still, Jackson had hopes for poor Callum. He wanted Joey's world to settle down, as his had. "So you have the rug. Was there enough blood left for evidence?"

"Oh yeah. A master criminal Sampson was not. He confessed to being there for his son's death, by the way, and giving him the sedative before Cormier bashed his head in. It was…." Kryzynski looked behind him, like he was tempting the gods when he said this. "It was creepy. Like… like he was grieving for a girlfriend or a lover or something, not a kid. A kid is… different. Deeper somehow. I…."

Jackson tilted his head back, his stomach roiling all over again. "He was a pedophile," Jackson said bluntly. "If you want to amuse yourself—and nail him for everything he's done—go interview the surviving kids of his business partners. Ash Carver's son was killed in a wreck—"

"He confessed to killing Carver, by the way," Kryzynski added. "I thought you'd want to know. He stashed the body in a vacant field by the levee. They've got cadaver dogs there now."

"Awesome." Because it wasn't. Nothing about Robert Sampson's damage path had been awesome. "Well, he might as well have killed the guy's son too. I'm pretty sure he fucked the kid up for life and pretty much put him on that road." Jackson sighed. "Just like he did to his own kid."

"Yeah," Henry muttered. "I... you don't ever think about what makes someone like Martin Sampson. It's... it's hard, knowing that a shitty world made a shitty person."

"But not at the end, though," Jackson said, hoping this was important. "I... I think seeing you defending the Johnnies guys, knowing you were David's brother—I think that meant something to him. That's why Cormier killed him. Not because he was a bad guy, but because he wanted to be a better one."

Henry looked stricken, and he blinked hard and swallowed rapidly, in succession. "I.... Dude. He wasn't supposed to be important to me. It's like... the more I learn about him, the more I feel like he was... like, a lost opportunity. Someone who could have been better."

"We can all be better." Jackson looked at Ellery hopefully. "We just have to, you know, keep at it. Don't backslide. Find something we don't want to lose."

Ellery nodded and looked away. He'd been quiet since he'd lost it in the hospital. "You don't need to be better," he said softly. "Just stay alive."

Jackson grabbed his hand. "Low standards," he replied. "Who knew?"

Ellery smiled a little, but his mouth quivered, and he didn't say anything.

"What did the doctor say?" Jade asked, sensing the tension.

Jackson grimaced. "She said the damage to my heart from last time is extensive enough to need surgery. The medication I was taking isn't enough, so she gave me nitro. Said she'll see me every two days until my weight's up enough to operate, and I can't eat crap anymore."

"She also said I should be here when he swims, and no more running in the heat," Ellery added, and Jackson grimaced, because that had been rough. A gentle swim, yes. Running in the heat, no. But he couldn't swim alone in case he felt distress.

Jade grunted, like she'd been hit. "I'll call Kaden," she said. "He can come down in a couple of weeks when you're ready for surgery. I'm sure Rhonda and the kids will want to visit too."

"There's no need to bother your broth—"

"Shut the fuck up," she said. "We're not having that discussion."

Okay, fine. "Well, make sure you tell them to come down next weekend instead," he told her. "We're still having the party to celebrate Ellery's business."

Ellery jerked his head. "We're what?"

"Have you or have you not been inviting the whole fucking world here to celebrate the new office?"

"Well, yes, but—"

"Are you going to not work there if I'm dead?"

The chorus of "Oh Jesus!" "Rivers!" and "Jackson, fucking really!" told him he might have gone too far.

"Okay, let's put that differently. I'm *proud* of you and your business. Keep inviting people. Make a list for us to do whatever we do. I can still run background checks and financials and shit. Henry and AJ can help with the physical stuff until I'm back on my feet. Man, we just wrapped up our first case, Ellery. Don't you want to celebrate?"

Ellery nodded. "Yeah," he said. "Yeah, I do."

"Party?" Kryzynski said wistfully, and Jackson caught Ellery's small smile.

"You're invited," Ellery said. "Next Saturday."

"Bring your boyfriend," Jackson said hurriedly. He darted his eyes to Ellery, heartened when he smiled a little wider.

"He'll be happy," Kryzynski said. "We never meet new people."

Jackson looked at Henry and winked. "Bring *your* boyfriend too," he said, and Henry scowled.

"I'll invite my friend," he corrected, and it was Jackson's turn to smirk. "And my brother and his husband," Henry added. And then he stopped, looking surprised.

"What?" Jackson asked.

"That doesn't sound weird to say anymore."

Ellery's hand fumbled for his under the table. "Yeah," Jackson said, glancing at him. "You never know when your heart will change for the better."

EVERYONE STAYED, surprisingly enough, and Ellery snapped out of his melancholy long enough to steam some vegetables and sauté some chicken for dinner. He made Jackson go outside, since the heat had broken and the air was cool, and they ate on the patio, talking about anything but what Kryzynski brought up at the end when they were eating donuts for dessert.

"So, uh, about Cormier."

Jackson put down his chocolate sprinkle. "What about him?"

"We have four eyewitnesses—all sitting here—who say he was shot by a random shooter that nobody saw."

"Yes?" Ellery said, eyebrow raised.

"I call bullshit."

"The deceased was a well-known criminal," Ellery persisted. "With many enemies. The possibilities are endless."

"And yet only one person did it," Kryzynski maintained. "And you guys smell like fish."

"Can you prove any other possibility?" Jackson asked with a feline smile. "Because I was busy having a heart attack, and you were driving up as he died."

Kryzynski rolled his eyes. "Look. We have two choices here. The first one is, I don't believe you and I investigate further and find the round that killed him. I know that it came from a big gun—bigger than something standard, so I'm looking for someone with a sniper rifle case. This will help when I look into all sorts of things like traffic cameras and phone records and such that might help determine what happened."

Jackson swallowed. Burton had done him a solid. That would be a shitty way to pay back a friend. "And your other choice?"

"You guys give me one good reason not to do that."

Jackson nodded at Ellery. He was the one who could do this.

"Because you'd run into a brick wall," Ellery said. "A military brick wall. And then you'd probe deeper, and you'd end up pissing someone off and maybe losing your job."

"And even though you could get one as a PI in a law firm," Jackson said, "we've already got two, and our other firm was a douche factory. You wouldn't want to go there."

"Nope," Kryzynski said, looking from Jackson to Ellery and back. "Military?"

"Yeah," Jackson told him.

"Like what got you guys into trouble in January?"

Jackson and Ellery met eyes, and Jackson shrugged. "Word gets around?"

"Jade shot a guy in her backyard," Kryzynski said dryly. "And there were military people there to cover it up. You guys show up a few weeks later looking like death—and yes, I was watching the house, sue me. I'm a cop. I'm asking if this is the same X-level shit."

"Yes," Jackson said. "And you don't want any part of it."

"Understood." He frowned for a moment, like this was hard to put behind him, but finally he looked up at them and smiled faintly. "And now do we have another chocolate sprinkle, or did Jackson eat them all?"

"We have two more," said Ellery. He looked at Jackson philosophically. "But we'll save one for you."

Finally, hours later, everyone went home, and they crawled into bed, skin on skin.

"Mm...." Jackson bucked up against him. "You thinking what I'm thinking?"

"That you need to give your heart a rest tonight?" Ellery asked, and Jackson subsided glumly.

"I am actually quite tired," he admitted, as defeated as he'd ever been.

"Tomorrow," Ellery murmured. "Tomorrow's Saturday. No work, no nothing. Your appointment is Monday, and tomorrow is all about sleeping in—"

"No," Jackson murmured. "I'm not the only one who's been backsliding."

Ellery stiffened. "I'm sorry, I don't know—"

"Temple. You made a big deal about it, Ellery, and about the same time I started fucking up, you stopped going."

"But—"

"You liked going."

Ellery sighed. "I did."

"Because even if you don't believe all of it, some of it gives you comfort." Jackson wanted to live—God, he really did. But he was a realist, and he'd gone through a lot of lives as it was. If Ellery had a source of comfort, Jackson wanted it waiting to catch him. Just in case.

"I felt guilty because you kept dodging Rabbi Watson." And now Jackson felt guiltier. Aces.

"Well, you go tomorrow, and tell him I'll meet him next week."

"Why don't you come with me?"

He sounded so hopeful—Jackson hated to burst his bubble. He kissed Ellery's cheek and snuggled. "I have something to do tomorrow," he said. "Don't worry. It's along the same lines. It'll be fine."

Ellery didn't ask what the thing was—but Jackson figured he knew.

HENRY HAD been the one who'd asked. They'd been standing over Martin Sampson's body, the wound in his head cleaned but not stitched, the flap peeled back onto his skull, the Y-incision in his torso wide open and exposing him, naked and cold, to the world.

"What happens to him now?" Henry asked.

"Well, he's not an organ donor," Toe-Tag had said, "and most of his organs are shot anyway. His father needs to contact a funeral parlor to have the body claimed for cremation, which he can do as soon as we release it."

Robert Sampson was in jail—probably getting ready to call a really expensive lawyer. And he'd never deserved a son anyway. Jackson had no idea about Hadley Sampson—but he knew the notification had been made, and she hadn't claimed the body.

The next day, Jackson made some calls, and then some more calls, and then the one hard call.

Monday morning, before Jackson's doctor's appointment, he stood holding a small vase of ashes with a surprising number of people gathered around him, at the local cemetery.

"So," Jackson said uneasily, looking at the attendant ready to bury the small pot of ashes in the open site. "We're here because the deceased was a douchebag. But that's not all he was. He was good enough to make David Worrall love him, to make John think he was a friend, and to welcome Henry to a new town. He did a lot of shitty things, because he was not just broken inside, he was so smashed he probably never could have been put back together. But in the end—the very end—he didn't want to be that guy anymore. And that's why it was the end, really. He was a person—he tried to be one, anyway—and he doesn't deserve to be just forgotten. So we're having a burial for him, and we're putting a marker down, and we're the few people in the world who are sad that this person was never allowed to be the man he could have been."

He looked around at the faces—David, Carlos, Henry, John, Galen, and Ellery. And one person, a thin, composed-looking young man with aging track marks on his arm and a sobriety chip clenched hard in his hand.

"Anybody else have anything to say?"

"Uh, yeah," Teddy Warburton said. "Me and Martin, we got high together when we were in high school. We fucked around when nobody knew we were gay. And I know that's not the beginning of a good relationship, but he was the best friend—and the first lover—I ever had. And you're right. He could be a shitty human being. But he could also be a really good one. And in the back of my head, I kept hoping me and Martin would find our way back to each other." He gave a faded smile. "It wasn't to be. But I'm glad in the end he found his inner hero, you know? Because he kept hoping one would save him, and that guy never showed up."

Jackson closed his eyes. There was so much to do. So much more to do. They'd missed Martin Sampson. Then again, maybe nobody could have caught him.

Jackson looked around at the other people in that part of the graveyard, all of them about to boil alive in their best suits.

"We were going to bury the ashes here," Jackson said. "Do you want to keep them instead?"

Teddy appeared to think about it, his hazel eyes getting a little shiny. "No," he said after a moment. "Maybe my best step in recovery will be by finding a way to say goodbye."

John let out a little laugh. "I chucked *my* best step into recovery by throwing his cookie jar into the sea. It was cathartic, but I don't think we'll do that here."

Galen eyed his boyfriend with undisguised affection. "My best step in recovery was following this redheaded goofball to Sacramento to watch him film porn. Recovery works in mysterious ways."

There was some strained and sad laughter then, and Jackson set the urn into the burial space.

"Bye, Martin," he said softly. "We'll try to do better."

Ellery's hand spanned the small of his back, and the two of them left to go to Jackson's appointment, while the people who'd known Sampson when he'd been alive settled their accounts.

THE NEWS from the cardiologist was mixed. Yes, his heart seemed to be behaving right now. No, the murmur hadn't gone, and yes, she advocated surgery once he'd gained eight more pounds.

But at the end, she gave him a kind smile. "Look, I get it. You have been hurt a lot, and I know you hate it here, and you cannot *fathom* a reason to come in here voluntarily and let us shoot a laser into your heart, am I right?"

Jackson shrugged. "Yeah, pretty much."

"Well, you seem like someone who can appreciate a tough old bird who takes no bullshit. And this tough old bird is telling you that you will walk out of here after surgery, spend six weeks in recovery like a normal person, and then you'll be mostly free to go running around stirring shit up. Does that make you feel better?"

Jackson thought about it. "Marginally. I have to admit, though— I've been in recovery since February—"

"November," Ellery muttered.

"November," Jackson corrected, "and I thought I'd be done by now."

Dr. Keller tilted her head. "You thought... honey, haven't you figured life out yet?"

Jackson glared back. "I have seen enough of it!"

"Well, if you've seen enough of it, go ahead and die before I go to the trouble of fixing your heart. Otherwise, take this one lesson in your teeth and don't let go."

"Hit me with it," he told her, kind of liking the way she lectured him. It was nice to have a doctor who cared.

"We are *all* in recovery. All of us. I could bore you with my life story, but let's just say when you're doing your residency at forty when people think a black woman shouldn't be a doctor at all, you have taken more than a few hits and gotten back up again. Do you understand me?"

"Yes, ma'am," Jackson said respectfully, thinking wistfully of Jade and Kaden's mother, who would have liked this woman. "Yes, ma'am, I do."

"It's taken me twenty-five years to recover from that, and in the meantime, I've won a lot, lost a few, and gotten kicked around some too. And I will *always* be in recovery from the things that hurt me. You can either deal with that and keep recovering, or you can give up on recovering and curl up and die. You ready to curl up and die yet?"

Jackson stared hungrily at Ellery. "No, ma'am. No, ma'am, I'm not."

She nodded decisively. "I will see you on Thursday, then, only because I think you are seeing sense right now. If you keep seeing sense, you can plan on surgery in two weeks. You may do everything you normally do, as long as you don't get out of breath—the bad kind of out of breath. I still recommend swimming over running in this heat, but again, make sure someone is with you. Have you been taking your medicine and vitamins?"

Jackson nodded dutifully. "Yes, ma'am."

"Don't stop that—not even after surgery, you understand? Recovery is working every day to be healthy. Am I getting through to you?"

"Yes," Jackson said, with another look at Ellery. Ellery couldn't look at him, but his eyes were bright and shiny and his breaths were hard and long.

Dr. Keller nodded. "Well, not everybody sees recovery like that, but those are usually the people who don't make it. Keep recovering, young man, and you may live to be a recovering old one, is that a deal?"

"Yes, ma'am."

"Then you can take your husband outside and get him some air. He's not looking too good."

They were supposed to go to the office, but Jackson texted Jade as they were walking out of the hospital and told her they were going home instead. She said good—they had a bunch of meetings with potential clients tomorrow, and they needed to rest up. Jackson booty-bumped Ellery out of the way when he got into the car.

"Where are we going?" Ellery asked as Jackson pulled out of the parking lot.

"Home."

"Why? Don't we have work today?"

"What is it you keep telling me about being the bosses? We've done a funeral and a doctor's appointment. I say we play hooky for the rest of the day."

Ellery let out a half laugh. "So what do we do when we get home?"

"Oh, Counselor, if you have to ask that, I am falling down on the job."

"But... but...," Ellery sputtered, trying to come up with reasons not to.

Because he was scared. Because he'd almost lost Jackson too many times. Because Jackson had backslid, and so had Ellery, and Ellery's faith was shaken.

Because it was up to Jackson to make things right.

"You finish that thought," Jackson murmured happily. For once, traffic wasn't being a rat bastard, and he was making good time. "Also think about what we can go out and eat that will fit into my whole new heart-healthy regime. C'mon... I know you're dying to try some place that serves chicken in a whole new way."

"Don't patronize me!" Ellery snapped. But Jackson was suddenly feeling the joy of the student who didn't have to be back in school for three whole days.

"I will patronize you with my dick in your ass, Ellery Cramer, so you had better get used to the idea and stretch!"

Ellery's caught breath told Jackson the merits of the idea had just hit him right in the groin. "Jackson, I won't be—"

"Nope, not trying to seduce you so you won't notice, Counselor. I'm trying to seduce you because I fucking want you." They were at a stoplight, and Jackson reached around to fondle Ellery through his slacks. "And I think you might have a thing for me." He gave Ellery a squeeze. "A good thing."

"A hard thing?" Ellery snarked back, and Jackson's own cock began to get hard too.

"Not as hard as my thing's gonna be," he taunted.

"Talk, talk, talk.... Shut up and fucking drive."

Jackson chuckled, liking the sound of that, and they pulled into the driveway ten breathless minutes later. They passed the tank and parked in the garage, practically running through the connecting door, slamming it behind them against the heat.

Jackson was on Ellery before they even passed the kitchen, a balls-out mauling as Ellery struggled for breath, for footing, finally clinging to Jackson's shoulders as they threatened to overbalance on the floor.

"Bedroom?" Ellery begged, feet sliding between Jackson's legs as Jackson pinned him to the wall.

"You gonna run away from me?" Jackson asked seriously. "You been running for three days, Ellery. I'm not going to stand for that anymore." He hadn't met Jackson's eyes since the ambulance. And Jackson was done with that shit.

Ellery squeezed his eyes tight now. "I love you so much, every close call we have fucking hurts me more."

"I know," Jackson whispered, touching his lips to Ellery's jaw, to his ear, to the side of his neck. "I'm hard to housetrain, I know it." He pulled up a mouthful of skin at the joint of his shoulder, under his polo shirt. He nibbled a little, enjoying the way Ellery moaned and squirmed, and then let it go with a pop. "But I'm worth the trouble," he promised. "I swear, I'll be like Billy Bob—beat the fuck up, but still here."

Ellery went for his neck, sucking his own mark, pulling back, letting it go. "I'll hold you to that," he breathed.

"Then come on."

Jackson helped him stand, and they ran to the bedroom, stripping as they went. Ellery kicked off his deck shoes as soon as they hit the hallway, and Jackson left his sneakers on the white tile of the kitchen. Jackson's shirt was ditched at the bedroom door, and his shorts fell to the ground with a thump by the side of the bed.

He looked up and saw Ellery stripped to the skin on the other side, and he slid his boxers right off his ass and dropped them on the floor and pulled back the covers.

And then he pinned Ellery underneath him before he could even breathe.

"Jackson!" he pleaded. "No—not like—"

Jackson pulled back from sucking on his nipple and smiled wolfishly. "Let me seduce you, this time," he said sincerely. "I am right here with you, and I want to hear every moan."

He pulled Ellery's nipple back into his mouth and sucked hard, and Ellery didn't let him down. One breath, one stretch of skin at a time, Jackson paid homage to the man who'd stood by his side, the man who was just a little bit afraid this time, because his heart was a little sore. He pulled Ellery into the present with him, into the sense of hope, of renewal that he had, because just this once, trying to do the right thing had been rewarded.

He was alive. He was here in bed with the only person on the planet he could think about spending a long, healthy life with.

He was going to make Ellery glad he was there if he had to by God make the man jizz out his eyeballs.

But that didn't stop him from getting lost in Ellery's cock, from sucking it so far back in his throat, he killed his own gag reflex, just to have more. He wanted the taste, the texture, the absoluteness of Ellery Cramer in his body, and his own arousal roared through his ears, amped in his groin, with every lick, every taste, every suck.

Ellery cried out too early, but Jackson swallowed anyway. All of it. He drank deeply, wanting Ellery to be a part of him. Ellery moaned a little, moving away, and Jackson moved up his body, claiming his mouth without hesitation, growling when Ellery gave in to him, holding nothing back.

They kissed. Jackson's cock drooled precome, and he ached for completion, but still they kissed. He reached under the pillows for the lubricant and only broke off when he had it in his hand.

"I'm gonna fuck you," he cautioned, and Ellery nodded.

"I know."

"And you're gonna be all mine."

"I know."

"And we're gonna be that way for as long as we're both breathing. You're mine."

Ellery's eyes spilled over, and he nodded, touching Jackson's jaw gently, cupping his neck. "I know. I've been all yours from that first time. Didn't you know that?"

"I know it now," Jackson whispered, kissing him again. He tasted brine, but he needed too badly, Ellery needed too badly, for him to stop and wipe his tears.

A quick pass with the lubricant and he was there, poised at Ellery's entrance, while Ellery tilted his head back in acceptance.

"Hey," Jackson whispered. "Look at me."

Ellery opened his reddened, shiny eyes. "What?"

"This is a good thing, us together."

Ellery nodded, and Jackson slid into his body, satin on satin, and Ellery made a little cry in the back of his throat. "More!" he begged, and Jackson kept thrusting, all the way in, and Ellery wrapped his arms around Jackson's shoulders and his legs around his hips and clung.

Oh, inside Ellery was his favorite place. Warm and tight—for maybe the first time, he believed Ellery was never letting him go.

"Move," Ellery begged. "Move. C'mon, baby, I'm dying here—*ah*! *God, yes, fuck me!*"

Jackson couldn't hold back, not anymore. He used to be so good at being selfless, at making a lover come, and come again, before he got his piece. But not with Ellery. With Ellery he needed—so bad it hurt, so bad he ached with the needing. There was no holding back, no making Ellery come again and again before Jackson felt entitled to his own release.

It was Ellery he just fucking needed.

He thrust into Ellery's body in a frenzy, and his heart held out, this once, as he fucked again and again, until Ellery cried out and came, just this once without trying to make Jackson come first. Jackson gloried in the heat of his come, the sloppiness, the way they both wore it without thinking. The thought of it bowed his back, tightened his ass, oh dear God, it made his cock hurt with the needing, the needing....

"Come, Jackson!" Ellery begged. "Please, just—oh!"

Jackson poured himself into his lover's body, eyes rolling back in his head, lost in orgasm as he never allowed himself to be lost with another human being. He rutted, still aroused, until another aftershock rocked him and he collapsed, his face buried in Ellery's neck, his own tears making a hot and sticky haven of his favorite fort in the world.

"Don't leave me yet," he begged. "I'm just starting to be worth your time."

"I could never leave you," Ellery whispered, smoothing his hair back from his face. "Dammit, Jackson, I can't even take a step back to breathe. You are my heart and lungs.... How could I leave you? You're the only reason I'm alive."

Jackson nodded and caught his mouth in a messy, briny kiss.

Ellery was here. In his arms. Jackson would recover for the rest of his life, if that's what it took to keep him there.

Look! A Castle!

IN A way, it seemed like the worst time in the world to have a party. Jackson was going into surgery in two weeks and the business was brand-new.

But as Ellery circled around his living room and made sure everybody was eating and drinking and happy, he had to agree with Jackson.

It did make him happy to be alive.

"So," Galen Henderson said, calling Ellery to his table as he sat and conversed with Crystal. Crystal was gazing at him like his aura was pure and lovely, and Ellery had to laugh as he thought of all the evil Galen would readily confess to, but apparently, didn't really do.

"Yes?" Ellery asked. "More sparkling water?"

"I just got a refill from this lovely woman here." Galen nodded, and Crystal giggled, and Ellery hoped someone had told her Galen was gay.

"He's going to fit in great at your office," Crystal said guilelessly. "Once he starts getting clients too, maybe you can afford to hire me."

Ellery's eyes popped open, and at that moment John wandered up, his red hair still damp from the pool, although his board shorts were mostly dry.

"Did you ask him?" John said. "Because I think it's a great idea. We've got an ex-model who's waiting for his bar exam results—he's going to be looking for a job soon. I was going to send him in for an interview, but in the meantime, Galen would love to be a full partner."

Ellery gaped, and Galen smacked John's arm.

"You," Galen said distinctly, "have no tact."

John grimaced. "Never have," he said by means of apology. "But what do you think, Cramer? Think you could let Galen come on as a partner after he gets his results?"

Ellery recovered his balance and smiled. "I think we should talk," he said, already liking the idea.

"Good," Galen told him. "That way, John and I don't have to break up because of his runaway mouth."

John grinned, all teeth. "You love my runaway mouth."

Galen smacked him again, and Ellery used that as a chance to escape. "On that note, I'll go. But call me in two weeks, okay?"

Their expressions sobered—two weeks would be after Jackson's surgery. "Of course," Galen said softly, and Ellery turned away.

He walked right into Reg Williams, who, like John, was still damp from the pool.

"Hey, uh, Ellery," Reg asked shyly, "where's Jackson?"

Ellery's eyes searched outside, where most of Kaden's family, including his adopted son, Anthony, was enjoying the pool. They weren't the only ones—Bobby was out there, along with Henry and his friend, the med student. David and Carlos were swimming with Frances, and Kryzynski and his boyfriend were blatantly ogling their bodies in surprise. Reg was dressed in board shorts as well, but he'd dried off and put on a shirt since he'd last been outside. Ellery had to laugh at all of the shirtless hot young men in his swimming pool. It was like every wet dream he'd ever had in high school.

"I'm not sure," Ellery said, scanning the people. "He's sort of disappeared."

"We just want to thank him," Reg said. "You know, for asking us. He said we could be friends, and I thought that was great, but then someone at work said he was just humoring me—"

"One thing I know about Jackson Rivers," Ellery said, "is that he takes being a friend seriously. He was thrilled you could come."

Reg's smile could light up a room. Hell, it could light up a city.

"That's real nice. I'm not so good on crowds, but I'll stay until I can tell him thank you myself."

"I'll make sure he knows to come find you," Ellery said quietly.

"Damn," Kaden muttered, coming out of the kitchen. In spite of Ellery's best efforts at air-conditioning, the kitchen was warm, and Kaden's shaved head reflected the light like shiny syrup. He smiled widely at Ellery, and Ellery hugged him, happy when the giant of a man hugged him hard back.

"Damn what?" Ellery grinned at him, genuinely happy to see Jackson's brother-of-the-heart. "Damn, your wife is outside with all those hot men?"

"Well, that, yeah," Kaden said with a laugh. "But I had no idea how many people you guys knew."

Ellery's mouth twisted, and he sought out Rabbi Watson, who was probably the only person there that he'd invited for himself. And the reason the rabbi had agreed to come was that he was worried about Jackson. Ellery couldn't spot him, but that didn't change the truth. He didn't see the rabbi, but he did see Crystal and AJ and AJ's friend—Ellery's former client—Jael.

"These are all Jackson's friends," he said. A year ago, he'd never had more than four people at his dinner table, and he'd been the only one to use the pool. Until he'd met Jackson, that had been enough.

Something about Jackson made Ellery's heart bigger. Made his *life* bigger. Made him want to open up his home to accommodate all these new people, to celebrate them.

"Are you still worried?" Kaden asked softly. Because of course Jackson had told him. Jackson didn't keep secrets from his brother.

"Aren't you?" Ellery asked, trying not to be bitter.

"Of course." Kaden shrugged. "But we've been worrying about him a lot longer than you have. You have to pace yourself or you'll get exhausted."

Ellery let out a bark of laughter. "*That's* hilarious. Every time I think I can step away and breathe and pace myself, he…." He made love to Ellery until every barrier between them broke down and they were left, broken heart to damaged soul, beating together as one.

"Are you strong enough?" Kaden asked seriously. "Because he thinks you're strong enough. And he hasn't put his faith in anybody but me and Jade for a long goddamned time."

"Of course I am," Ellery snapped back. He laughed then, less bitterly. "I am. I guess it's like recovery. He's recovering from the rest of his life, and I'm just recovering from being scared for him."

"Welcome to the club," Kaden said gently. "Call me if you ever need to talk."

Ellery found his smile then, and it was whole and unfettered. Kaden had hated him once—but not anymore. Now they were family. "I'll do that," he said genuinely. "But first, I need to find him."

Kaden looked around at all the people. "Uhm, I hate to suggest this, but maybe he's hiding. I mean, this many people might freak him out a little, you think?"

"Who, Jackson?" Jade asked, coming to talk to them, with Mike at her elbow. "Yeah. He's never been great at parties—especially meant for him. Remember when Mom tried to throw him a bash for his eighteenth birthday?"

Kaden's smile went sweet and sentimental. "We had to drag him out of the laundry room, and that was just us and some kids from school."

Ellery's eyes darted to their bedroom, where they'd stored purses and backpacks and changes of clothes. "Actually," he said, "I think I've got an idea."

They let him go, which told him that he was the one they trusted to take care of Jackson and that he was probably the right man for the job.

He found Jackson sitting cross-legged on their bed, Billy Bob in his lap, while he talked quietly with Rabbi Watson.

"Ellery!" the rabbi said, smiling through his neat brown beard. "How nice to see you. We were just talking about me resuming my visits next week. I think that would be terrific, don't you?"

Ellery grinned at him, charmed as he always was by the rabbi's attempt to sound older than his maybe forty years in order to be a more "rabbinical" presence.

"I think Jackson talking to anybody is a really good idea," he said, meeting Jackson's green eyes across the muted room.

Jackson smiled and looked away.

"Well, I'm going to go inside and try some of those wonderful canapés," Rabbi Watson told him. "And how kind of you to make a plate that was kosher, and one that was halal."

The halal plate was also vegan—Ellery liked to cover his bases.

"Enjoy the food," Ellery told him, his public face and voice very much to the fore. The rabbi left, and he felt that slip away as he sat down on the bed next to Jackson, taking his hand.

"Overwhelmed?" he asked perceptively, and was rewarded by Jackson's quiet smile and a finger touching his nose.

"Got it in one."

"It's good that you made an appointment with the rabbi again."

Jackson nodded. "I meant it about recovery."

Ellery nodded. "I know you did. Just… just remember. Even if you fuck up again, don't… don't hide it. Not out of shame or a misguided sense of trying to protect me. I can't do this if I'm afraid you're not being honest with me."

Jackson nodded soberly. "Understood." Someone outside their door laughed loudly, and he grimaced. "All those people," he said, sounding like a child. "I can't believe you know all those people!"

"Uh, no." Ellery smirked. "The only people I knew were at our old firm, or at the courthouse. And truthfully, Carlyle Langdon *did* call me this week, but it wasn't to socialize."

"Uh, what'd he want?" Jackson asked, curious. His hand stilled in Billy Bob's fur, and Billy Bob swatted at him so he'd resume the petting.

"He wanted to tell me he was defending Robert Sampson and wondered if there was anything he should know."

Jackson's eyes got really big. "Oh my God, really? When was that?"

"Thursday. You were at the doctor's, and when you came out, well, your news was all I wanted to hear."

Same prognosis—surgery in two weeks. But Ellery had still needed to know.

"What did you say?"

Ellery couldn't help his grin. "I told him he'd need a scuba suit to swim through the slime. Then I told him everything Sampson had done, including the stuff the police haven't been able to prove yet." Proving the sexual abuse had been the hardest. Nobody wanted to come forward, and Martin and Ash Carver's son were both dead.

"What did *he* say?" Jackson asked curiously.

Ellery's grin of satisfaction went nuclear. "He said he'd plead for twenty-five years and get the life sentence off the table, but that was as low as he'd go."

Jackson nodded. "Not perfect. I'd love to see him locked up for life. But twenty-five years ain't bad."

Ellery grinned. "I thought so. I'm sure Siren Herrera will be pleased. Not a bad week's work, Detective."

"You too, Counselor."

They sat in the quiet for a moment, and Ellery said, "They're all your friends, you know."

Jackson shook his head. "No, no, they're your people too—"

"No. They're yours. Because I didn't feel like I needed people before you came into my life."

Jackson blinked. "Because your life was perfect before I showed up."

Ellery snorted. "Maybe. But it was lonely. And it was cold. Besides, listen to all those people outside, happy to be here. That's what you did."

"That's what we did," Jackson said softly.

Ellery leaned forward and brushed their lips together. "That's what we did." He pulled back and smiled. "And we need to go back out there and take care of them."

Jackson nodded and gave Billy Bob one final pet before hefting his buddy onto the bed, where he curled up for a solitary snooze.

He stood and stretched. "Come on, Counselor. Time to move."

"I know it," Ellery said, taking his offered hand and leveraging off the bed. They would be okay. Jackson would be okay. Recovery was nothing more or less than changing, every day, to adapt to your life without the bad things and embracing the good. "Come on," he said, tugging gently. "We've got a lot to do."

MoonFish—A Surprise Visit

BONUS READ!

Remember Ellery and Jackson talking about the time Ellery's mother came to visit?

This is what *really* happened....

MoonFish—A Surprise Visit
Holy Fucknuggets

BURTON LOOKED at the information on his screen and blinked. He knew that name.

"Uh, Jase?"

Jason Constance looked harried, his appealing square-jawed features pale and haggard under his neatly trimmed goatee. Tracking down the trained mercenaries who'd been "modified" into psychopaths had taken a toll on them all these past months. Constance needed to get the hell away from headquarters, even if it was just to get laid and have drinks on the beach.

"Who is that?" he asked, blinking hard.

"Man, you are looking like shit. Can you get away from here for a minute?"

"Depends on who that is."

"Remember Rivers and Cramer?"

"Taylor Cramer, Esquire—his father?"

Burton stared at him. "His mother. Man, I told you about meeting her two months ago. Look where she popped up."

Jason sat up as though stung. "Holy fucknuggets!"

"Yes, sir, that is mercenary chatter, and yes, she does seem to have a hit out on her. Why do you ask?"

"Who's taking the contract? One of Lacey's guys?"

Burton frowned as he tried to interpret the chatter on his screen. "Looks like one of the guys working for Corduroy. It says something about Mrs. Cramer putting pressure on the military to investigate the organization and see if any of the branches are utilizing them as a resource."

Jason's quiet snort told Burton that yes, a number of high-ranking military intelligence officers were not looking forward to having Ellery's mother shove a magnifying glass up their sphincters.

"Only one?" he asked.

"Mm… nope. Two. But they're under strict orders to make it look like an accident, and to have no witnesses and no other casualties.

Anything looking like a hit that takes out civilians or other members of the family negates the contract."

Jason looked thoughtful. "So, uh, Rivers and Cramer. Think they can handle themselves?"

"Rivers, absolutely. Cramer follows Jackson's lead and tries to stay out of the way." Unless he lost his temper, but Burton kept that to himself.

"Okay, do you have a relationship with Mrs. Cramer?"

Burton's eyebrows did something complicated that made his face feel scrunched. "Define relationship."

"Does. She. Know. You? Oh my God, Burton—Ernie would skin you alive!"

They were alone in the room or he wouldn't have said that, but Burton smiled. His face went soft when he thought about Ernie—he couldn't help it. He'd trusted Jason with that info too. He and Ernie had had Jase out to dinner once or twice, always under the strictest of secrecy, and Ernie had been as gentle with Constance as he had been with the feral kittens he cared for on a regular basis. You'd think Burton's CO, hard-bitten, tough as nails, as cold a killer as Lee had ever seen, wouldn't need to be treated with kid gloves, but Burton could see it too.

Constance was getting frayed at the edges and thin in spots. The trained-serial-killer thing had taken it out of all of them.

"She's met me before, sir. She wasn't at her best, but she'd remember me." You didn't forget the people you met in the waiting room when you were hoping to hear your son would live. Particularly when your son's lover was hanging on by a thread, as well.

"Good. I need you to make contact and get her to the West Coast. Ask her if she wouldn't like to visit her favorite kid. I want her in their company at all times—and you and me, we're going to be their shadows."

Burton blinked. "Are we taking out the targets, sir?"

"They're Corduroy, right?"

"Yessir."

"Then we capture and question and see if we can negate the contract. Unless their targets are in imminent danger, understood?"

"Understood."

"But first…."

Burton sighed. Even upset and holding Jackson Rivers together by force of will, Taylor Cramer was a formidable woman.

"YOU'RE GOING where?" Ernie was pretty psychic, but he didn't always know the details of Burton's little trips.

"Sacramento." Burton ran his palm from Ernie's shoulder blades to the hollow above his round bottom. "Tomorrow morning. Me and Jason."

Ernie relaxed into the caress. "Well, if Jason's going with you, that's okay." He looked up from the vat of boiling oil he was cooking pastries in. "And the apple fritters will still be fresh. You can take them with you!"

Burton blinked slowly. "Uh, why would I—"

"They're Lucy Satan's favorite," Ernie said. "If I make them and ice them tonight, they'll be ready tomorrow, but you'll probably have to wait until the next day to deliver them. You'll be talking to the bad guys. Anyway, here!" Ernie took one of the cooled, iced fritters off the drying rack and pulled a piece from it. "Want a bite?"

Burton took the pastry from Ernie's fingers, completely entranced. The fritter was amazing—because Ernie could cook desserts and donuts like nobody's business—but it was Ernie himself who he found mesmerizing.

Ernie caught the look and popped a piece of fritter in his mouth, blushing. "Uhm, Cruller?"

Burton moved behind him and started to kiss his neck. "Mm?"

"Do you want to do this before or after I finish with the fritters?"

"Before."

"Okay. I'll turn off the heat." He reached out and did that, and put a lid on the deep fryer, as Burton kissed down his spine, rucking up his shirt when it got in the way. Ernie's body, lean, pale, with a few freckles dotting his shoulders from recent forays into the Southern California sun, was still as tender and delicious as the day Burton had first devoured him, back in October. Ernie dropped his chin to his chest and leaned into Burton's hard embrace. "Mmm... do you have plans for us to get more naked?"

"Oh yes."

"Do you want to sit in the hot tub first?"

"Nope."

"Shower? I'm all sweaty from cooking."

"Sure."

They'd purchased the house built in the middle of Victoriana for a song. The suburb had been meant to grow out in this direction, but businesses had failed, and people decided that the desert was just not that exciting a place to live in. As a result, Burton had about an hour's commute to the secret military base in Barstow where he and Constance were not stationed.

Also, he and Ernie had a home, one with a really awesome hot tub and a shower built for four. But those days were over for Ernie, and all Burton had ever wanted was the one.

The one lover—Ernie, as it turned out—who knew who and what he was and what he did for a living and saw the warm beating heart under Burton's badass exterior. And who melted in Burton's hands like Burton was made to wear him like a second skin.

Burton soaped Ernie's body thoroughly in the shower, all his crevices, cleaning him, teasing him, chafing his nipples and slowly jacking his cock with a soapy washcloth. "Is that all you want clean?" Ernie taunted, spreading his legs and planting his hands against the wall. Burton took the washcloth and parted his cheeks, cleaning and then poking and then stretching with soap and three fingers, while Ernie urged him on.

Finally, Burton pulled out his fingers and rinsed them both, and then, when he would have toweled them both off and taken him to the bedroom to make slow love to him, Ernie leaped into his arms instead.

The temperature in the shower jacked up to about a thousand degrees, and Ernie clung to Burton's body while Burton positioned his cock at Ernie's cleaned and stretched entrance. Ernie slid down ecstatically. Burton's knees trembled, and he shoved Ernie's back against the shower wall and held him in place while he undulated his hips, slowly, slowly, until Ernie reached between them and grabbed his own cock, squeezing hard enough to come.

The ejaculate fountained up to hit Ernie on the chin, but Ernie's head was back against the wall and his limbs were going slack around Burton's body. Burton had no choice but to rocket his hips and rut into Ernie's ass until he came too, his knees going out and both of them sliding to the floor in a not-so-clean heap of repletion.

"Burton?"

"Ung?"

"Water's going cold."

"You wreck me, kid. You wreck me every fucking time."

"Good. You're leaving me for a week, and I hate that."

"I'm sorry." And he was. Ernie had known this would be their lives—and for the most part, their lives were pretty good. There was a surprising amount of time to have sex in the shower and other unusual places in their spacious ranch-style house in the middle of the fucking desert.

But leaving him was never easy.

"I know, baby," Ernie consoled him. "Let's get out and go enjoy round two in the bedroom. I want to rim you until you cry."

Burton's cock started to grow hard just thinking about it. He struggled to stand up without slipping and knocking his head and fucking up the op before he had a chance to leave for it.

They made it to the bedroom, and Ernie made good on his promise. And this time he topped, and Burton gave himself over—the few moments of his life not in control—and Ernie saw him to the finish, as he always did.

They ate dinner then—soup Ernie had made earlier—and ate some more of Ernie's donuts while the apple fritters were cooking. It wasn't until they were eating the donuts, big glasses of milk next to them on the table, that it hit Burton.

"Hey, did you know I was going?"

Ernie took a nibble of crispy outside with icing. "No. But I knew I had to make apple fritters."

Burton took his own bite, going for the tender apple filling inside. "Because they're Ellery's mother's favorite?"

"Oddly enough, I didn't know that until you said you were going to Sacramento. It's an imperfect system, Cruller. I'll let you know when I fine-tune it enough to be useful."

Burton grinned at him. "You're pretty useful without the woo-woo stuff, Ernie. I'd rather have you fuck me like the god you are than tell me what my next op is."

Ernie grinned back. "Yeah? Good, because I always thought sex was way more fun than woo-woo shit." He took another bite of his fritter. "But that doesn't mean I won't clue you in if I get a flash on your next op, okay?"

"Deal."

After one more sleepy bout of lovemaking for the road, they fell asleep early so Burton could get up two hours before dawn. Ernie must have gotten up sometime in the night, because he'd taken a pink pastry box from the stacks he'd ordered and filled it with fritters. He'd filled another one with crullers and written *For Jason and Lee* on top of it, which was nice. The one with the fritters said, *Don't throw away, I'll know.*

Which was a nice way of telling Jackson and Ellery who sent the donuts without writing his name.

Burton sighed and put both boxes on the seat of his truck before starting off into the blackness of morning. Ernie had looked so sweet as he'd left—asleep, his black lashes fanning his cheeks. Like an angel.

Devious little shit. He'd managed to convince Burton to make a six-hundred-mile donut delivery while Burton was running an op.

But then, anything Burton could do that would let Ernie keep thinking he was a hero was okay with Burton.

Woo-Woo Shit

AFTER BURTON left, Ernie wandered around disconsolately, fed the cats, cleaned up after baking, and then, as always happened when Burton left on business, his feet led him back to Ace and Sonny's.

"How long's he been gone?" Ace asked good-naturedly, feeding Ernie the last of the tamale pie Ace had made on his night to cook. Ace had muscles like cannon shot and a handsome good-ol'-boy face with a dent in his chin. He didn't look like he'd even admit to having a boyfriend, much less cook for the one he had, but Ace was surprising that way.

"He left this morning," Ernie said, huffing out a sigh. "Ellery Cramer's mother is in danger. He convinced her to go to Sacramento so he can watch all three of them."

"Jesus," Sonny muttered. "Are we even supposed to know shit like this?"

"'Course we are." Ace sat down and sipped his after-dinner coffee slowly. "We're invisible. Like, nobody even knows we're here."

"How do you even say that?" Sonny demanded. "We make more noise than a sonic fucking boom. We blew up an Army base, Ace. How does nobody know who we are?"

Ernie snickered. "Because me and Burton and Jackson and Ellery and even Ellery's mother, I think, have worked very hard to make it that way," he said, surprised that Sonny hadn't realized this.

Judging by the blank look on Sonny's face, he really hadn't. "Why would they do that?" he said in a small voice.

Jai—who was there because it was Tuesday night and apparently Jai appreciated Ace's cooking too—smiled softly at Sonny, but Ernie wasn't fooled. Jai was a ginormous ex-mob enforcer who had been "loaned" to Ace after Ace had risked his life to save Jai's boss's niece. Ace and Sonny had kept him, and Jai's loyalty to the two of them transcended life. For a while, he'd mooned over Sonny Daye in an unsubtle, painful way. But in the last few months, his tightly held torch for Sonny Daye had changed to an out-and-out fondness, a soft spot that would never heal, but that didn't pain him anymore.

Two months ago, he'd lied to Ernie about having a booty call that he met camping. Oh yeah, he had the booty call, all right, but the guy wasn't married, and Jai did like him, and even though Ernie knew the truth, he was highly curious as to what had caused the lie.

"Because they see your value when you're free to work on cars and not locked in a cage," Jai said, and Sonny looked at Ace with troubled eyes.

"That sounds like charity," he muttered stubbornly.

"It's more like love," Ace said bluntly. "And it keeps my criminal ass in the free and clear, so I'm really fucking grateful. Do you know how long Burton will be gone?" Ace asked, obviously to change the subject, but also because he wanted to know if he should prep Burton's old room so Ernie could stay there.

Ernie thought about it. "A couple of days," he said, not sure what prompted him but trusting it, just like he'd trusted his urge to make apple fritters. "And yes, thank you, I would very much appreciate a place to stay until he gets back."

Ace nodded. "Sonny, stop pouting about people taking care of you and help take care of Ernie. Also, one of you may want to take Duke for a walk—you know how excited he gets when Ernie comes over."

Back in the days before Burton had committed, Ernie had spent his time with Duke the Chihuahua, wandering the desert at night. Duke had enjoyed their little forays—and probably missed their time together now—so Ernie made sure to come take him for a walk once or twice a week, just for old-time's sake. When Burton was there, they'd go together and talk desultorily about the way the desert smelled and what the stars could possibly mean. But without him, Ernie's brain—and therefore his psychic ability—tended to reach out into the vast world and bring back things Ernie was never sure what to do with.

There was nothing he could do to stop a bus crash or a bank robbery. He would tell Burton and hope for the best. Occasionally his brain came back with stories of the serial killers he'd been asked to assess when Karl Lacey's illegal behavior modification project to create the perfect soldier had been up and running. That, he'd reported immediately, via text if Burton wasn't home. Burton always told him when his contact with the "bugs," as he called them—because their brains were crawly twisted places—panned out.

So far Ernie was eight for eight as a reliable bug catcher, and he was glad he could help. But he really hated stumbling into a bug's brain when he was all alone and unprepared.

"I'd love some company," he said a little desperately, and Ace tilted his head, as if he heard the things Ernie wasn't saying.

"Jai, go with him," he said. Ernie still did the books for the gas station, and while Ace was their friend as well as their boss, it was obvious this was an order.

"Da," Jai said, not even bothering to complain.

THEY WERE about a mile out from Ace and Sonny's place when Jai said his first words. "You haven't said anything."

Ernie knew what he was talking about. "About your friend in the mountains? No. You lied to me so I wouldn't know, and I figured that meant you didn't want everybody else to know. Why not?"

Jai shrugged. "George is… he's a nurse. A good guy. I am not."

Ernie snorted. "That's hilarious," he muttered.

"No, no—I have—"

"Killed people. I know. You don't understand. I keep running into serial killers in my mind. That's why I wanted your company, you know. Their brains are awful. Like bug warrens. Like little shit beetles crawling through their head."

"Lovely," Jai said, shuddering with revulsion. Jai was well over six feet tall, with a shaved head and a black goatee. Watching him shudder was a treat in itself.

"Yeah. Well, I've known you for a while now, and your brain isn't like that. Your brain is all these neat little boxes. Well, one of your boxes has a guy named George in it, and he's bursting the box's seams. You're going to have to share him with Ace and Sonny soon or he's going to break your brain."

Jai groaned. "Ugh. Could we go back now? I don't want to think about this."

"Sure." To tell the truth, Ernie didn't want to either. He wanted to think about Burton, under the same sky he was under, looking out into the cloud of mottled stars and thinking about Ernie, the way Ernie was thinking about—

"Burton's going to have to pull that thing," Ernie said, suddenly right back in the present. "And yell at Jackson to duck. Jackson's going to duck and roll, and there's going to be a crash, and then Burton can come home."

Jai was staring at him.

"What?" Ernie said, shaking himself all over.

"That was the fucking creepiest thing I've ever seen."

Ernie groaned. "Well, keep it to yourself, okay? I've got to text Burton so he knows what's coming."

"How on earth can he know what's coming from that?" Jai asked in wonder.

"Same way I knew how to make apple fritters, Jai. Shit just comes to us."

He typed as fast as he could, and when he was done, he let out a breath.

Thanks, kid.

Now, some boyfriends would blow him off—but Burton had learned to trust him in the past six months.

And now they just had to wait.

For his part, Ernie was very curious as to what it all meant.

Hail, Lucy Satan

"ELLERY!" ELLERY'S mother looked impeccable. With her hair pulled back into a shortened bun, makeup done with razor-line perfection, a cool linen suit, and sensible ecru pumps, Taylor Cramer never traveled with anything less than aplomb.

"Mother?" What in the fuck was she doing here?

"Ellery, who's at the door at fuck all y'all in the morning?"

"Jackson, could you get my bags, please?"

Ellery turned to find Jackson, mid pit-scratch, in his boxers, having a panic attack.

"Oh, dear God."

"Jackson, my mother's here."

"For sweet fuck's sake!"

Ellery grimaced. The weird thing was, he was almost certain Jackson liked his mother. Revered her, in fact. But that didn't mean she didn't scare the crap out of him. "Jackson, maybe come get her bag like she asked."

"Hello, Lucy Satan," Jackson muttered as he came to the door. "Are you moving in?" His eyes bulged out, and Ellery managed to look behind his mother.

"You brought a trunk?" Ellery asked, his voice pitching in dismay.

"Don't get too excited, Ellery. Some of those are gifts for Jackson's family. Thank you so much, Jackson. I'll take the guest room, per usual."

Well, yeah, but usually Ellery's mother stayed with them when there was something wrong.

"It smells like dead grandmas," Jackson mumbled, wrinkling his nose at the trunk.

Taylor Cramer smirked, and Ellery had to look twice to make sure it was his mother. "That's the perfume you bought me for Hanukah, sweetheart. I'm so glad you like it."

"I thought it was Christmas," Jackson mumbled, still pulling the giant wheeled case behind him. "I am so confused."

Ellery took his mother's smaller case and kissed her cheek, ushering her in. "It's lovely to see you," he said diplomatically. "Is there an occasion?"

"Mm…," she said, smiling serenely, which told Ellery that yes, there was, but she had no intention of telling him. "Let's just say that I've become enchanted by your charming little valley, and I understand there are all sorts of outdoor spring activities that we should partake in. Jackson? Did you hear that?"

"I don't understand a word of it!" Jackson called back. He came plodding into the living room as Ellery passed him on the way to the bedroom with the smaller case. "You're here so we can go outside?"

"Exactly," she said. "And I understand you have a new vehicle."

Jackson's eyes widened. "The tank?"

"The tank?" Ellery echoed, having settled as much as he could in the guest room.

"Yes. It's new, isn't it? Weren't your friends going to outfit it to make sure it was the last vehicle you would ever need?"

Sonny and Ace had retrofitted the SUV—an Infinity QX30—and reinforced the panels, removed padding, added bulletproof glass and custom seat belt webbing, not to mention the several highly illegal things they'd done to the suspension and engine itself. The result was… well, a very sturdy vehicle.

"It might be," Ellery said diplomatically, "but I always thought it would be the last car you'd ever be caught dead in."

His mother patted his cheek. Patted his goddamned cheek. "Oh, Ellery. Son. That only shows how much you really know about me. Now it's a lovely April day. The sun is shining. The birds are singing. Let's find some donuts and go to the zoo, shall we?"

Jackson's eyes hadn't gotten any smaller, not since he'd opened them to see Taylor Cramer on the doorstep. "The zoo?"

"Donuts?" Ellery squeaked. "You showed up on our porch to… to…."

"To go see the zoo and have donuts," she said happily. "I'll just make some coffee while you two shower and change. Hustle, boys. There's so much I want to see!"

The two of them stumbled into the bedroom, Ellery in the pajamas he'd been wearing when he'd opened the door, Jackson in his boxer shorts, both of them wearing the veil of confusion like a miasma.

"I...." Ellery struggled. Jackson's warm hand on his waist was not reassuring. "Please don't leave me because my mother has just done the first spontaneous thing I've ever seen her do in thirty-one years."

Jackson half laughed and kissed his neck. "I won't leave you. But you know, this doesn't seem spontaneous in the least. I'm pretty sure she's hiding something from us."

Ellery stared at him. "How would you even guess that?"

Jackson shrugged and gave a soft smile. "Hunch."

"But what do we do?"

"What would we do under normal circumstances?"

Ellery sighed and let his shoulders slump. "Anything my mother wanted."

Jackson nodded and kissed his neck again. "And hurry, Counselor, or I'm going to do one or two things she might not want me to do at all...."

Ellery hustled to the bathroom and heard his mother cooing at the cat in the sudden quiet.

His mother. Staying with them indefinitely. Oh dear Lord, what had they done to deserve this?

Two days earlier...

BURTON BLEW out a breath and dialed the number.

"Taylor Cramer," said Ellery's mother, her voice crisp and no-bullshit.

"Yes, ma'am. This is—"

"I remember you from the waiting room," she said with hardly a wobble in her voice. "Is anything wrong with my son?"

God, she was quick. "No, ma'am. We just... I'm on a secure line, but I don't think you are."

"Understood. Where would you like me to call you from?"

"Sacramento," he said promptly. She would know what that meant.

"Indeed? Anywhere particular in Sacramento?"

"As many public places as possible." He and Jason had it on good authority that this particular death squad liked to work in secret and make things look like an accident. Well, that would be hard to do if Ellery, Jackson, and Taylor were touring the outdoor delights of the city in the spring.

"How long should I call you from there?"

Burton had no idea. "An indefinite length of time. I'll contact you when you can go back to using your home phone."

There was a silence. A long, *uncomfortable* silence, during which Burton squirmed *uncomfortably*.

"When you contact me, you'd better have a damned good explanation for that, young man."

Burton blew out a sigh of relief. Well, yeah. She deserved no less. "You will, ma'am. I promise."

"Of course. Now, if you'll excuse me, I must procure some plane tickets and go shopping. I'm not showing up without copious amounts of random gifts, you understand?"

"Understood, ma'am. Happy travels."

"You too, young man. And say hello to your young baker, while you're at it. I did enjoy meeting him, as well."

Burton thought of Ernie, at home, making donuts. "I'll give him your regards, ma'am."

"Thank you."

Burton hung up and looked in agony at Jason Constance.

"So, she's going to be with her son and his friend before the team gets to town."

"Confirmed," Burton told him and then slumped forward. "Sir, are you ready for tomorrow?"

Constance frowned, obviously surprised. "Certainly, soldier. Why wouldn't I be?"

"Because you haven't met these people. There is no telling what comes next."

Constance didn't seem to believe him, but Burton was actually relieved when he got home and Ernie was making apple fritters. It meant they had Ernie's witchiness on their side.

Dollars to Donuts

JACKSON SAW the shadow outside his window as Ellery got into the shower, and he hurtled past a surprised Lucy Satan and out the front door before Ellery's mother could so much as gasp.

A pink box sat on the stoop. If Jackson hadn't paused to make sure it wasn't lethal, he might have caught Burton as he left from putting it there.

Don't throw away, I'll know.

He opened the box and took a deep breath. Mm… apple fritters. Ellery's mother's favorite.

Sent by someone who'd know if he threw them away.

And delivered by someone who could leave them on the porch without triggering the alarm and get away like a ghost.

"Jackson?" Ellery's mother was not going to let him rocket out of the house without an explanation. "Jackson, what on earth—"

Jackson turned to her grimly, box in hand. "You and me have got to have a talk," he said quietly.

She pursed her lips. "Is that a donut box?"

"Apple fritters. Your favorite."

She looked confused. "Why is that a—"

"Remember Ernie?" he asked pleasantly.

Her eyes got big. "I do."

"He came to visit me and Ellery a couple of times when we were in the hospital. Smuggled me éclairs that would make a saint come. I never told him they were my favorite. He just knew."

"We should go inside," she said pleasantly. "I'll get some milk."

He took one more hasty look around his neighborhood and spotted the flash of something shiny behind the fence three houses down—the neighbors who had gone to visit their daughter in Florida over spring break, the sadists.

He gave the shiny thing a two-fingered salute and followed Ellery's mother inside.

"We can't tell Ellery," Lucy Satan said softly as they neared the kitchen. The water was still running—Ellery could take an epic shower when he didn't have to be somewhere. Or when his mother was in the house.

"Can't tell him what?"

She grimaced. "When was the last time you swept the house for bugs?"

Jackson blinked. "Two days ago." After they'd found them in January, he and Ellery did it once a week—vacuum, dust, scrub the toilet, check for bugs. It was the new housecleaning regimen.

"Oh," she said, nodding. "So nice to know you're sensible about things. But your friend"—she nodded toward the donut box—"simply said I should come here and spend some time in your company." She grimaced. "In public. So I looked up some activities for the next week. How do you feel about craft fairs?"

Jackson's eyebrows went up to his hairline. "I actually don't mind them." He'd furnished his duplex with thrift store finds and the occasional handicraft, but he was the first to admit his taste was eclectic and… well, not suited for Ellery's gracious, masculinely furnished home. "But—"

"Good. Tours of the capitol building?"

"I'm not even sure they'll let me in—"

"They will if I'm there. How about sporting events?"

"I can get us some Kings tickets and some Republic tickets and some Rivercats tickets—" It was late March. Everything was in season.

"Be sure to put them on my credit card," she said smoothly.

"I can pay for my own goddamned ballgame," he muttered. Ellery did the same thing, and it drove him batshit.

"But this time, I'm paying for it," she said with a pleasant smile.

"Not if I'm getting the tickets. Anything else you're on for? Wine tasting? A bus tour of San Francisco?"

"All of the above," she said, without blinking an eyelash. "You go to work on that while I unpack. I think today we should stay local, tomorrow maybe go to San Francisco, then Saturday we could visit your brother—"

Jackson's eyes got big. "For fuckin' real?" Because Kaden loved surprise visits as much as Jackson did. Which was to say if Jackson hadn't walked by the hallway when Ellery opened the door, he seriously would have gone out the back door and over the fence and run across town in his boxer shorts so he didn't have to do what he was doing right now.

Which was anything Ellery's mother asked him to do, apparently, without getting any answers as to why.

"Of course. I brought gifts for his wife and the children. The day after we should attend some sort of sporting event with your sister and her boyfriend—"

"Jade hates sports," he said blankly.

"But her boyfriend adores them. And of course, we should eat out. Except for this morning, when I shall indulge in some lovely donuts."

As she'd been speaking, she'd invaded Ellery's kitchen, poured two glasses of milk, and put the apple fritters on a plate. Jackson cleared the table of everything except his laptop, which he put at the end, and helped her set breakfast up, then looked longingly at the coffeepot, which he had been about to turn on when she'd knocked.

She ran a knowing look up and down his scrawny recovering body. "How is your heart murmur?" she asked, and he grimaced. He'd acquired scars on more than the outside in November when his heart had stopped. Since he and Ellery had returned to Sacramento in February, he'd been trying to be good about seeing a cardiologist.

"Caffeine isn't forbidden yet!" He crossed his arms over his chest defensively. Only in small doses—that's what Dr. Keller had said. He had yet to ask her to quantify "small doses." He assumed a pot a day was a small dose, if you eked it out with lots of cream and sugar, with only one or two sodas on the side.

"Fine. I'll start the coffee and unpack. You start our itinerary and wait for Ellery so we can eat. You may proceed."

Jackson sat down at the table and grabbed his laptop. Yeah, he still had no idea why Burton wanted her there, but honestly, doing all that shit she had him planning was a damned sight easier than arguing with her, that was for sure. She was already talking about his caffeine intake and diet—he needed to keep her busy now before she started making him kale shakes for breakfast and serving him nothing but tofu and fish!

SHE HAD arrived on a Wednesday, which meant they had a poetry reading at the local library in the late morning, a tai chi class in the afternoon, and a Kings game that night. As Jackson and Ellery fell into bed, exhausted from running around town—and by just being with Ellery's mother— Ellery moaned, "She's got the entire week planned out?"

"It's not my fault," Jackson mumbled. He'd liked the tai chi class, hadn't minded the Kings game, and had napped during the poetry reading. What had really knocked him out was that Ellery's mother seemed determined to smooth out all of Jackson's... Jacksonness while she was there.

"Jackson, do stand up straight. You'll ruin your posture." "Jackson, I understand you can use that word as often as you like, but part of being an adult is only using it as often as you need." "Jackson, I do believe if you and my son plan to work full-time again, you should either procure a friend for this animal or find someone who doesn't mind feeding him while you are gone. I think he might be lonely."

"I know it's not your fault," Ellery soothed. "I just don't know why we're doing this, that's all."

Jackson closed his eyes, thinking about the fritters. Ellery had been so discombobulated, he hadn't even asked where they'd come from. And Jackson just couldn't tell him that someone had put a hit out on his mother. That seemed rude, somehow.

"Lucy Satan works in mysterious ways," he grumbled.

"Well, I need her to work her way home," Ellery said. Then he sighed. "But while she's here, maybe we can have her look at some of the properties for the new office."

Jackson perked up. "So we don't have to go to San Francisco tomorrow?" Because driving the tank down there would cost a fortune, the parking would be horrific, and the car was loud enough to wake the dead.

"No, Jackson. I'll talk to her over breakfast. Do you think you can hit that donut place again? Those fritters were amazing."

"No," he muttered. "I'd rather have fruit." Ellery was warm next to him, and Jackson kissed his shoulder through a softly laundered T-shirt. "And you," he said, meaning it.

Ellery kissed him chastely on the mouth.

And then not so chastely.

And then they were sliding their hands over each other's chests and Jackson had a handful of Ellery's taut backside and was kneading and spreading and grazing the sensitive bits and then—

"Jackson?" Ellery's mother said as she knocked. "Jackson, your inappropriate cat seems to want to sleep with me. I insist you take him."

Ellery made sobbing sounds, and Jackson rolled sideways. "You get the door," he whispered. "You can pull a T-shirt over your boner!" Jackson wasn't wearing a T-shirt, but he definitely had the boner.

Ellery grunted and pulled his T-shirt low over his boxers and went to let the cat in, because apparently, the big loser was still sore about getting fixed and they hadn't known it until now.

THE NEXT day, they ran all over town looking at office rental properties, which was actually pretty awesome, considering.

The one in the strip mall on Howe was a big no. The location was great—right next to a bail bond place—but it wasn't the sort of vibe they were going for.

The one a block away from the capitol building was nice—but really pricey—and, in Jackson's words, "Built like a Republican was given a bunch of tan Legos."

There was one off the river, in what had once been a residential building but was now separated into office spaces, but Ellery had balked at both the drive down the Garden Highway and the lack of amenities nearby.

The final one they looked at, on the edge of downtown around 9th and F Street, had seemed okay. It sat at the top of a flight of stairs, which might have been inconvenient if it hadn't been for an elevator to accommodate those with disabilities. The space itself was large, with four offices and a conference room, as well as a reception area that had a counter and a recessed kitchenette sort of space that Jade could definitely make her own.

The walls were a sort of muted beige that Jackson said had to go, and the carpet was teddy bear brown, and Ellery wasn't going to live with that either. It needed paint and carpeting and a solid redecoration. All of that might not have fazed Jackson except....

"Parking," he said, looking out the window. "There's only one parking space next to the building. Ellery...."

"But look at the ceiling in the corner office!" Ellery begged. "Look at it! And it's got moldings—"

"I don't actually give a shit about beveled moldings," Jackson told him. "Hardwood floors, yes. I can see some nice hardwood here. Moldings can kiss my ass. But parking...."

"We have six more offices to look at," Ellery's mother told them crisply. "Two more before lunch?"

Outside, they heard the unmistakable sound of a car smashing into another one, and then a rather ambiguous sound of what they found out later was a light pole collapsing for no reason at all.

"Maybe lunch now," Jackson muttered. "Somewhere across town."

He and Taylor Cramer met eyes, and she nodded imperceptibly. "After you," she said, and he nodded, leading the way while Ellery's mother made peace with the real estate agent, who had sat in the back of the room and let them bicker over this one.

"Ellery, take the rear," Jackson said, forgetting that Ellery didn't suspect what he did.

Later, it would occur to him that Ellery did exactly what he asked without question and continued to move like that, Jackson first, Ellery bringing up the rear, with his mother and the clueless real estate agent in the middle. All day. He did that all day.

But of course, there'd be hell to pay that night.

Brooding in Company

ELLERY MANAGED to wait until his mother was—hopefully—asleep in the next room.

"You weren't going to tell me?"

"Tell you what?" Jackson sat on the bed in his boxers, looking ridiculously sexy for a guy who'd spent half of the last year in the hospital, and made moon faces at the cat. Billy Bob batted his lips, claws retracted.

"Tell me there was a hit out on my mother."

Jackson didn't even look up. "Why would there be a hit out on your mother?"

"I don't know—you tell me!"

"Well, since she hasn't told me, I don't know what else I can tell you!"

Ellery had never really considered homicide until he'd fallen in love. "What. Did. She. Say?"

Now Jackson did look at him, his green eyes open and sparkling and as innocent as a lamb's. "She said she was here for a visit."

"I will beat you," Ellery threatened, which was a laugh and a half because they were both only just getting their wind back enough to run around the neighborhood.

"Would you like equipment for that, or are you going to use a household item, like a wooden spoon or a shoe?"

"Augh!" He didn't control his volume either, and Jackson flailed his arms.

"You will wake the beast, and we'll both be fucked!" he hissed.

"No we won't, because we don't have sex while my mother is here, remember?"

Jackson pursed his lips. "Look, this isn't my fault. She showed up on the doorstep. That's all I know."

"That's obviously not all you know, because we've been walking around Sacramento with you running point and me running cleanup like an actual police detail, all day. Care to explain that?"

Jackson gave a sigh, and Ellery thought, *Oh ho! The jig is up! I shall have some answers! Ha!*

"All I know—all I know—is that Burton left Ernie's apple fritters on our doorstep yesterday, and your mother was told to stay in public places."

Ellery blinked. "That… is not reassuring."

"You are telling me."

"Give me one good reason not to put us all into protective custody."

Jackson shrugged. "Because he sent donuts and not directions for burying our remains?"

"I'm having mine donated to science," Ellery muttered. "The rest you can burn and scatter."

"I could donate my remains to science too," Jackson said helpfully, but Ellery just rolled his eyes.

"Most of your remains have already been stitched together and replaced. I don't think you have anything left to give. Now scoot over. I need to brood."

"You need to get into bed to brood?" But Jackson was scooting over.

"No, I need to get into bed to touch you so that we can think together. Jackson, there's probably a hit out on my mother! What are we going to do?"

Jackson shrugged. "We're going to turn on the house alarm—"

"Done."

"And let the hit men watching over us do their job. Also, we're going to take your mother places because she was told to stay public."

Ellery narrowed his eyes. "It's like you're on her side."

Jackson glared back. "Ellery, she was threatening to take my coffee away from me. Not in so many words, but—"

"She did not, you big baby."

"You pretend not to hear it, but we know what this means. 'Jackson, I think you would enjoy tea so much more than coffee. Has Ellery allowed you to taste some of the more robust blends with almond milk and honey?' What do you think that means?"

Ellery tried to hide his pleased expression and failed.

"See? It means she's trying to take away my coffee! No! Not even the doctor has tried to do that!"

"That's because you lied to the doctor about your intake!" This had been a sore point between them. Their idea of a "moderate" amount varied vastly.

"One pot is not excessive!" Jackson defended, wounded. "And see? Now she's got you on her side! Just let the professionals take care of it, and don't press her any further!" He flounced over onto his side, beat up his pillow, and settled in for the night.

Ellery let out a breath. "Do we even know who it is?"

"No."

"Did you ask?"

"I'm not taking the chance. Why don't you try sacrificing something you love? Watch. You ask her, and she'll figure out a way to take away your Lexus."

Ellery sat up in bed. "She would not!"

Jackson threw a pout over his shoulder. "Want to risk it?"

"No." Ellery slid back down into bed again and kissed the back of Jackson's neck. "Damn."

"Yeah."

"We were on a hot streak."

They'd both been recovering, but yes—somebody had come at least once a night since they'd gotten out of the hospital. Jackson hadn't had this much sex when he'd been banging everything that moved—and Ellery knew because Jackson told him so.

"I know," Jackson said glumly. "We're going to have to think of something else to do before bed."

Ellery laughed. "We could start reading books."

"Dirty ones?"

"How about Jane Austen?"

"I hate you."

"I love you, Jackson."

"I love you too, Counselor. What are we doing again tomorrow?"

"God, I forget. We'll remember when she wakes us up in the morning."

"Fine."

Jackson rolled over just enough to kiss him.

"Night."

Except whatever it was she had planned never got done.

Jackson's phone rang in the charger that morning, and he snagged it before Ellery could crawl over his body and claw out its eyes.

"Kaden?" Jackson mumbled. "For real?"

Then Jackson sat up in bed, looking panicked. "No, seriously, did you look for him?"

"Who?" Ellery asked, rolling out of bed and looking for the khakis he'd worn the day before, as well as a sweater and some sturdy shoes. "Who's missing?"

"Anthony," Jackson muttered, hopping out of bed to get dressed too. "Yeah, K. Keep us briefed. We're getting in the tank now." He paused and looked at Ellery apologetically. "Why the tank? Because it's a long story that we can't talk about and Ellery's mother is coming."

Ellery moaned. "Goddammit."

"Yeah, Ellery. Go tell your mom that she's coming with us up to Foresthill." Jackson spoke back into his phone. "Don't get too excited. I think we were coming up tomorrow anyway. And tell Rhonda we can't stay, so she's off the hook. Keep us briefed. See you soon."

He hung up and started his own search for yesterday's jeans and a fresh pair of undershorts, while Ellery dressed as quickly as he could.

Oh man. Their day had just gotten a whole lot more complicated.

View From on High

THE TRIP up was surprisingly quiet, and at first, Jackson thought it was just because the damned tank was so loud without the extra padding and insulation that Sonny and Ace had pulled out to make it slightly more fuel efficient.

Then he'd glanced in the rearview mirror and seen Lucy Satan asleep, hands folded in her lap, head against the headrest, perfectly composed like a vampire.

But still vulnerable.

He felt bad for a moment. Ellery's mother didn't deserve a hit out on her, but then, she was fighting the same people in court that Jackson and Ellery had fought on the ground that winter, so maybe what she deserved and what was happening had no relation whatsoever.

"What?" Ellery practically shouted in his ear.

Jackson just shook his head, unwilling to tell Ellery that his mother looked helpless, because as far as Ellery was concerned, Lucy Satan was invulnerable and perfect, and Jackson didn't ever want to change that for him. It was wrong on a cellular level to let Ellery think his mother could be harmed.

They made it to Kaden and Rhonda's house, which was back in a little development called SugarBaker's Cove. The houses were on four-to five-acre plots, most of the land filled with dense woodland beyond whatever yard development the homeowner implemented. Some people had four acres of swimming pools and tennis courts, but Kaden and Rhonda weren't rich, only prudent. They had a backyard big enough for the kids to play kickball in, and a lot of fucking trees.

Kaden and Rhonda, and their children, River and Diamond, were out in front, nervously pacing as they pulled up. Two ginormous fucking American boxer-Labrador retrievers were sitting patiently at their heels, waiting for the occasional pet so they could slobber on whoever offered attention first.

"Uncle Jackson!" River had grown. She was, what? Ten this year? A beauty like her mother, she wore her hair back in thick braids and had gotten tall enough for Jackson to rest his chin on her crown when he lowered his head.

"Hey, pretty girl," he murmured. "What's going on? You haven't found him yet?"

River shook her head and wiped her eyes. "He was weird all week, like freaking out and crying. And Mom and Dad couldn't get him to talk. This morning, we were supposed to go to school, but he was gone before we woke up!"

"It's a good day at school!" her brother, Diamond, told him. "We get treats and stuff, but maybe not...." He looked at his sister nervously. "Maybe not in the sixth grade."

"We get them in the sixth grade," River sniffed. "I don't see why Anthony wouldn't get them in the seventh."

Anthony had started out as a lonely kid who'd taken a job to bug Jackson and Ellery's car. But once Jackson grabbed him—and realized that the one witness to the transaction had been killed—he'd become in need of protection. Kaden and Rhonda had stepped up because Jackson had asked them to, and because the police hadn't seen the need at first.

But Anthony, who'd been a foster child most of his life, had fit into the Cameron household as if he'd been born into it. Kaden and Rhonda had asked if they could take over his fostering, and had been looking into an actual adoption—as well as the happily ever after that Anthony had cynically believed would never happen to him.

Jackson had no idea what would make the kid take off and leave. Except....

"Don't report cards come out today?" he asked the kids.

"Yeah." Diamond looked at his father. "I don't get real grades yet," he said ingratiatingly. "But if I did, I'm sure they would be A's." His smile—wide and white against the ebony of his skin—was extra sugary sweet.

Kaden rolled his eyes and looked at Jackson. "I so believe that," he muttered.

"Yeah, that totally wasn't a line." Jackson tried to look sternly at his nephew, but Diamond's smirk was just so transparent, he couldn't. "God, kid, you'd better get your act together for seventh grade."

Diamond laughed outright. "Well, yeah. They use percentages and letter grades in seventh grade. I know bad things happen to people who can't figure that out!"

The laughter relaxed the little family for just a moment, and then they sobered.

"Well," Ellery's mother said, a big bag of all sorts of treasures over her shoulder, "I'm sure you can completely explain to me why it's okay to not do your best in school when you're obviously smart enough to fool the system. But in the meantime, how about I take you children inside and we make some breakfast and let the adults try to find your foster brother."

"Our brother," River said fiercely. "He says 'foster brother' like he's afraid he's going to get moved to another home, and we keep trying to tell him we want him forever." She pulled away from Jackson to look at him with pleading in her eyes. "Uncle Jackson, we're the only family he's ever had. I don't even know where he thinks he'd go."

Jackson nodded. "I would bet he's not far away," he said softly. In fact, he'd put actual money on it. "Go in with Lucy... uh, Mrs. Cramer, and see what she's got for you." He met Lucy Satan's eyes, and she nodded. "She came from a long ways away, just to bring you some good things."

Lucy nodded and disappeared inside with the children, and Rhonda gave a sigh of relief.

"Oh good, they're gone now and I can tell you we are losing our fucking minds. Jesus, Jackson, where in the hell could that kid go?" Her eyes got bright again, like they had when they'd pulled up. "He was so happy until about a week ago. Then he started slinking around like he was afraid we were going to drop the hammer on him at any moment. I caught him crying when I went to tuck him in, and he just said he was sad. But it's got to be something."

Jackson nodded. "I, uh... look. I've got an idea." He pulled out his phone and punched some buttons. "And better yet, I've got a tracker on him."

Kaden's mouth fell open. "You've got a what?"

Jackson shrugged. "Remember? I bought him that phone when I brought him up here. He took it with him, right?"

They both nodded. "He doesn't go anywhere without it," Rhonda said. "Those games you let him buy are like his favorite things."

Jackson smiled a little. "Does he have a charger?" he asked, and Kaden clapped his hand over his eyes.

"He's got *my* charger! It disappeared last night!"

"I bet he packed a lunch too," Jackson said.

Rhonda—who was Kaden's smarter half—looked at Jackson compassionately. "What is this about?"

"You guys, report cards are coming out. This kid hasn't had you for parents very long. How good do you think his grades are going to be?"

Kaden groaned and pinned Jackson with a frustrated glare. "Oh Jesus—I should have known."

"Kaden," Rhonda said kindly, "it's not your fault. How would you—"

"Oh, trust me," Kaden muttered. "I'd know. Well, Jackson, where is he?"

"Let me go find him," Jackson said. "I… you know. I've got a little experience with this."

"Text us when you see him. I need to go have a heart attack."

"Yeah, he's somewhere in the backyard."

"We've been back there. We spent the morning with the dogs going through the area. There's nothing there but trees." Kaden looked at the dogs. "By the way, you two were a terrible disappointment in the search and rescue department. I thought you liked that kid."

The dogs looked up at him, tongues lolling, and waited for more attention.

"Morons," Kaden muttered.

"Anubis, Orion, door!" Rhonda commanded crisply, and the dogs ran to the front porch and turned around, ruffs bristling, eyes alert for any danger.

"Yeah, honey. They're the dumb ones," she said sweetly. Then, to Jackson, she said, "You can find him?"

"I promise," he said. "But maybe let me go alone."

Ellery grabbed his hand. "Alone?"

Jackson winked at him. "Trust me. We'll be fine."

There wasn't a hit on Anthony anymore, but the more people around Ellery's mother, the better.

Ellery kissed his cheek and let him go, and Jackson kept his eye on his phone and sauntered around to the backyard.

Kaden wasn't kidding about there being a lot of fucking trees, but some trees are more memorable to an agile twelve-year-old than others. Jackson spotted the appropriate tree immediately, then went to stand near the bottom.

"Anthony," he called, looking up, "would you care to explain?"

He wanted to yell—he really did. The kid had dragged him and Ellery out of bed, had scared his entire family, had caused all sorts of trouble, and dammit, over a report card?

But Jackson looked into the kid's tear-ravaged face as he peered down from about twenty feet and couldn't be mad. He'd been that kid before, so surprised that anybody would give a shit about his grades that he couldn't figure out how to fix them before he let that person down.

"You can't tell them," he said, hiccupping. "You can't."

"Yeah, kid. Sure. Here, I'm coming up." It wasn't a bad climb, really. Jackson was wearing a sweatshirt in deference to the coolness of the hills near Truckee, and his jeans were relatively hole free. With a jump and a pull and some scrambling, he managed to make it as high as the kid was, and he stood, holding on to the trunk of the pine tree, wondering if he was going to have to cut his hair to get all the sap out.

Anthony had curly brown hair that framed his pale face, and a lot of that was matted together with pine tar. Poor kid was probably going to miss that hair when Rhonda had to shave his scalp.

"So," Jackson said conversationally when he'd caught his breath, "what class are you flunking?"

Anthony looked at him with red-rimmed eyes and a wobbling lip. "All... all of them!" He burst into sobs, leaning against the trunk of the tree by Jackson's knees, and Jackson reached down and stroked his sap-sticky hair.

"Oh, kid," he said softly. "Why wouldn't you tell them? Rhonda's a teacher—"

"She's a teacher," Anthony wailed, "and I'm stupid! How could they ever want me if I'm stupid?"

Jackson sighed and scrambled down to a sitting position on a limb about two feet lower than Anthony's. "You're not stupid," he said softly. "You've just had other things on your mind these last few years. Which home you were going to, whether you'd have clothes or food, whether your next set of parents would be dicks.... Man, you've had a full plate."

"But everything's perfect now," Anthony hiccupped. "And I'm a loser who can't pass math! Or English! Or history! Or science!"

"You passing PE?" Jackson asked, hoping for a win.

"I keep forgetting my shoes," Anthony said glumly, and Jackson held back a smile.

"Well, yeah, some years are like that. Look. Anthony?"

Anthony stared at his tennis shoe as it dangled over the ground. "Yeah?"

"You had a raw deal. And you lost out on a lot of school. It's March, and you didn't start school until December. Back then, your life was so damned up in the air. You missed out on stuff. That's not your fault. But Kaden and Rhonda can't help you if you don't tell them what's wrong. I bet you had progress reports, didn't you?"

Anthony nodded. "They're the old-fashioned ones that come in the mail," he muttered.

"And that's why computer grades were invented. Believe me, nobody's going to make that mistake again. And that's fine."

"But I'll have to repeat seventh grade! River and I will have to graduate at the same time, and that's embarrassing!" he said. "I mean, she's my sister, and I don't have anything to teach her. She knows everything, and I'm so fucking stupid—"

"Okay, we're done with that word," Jackson said firmly. "You're not stupid. You needed help. And of course you were afraid to ask for it. Nobody's ever stepped up to help you before. But man, I've got to tell you that those people I just met in front of the house weren't worried about your grades. They were worried about *you*. River told Mrs. Cramer she couldn't call you her foster brother—she had to call you her brother. Because they love you, kid. And loving someone means forgiving them when they screw up. Screwing up is what people do. But if you're afraid to admit it to the people you love, you'll never see how much they love you, you understand?"

Anthony nodded. "You think they love me?" he asked sadly.

"You love them, don't you?" Jackson stroked his head again, heartily wishing he could get out of the damned tree.

"Yeah." Anthony actually looked at him and then wiped his nose on the sleeve of his T-shirt. "How did you know?"

"Because, kid, you couldn't even run that far. You just climbed a tree where you could see the house. Did you even have a plan here?"

Anthony's stomach grumbled. "I was going to sneak back in after dinner and come back out to the tree," he confessed.

Jackson started to laugh. "That, son, is the shittiest plan in the world."

After a moment, Anthony snorted, like he hadn't been planning to laugh but it had just snuck out anyway. "It really is. See, I told you I was stu—"

"Shut up, kid. Not stupid. New. I was new once. Kaden's mom taught me how to be loved. I'm not great at it, but she taught Kaden everything he knows. You're smarter than I was at your age. I'm sure you'll catch on faster than I did, okay?"

Anthony nodded. "Okay. Thanks, Jackson."

Jackson's pocket phone buzzed, and off in the distance, up in another tree, he saw the flash of what could have been the scope of a rifle. He pulled his phone out of his pocket and read the text.

Get out of the fucking tree, Rivers. You are giving my boss the heebie-jeebies just watching over you.

Jackson rolled his eyes. Fucking Burton.

I am talking the kid down, here. Are there any hit men nearby?

No. Apparently hit men don't know how to react to a fucking tank. They followed you until Roseville, then buggered out. But we're here, and you need to get out of the fucking tree.

Jackson snorted and put the phone back in his pocket. "Anthony?"

"Yeah?"

"How's about we get out of the fucking tree?"

Anthony took a breath that was mostly snot. "Jackson?"

"Yeah?"

"I don't know how."

Jackson let out a cackle. "Okay. So here's what we're going to do. I'm going to lower myself down to the next branch, and you are going to follow my lead. Think you can do that?"

"Yeah. What about my backpack?"

"Put it on your back, kid. Let's get down."

It took them twenty minutes of breathless swearing and a bunch of scrapes on their hands and one on Jackson's cheek, but they eventually got down. By the time they landed, they'd alerted the people in the house, and there was a crowd around the base of the tree, ready to help Anthony into the house and get him warmed up—and cleaned up—and to discuss a shit-ton of summer school. Jackson only guessed at that last part, but he figured Rhonda and Kaden would have a contingency plan for a kid who hadn't taken the time to learn how to be a kid.

Jackson finally dropped to the ground, and only Ellery was there, but he had a warm washcloth for Jackson's scrapes and the promise of coffee in the house.

"What was the problem?" he asked quietly as everybody went inside, the babble ensuring that Anthony would be king for the day.

"He's failing all his classes," Jackson said. "Poor kid. I was him once."

Ellery nodded. Jackson had told him how Jade and Kaden's mother had made him make up a semester's worth of work in a week so Jackson could graduate and go on to high school. "Did you tell him that story?" he asked curiously.

"No. I needed to listen to his story. I mean, we're grown-ups. It feels like the same story to us, but to him, it was brand-new."

Ellery nodded quietly, and then, before they could get to the porch, he stopped and pulled Jackson down for a kiss. It was tender and carnal at once, and it reminded Jackson of all the lessons he still had to learn about accepting love. It also brought home the fact that he and Ellery hadn't had time alone in their own house for three days.

But mostly it told Jackson that he was loved, and he was grateful for it.

"That was a good kiss, Counselor."

"You're a good man, Detective."

They both felt Jackson's pocket buzz, and Jackson grimaced.

"Who is it?" Ellery asked curiously.

Nice. Now get the fuck inside so I can get my boss out of his damned tree and give him a sedative. You people are driving him batshit crazy.

"Burton says hi," Jackson told him without inflection.

"Really? He followed us up here?"

"He'd really like us to go inside now and stop climbing trees," Jackson added.

Ellery's eyes grew big. "Anything else?"

"We owe Sonny and Ace big for the tank."

"Fantastic. Are you driving back?"

"Yes," Jackson told him. Ellery didn't even want to touch the tank. "Why?"

"Think Kaden and Rhonda have any alcohol?"

Jackson laughed as they hit the porch. "You don't day drink!" he protested.

"Oh, I am about to start."

Jackson kept laughing. Yeah, sure, Ellery threatened a lot, but Jackson was pretty sure he wouldn't have missed that morning for the world.

Done, So Done, and Really Done

"OH, DEAR God," Jason muttered, struggling to sit up in the bed of the house they'd co-opted for the operation. "What now?"

"Craft fair," Burton told him from the computer console that tapped into all the cameras they'd placed around Ellery Cramer's house in the past week. "Jackson texted last night after we got in."

"He what?"

Burton grimaced. Technically he never should have contacted Rivers at all, but after things like, say, an emergency trip to the Sierras to rescue a kid out of a tree, he figured maybe Jackson's pithy advanced notice comments did more good than harm.

"He wanted us to know. They're going to a craft fair during the day and a Republic game at night. I already got us tickets."

"A Republic game? Is that like a politics thing?" Jason blinked hard, trying to wake up, and Burton let out a sigh.

"It's soccer. And boss?"

"Yeah?"

"You need a break."

And maybe because they'd been working the op together for four days and Jackson had almost given Constance a heart attack when he'd climbed that fucking tree, Jason actually said something real.

"I am having nightmares."

Well, of course. The things they'd seen, the things they'd known had happened, and, worse, the things they were anticipating but hadn't happened yet. Burton had Ernie to go home to, but Constance, he watched over the whole lot of Psycho Unit USA (as some asshole—whom Burton would never forgive—had dubbed their detail).

"I…. Ernie helps," Burton admitted, because hearing his CO and boss and friend admit that he wasn't handling shit was a big admission. Nobody took advantage of the free psych program in their detail.

Nobody.

"Burton, can I ask you something?"

"Sir, yessir."

Constance rubbed the sleep out of his eyes and scowled. "Very funny. How did you know? About being... gay?"

"Bi?" Burton protested but then took pity on his boss. "I knew. Girls were easier. And since, you know, in this job, relationships are not a thing, I went for easy."

"Then why Ernie?"

Ernie hadn't been easy at all. Ernie had been a spacy, bitter, kind mass of contradictions—who had known deep in his witchy bones that they were destined to be lovers from the moment he'd first heard Burton's voice.

Which was about three days before he'd seen his face.

Burton blew out a breath and smiled. "He, uh, wouldn't take no for an answer."

Constance's look of surprise made him laugh. "Really."

Well, Burton had cultivated his silence, his body, his entire demeanor, to be the guy people didn't mess with. But then, Ernie had cultivated his spaciness, his flexibility, his quiet yielding to the brutal winds of the world to be the guy people didn't notice.

And yet Ernie had kept bending Burton to his will. Burton had just looked at him and melted. And every time he tried to put up a barrier or put the brakes on, he'd thought about living without Ernie and....

Couldn't.

"I can't explain it," he said humbly.

Constance let out a bark of laughter. "And I came to you for advice?"

Burton rolled his eyes. "About what?"

Constance shook his head. "Nothing. It's unimportant."

Burton let out a sigh. "Jason, do you see those screens?"

"Yeah?"

"To the left of screen four, we've got a bad guy waiting in a follow car. At nine o'clock, our three targets are going to leave the house in that ridiculous SUV of theirs and drive through this weird-ass city to go to a craft fair in the Rainbow District. Which means that in forty-five minutes, one of us is going to go first and set up, and the other one is going to follow, and we're going to be kind of busy for the next couple of hours. But until then, you and me got nothing but time. Now what? We've worked together for five years, and you are one of maybe seven people—including my parents—who know about me and Ernie. So what is it you can't tell me?"

"Fine." Jason blew out a breath. "I'm not bi, Lee. Gay. Me. Gay. And I haven't hooked up since I became your CO. Because I'm ten years older than you, and ten years ago, that sort of thing could have gotten me fucking killed."

Burton was conscious that he had to close his mouth. He did that and swallowed to get rid of the dryness. "Really?"

"Would I fucking lie—"

"No. Not about this." Burton held up his hands. "But you heard me calling out for Ernie…." Neither of them liked to talk about the early days in Psycho Unit USA. Knowing who was out there, knowing what they'd been trained to do, knowing that someone from their military had basically set monsters loose on the world—nobody in their unit was okay.

"I guessed. I was right. And so I can talk to you."

Burton grimaced. "Look. You know that place I don't talk about?"

"Yeah?"

"It's home. I… I made myself a home, even before I had myself an Ernie. Do you still live at the base?"

Constance scrubbed his face. "Yeah. God yeah."

"Make yourself a home. Take your own advice. Get the fuck off the base and find a thing that's human and real. You don't need to hook up—you need to connect. And that's a whole different thing."

Constance gave half a laugh and nodded. "Those are… those are some wise words," he said softly. "I'll remember that."

"My pleasure, sir," Burton said dryly. "You want to shower before we have to get to it? This house we're borrowing has a shower with a steam setting. It makes me feel like all my dangly parts are clean, you know?"

Constance laughed outright then. "I'll try to make it quick."

"You completely missed the point. Now go!"

Burton watched his CO disappear into the bathroom and looked back at his screens. Nope, nothing yet. He knew they were out there—he'd seen flashes of one guy, shadows really. He and Jase had to get them both. Taking out one wouldn't do it. But stopping both would help them put pressure on the people who issued the contract.

He was ready for this detail to end already.

Usually, when he was sent to guard a target, there was a hint of wrongdoing—some sense that this person had agreed to live dangerously. Ellery Cramer's mother had done nothing more than issue a few delicate inquiries as to where Karl Lacey had gotten his money. Yes, it was officially poking her nose where it didn't belong. But issuing a hit wasn't usually the protocol for that kind of thing. A runaround would have done just fine.

He thought about the way the woman had ruthlessly dragged her son and his boyfriend through pretty much every public experience known to man. If Sacramento had an amusement park, he was sure he'd be spending part of his life in Disneyland.

Well, maybe not the runaround—but at least try a sternly worded letter of discouragement before signing her death warrant, right?

At his belt, his pocket buzzed, three short bursts, like he'd programmed his phone to do with Ernie and Ernie alone.

See you tomorrow, Cruller. Can't wait!

Burton blinked, and a buzz of excitement hit his stomach, like it had when he'd been deployed and action had been in the air. He didn't ask if Ernie knew that for certain, and didn't ask how he knew.

He took Ernie on faith, which was the only way to take his flaky, witchy, sexy as hell boyfriend.

Me neither. Love you.

Love you back.

Burton smiled softly at the phone, not feeling dumb in the least. One way or another, he would see Ernie tomorrow. And he'd be damned if he'd let grieving over friends ruin his homecoming.

He was going to get these bad guys, and he was going to leave Rivers, Cramer, and the woman he was starting to think of as Lucy Satan in his rearview mirror, safe as bunnies on his watch.

Over the Rainbow

JACKSON COULDN'T keep his eyes off the monstrosity dangling over his head.

"Really?" he asked nobody in particular.

"I was about to say the same thing," Ellery muttered, staring in the same direction. "I mean, apart from being hideous—"

"It's gonna fall on our heads and kill us all?"

The hideous thing in question was a large plywood rainbow arch, painted in neon colors—badly—and suspended about thirty feet off the ground using nylon cord in the branches of trees, and a nearby cherry picker. Besides looking garish and unhealthy, it also looked… precarious. Damned precarious.

Jackson looked at Ellery, and they both looked at his mother, who was lingering over a table of admittedly lovely blown-glass baubles that had caught her eye.

"We need to get her away from this thing," Ellery said, and Jackson nodded in return, his blood running just the tiniest bit cold. This had been the longest four days of his life—but he was damned if it would end with Lucy Satan's blood on his hands.

He gave the sign, which read, "Crafty, Free, LGBQT!" another dubious look and caught a flash of something shiny from a gap in the cherry picker.

Fucking aces.

With a shake of his head, he turned toward Ellery's mother, who was charmingly terrorizing the poor blue-haired waif behind the counter.

"So, these were blown by your wife? That's wonderful. Is that her there?"

"Yes, ma'am." She nodded at a tanned, wiry woman waiting on another customer. "She's been learning the craft from her uncle since she was in high school."

"Well, this must be her calling, then. And did you make the felted bags they go into? Because they complement the artwork so very well."

The blue-haired waif smiled weakly and looked toward her wife, who was not in rescuing position. "Thank you," she squeaked. "We, uh, like color."

They did indeed. The glass globes were done in a variety of techniques, from color diffused throughout the glass, to the kind that looked like flowers in the center, to the kind with abstract shapes drawn throughout the sphere, the colors undulating and receding with the angle.

Jackson smiled and winked at the poor woman, not talking because he sort of got that wasn't her thing. Instead he peered at the artwork, as fascinated by the colors as Ellery's mother seemed to be.

"Which one do you like?" Lucy Satan asked, and for once he didn't get defensive or snark at her. For one thing, the girl watching them was fragile, and she might not get that with them, being bitchy was a bit of a dance.

"Mm...." Jackson ran his finger down one that was a cluster of white and ebony flowers, with hints of green. "That one's very Ellery, except it's a little girly. But pretty." He smiled at the waif again. She smiled back gratefully. "This one...." He had to reach out and touch it. The colors were rich brown and bright magenta, and they reminded him of his sister's hair. Back before it had been a thing, Jade had found a way to put a strip of that bright purplish pink in her gorgeous hair. She'd done it as tightly kinked curls; she'd done it as waves. Even when they'd been in high school and she hadn't had the money to get her hair "done," she'd bought a box of something totally inappropriate for her hair and combed it through her tight mahogany-bronze ringlets. The dye had lasted until her next wash, of course, and she'd needed to cut the ends off because it had fried them completely. For the rest of high school she'd bought extensions and had them woven in—she'd loved that color.

His sister-of-the-heart—he'd put her and her boyfriend through a lot this past year. And she hadn't wavered, not once. It had been her idea to break off the on-again-off-again thing between them, which was good, because they'd both fallen in love with other people. But she was a lesson—a true, good lesson—in how love, real love, wasn't something you could just fuck away.

"This," he said thoughtfully. "It reminds me of Jade."

"It does indeed," Ellery's mother said.

Jackson risked a look at her, and she was regarding him thoughtfully.

"Did you and Ellery decide on the office?" she asked, catching him by surprise.

"The one on F Street." He sighed. "The parking is going to suck, but you know, he really loves the inside."

"And you'd do anything for him, wouldn't you?"

Jackson nodded. "Well, yeah."

She patted his hand. "I appreciate the two of you doing what I asked this week. Not asking questions." She let out a little sigh, and he wondered if she was as tired as he was. "I think I was asked to come here because you and Ellery could handle this situation, and Ellery's father...."

"Is too sweet for words."

She gave a throaty little laugh. "It's really so very much easier for us to be in danger, isn't it? Than to let our loved ones be?"

Jackson nodded, and out of instinct, he looked up at the cherry picker.

Burton was standing up in full view of the entire goddamned world!

Jackson grabbed Ellery's mother and wrapped himself around her, hating that she was six inches shorter than he was, even in her pumps. With a quick look around, he saw Ellery, standing under the sign, his head cocked as if he couldn't figure out what in the hell Jackson was doing.

And beyond him, he saw a motorcycle, veering toward them, ready to go up and over the sidewalk and into the crowd, as if out of control.

From far away, he heard Burton shouting, "Rivers, get down!" at the same time he said, "Ellery, move!"

And then....

BURTON HAD never almost frozen in his entire life.

He'd had them all in his sights. The happy little family, looking at doodads. Ellery was standing a few paces off, apparently entranced at the sight of his mother and Rivers making nice. Wasn't that fucking adorable, right?

Then Jason had spoken up in his earbud. "I got Charley One, repeat, I got Charley One. Charley Two is inbound on a motorcycle, heading east down K Street. He has no options, repeat, zero options."

Uh-oh. Bad guys with zero options often got desperate and forgot the finer part of their orders, focusing in on their targets with complete disregard for anyone in their way. Burton fucked invisibility and stood up to locate the motorcycle when he saw two things.

One was Jackson wrapping his body around Ellery Cramer's mother, and the other was Cramer, standing right in the way of the motorcycle headed straight toward him.

And then the last thing—the big-assed nylon cord, the granddaddy of sailor's knots that held the entire hideosity of a sign up from this side, was within his grasp.

He screamed, "Rivers, get down!" at the same time Jackson screamed, "Ellery, move!" and then he prayed for timing and pulled the cord.

ELLERY DIDN'T give a shit what everybody was yelling. Jackson was protecting his mother bodily, and Ellery had to go help him. He lunged for the two of them, knocking them both to the ground just as the giant piece of plywood swung down and knocked some poor asshole on a runaway motorcycle across the concrete.

The cycle went sideways and slid across the concrete, coming to a stop about a foot away from Ellery's backside as he lay sprawled on the sidewalk feeling foolish. The rider—wearing black leathers with a yellow helmet—got unsteadily to his feet and was reaching around behind him for something, when suddenly he fell to his knees and then on his face.

Ellery's eyes went wide as a thin trickle of blood came out of his helmet and a gun went skittering across the sidewalk.

And out of nowhere, an ambulance pulled up.

Jackson and Ellery's mother were still climbing creakily to their feet as the ambulance guys—no medics Jackson or Ellery had ever met, and they knew this beat pretty well—gathered the cyclist up and put him on a gurney without even taking off his helmet. Given the lack of movement as a whole, Ellery suspected the helmet was probably holding all the cyclist's brains in, after the bullet had liberated them from the rider's skull.

As they clambered to their feet and checked for bruises, Ellery caught Jackson looking over their heads and nodding, before going back to make sure Ellery's mother and Ellery didn't have any scrapes.

Jackson, of course, had bloodied his elbow going down, because Jesus Christ, that man.

As the crowd started muttering to itself and stopped looking for police—who didn't appear to be coming—and nobody noticed that the motorcycle had just seemed to pick itself up and drive away, Ellery looked a question at Jackson.

"So…?"

Jackson shrugged and smiled wearily—and then jumped and checked his pocket. "Uh, so, Lucy? We can go the fuck home now."

For a moment Ellery's mother sagged, looking a little older, and a little fragile, and a little like she'd actually needed their protection after all.

Then she stood upright and gave Jackson a level look. "Of course, dear boy. But if you will excuse me, I have a purchase to make. And I'd really love to see the rest of the booths here, don't you think?"

Jackson let out a little laugh. "Of course, Lucy Satan. Of course."

They stood back and let Ellery's mother make her purchases, and Ellery put his hand solidly on the small of Jackson's back.

"So, is it over?"

Jackson pulled out his phone.

One bad guy dead, one in custody. Will text you tonight with the all clear. Nice reflexes, by the way.

As Ellery watched, Jackson texted, *Thanks for the apple fritters.*

And that was all. "Wow," Ellery muttered. "So, do we still have to go to the game tonight?"

Jackson just looked at him. "After we've invited Jade and Mike? Do you really think your mom is going to cancel now?"

Ellery groaned.

No. No, she would not. But they would get to go home and have dinner there and spend some time on the couch. And since his mother couldn't get another flight out until the day after tomorrow, they had an actual day to sit quietly and visit, while Jackson swam laps in the pool and tried really, *really* hard to forget the last five days had ever happened.

Good luck with that, though.

Before she left, Ellery's mother gave them a charming hosts' gift.

A hand-blown paperweight, with the unlikely color combo of bronze and magenta mingling in the center. Jackson had smiled as he'd unwrapped it, and set it down on its felt coaster with surprisingly respectful fingers.

Ellery had just cocked his head.

"You don't like it?" his mother inquired.

"Mm… not my colors," he said diplomatically.

"Well then, think of it more as a gift for Jackson."

And Ellery did. But that was okay. He gave his mother a genteel kiss on the cheek. "Something that makes him happy is a gift for me," he said, feeling sappy.

But his mother just smiled and patted his cheek. Then it was time to take her to the airport.

They got back and collapsed on the couch in complete relief.

"Please tell me you won't miss her," Jackson begged.

Ellery looked at him, wearing the waterproof bandage on his elbow like a badge of honor. "Jackson?"

"Yeah?"

"If I stripped naked and bent over the couch, would you get the lube from the bedroom? I'd really like to celebrate being alone."

Jackson's chuckle, ripe and filthy, was enough to get him to stand up and start toeing off his shoes.

Constant Worry

JASON CONSTANCE had learned to sleep on a helicopter a long time ago—but he couldn't. Not today.

"You dropped a sign on his head," he said in disbelief.

Burton opened one eye, because he had been sleeping. "You taught us to use whatever weapon there was at hand," he replied, voice mild.

"I don't even believe how that went down."

Burton snorted. "I don't believe you subdued your guy without killing him. It took an awful lot of fun with knives to get that guy to talk."

Constance shrugged. Like Burton, the physical things—the running, jumping, shooting people while you did it—that had been the easy part.

It had been holding on to the tiny fragments of his soul that was hard.

"But a sign!"

Burton blew out a breath. "If I tell you a secret, will you shut up about the fucking sign?"

"Sure."

"Ernie texted me the day after we left. He said, 'Rivers, get down,' and 'Pull that thing!' Guess how it played out?"

Constance started to giggle. "Really?"

"Really."

The giggles died abruptly. "Let me know if he texts you anything about me, okay?"

Burton just stared at him, and Constance got an uneasy feeling in the pit of his stomach.

"What? What'd he say?"

"He said that in the end, when it's all over, you're gonna be okay."

And for the life of him, Jason Constance, who'd had a plan all his life, couldn't think of another thing to say.

AMY LANE lives in a crumbling crapmansion with a couple of growing children, a passel of furbabies, and a bemused spouse. She's been a finalist in the RITAs™ twice, has won honorable mention for an Indiefab, and has a couple of Rainbow Awards to her name. She also has too damned much yarn, a penchant for action-adventure movies, and a need to know that somewhere in all the pain is a story of Wuv, Twu Wuv, which she continues to believe in to this day! She writes fantasy, urban fantasy, and gay romance—and if you accidentally make eye contact, she'll bore you to tears with why those three genres go together. She'll also tell you that sacrifices, large and small, are worth the urge to write.

Website: www.greenshill.com
Blog: www.writerslane.blogspot.com
Email: amylane@greenshill.com
Facebook: www.facebook.com/amy.lane.167
Twitter: @amymaclane

Choose your Lane to love!

Orange

Amy Lane's Dark Contemporary Romance

Guess who's swimming in the same pond...

FISH
OUT OF
WATER
Amy Lane

Fish Out of Water: Book One

PI Jackson Rivers grew up on the mean streets of Del Paso Heights—and he doesn't trust cops, even though he was one. When the man he thinks of as his brother is accused of killing a police officer in an obviously doctored crime, Jackson will move heaven and earth to keep Kaden and his family safe.

Defense attorney Ellery Cramer grew up with the proverbial silver spoon in his mouth, but that hasn't stopped him from crushing on street-smart, swaggering Jackson Rivers for the past six years. But when Jackson asks for his help defending Kaden Cameron, Ellery is out of his depth—and not just with guarded, prickly Jackson. Kaden wasn't just framed, he was framed by crooked cops, and the conspiracy goes higher than Ellery dares reach—and deep into Jackson's troubled past.

Both men are soon enmeshed in the mystery of who killed the cop in the minimart, and engaged in a race against time to clear Kaden's name. But when the mystery is solved and the bullets stop flying, they'll have to deal with their personal complications… and an attraction that's spiraled out of control.

www.dreamspinnerpress.com

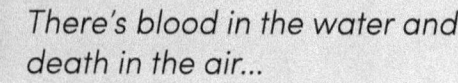

*There's blood in the water and
death in the air...*

RED FISH,
DEAD
FISH

Amy Lane

"Deliciously tense . . .
a satisfying mix of sweet
angst and steamy suspense."
KAREN ROSE,
NYT Bestselling Author

Fish Out of Water: Book Two

They must work together to stop a psychopath—and save each other.

Two months ago Jackson Rivers got shot while trying to save Ellery Cramer's life. Not only is Jackson still suffering from his wounds, the triggerman remains at large—and the body count is mounting.

Jackson and Ellery have been trying to track down Tim Owens since Jackson got out of the hospital, but Owens's time as a member of the department makes the DA reluctant to turn over any stones. When Owens starts going after people Jackson knows, Ellery's instincts hit red alert. Hurt in a scuffle with drug-dealing squatters and trying damned hard not to grieve for a childhood spent in hell, Jackson is weak and vulnerable when Owens strikes.

Jackson gets away, but the fallout from the encounter might kill him. It's not doing Ellery any favors either. When a police detective is abducted—and Jackson and Ellery hold the key to finding her—Ellery finds out exactly what he's made of. He's not the corporate shark who believes in winning at all costs; he's the frightened lover trying to keep the man he cares for from self-destructing in his own valor.

www.dreamspinnerpress.com

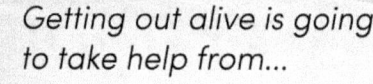

*Getting out alive is going
to take help from...*

A FEW
GOOD
FISH

Amy Lane

Fish Out of Water: Book Three

A tomcat, a psychopath, and a psychic walk into the desert to rescue the men they love…. Can everybody make it out with their skin intact?

PI Jackson Rivers and Defense Attorney Ellery Cramer have barely recovered from last November, when stopping a serial killer nearly destroyed Jackson in both body and spirit.

But their previous investigation poked a new danger with a stick, forcing Jackson and Ellery to leave town so they can meet the snake in its den.

Jackson Rivers grew up with the mean streets as a classroom and he learned a long time ago not to give a damn about his own life. But he gets a whole new education when the enemy takes Ellery. The man who pulled his shattered pieces from darkness and stitched them back together again is in trouble, and Jackson's only chance to save him rests in the hands of fragile allies he barely knows.

It's going to take a little bit of luck to get these Few Good Fish out alive!

www.dreamspinnerpress.com

Hiding
the
Moon

AMY LANE

Fish Out of Water: Book Four
A Fish Out of Water/Racing the Sun Crossover

Can a hitman and a psychic negotiate a relationship while all hell breaks loose?

The world might not know who Lee Burton is, but it needs his black ops division and the work they do to keep it safe. Lee's spent his life following orders—until he sees a kill jacket on Ernie Caulfield. Ernie isn't a typical target, and something is very wrong with Burton's chain of command.

Ernie's life may seem adrift, but his every action helps to shelter his mind from the psychic storm raging within. When Lee Burton shows up to save him from assassins and club bunnies, Ernie seizes his hand and doesn't look back. Burton is Ernie's best bet in a tumultuous world, and after one day together, he's pretty sure Lee knows Ernie is his destiny as well.

But when Burton refused Ernie's contract, he kicked an entire piranha tank of bad guys, and Burton can't rest until he takes down the rogue military unit that would try to kill a spacey psychic. Ernie's in love with Burton and Burton's confused as hell by Ernie—but Ernie's not changing his mind and Burton can't stay away. Psychics, assassins, and bad guys—throw them into the desert with a forbidden love affair and what could possibly go wrong?

www.dreamspinnerpress.com

Racing
for the
Sun

AMY LANE

Racing for the Sun: Book One

"I'll do anything."

Staff Sergeant Jasper "Ace" Atchison takes one look at Private Sonny Daye and knows that every word on paper about him is pure, unadulterated bullshit. But Sonny is desperate, and although Ace isn't going to take him up on his offer of "anything," that doesn't mean he isn't tempted.

Instead, Ace takes Sonny under his wing, protecting him when they're in the service and making plans with him when they get out. Together, they're going to own a garage and build race cars and make their fortune hurtling faster than light across the desert. Together, they're going to rewrite the past, make Sonny Daye a whole and happy person, and put the ghosts in Ace's heart to rest.

But not even Sonny can build a car fast enough to escape the ghosts of the past. When Sonny's ghosts drive them down and run their plans off the road, Ace finds out exactly what he's made of. Maybe Sonny was the one to promise Ace anything, but there is nothing under the sun Ace won't do to keep Sonny safe from harm.

www.dreamspinnerpress.com